Double Bluff

Ruby Vincent

Published by Ruby Vincent, 2025.

Copyright © 2025 by Ruby Vincent

All rights reserved. No part of this publication may be reproduced, stored in a retrieval system, or transmitted in any form or by any means, electronic, mechanical, recording or otherwise, without the prior written permission of the copyright holder.

This is a work of fiction. Names, characters, businesses, places, events, and incidents are either the products of the author's imagination or used in a fictitious manner. Any resemblance to actual persons, living or dead, or actual events is purely coincidental.

Chapter One

"The trapdoor was sabotaged. When Colin stood on it, it gave way and he fell eight feet... onto the small steel pipe sticking out of the floor—"

"Ms. Kim—"

"It impaled him through the throat," I cried. "He's been paralyzed from the neck down ever since, changing the course of his life forever. And mine."

"Ms. Kim, I—"

"But it turned out students had been sneaking under the stage to smoke, drink, and hook up for years, so a couple months before it happened, the headmaster had the whole place rigged with cameras. And when they checked those cameras, who did they see sneaking around under the stage, messing with the trapdoor?

"Me!" I burst out, making him jump. "He saw me, except it wasn't me! It was Sue. *She* sabotaged the stage. *She* nearly killed Colin. And *she* set me up to fall for it, knowing that no one was going to believe it was the fault of my evil fucking twin."

He sighed, rubbing the bridge of his nose. "I understand that—"

"Do you?" I sliced in. "Do you understand that the headmaster grilled me for hours? Demanding to know what possible reason my sister would have for entering the grounds of a school she didn't even go to, just to play a vicious prank on a guy she didn't even know? A guy who just happened to be beating *me* out for valedictorian?

"He didn't believe a word out of my mouth," I scoffed. "And it didn't help that my own mother sat in his office and said my accusations were ridiculous. Sue was across town working on her lessons with her math tutor. She was never anywhere near Titan Prep.

"I tried to tell them that she absolutely could and would do those horrible things. That any alibi she gave was false and coerced, and that Soo Min Kim is the most evil, manipulative, cold-hearted bitch that ever walked the face of the earth. *I told them*," I cried, speaking over another attempt to interrupt me, "that only a few days before Colin's accident, Sue cornered me coming out of my room.

"She hissed at me that I didn't deserve my acceptance to Yale. That I only got in because I forced Omma to send me to a different, and better, high school. I got to 'cheat' my way to the top without her there to outshine me, and if it wasn't for that, she'd be going to Yale and not me.

"I dismissed her as the jealous bitch she was, but—but I should've known," I rasped, voice cracking, "that Sue always gets the last word."

"Ms. Kim, please—"

"The headmaster expelled me," I whispered, eyes stinging, "Yale rescinded my acceptance. No other college would take me, and then Colin's family sued ours.

"Omma paid them everything they asked out of my trust and college funds. Then, she threw me out." My voice was dead. "The shame was too much for her. She wanted nothing to do with me. And just like that... my life was over."

"Ms. Kim," he said gently. "I truly am very sorry for what happened to you, but, I confess, I don't understand why you're telling me this."

I looked around the small, but cheerful office. Bright, blue walls enveloped us instead of clinical white. Everywhere I looked, there were adorable child-made drawings, and pictures of the babies who grew up to draw them.

"I'm telling you this, Dr. Cormac, because every dream I've ever had has been stolen from me. Every single one, except this one. I've wanted kids since I was a kid, and I'm tired of waiting. Tired of waiting for my life to start. Tired of waiting for permission to be happy. I want to do this," I pressed, "but I can't for thirty thousand dollars."

I waved the price sheet he handed me in the air. "IVF cannot possibly cost this much."

"I'm afraid it does."

"But—but there must be payment plans," I cried.

"There are—"

"Great," I pounced. "I'll do that—"

"—for those with a credit score of seven hundred or higher. Your score is four hundred and two."

I bit my lip hard, refusing to deflate like the hopes he just popped a hole in. "Please," I said when I trusted myself. "There has to be something you can do."

"Well, we haven't discussed IUI." Dr. Cormac was as kind as his gentle green eyes, and the smile that was never far from his lips. That's why I chose him as my doctor. I could hear in his voice that he wanted to help me. "The costs for IUI are greatly reduced. We charge only one thousand two hundred per cycle."

I was shaking my head before he finished. "I can't do IUI. One of my tubes is blocked, and the other is badly scarred from the endometriosis. IVF is my only real option."

"I'm so sorry, forgive me." He flipped quickly through my file. "I didn't see that in your file."

"Because the last doctor I went to would've been better off selling snake oil behind a donkey's ass."

He barked a startled laugh.

"He was completely disorganized, unreliable, and not good about updating patient files," I said, flapping my hand at the papers. "That's why I spent money I don't have for this consultation with you. You're the best fertility doctor in three counties. There must be something you can do for me."

He smiled softly. "You flatter me, Ms. Kim, and believe me when I say that I want to help you, but it appears that IVF is simply something that you cannot afford at this time. When your financial situation changes, please return. When you do, I swear to you that no matter how busy my schedule is, I will make time for you."

"I'll help you make this dream come true."

"But—"

"I'm afraid that's all we have time for today." He rose out of his seat. "Allow me to escort you to the door."

Abrupt. Direct. Not unkind, but firm. No doubt the tone and dismissal he used on many a person or couple that came in here hoping that a sob story would persuade him not to force them to mortgage their home for their future.

Swallowing my protests, I turned off my recorder, stood, and let him walk me out the door.

My wedges hit the sidewalk by the time my phone went off. I declined the call without even looking at it, trudging to my car. The 1987 Dodge Charger was a sleek, black beauty back in its day.

But now it was a dented, rusted-over piece of crap that groaned every time I turned the key. Loud and clear it demanded to know why I wouldn't let it fall apart in peace, but it wasn't allowed to take the easy way out.

That car was the only thing I was allowed to take when Omma threw me out. She barely let me have the clothes on my back, and even those weren't left unscathed. I rubbed my throat, slowing down as I was thrown back to the night Omma ripped my shirt tearing Halmeoni's necklace from my neck.

She had no right to it. My grandmother left me that necklace in her will, but when I unwisely made that argument, my mother slapped me so hard across the face, my head nearly popped off.

I wasn't worthy of Halmeoni's necklace. I wasn't worthy to walk the halls where she once lived. And I wasn't worthy to stand before her then, crying about what I was entitled to after shaming myself and my family in the most hideous way.

All of that my mother screamed at me... as my sister watched from the shadows—laughing.

I ripped out of the memory when my phone went off again. Checking the screen, I bit off a curse and accepted the call—hitting *record* before I said a word.

"What."

His oily, skin-crawling laugh oozed through the phone. "Now, now, Sarah. Is that any way to answer your boss? I would've thought *I'm so sorry, Dan, please tell me what I can do to make it up to you* would've been much more appropriate considering you're three hours late for your shift."

I continued to my car, riffling around in my bag for my keys. "So fire me."

"I'm not doing that. And you wouldn't want me to do that."

I tensed. "What wouldn't I want you to do, Dan? Release sex tapes we made when we were dating and I thought we were in love—"

"We're still dating and we're still in love."

"No, we're not! We haven't been since I walked in on you screwing the line cook!"

"I apologized for that a dozen times."

"No, you didn't," I hissed. "You said *I'm sorry you had to see that* and *I'm sorry you were hurt.*"

"Exactly."

"No, not exactly, dumbass. We've been through *that* a dozen times, and I've got the recordings to prove it, so cut it out with your gaslighting garbage. Fake-ass apologies like that put all the responsibility on me for what happened, instead of on you."

"Fine, then I take all the responsibility. I'm sorry. End of sentence," he said. "We good?"

If I could've reached through the phone and punched him, the dickhead would be missing five teeth. "Okay, yes, fine," I gritted. "We're good. Apology accepted. Now we can break up and move on from each other with no hard feelings."

"If that happens, then I've got no reason to keep these little home videos we made to myself."

I tossed my head. "It amazes me how you have no shame over blackmailing me, even when you know I'm recording every word you say. Danny boy, if you release those videos, I'll sue you for everything you have. The judge won't be too sympathetic when she listens to my home records."

"True," he breezed, "but how is the two hundred and twelve dollars I've got in my bank account going to lift your spirits when the whole world is watching your flat ass bounce on my lap? The future Little Kim is going to have quite a hard time at school when all the bullies are flashing your tits in their face—"

"Stop!"

"Sure, I'll stop." I heard the triumph in his voice clear as day. "As long as you stop being a bitter old hag, and move on from the past. I love you, I made a mistake, it'll never happen again, so let's move the fuck on. Deal?"

The word was acid on my tongue. "...deal."

"Awesome. Then, I'll see you tonight, baby. My place."

"Fine."

"You—"

I hung up, not letting him drip another poisonous word in my ear.

Walking up to my car, I dropped my head on the hood—letting the warmth seep into my skull and banish the oncoming headache.

That evil, fucking, miserable bastard was right. Suing him wouldn't get back what he planned to steal from me—my privacy, my safety, my last chance to ever make it home. If Omma was shamed by a vicious prank I wasn't a part of, what would be her reaction to a sex tape I was a part of?

That question didn't need answering. I already knew.

Standing there slumped over my hunk of crap, the words of another miserable bastard roared in my ear.

"You're a twenty-eight-year-old waitress making fourteen dollars an hour. You live in a terrible neighborhood, that car you pulled up in is older than you, and you think that you can pay medical bills with sob stories.

"So I'm going to do you a favor and give you what you need more desperately than a baby. A wake-up call."

I cringed then like I did the first time I heard it.

"You're not ready to be anyone's mother, Ms. Kim. Come back when you get your life together."

Tears stung my eyes as my closing throat strangled a sob. The last fertility doctor was a disorganized, inappropriate, irresponsible jerk, but maybe it was possible... that he wasn't a liar.

"How can I give a child a good life... when I can't give one to myself?"

The car hood had no answers for me.

Eventually, I slid myself off and got into the car. Checking in for my shift was a no-go after a morning like that, so instead I drove straight home, letting the slow, sleepy town of Willingsworth dance outside my window.

Willingsworth.

I'd never heard of the place before I broke down in it. After Omma threw me out, I bounced around from place to place, taking any job that would hire a kid that was expelled from high school. When I was twenty-four, I left Chicago and found myself driving east toward home—dreaming of making something of myself in the one and only New York City.

My crappy car got as far as Willingsworth, Nowhere, USA.

I broke down in front of the diner where I made a pit stop, and the sweet couple who owned it offered to get it towed to the auto shop, promising the tow would be free of charge. The next day, when I went to the shop to pick it up, I discovered the same couple also paid the bill.

It had been so long since anyone, anywhere, had shown me any kindness, that I decided I'd stay in Willingsworth—make a real home here.

That was until I met Daniel Mills.

I should've known that no matter where you are, or how far you run, you're never too far from a gaslighting, self-obsessed narcissist.

I also should've known nowhere is paradise.

My hometown of Lantana looked like a nice place to live too. Mansions as far as the eye could see, and so many smiling, well-dressed people walking among them. You'd never know that a street over from where I grew up, Nick Russell found out his neighbor drained his bank account because he was planning to use that money to run away with Russell's wife.

So Russell crossed the lawn and shot both the neighbor and his cheating wife in the face.

Nothing like that had happened in Willingsworth, of course—no doubt because Daniel perfected his cheating game after I walked in on him—but, even so, we weren't headed anywhere good.

After the bypass was put in and tourists stopped passing through town, all of the businesses and incomes dried up, so a new business had taken over the town. One we all knew about, but never spoke of in public.

Drugs.

I slowed before my turn, eyeing my apartment building looming in the distance.

Nicky loitered on the street corner, expertly faking at being nonchalant while he messed around with his phone—texting his bosses above whether the coast was clear.

Not that clear, I thought, sliding a look in the other direction to my diner.

The same diner that I broke down in front of—owned by the same couple who showed me even more kindness by offering me a job. For a whole year, life was pretty nice.

That was until Maybelle and Charles Mills retired and left the business to their devil spawn.

Now I got to spend my days enduring Dan's leering while serving two undercover cops who couldn't remember to leave their badges in the car while they spent all day posted up in the diner across the street from a known drug den.

Sighing, I turned at the green light—heading for my craphole above the drug den.

Parking, I got out of my car, fished out my bag, and climbed the stairs without looking left, right, up, down, or even straight ahead for too long.

One thing I learned the hard way about drug dealers, they're real fucking paranoid. They don't like people who stare.

I made it to my apartment unaccosted and shoved inside. Looking around, I sighed for what felt like the fiftieth time in an hour. I was being generous when I called this place a shithole.

The gross, puke-green wallpaper peeled off the walls, revealing the even grosser poop-brown paint underneath. The laminate floors were cracking. There was no hot water in the kitchen. There was something that very much did not like being disturbed living under my sink, and the black mold creeping up my bedroom walls forced me to sleep on my threadbare, falling-apart living room couch.

I tried for something resembling positivity as I changed out of my clothes and began preparing lunch. Setting my phone down on the table, I pressed *record,* then began my daily mantra.

"I am in control of my life. No one makes me their victim. No one has power over me that I don't give them. Soon, I will have a job that fulfills me, a home that delights me, a family that loves me, and a love that completes me."

I repeated that three times while I brought the glass noodles to a boil. By the final time, I almost believed it.

"First, Dr. Cormac didn't say it was impossible. All he said was I needed to stump up the cash, which I knew," I cried. "I knew IVF would be expensive, I just didn't know how expensive. Either way, I was always going to run into this issue, so instead of wallowing, I need to figure out how to make it work.

"There has to be a way I can come up with thirty thousand dollars. Some way... Something..."

I trailed off, letting my mind focus on chopping the vegetables so I could pretend I wasn't stumped.

"I've got to think of something," I whispered. "This is one dream I can have. I won't let money of all things stand in my way."

A knock sounded at the door.

"You're early." Setting down the knife, I padded out of the kitchen and unlocked the door. "Lunch isn't ready, Nicky, but I'm making your favorite," I tossed over my shoulder as I returned to my meal. "Japchae. And yes, I'm leaving out the mushrooms, but I'm telling you, it doesn't taste as good without them."

"I don't know," replied a voice that definitely did not belong to a fifteen-year-old boy. "I'm kind of partial to mushroom-free japchae myself."

I spun around, heart shooting into my throat. Our eyes connected... and I stopped.

My lungs stopped expanding. My heart stopped pumping. My mind held fast—stuck in this one moment and single realization that I was looking at me.

Long, shining, healthy hair flowing past my shoulders. Designer cashmere dress clinging to a body thin and toned from exercise and healthy eating, and not from skipping meals to make rent. Makeup applied with an expert hand. Orange lipstick both bold and suitable in how perfectly it drew attention to my mouth—

—until I looked at that mouth, and saw its smirk.

I snapped back, gasping as air, blood, and sense rushed into me once again—jolting me to reality.

"What the fuck are you doing here!"

Sue hissed, a slight frown cracking her perfect mouth. "Really, Sarah? We haven't seen each other in ten years, and the first thing you say to me is *what the fuck are you doing here?* At least give me a hug first."

She stepped forward and my hand flashed.

Snatching my knife off the cutting board, I brought it up between us so fast, she flung back—nearly colliding with the open door. All trace of her smirk was gone now.

"Fuck's sake, what are you doing! Put that away!"

"This isn't any concern of yours"—I flashed the knife—"because you're turning around and walking out that door."

"Dammit, Sarah!" She flung her arms down like it pissed her off that I made her throw them up. "I'm not here for this," she snapped. "I've been searching for you for months. I wouldn't have done that and come all the way here if it wasn't important."

"Sucks for you, because I'm not interested." I tossed the knife back on the cutting board without issue. It wasn't like I was actually going to kill the bitch in my apartment with my knife covered in my fingerprints. Sue had already ruined my life. I wasn't going to prison because of her on top of it. "Get out."

"Just let me say what I came here to—"

"Get out."

"—you'll regret it if you throw me out before—"

"Get out!"

Frustration bled into her tone. "This is life or death—"

"GET O—!"

"Omma's dying," she shrieked. Sue punched the door and slammed it against the doorjamb—rattling the decayed building. "She's dying, and she wants to see you before it's too late! It's the only thing she wants!"

Her screeching went in one ear and out the other. "Bullshit." I finished chopping my vegetables and transferred them to the sauté pan. "That woman can't die. She'll survive on malice and self-righteousness long after the human race dies out."

"Witty comeback as usual, Sarah, but this is serious." I heard cautious footsteps approach the kitchen. "It's cancer. She was diagnosed a couple years back. We thought she beat it, but then it came back hard. She doesn't have long, and she knows it."

I said nothing—engrossed in my cooking.

"She wants to see you before it's too late."

Silence.

"She's our mother," Sue cried. "The only parent we've got left— The only *family* we've got left other than each other. I tell you she's dying and all you can do is stand there playing with your noodles?"

Still, I said nothing. I didn't so much as lift my head.

"What is wrong with you!" A rough hand spun me around. "Do you think I'm lying or—"

"Yes."

She blinked. "What?"

"Yes. I think you're lying through your bleached teeth. You forget that I know you, Sue. I do," I hissed, "and that's why you've always hated me. Everyone else has looked at you and seen the pretty, sweet, charming person you've always pretended to be, but me..."

She backed away, expression hardening.

"I know you're nothing but a monster in a candy-coated shell." I flicked her forehead, making her jerk. "And you're already starting to crack."

Sue straightened, clearing her throat. "That's very hurtful, Sarah, and completely uncalled for. I came here not as your enemy, but as your sister. Your only sister. All I want is for the three of us to be together one final time. Please, can't you just for once leave the past in the past? What good is it doing you, sitting here in your hovel all day, frying up a side of resentment to make your Korean cheap eats go down easier?"

I clenched my teeth, fuming as my own words came back to haunt me. *Fake-ass apologies like that put all the responsibility on me for what happened, instead of on you.*

But, of course, Sue didn't even apologize. Why would she when I was the one holding on to *resentment* and *refusing to leave the past in the past*? It really had to be nice in the mind of a narcissist. They got to live an entire lifetime never doing a single thing wrong—or so they would go to their graves swearing.

I smiled winningly. "Me and the past are living quite happily in this hovel. And I'll have you know that resentment is a tasty spice, but my cheap eats don't need it. I always was the better cook than you."

"No, you weren't!" she barked, lip curling.

I smiled wider.

Sue saw it and fixed her face in an instant, internally cursing herself for the slip—and I didn't need to be in her head to know it.

I was eight years old when I figured out that my sister was a twisted, duplicitous snake. Nine when I stopped taking her crap, and made it my mission to ensure the world saw her for what she truly was. And ten when

Omma realized that the only way for us to live in a peaceful home was for her to put Sue and me at opposite sides of it.

She cleared her throat. "You know what? Have it your way, Sarah. Pick a fight. Be a bitch. Whatever it takes for you to feel like you're winning a game you're only playing with yourself."

"The only reason I came was for Omma. She wants to see you before it's too late. Are you coming or not?"

"Not," I breezed, turning back to the stove.

"Why? Don't you care about your own mother?"

"I would, if she were really dying." My tone couldn't be flatter. "But since you're lying and she's not, I'm not rushing off anywhere with you."

She choked. "I— I'm not lying! What kind of a nutcase do you think I am? Do you really believe I'd come all this way just to make up a story about our mother being on her deathbed?"

"Yep," I replied, popping the "p."

She blew out a rough breath that tickled my hair. "Fuck's sake— Fine," she snapped. "I thought you'd make this difficult, so here." I heard shuffling behind me. "I brought proof."

"What proof?" I didn't turn around. "Medical reports? Scans? Might as well put them away now because you could've easily doctored those. That's not proof of anything."

"Will you just look?"

My stirring slowed down. *There's no reason for me to look at anything she has to show me. Sue used to call Omma a poisonous prune whenever her back was turned, and I doubt her feelings toward her changed much in the last decade.*

She doesn't give a shit about honoring her dying wish, because that would require her caring about someone other than herself.

Don't get caught in her web, sense whispered in my ear. *Remember everything you learned about dealing with narcissistic abusers. Remember that no matter how much you wish, beg, plead, want them to... they never change.*

Just tell her to go.

"What is it?" I turned around and snatched the folder from her grip. "A letter *from Omma* that you wrote yourself? Pictures from the bad old days?

Or is it...?" I trailed off, reading four uppercase words across the top of the document that shut me down better than an explanation.

LAST WILL AND TESTAMENT

"What is this...?" My whole body went numb.

"Read what it says under Disposition of Property."

My hands moved of their own accord, flipping through the pages, they took me to the second to last page.

"She's leaving it all to you." Sue's voice whispered against my ear. "Yes, all that she has. Omma made some bad investments in the last couple years, and that was before she found out about the cancer. Between the chemo and experimental trial after experimental trial, she doesn't have much, but still, she's leaving it all to you. Ten thousand dollars, her car, and even Halmeoni's necklace."

"We bought the house from her to help her cover the medical bills," Sue confessed. "That belongs to me now, but you get her book collection and most of her furniture. You can keep it or sell it—up to you."

She didn't have to tell me that. I could read it all in fine, black ink. All of Omma's *earthly and monetary possessions bequeathed to my youngest daughter, Sarang Kim.*

"It's not fake," Sue blurted out in the stretching silence. "You can see for yourself that she and the witnesses all signed it. It's her real will."

Sue didn't have to tell me that either. I once dreamed of becoming a lawyer until Sue saw to the end of that. I knew when I was holding a legal document in my hands.

"You know what this means, don't you?" Sue asked when again I didn't speak.

"Yes," I rasped, holding the papers in my trembling hands. "It means Omma did something she's never done in the eighteen years I lived in her house. She... admitted she was wrong." I raised my head, gazing at her for the first proper time since she walked into my life. "And not even your lies, schemes, or tricks could ever get her to do that.

"She really is dying."

She nodded. "So... will you come?"

My grip tightened on the will, crumpling the paper between my fingertips. "Why now?"

"She's on hospice. The doctors have her on so many meds to stop the pain, they're making her loopy and confused. Some days she doesn't know what year it is or even who she is," she said. "She'll ask where you are, forgetting that she sent you away, and then when she remembers... she cries." Sue looked away, her jaw clenching tight. "She's just reliving one of the worst days of her life over and over and over, and it's hell.

"Omma is already in enough pain. She doesn't need to carry the regret of never making it right with you to the grave as well." Sue snapped back to me, glaring. "I know you think I'm some kind of monster, but not even I can watch my own mother suffer like this. I can't do anything to help her, except bring her you. So," she barked, making me stiffen. "Are you coming or not?"

I stared at her—my expression blank but my mind racing.

Why should I go with her? My own mother didn't believe me when I told her through snot-covered lips that I wasn't some psychopath who left innocent people paralyzed for life. She threw me out onto the street with nothing, ignored my calls and letters, hasn't spoken to me in ten years, and now that she wants to make up, instead of reaching out herself, she sends the last person on earth I'd ever want to see to be her message girl.

I owed Omma nothing. Less than nothing. I played the good, dutiful daughter for eighteen years, and it didn't save me from living under the constant cloud of her disappointment and its acid rain of her impossible expectations. The truth was, Ha-eun Kim was never anything approaching a good mother. I gave up on her long before she gave up on me.

"Yes," I said, turning off the stove. "I'm coming."

Chapter Two

"Are you done now?"

Her superior tone clenched my jaw.

"How much more time are you going to waste?"

"I'm not wasting time," I snapped over the wheezing engine. "I'm trying to get my car to start!"

Sue stood outside my window, hands on hips and tapping her Gucci boots. She watched me try, and fail, to start my car with a mixture of annoyance and amusement.

"Come on, baby," I whispered. "Don't give up on me now."

"I told you I'd drive you."

"And I told *you*, there's no way I'm getting in a car with you."

Sue rolled her eyes. "Okay, then drive out of the parking lot. I'll follow behind you."

The taunt cut particularly well since my engine chose that particular moment to hack up an ear-splitting cough, and then die completely.

Sue smiled at me. "Shotgun?"

Swearing, I shoved out of the car, snatched my bag from the backseat, and stormed over to the only Porsche parked in the lot. "No," I said, covertly reaching into my bag and turning my phone recorder back on. "I'm driving."

"Suit yourself."

She handed over the keys without issue, which was good because I would've fought her for them.

For as long as I was forced to endure Sue's presence, not only would I record everything she said and did, but I wouldn't put myself at her mercy in any way, shape, or form—and that included being her passenger. She might drive me home, or she might drive me across the border to the sex traffickers she sold me to for the low, low price of twelve bucks.

This was the same person who almost killed an innocent eighteen-year-old boy, and her only response was to laugh over getting away with it.

I'd put nothing past her.

Pulling out of the parking lot, I stopped just short of the street, and leaned out. "Nicky?"

The kid stopped faking like he was texting and looked up.

"I've left your lunch in the fridge. I made plenty for your sisters, so take some home to them too." I tossed him my apartment key without blinking. "No *product* in my apartment, but if you ever need a safe place to stay for the night, it's all yours."

His hard act softened for the barest moment, letting through a shy smile. A reminder that whoever he worked for, he was still just a kid. "Thanks, Ms. Kim."

"Can we go now?" Sue demanded.

I ignored her. "Also, there are two cops clocking you across the street."

"Ah, don't worry." He winked. "I clocked them first."

We said goodbye, then I set off—starting the eight-hour drive back home.

I didn't need directions. I knew the way back to my old life by heart.

***

"You must be wondering what I've been up to since you went away."

Twelve minutes. That's how long it took Sue to break the silence after the *fifth* time I told her I didn't want to talk.

"Nope," I replied simply.

"Obviously I got accepted into a string of Ivy League colleges," she plowed on. "Nearly did the full sweep. Harvard, Brown, Cornell, Columbia, Penn... Yale."

I felt her eyes on me, but mine stayed glued on the road—my expression as bland as the gray stretch of road before me.

"I'm sure I would've gotten into the others if I applied, but I decided to only entertain universities near Omma. She lost Appa and her youngest daughter took off. I couldn't abandon her too."

"Does this car take regular or premium gas?" I asked, not rising to the bait. It was wild how quickly she tried to drag me into our old routines. Sue used to love making her little, biting digs, but when I called her out, she'd spin it on me so fast—saying I was too sensitive, and attacking her for telling the truth. Some people change over a decade.

And some people don't.

"Or is it electric?" I continued. "If it is, good for you looking out for the environment."

"Well, I should," she returned, a tad snappish. "I've built my entire brand on natural and sustainable methods and products."

"Admirable."

"Yeah, it is admirable, Sarah." Temper leaked into her voice. The poor thing finally got her favorite punching bag back, only to discover it's nothing but a damp old sock.

No fun to hit.

"Some of us are trying to build things that last." She snapped her fingers in my face. "Leave a legacy that makes the world better than we found it. What do you have to show for yourself? Did you even go to college? Or was that rathole what your prestigious law firm gives you when you make partner?"

I burst out laughing. "Hardly," I chirped. "Can you imagine? *Here's a raise and a smallpox-laden apartment. Try not to think too hard about why there's a chalk outline on the floor.*" I howled. "Everyone turning to random strangers on the internet for legal advice has really hit the profession hard."

Sue tsked, turning away. "Always the clown, Sarah. That's forever been your problem. You could never take anything seriously."

I snapped up straight, setting my chin. "You're right, Sue. Tell you what? I'll take the next six hours we're going to sit in silence seriously. You won't get another word out of me." I made a show of zipping my lips and throwing away the key.

True to my word, I didn't utter another syllable to Sue, even when she made two more attempts to drag me into a conversation where she could brag about how great her life was. When I still didn't respond, she went ahead and did it anyway.

"—that's why I ended up leaving the influencer space," she said. "While I loved being an inspiration and role model to young Asian girls and women, I couldn't get past the fact that I was pouring so much of my time and energy into uplifting other people's brands, when what I really needed to do was create something of my own."

Biting hard on my lip, I flicked to the clock—my nostrils flaring. We were now at hour six, and Sue had spent three of them droning on about herself.

"When I was at Columbia— Oh, did I mention I went to Columbia?" she asked, nudging my shoulder. "I know you were all about New Haven, but there is nowhere on earth like New York City, and no better place to go to college. When I lived there, I met people from all walks of life, from so many different cultures and countries.

"The one thing they had in common was a desire for clean, healthy, sustainable products that they could afford, and that's what SueNation is all about. *Clean. Healthy. Affordable.* That's my motto."

I turned off the highway, setting down the road that would take me to Lantana—a town that I still found unique after ten years of living in many different places.

A wealthy, insular community, it backed onto the rocky, mountainous coast. Flatter land and smaller bank accounts made for closer neighbors, but as it was, the richest, longest-dwelling residents had acres upon acres to themselves—even whole chunks of the coast.

The Kim family was one of them.

I could walk our estate for an entire hour, and not reach the end of it. I also wouldn't see another soul who wasn't staff or family.

I didn't mind that so much at first. I made friends easily with the staff's kids, and we'd run through the forest—playing hide-and-seek, and stashing secrets under the rocks. It was nice... until a jealous Sue drove them all away from me with lies and bribes. Even at ten years old, she knew how to get people to do what she wanted.

After that, every minute in my own home felt cold and lonely, making me wish for the bustling, vibrant vibe of a city like New York. But even though we lived only a few hours away, Omma never took us. She used to say it was a dirty place for dirty people.

She wouldn't pay for a weekend trip to the place. I slid a look at my sister. *But now you're claiming she paid for you to go to college there? Did my mother do a complete one-eighty? Indulging Sue's every wish and whim once she became her only child? Or is Sue lying through her teeth?*

That was my car game as ten minutes of her droning turned into an hour: *Fact or Fiction?* How much of her boasting was true? How much was only true in her daydreams?

I got a break when we made a pit stop to fill up. I stayed at the pump while Sue went in to get snacks and use the restroom. I hadn't noticed she came back until I bent over the car window, and saw her messing with my phone through the glass.

"Hey!" I shot inside, snatching it from her grip and tearing a tiny scream out of her. "What the fuck do you think you're doing? Don't touch my stuff!"

"What the fuck are you doing!? You scared the shit out of me!" She threw something at my head. "I only touched it because I heard it beeping. Your phone died. I was trying to charge it for you. You're welcome!"

I flicked down to the thing that bounced off my face and saw it was indeed a phone charger.

"No one asked for your help." I flung it back at her. "Boundaries, Sue. Learn about them."

"Losing, Sarah," she mocked, adopting a high-pitched tone. "Learn about it. Because you just lost your little silent game."

"I wasn't playing a game with you, so how could I have lost?"

She smirked. "Life's a game, and you're always losing. That's why you can't tell the difference. It's second nature to you by now."

"Bitch."

"Slut."

"Cunt." I slammed the door before she got in her comeback, leaving her to scream unintelligibly through the glass.

I went inside, got some snacks because of course she didn't buy me anything, then went back to the car.

"Failure," she greeted me before my butt hit the seat. "You broke, miserable waste of life that privilege expelled into the shitter like explosive diarrhea. You have no future, no friends, no family, and no one who loves you—that's why the only one who'll miss you when you're gone is some leeching, gangbanger brat.

"And even he only likes you for your cooking."

Pale knuckles strangled the wheel—as choked as the lump pressing in my throat. A lump filled with all the insults and profanity I wanted to drown the bitch in. But what was the point? Sue would only laugh and say she was just telling the truth.

"*You're not ready to be anyone's mother, Ms. Kim. Come back when you get your life together.*"

And she'd be right.

Pushing that lump way down, I started the car, plugged my own charger and phone into the port, and then set off—resuming my silent game as Sue's laughter filled my ears.

***

Welcome To Lantana: The Only Thing Nicer Than The Scenery Is The People

I blew past the welcome sign, officially entering the town limits of the only place I'd known for eighteen years.

Night chased the sun over the horizon, blanketing the world in an inky, shining duvet.

Sue had long since tired herself out from her nonstop self-congratulating and fell asleep, her head resting on the window. The peace and quiet was almost meditative—allowing my anxious, irritated mind to relax, and imagine the scene waiting for me at home.

I wasn't kidding when I first dismissed Sue's news, not believing that my mother was dying. Wasn't it just an eerie fact of life that spiteful, cruel people got to live forever while those who tried to be good struggled on to a miserable end?

No? Okay, maybe that's too cynical, but I did always believe my mother's stubbornness would outlast my life. I would die before ever getting her to see the truth. I believed it, and now here I was… going home.

I halted at the stop sign, looking up and down the three-way stretch of road cutting through the dark and shifting forest. On one side was more forest, but on the other were the cliffs, and the sea.

What do I say to her when I see her? I turned right, taking the final street that spilled out onto the Kim Estate's private road. *Do I bring up the past? Do I ask if she finally believes that I had nothing to do with that evil prank?*

I sped along the natural bend in the road.

Or do I just thank her for making a real gesture and welcoming me bac—

A deer shot through the trees, racing out onto the street.

"Ahhh!" I slammed on the brakes.

Bang!

The last thing I saw before the deer's body flew to meet me, was the steering wheel rising to meet me first.

Chapter Three

Ring, ring, ring.

Ring, ring, ring.

A heavy, crusted lid peeled open, letting in the darkness.

Ring, ring, ring.

Discordant jangling rattled in my pounding brain, dragging me groaning out of the fog.

Slowly, achingly, I scraped myself off the steering wheel—flopping back onto the seat.

Ring, ring, ri—

The noise finally stopped, allowing silence to give way to the screaming in my head.

"Aghh." A shaky hand rose to my temple.

It came away tacky with blood.

"S-Sue?" I croaked. I blinked through the blood, straining to see through the dark, dark, and more crushing dark. "Sue? Are… you o-okay?"

The noise started up again, making me cry out.

Cellphone, my sluggish brain supplied. *It's my phone. Call for help.*

"Need help—" I turned my head, and screamed.

Wide, unseeing eyes stared at me through a red mask… even though her body faced the other way.

"Ahhhh! Ahhhhhhhhh!" I shoved against the car door, screaming, pounding, and pulling until the latch popped free—spilling me out onto the forest floor. I crawled a single inch before showering the dirt in gas station potato chips and diet soda. "Oh my God, oh my God, oh my God," I cried, crawling farther still.

Sue's eyes followed me the whole way.

Sobs wretched my throat. I cut ever more slices into my skin, clutching my face with clawing hands.

Sue was dead.

I didn't need to check. I didn't need to question. No one survived after gaining the sudden and tragic ability to tap their spine with their chin.

"Oh my God. Oh my God!" I screeched, screaming into the forest. *She was sleeping. She couldn't brace herself. Protect her head. She had no chance. She had no chance at all.*

I threw myself back, pounding the leaves and twigs—screaming myself hoarse.

How often I wished that bitch would get what was coming to her, but not this. NOT THIS!

"Oh, God, no," I cried. "Why? Why n-now? Why like this? Why me! How much can you shit on me in one day! How much?!"

My raw, strangled throat gave out, but shrieking raged on in my head.

How could this happen? I was so close—*so close*. And now I had to go back to my dying mother... and tell her I killed her eldest daughter.

Loud, hiccupping cries heaved my chest—shredding the last flicker of hope in my soul. Nothing could ever be the same again.

The person I entered the world with—the one whose soul shared mine until nature tore us in two—she was gone. And the only thing that was certain now was that my life could change, it could even improve. But it would never be whole.

Ring, ring, ring!

"Fuck's sake." I shoved up, tearing across the ground. "What do you want!?" I snatched up the phone, reading *Satan* clear and shining on the screen. "Ugh! Fuck off, Dan!"

I reeled back to fling my cell as far as I could—

Stop! I halted with my back arched in half. *Take a breath. Think. Call for help.*

Sucking in a shuddering sob, I lowered the phone on my lap—breathing in and out, slowing my thumping heart as the ringing came to a blessed stop.

A glance around didn't reveal much other than trees, dirt, dark, and more trees.

Back in high school, there were a spate of accidents on the backroads, and my friend Courtney organized a petition and protest to get more streetlights in Lantana.

They must've missed this street because I couldn't see anything beyond the glow of my phone light.

But we can't have veered far from the street. I tried to stand and fell forward, clutching my spinning head. *I'll wait by the road for the police.*

I gazed into the gloomy blackness that swallowed Sue. *They'll know what to do.*

Pressing call, I typed in *9-1-*

My phone went off again, flashing Dan's true name across the screen. Rage flared in my soul and ripped a snarl from my lips.

I'm bleeding in the dirt next to my dead sister, and this evil, predatory piece of shit was blowing me up because I missed the date he blackmailed me into.

"I'm not fucking coming, you controlling dung-licking shitbag!" I screamed, or tried to. A raspy croak was the most my ruined throat could manage. "Release all the videos you want, my life can't get any worse than this!"

I slapped *End Call* and went back to the call screen, my thumb hovering over the final digit.

I didn't move.

When the police came, they would know what to do, but... I also knew what they'd do.

They'd tell me everything was okay. That there was nothing I could've done, and that Sue's death was a tragic and unavoidable accident, but...

My mother wouldn't.

The cops would drive me to that house. To my mother. And she'd demand to know why.

Why couldn't I swerve in time? Why wasn't I paying attention? Why was I driving so fast? Why wasn't I careful? Why wasn't I safe? Why didn't I try to save her? Why did I drag my sorry ass into her home with nothing to my name but my sister's corpse and a sex tape currently trending on the Ajumma Gossip Network? Why was I a fucking failure who couldn't even get a family reunion right?

Why didn't I die too?

I rocked back, tears springing to my eyes as my phone sounded off again.

The big, triumphant moment that I'd always been waiting and wishing for—the day my mother apologizes and welcomes me back—would end with her throwing me right back onto the street.

Maybe she would let me hang on to her final gesture and not remove me from her will once again, but even if she didn't, ten thousand dollars and old furniture weren't enough to cover IVF, and it certainly wasn't enough for what happens after IVF.

It wouldn't cover getting me and my baby out of a drug-infested apartment building surrounded by cops. It wouldn't pay for me to go back to school and get my degree. And it wouldn't pay for me to give my baby the good parts of my childhood, like flying back to Korea for Chuseok with the whole family, or drama summer camp with her best friends.

I turned my head, gazing in the direction of the manor. "There's nothing waiting for me there..." My eyes drifted back the way I came. "...and there was never any life worth living back there."

Dan blew up my phone again, drowning out my whispery croak.

"I'm the one who should've died."

Dropping my head in my hand, I answered the fucking phone.

"Hello."

"Sar—! Wait, hello? Who is this?" His irritation filled my ear. "Who the fuck are you, man? Why are you answering my girl's phone?"

My mouth wanted to snap that I wasn't his girl...

...but nothing came out.

He doesn't recognize the smoker's hacking cough that's become my voice.

"Hello?! I said who is this? Where's Sarah?"

I dropped my hand, slowly lifting my head up, and up, and up—my gaze latching on eyes I couldn't see.

"Hey! You better fucking answer me!" he roared. "I swear, if that bitch is fucking around on me, I'll—!"

"She's dead."

"What?" His anger snapped like a cold front—all heat and fire doused under frigid shock. "Wait, what did you say?"

"I... I..." My mind raced a mile a minute, throwing words at me like a dealer tossing product out the window with the cops on his tail. "There was an accident," I rasped. "I pulled over to see if everyone was okay, and if they needed help and... she's dead, man. There's nothing anyone could've done. I'm sorry."

"No, no, no, stop," he cried. "Just stop!"

I'd give the bastard something. He actually sounded stricken.

"I don't understand what you're saying. What accident? Where are you? Where is she!"

"I'm out on some road in the middle of nowhere," I confessed. "I was driving cross-country when I saw a dead deer on the highway and skid marks. I had a bad feeling, so I stopped to look and..."

"Oh, God, no. Oh my God! No," he barked. "No, that's not possible. You've got it wrong. Why the fuck would Sarah be out on some highway in the middle of nowhere? You've got the wrong person."

"This is literally her phone, guy." I was almost impressed with myself for sticking to the ruse. Part of me believed what I was saying. "You called her yourself—"

"No! She's not dead! Whoever the fuck's in that car stole her phone."

I tossed my head. "I don't know anything about that. All I know is I need to call the police, and get out of here. I don't want anything more to do with this. I'm not going to be in a police station all night, questioned about why I was found next to a dead woman." The bullshit just kept falling and falling out of my mouth.

"No one's going to care about why you stumbled on some junkie thief. That's not Sarah, and—and— I'll prove it!" he burst out. "Send me a pic. I'll tell you it's not my Sarah."

I was still shaking my head even though he couldn't see. "The phone's locked. How am I supposed to—"

"Three-seven-eight-one," Daniel snapped, shocking me.

I had no idea the guy knew my phone passcode. But then, he was always hovering and following me around at work. Why should it surprise me that instead of doing his job, he stole a minute to peek over my shoulder and sneak my code?

Still, I hesitated.

Of course he was going to ask for proof. He knew how desperately I wanted to get rid of him. A part of him had to be thinking this could be all some horrible trick, but still, this was my sister. My evil bitch of a sister, but still, my sister—and she deserved basic respect in death. And the one thing she would hate above all was to be seen the way she was then.

From the split second I looked at her before flinging myself out of the car, I saw her airbag's failure to deploy left her to smash her face into the dashboard at the seventy-five miles an hour I was driving.

The force snapped her neck and ruined her face, leaving nothing recognizable behind except a mask of blood, and our eyes. Letting her body be something Dan swiped past while he was searching for our sex tapes was just obscene but I had to be rid of this fucking leech for good.

This horrible life had to be done. In every way, I wanted Sarang Kim to die.

"Hello? Hello!" Dan shouted. "Are you there?! You did not seriously just hang up on—"

"Calm down, man." Shakily, I pushed to my feet. "I just needed a minute. And you're going to need a minute too," I added. "If this is your girl, what you're going to see will... change you forever."

"I'll be fine. Because it's not Sarah," he said. "Just send the picture."

I slowly moved to the car door, unlocking my phone. Daniel didn't know I had a twin sister. It wasn't a secret. Honestly, I had no problem ranting about Sue and how she ruined my life. But the first time I brought up my mother, how she treated me, and that she threw me out of the house for a prank I didn't commit, all Daniel did was defend her.

He went on and on about how it wasn't her fault, she was doing the best she could, and that *I* should forgive *her*, because she's the only mother I've got.

Before he finished, I made up my mind not to even mention Sue. If I did, he'd want to know why I never talked about or saw my twin sister, and I for damn sure wasn't going to be subjected to a bunch of excuses for her behavior.

So, no, there was no reason Dan would look at a dead body that resembled me, and think anything other than I was dead.

At the last second I turned away, letting the camera and automatic flash do its terrible job.

I sent Daniel the picture.

"Okay, I got it," he said after a beat. "So I can tell you right now that whoever that is… isn't my… Oh, no. No. No! Sarah, no!"

I pulled the phone away, letting Dan pour his shouts, wails, and grief into the forest. As much as it wanted to, his pain didn't touch me. I gave myself to him in every way. I loved him, and he treated me like a toy he abandoned in the backyard, and then came back to kick around when he got bored.

"—no, Sarah," he wailed. "How c-could this happen? Where are you? Why is she in the passenger seat?"

I tensed. *Of course he noticed that. Why wouldn't he?*

"I don't know. I was on the I-102 going north when I saw the accident. The last town I passed was called Cordell. As for the driver, there must've been one, but they took off before I got here. Now, I really have to call the police and get out of here," I said, rushing over him when he tried to cut in. "I'm really sorry about your girl. By—"

"No, check the glove compartment," he shouted. "Get the registration and tell me the name of the rich fucking bastard who drove my girl around, and then left her dead on the side of the road!"

"Check the— Are you insane! I'd have to move her to get to the glove box. I'm not touching a dead body, man!" Those drama camps really paid off. "What the hell is wrong with you?!"

"Okay, okay, you're right," Dan said. "I— Fuck, that was too much to ask. But, come on, you have to tell me something about this guy. He can't get away with this."

"Well, I… I can tell you he is most likely a she."

"What? A girl?" Skepticism laced his voice. "How can you tell?"

"Because the seat is pushed all the way up, so they've got to be super short. And," I added, "there're a bunch of shopping bags in the backseat. Gucci, Prada, and all that shit. Could that be your girlfriend's stuff?"

"No," he dismissed. "I know better than anyone how much Sarah makes. She couldn't even afford the parking meter outside of those rich-bitch stores."

"That's all I can see." I pressed my fingers to my temple. My head was really starting to pound. "Now, I've got to hang up and put this phone back."

"Okay, but text me your number before you do." I heard shuffling on his side of the phone. "I'm looking up Cordell now, but you can drop me a pin—"

"I said no, man. I don't want anything more to do with this," I said. "Besides, you don't need me. The cops will get her phone and her license, they'll reach out to you, and they'll tell you everything—including who owns this car.

"Now, I've got to get out of here. You cool?"

"Uh, I— Yeah, I'm good." Daniel sounded more than a little put out. "I get it. You've got your own shit. Go ahead and call. Let them get her out of there. I'm sure they'll call me right after."

"All right." I hung up before he could say more.

Stepping back from the car, I stood there for a long time—staring down at my phone.

Just like that.

A picture and some silken-spun bullshit, and Daniel Mills was finally out of my life.

Or at least he will be until I return to the apartment building literally across the street from his diner, he sees me, and then he blows up at me for letting him believe I was dead.

Daniel's pain always became my bruises, and this would be no different. He'd flood the internet with my flat ass to punish me. Of course he would, unless—

I never go back.

My breaths came too fast, heaving my chest against my tight top.

But I'll have to go back, another voice argued. *There are some things that not even dying will change about Omma, and in her mind, there're no such things as accidents or mistakes. Someone is always to blame, and she'll blame me for this. There's no way she'll let me stay.*

A memory floated to my mind unbidden.

"The doctors have her on so many meds to stop the pain, they're making her loopy and confused. Some days she doesn't know what year it is or even who she is."

I nodded slowly, letting the voice talk. Letting it whisper through my jangled mind.

She's on hospice. She doesn't have much time. If I can just keep her calm and happy for her time remaining. Tell her that Sue was away and she'd be back soon. In the meantime, she sent me here to be with her, so she wouldn't be alone.

I can just keep repeating that story every time she asks until she drifts off to rest. And with Omma content and happy, she won't notice that I've used the resemblance nature gave me to borrow a bit from Sue's bank accounts, possibly to the tune of the trust and college fund she cost me with her psychotic prank. I won't be taking more than what she already owes me, that voice whispered.

Besides, when Omma's gone, everything will revert to me anyway—chiefly the manor. A manor worth a whole lot more than ten thousand dollars and an old car. All I'll have to do is sell the place, and then I'll have the money to go anywhere. Live anywhere—with my baby. There'll be no reason at all to go back to Willingsworth.

"This could work," I whispered. "This could really work."

I lifted my head, my gaze piercing the gloom into the car, and then slowly moving to the direction of the cliffs. "This is my last gift and honor to you, big sister. The promise that from this point on, you will only be remembered as young, beautiful, and successful. Exactly the way you always wanted it."

Chapter Four

"Walk us through what happened."

I hung off the back of the ambulance, wincing when the paramedic came at me with the antiseptic.

"There isn't much to tell," I replied as he dabbed the gash on my forehead. "I was driving and a deer ran out into the road. I tried to swerve, but there wasn't time. I hit the poor thing head-on, blacked out, and woke up with a busted car and bleeding head."

The officer nodded, jotting down my account in his notebook. He was a short man with sandy hair, muddy eyes, and a dusting of freckles on his cheeks. Behind him, his partner circled the remains of the deer. "How fast would you say you were going?"

"Seventy-five."

"And where were you headed?"

"Home."

He opened the wallet he took out of the car. Unzipping it, he met my eyes—looking deep into my shifting gaze. "Can you confirm your name and address for me, please?"

"56 Coral Reef Road, Kim Manor. And my name... is Soo Min Kim."

Officer Davis put Sue's license back in her wallet, and then handed it right to me. "Thank you, Ms. Kim. From the... pieces of the animal in the road and the single set of tire tracks, your story matches the evidence.

"This was clearly an unavoidable accident, and we're ready to wrap things up here. If you give me a few minutes, I'll get the accident report for your insurance."

"Thank you," I croaked. My heart pounded so hard against my rib cage, I was sure he could dance a tune to it all the way to his squad car.

Okay, he bought it, but he was never the challenge.

The paramedic glued the cut closed, then bandaged it. By the time he was done, Officer Davis returned.

"All right, Ms. Kim." He gestured to his car. "After you."

I blinked. "After me? After me where?"

"To the car." He laughed. "I'm sure you're eager to get home."

Understanding dawned. "Oh! No, that's okay," I blurted. "I'll wait here for the tow truck."

"Absolutely not." Davis handed me the accident report. "The town only has the one, and he's tied up on another job. He won't be here for hours, and there's no way I'm leaving an injured woman on the side of the street for that long.

"Here," he said, taking my arm. "Let me help you."

I wanted to argue, but didn't know how to do that without coming off strange.

Leaving anyone else alone with the car seemed like an extraordinarily bad idea. I used the clothes I found in Sue's shopping bags to clean up the blood on the passenger side—fueling the lie that I was alone in the car, but what if I missed a spot? What if they did their CSI luminol shit? What if—

"Ma'am?"

I jerked to attention, realizing Davis was waiting for me to move. Swallowing hard, I let him lead me to the car—passing his partner as she moved back to the accident scene, examining Sue's sports car.

We drove away as she opened the passenger side door and ducked inside.

I leaned back in my seat, eyes darting this way and that—taking everything in. The squad car was as immaculate as I expected of the serious man who took copious notes while I gave my story, and whipped out a tape measure to compare the skid marks on the road with Sue's tires.

I eyed him, relaxed and whistling behind the wheel. *A guy this by-the-book wouldn't be so chill if he suspected something, would he?*

I peeked inside my bag, making sure the recorder was on. *If he starts asking me weird and specific questions, I'll have proof he questioned me without a lawyer present. That'll get anything I might stupidly say thrown out.*

Although if I learned anything from living vicariously through lawyers on TV, it's that my best play right now, is to shut the fuck up.

"So," he spoke up, nearly popping me out of my seat. "Are you sure you don't want to swing by the hospital? Head injuries can be very serious."

"I'll go," I replied, holding tight to my phone. Resting beneath it was Sue's. "But I need to see my mother first. She's ill and elderly. I can't imagine how worried she's been waiting for me to come home. I need to reassure her I'm alright."

"Right, of course." He tipped his chin. "I completely understand. My first thought after a near-death experience would be to hold my family too."

I chewed my lip, eyeing him out of the corner of my vision. Am I supposed to say something in response? Is he trying to bait me with normal conversation, or is this really just a friendly chat?

If he suspected me of something, wouldn't he be driving me to the police station?

Not if he suspected you of something he couldn't prove, that whispering voice slithered in. *He'd just try to catch you off your guard, then. Get you to say something you shouldn't.*

"You take this road down to Fifth Street, then turn left on Coral Reef," I finally said, then I shut my mouth. If I could sit in silence while Sue baited me every which way from Sunday, then I could certainly keep my mouth shut with a random cop.

He nodded.

Quiet permeated the car—smothering even to me. Our route was still gripped by the trees and the occasional break through the leaves, revealing the shining sparkling sapphires that were the ocean.

In other words, there wasn't a damn thing to look at other than a mess of trees and water. Hardly engrossing enough to prevent conversation, which just made it weirder that we weren't talking.

You don't need to fill the silence. You don't need to fill the silence. You're almost to the manor. Just keep your mouth—

"So what brought you out so late at night?"

I stilled. "Excuse me?"

"What took you out of Lantana?" I felt his eyes on me. "There was a receipt in your car for a gas station in Charlesbrook. I'm assuming you were on your way back when you hit the deer."

"When the deer hit me," I corrected, then fell quiet again.

I could sense Davis waiting for me to say more.

"When it hit you," he gave in. "So, do you have family out that way? Near Charlesbrook."

"No." I pointed the way we were headed. "The only family I have is that way."

"So—"

I was really starting to hate that word.

"—if it wasn't family you were out there to see, were you out on business? Or maybe seeing friends?"

"I don't have many friends," I said to the window. "It's actually a sore subject. I cry just thinking of how lonely and isolated I've become, *so* I don't like talking about it."

"Oh, uh…" Davis stalled, his eyes lifting off me and returning to the road. "I'm sorry to hear that."

If he was really determined to have a conversation with me, I'd make it as uncomfortable as possible.

I got my wish for a whole ten minutes, then I saw his jaw crack in the rearview mirror.

"So, business, then," he concluded. "What do you do?"

"I'm a failing entrepreneur," I dropped. "I could be good at it, but I'm a parakeet—hopping from one shiny thing to another—getting bored as soon as the one before loses its shine. I might be headed for bankruptcy actually. At some point the mountain of credit card debt gets too high to bail you out."

"Oh… I see."

Another awkward silence took us as far as the final turn to the manor.

I rested my head on the cool glass, eyes fluttering shut. It had been a long and horrible night. The only thing I wanted to do was sleep—

"So—"

My lids sprung open, peeling back as far as my lips. First, I would snarl. The next thing I'd do if this fucker didn't shut up was bite.

"—if things are so bad, I'm guessing all those bags in your car were the result of some serious retail therapy."

I froze. "Bags?"

He laughed. "Your trunk was overflowing with every single designer brand my girlfriend dreams of." Davis raked me up and down. "Were the clothes, shoes, and jewels for… your mom?" he asked like he already knew the answer. "Pretty fancy for an ill and elderly woman."

Stiffly, I turned—meeting his searching eyes before they flicked back to the road. "Why would those things be for my sixty-eight-year-old mother? Why couldn't they be for me?"

Davis merged onto the dirt road, rumbling down Coral Reef. "You're dressed modestly for someone who—"

"And there it is," I snapped. "You've finally arrived at your destination."

"Excuse me?"

"Excuse you? You want to be excused? I thought I was the one who should be begging your finest pardons for not getting dressed up and put together before you found me bleeding on the side of the street?"

"What?" he cried, eyes bugging. "That's not—"

"What would you have liked to rescue me in, Officer? Should I have been wearing the tight miniskirt? Or the pumps? And you must definitely hate this saggy, old bra that I've worn for the last week?" I popped my breasts up, sending Davis careening into the side of his door. "Why oh why didn't I peel my cracked head off the steering wheel in time to change into something more uplifting, and low-cut?"

He sputtered. "I didn't say a thing about—"

"About why you didn't drive up and find me flashing my best come-hither smile?" I scoffed. "You didn't say it, but I'm sure that was your next question."

"Ms. Kim! There— There has been a terrible misunderstanding," he cried. "I, in no way, meant to imply a negative about your clothing, or what you should or shouldn't be wearing. Obviously, it is no business of mine how you choose to dress on any given day."

I sniffed. "Look, my head is killing me. I'm tired, I'm freaked out, I'm looking at a massive car repair bill. Do you think we could take a break from discussing what a friendless, broke, slovenly, living-with-my-mother loser I am?"

Davis's cheeks glowed neon red.

I really should've been a lawyer. Anyone with my ability to make a cop this flustered was destined to be.

"Of course, Ms. Kim, please rest. I apologize for..." He tossed his head. "I'm just sorry."

Accepting that, I rested my head back on the glass and closed my eyes.

Eeeeee!

I shot up, blinking under the stabbing sunlight. *I fell asleep? How? When?*

"We're here," Davis said, raising his voice over that horrible screeching. "If it's all right, I'd like to escort you inside. Get you settled."

"In... inside?" My sluggish brain sputtered and stopped, and started up again—focusing on my surroundings long enough for me to put together the picture. "Oh, no..."

The manor—

My home for eighteen years. Once photographed for the cover of *Lantana Lifestyle Magazine*. The pride of my mother's eye.

—looked terrible.

Gone was the manicured lawn. Grass and weeds hip-high grew with abandon, defiantly raising a million middle fingers to the riding mower that clipped their growth. The night I left the manor behind forever, I shot down the circular gravel path—blowing past our marble fountain, the centerpiece of our landscape. Beautiful, dancing women in flowing hanboks posed, smiled, and beckoned to the coming guests—streams of crystal-clear water dancing from their palms.

Not anymore.

The marble cracked in a dozen places—splitting their smiles, stealing their noses, dismembering their fingers and limbs.

No water was running, which was just as well. The fountain basin held nothing but dirt, leaves, and trash. Running water would only gift us a feature as muddy as the path surrounding it. Clearly, the gravel had blown away long ago, and nobody bothered to have it redone.

And still, all of that was a better sight than the manor itself.

The flower garden that used to circle the mansion, once my mother's pride and joy, was now nothing but weeds and dead bushes. The plaster was peeling. The roof was missing shingles. And a few of the windows were boarded up like an abandoned asylum, instead of a lived-in home.

Twisting around, I realized the screeching was a gift from the gate. Now unmanned, it seemed it was replaced by an automatic gate sometime after I left. And that replacement was the only upgrade that gate has gotten since, because I was now looking at a rusted, wheezing thing that wanted to be put out of its misery.

"Ms. Kim?" He stopped the car and killed the engine. "Would you mind?"

It took me a second to remember his question. "Oh, uh— Yes. That would be fine."

Climbing out, he came around to my side, opened the door, and guided me out. I leaned on him, letting him prop me up more than I needed him to. Coming across weak and fluttery would dissuade him from asking any more questions. How could I deal with his questions when I couldn't handle my own?

How did the manor get this bad? Where were the staff? The groundspeople? The gardeners? The housekeepers? Anyone?

Davis led me up the brick staircase.

Loose stones wobbled beneath our feet, welcoming us officially into the house of disrepair.

If it looks this bad on the outside, how bad is it on the inside? Another, harsher, thought occurred to me. *It must be falling apart inside too. That's why Sue didn't care that Omma left me all her furniture and the manor's contents.*

The real wealth is in the building and in the land. Why would she be jealous when she knew when it came to the inheritance game, she still won?

The thought crossed my mind, then I shoved it out. What did it matter now? Any games she may or may not have been trying to win? Any manipulations she thought she was running on me? None of that mattered.

Sue was gone.

She was more than gone. Because of me, she was a battered corpse on the ocean floor. I robbed her of a proper burial. I was erasing her from her own life. The least I could do was think more charitably of her now, and let the past finally be the past.

"Ms. Kim?" Davis looked at me like he'd been trying to get my attention for a while. "Your key?"

"Oh, right." I fumbled in my bag, fishing out Sue's housekey.

Passing it over, he pushed inside and helped me in.

Our eyes locked immediately.

Time slowed, then ground to a screeching halt—trapping me in this single moment. With a single thought.

I know you...

The man paused on the staircase, clearly in the middle of descending them when we burst inside.

Curly hair that was a cheek-tickling, dusky brown. Glinting, melty hazel eyes, and that tight, muscled body that somehow got tighter and musclier. His handsome, angular face crumpled in a frown—stealing the breath from my lungs before he, or I, even got a chance to speak.

"Sue?" He fixed on Davis. "What's going on?"

"Excuse me, sir," Davis said. "May I ask who you are?"

His frown deepened. He came the rest of the way down the stairs, stepping from the shadows into the light of the early morning. "Who am I?"

"No..." I whispered. "Please, no..."

"Who do you think I am? I'm her—"

Don't say it.

"Husband," Alexander finished, pulverizing my heart into dust. "What happened to her—? Sue, what happened to you?"

I couldn't move. Couldn't speak.

"—in a car accident..." Davis's voice reached me from far away. "...hit a deer... wanted to come home instead of the hospital—"

"What? And that didn't seem like a bad idea to you?" Alex rushed me, taking me stiff and unmoving into his arms. "Sue, are you okay? Why would you refuse to go to the hospital? You know how serious head injuries are." He twisted around. "Guys? Guys, get in here!"

Sounds muted—smothered under the roaring in my ears. The thundering of rushing footfalls tried to penetrate, but it did not do so as successfully as the sight of two other handsome, dazzling men rushing into the front room.

Long, raven hair, and razor-sharp cheekbones. Eyes that weren't laughing at the moment but were still tantalizing lady-trappers.

"Sue, you okay, baby?" Micah dropped a kiss on my lips before I could squeak. "What happened to your head?"

Coiled, tight brown curls rose over Micah's head like an umber-drenched sunrise. Dark, almost black ink stole all the color from his iris, but not the concern in his eyes.

I did get out a squeak when he reached around Micah and kissed me too.

"Is this why you didn't come home last night?" Rhodes asked. "Are you hurt?"

My lips parted—to say what, I wasn't sure—

—until I heard her voice.

"Mommy?"

The world stopped.

A tiny purple torpedo shot down the stairs and barreled through the crowd forming around me. Throwing her arms around my waist, she looked right up into my eyes—tearing a cry from my lips.

My baby...

In front of me. In my arms. Drowning me in her calla lily eyes.

She was mine.

My angular face. My full lips. My button nose. Even my thick, bushy brows. The only features stolen from me by her father were her thick, curly hair and round, blinking eyes. But everything else was me. *Mine*. She was—

Sue's.

Not my baby. Sue's baby. Her daughter. That she lived with in a house with Micah, Rhodes, and Alex—all of whom touched and kissed the woman they thought was Sue without a trace of jealousy between them. And in that moment... I knew.

I knew why Sue spent eight fucking hours in the car talking about herself but didn't once mention she was in a relationship, or three, and that she had a daughter.

I knew she didn't tell me, because she wanted this. She wanted this exact moment where I stood there—eyes blown and mouth gaping like a fish—shocked down to my very soul that Sue went out and landed the only three guys on the planet I truly fell head over heels for.

She wanted to see the look on my face when I realized just how much she stole from me—just how much she won.

The mother's love I lost. The baby I couldn't have. The home I never really had. And the men who made my heart skip three beats even then—no matter all the time that passed.

She took it all. And for all her bullshit about wanting to bring me home and make things right with Omma, she still couldn't resist another opportunity to laugh at my pain as she twisted the knife in.

My promise and resolution to forgive her burned away in an eruption of white-hot hatred.

Looking into Micah's, Rhodes's, and Alex's eyes, I had only three words to say to their worries and concerns.

"That fucking bitch."

Pitching to the side, my head rushed to meet the floor. Darkness took me before it finished the trip.

Chapter Five

I lay in the middle of the bed, trying not to look left, right, or forward as the doctor checked me out.

"Hmm." She flashed that annoying light in my eyes. "Any numbness or dizziness?"

"No."

"Nausea or vomiting?"

"No."

"You said before you fainted that you had a pounding headache." She drew back, which gave my newly acquired niece room to move in and snuggle under my arm. "How's your head feeling now?"

"Fine. The headache's gone," I replied. "The impromptu nap helped."

"But she should still go to the hospital, shouldn't she?" Rhodes spoke up from his position on the left side of the bed.

Micah was posted up on the right. Alex had the foot of the bed covered. And even worse, Davis was posted up against the bedroom door.

There was no escape.

"I... I am a little confused," I confessed. "And my memory..." I swallowed hard. "There are blank spots."

Doctor Martin was short, bespectacled, and freckled. Her glasses popped up when she scrunched her dotted nose. "Blank spots? Meaning what?"

"Meaning..." I lifted my head, peering at the guys through my lashes. "What... what exactly is our... relationship?"

Rhodes frowned. "Our relationship?"

"Yeah, I mean... What...?" My mouth was paper dry. "What are the four of us... to each other?"

Micah's brows blew up his forehead. "That's it." He advanced on me. "We're taking you to the hospital."

"Wait, please," I cried. I threw my arm around the little girl protectively—as if Micah was about to snatch her from the crazy lady. "Just answer me first."

"Answer you fir— Sue, you know who we are? And if you *don't* know who we are, something is very, very wrong."

"Micah, Alex, and Rhodes," I blurted, cutting off whatever he was going to say next. "I know who you are. Of course, I do. There are just some blank spots," I said again. "Help me fill them in."

"Some confusion and memory loss can happen following a concussion," Doctor Martin put in. "It's called a traumatic brain injury for a reason."

Micah looked from her to me, then he glanced at Alex and Rhodes.

Alex shrugged, clearly not knowing what to do in this situation any more than he did.

That makes three of us.

Micah sighed. "We're your husbands, Sue. We've been married for seven years."

I bit my lip hard, penning in the tears that sprung to my eyes. I knew it had to be something like that, but still, hearing it crushed my heart to pulp.

"Uh, excuse me?" Davis came alive. "Did you say *husbands*? Plural?"

"Relax," Alex shot back. "She's only legally married to one of us. No bigamy here."

"And I'm sure when I look into the matter, the truth will bear that out."

Alex's eyes flashed. "Are you kidding me? You're standing by my wife's bedside after she was nearly killed, and you've summoned so much pity in your heart it amounts to threatening her with an investigation?" Alex scoffed. "What happened to you, man? Is this the person you wanted to be when you signed up for this job?"

Davis looked truly offended. "The person I wanted to be when I accepted this badge is a person who lets no one escape the—!"

I tuned him out, taking a chance to take a proper look around the bedroom.

I already knew I was in Sue's room. It was the same room she grew up in. But if that accident had conked the memory out of my head and I needed a reminder, I would've gotten the hint from the many... many... many photos of Sue plastered up literally everywhere.

Photos of Sue frolicking through the Tuscan fields. A photo of her posing in front of the Colosseum. A photo of her eating gelato on a gondola in Venice. Parasailing in Interlaken. Riding elephants in Chiang Mai. Hiking

Uluru. Beaching it up in New Zealand. Dancing in Rio. And a few adult photos of her in Seoul and Daegu—replacing the childhood photos of her in Seoul and Daegu, standing next to me.

The photos taken in Korea I knew with a single glance. But the reason I knew where the other photos were taken was because Sue helpfully pinned them to the corresponding places on the massive painted world map taking up the entire east wall. An addition that definitely wasn't there when we were kids.

Truthfully, the map was stunningly beautiful. So beautiful it dwarfed her expensive furniture, antique wardrobe, four-poster king-sized bed, plush cream carpets, and large vanity weighed down with makeup, perfumes, and accessories that cost more than my life.

The map artist made their work come alive with rolling ocean waves, undulating green fields in the rural parts of the world, and stretching skyscrapers in the cities. All of the countries with famous landmarks had them proudly displayed with the Eiffel Tower for France, and the penis building for England.

There to make the creation more beautiful were all the smiling, happy, gorgeous photos of a woman who crisscrossed the earth.

I could just imagine Sue's face if she'd gotten the chance to give me a tour of her new room. She'd have smirked her ass off while forcing me to see that she'd gotten to travel the world, searching for adventure. While I traveled the backroads of the States, searching for a home.

Shoving that mental smirk away, I flicked down to the little girl smiling up at me. Lowering my voice, I whispered, "And what's your name, beautiful?"

She giggled. "Mommy, you're silly. You know my name."

My chest tightened. Of course it was wrong to trick a child. Let her believe I was her mother, when her actual mother was trawling the ocean floor. But if Sue had been able to take a break from being an evil, manipulative bitch for five minutes, I wouldn't have walked in here with the wrong name on my lips, and the wrong wallet in my purse.

What was I supposed to do when Alex, Rhodes, and Micah came at me, calling me their wife and showering me in relief and concern? Was I supposed to say, *oh, sorry, I'm not actually your wife. I'm her twin sister who is currently impersonating her to get back the life she stole from me?*

What? You want to know where the real Sue is? Well, funny thing is, I threw her broken body off a cliff.

There was no ending to that conversation that went well. Davis would've turned me right around and marched me to the nearest jail cell.

On top of that, this little girl believed her mother was sitting right next to her. How could I be the one to tell her she was dead, and she'd never see her again?

I gazed into her eyes, my broken head wrecked for reasons that had nothing to do with its meeting with the steering wheel.

I just have to go along with it for now until I figure out the best way to handle this without ending up in prison. I'm not after anything that isn't already mine. When it's all said and done, I'll make them understand why it all got so screwy.

Sighing, I smiled at her. "Yeah, Omma's silly sometimes, but I like to be silly every now and then. Do you like to be silly?" I asked as the argument between the guys and Davis got louder.

She nodded.

"Then, let's be silly and ask each other lots of silly questions." I winked. "I'll go first: what is the name of the prettiest girl in the world?"

She giggled again. "Nari!"

"Nari," I whispered. "That is a beautiful Korean name. So, let me guess, your other name is Lily."

"Uh-huh."

"And how old are you, Lily?"

"This many." She held up six fingers.

"I see, and..." I lowered my head, speaking softly in her ear. "Which one is your daddy?"

Lily cocked her head, brows crumpling.

I tried another way. "What's your last name?"

"Nari Kim!"

Chewing my lip, I let it go. They probably hadn't gotten too far into the discussion of biology and one-sperm/one-egg discussions with a six-year-old, and that was okay. It was only a teenage girl's obsessive curiosity that made me ask.

I spent an entire year of high school doodling Sarah Newbury, Sarah Spencer, and Sarah Montgomery in my notebook, and that was only when I was taking a break from imagining what versions of our children would look like. My little cherub face with their everything else? The only result of that union would be completely, off-the-wall adorable—

—and she is, I thought, stroking Nari's hair.

A small part of me wanted to know which version of my fantasy came true—

—with the wrong sister.

I let out a rough breath, feeling the question I truly needed to ask coming up my throat. "Do you have any brothers or sisters, baby girl?"

She tossed her head. "No. I want a sister, but you won't let me have one."

I barked a startled laugh at her directness. Oh yes, I loved this girl.

"And does... Omma have a brother or sister?"

She cocked her head the other way. "Grandma?"

"No, me," I corrected. "Do I have a brother or sister?"

"Nuh-uh." Her denial crashed on my head like a ton of bricks. "Just Mommy. Grandma wanted one perfect child, just like Mommy wanted one perfect child." Nari said it in a tone like she was repeating something she'd been told many times before. "So I can't have a sister because you don't have one, but that's not fair, Mommy. I still want one."

I didn't lose my smile. "Of course you do, baby. I always wanted a brother too."

Leaning back, I tipped my head to the ceiling so Nari wouldn't see me seethe.

The worst part was that I wasn't even surprised, and I didn't even blame Sue.

Sue couldn't erase me from my childhood home and my hometown... unless my mother did it for her.

How could you live in the same home as your grandmother and believe she only had one child, unless she let you believe it?

It's also the only explanation for why her husbands don't know they're not talking to their wife.

When a carbon copy of your wife walks through the door, your brain takes a shortcut to the simplest explanation: *This is your wife.*

It doesn't think *this is your wife's secret twin sister that she brought home to surprise us so she could also get off on crushing her sister's feelings one last time.*

It also didn't help that ten years didn't change the two of us much at all. We still cut our hair the same length. Our body types were still the same, and we didn't gain any new or visible piercings or tattoos. There was nothing about me to make a person think I wasn't Soo Min Kim.

Our differences had always been on the inside.

"Okay," I breathed, returning to Nari. "Do you have any silly questions to ask me?"

Her brows blew up, mimicking the little "o" her pink lips made. "I can ask too?"

"Sure can."

"Hmm."

Her look of concentration was so adorable, it made my heart burst. There was a hundred percent chance that if my baby-crazy self had known about Nari earlier, I would've bankrupted myself a long time ago, because I would've showered her with gifts and attention at every possible opportunity.

"Uhh, how... old are you, Mommy?"

I laughed. "I'm twenty-eight, but that's not a silly question." I tickled her, making her squeal so loud Doctor Martin spun away from her laptop to check on us. "You have to ask a silly question, like am I a flying purple people eater, because the answer is..." I roared, pouncing on her. "Yes!"

Roaring, groaning, growling and carrying on, I tickled Nari all over—peppering her face with kisses.

She flat-out screamed with laughter, kicking and twisting to get away.

"I'd say you're going to be just fine." Dr. Martin tapped my shoulder, drawing my attention to the pill cup in her hands. "Wouldn't hurt to go to the hospital for an MRI, but your symptoms fit with a concussion, and they're only going to tell you what I'm telling you now.

"You need to rest for the next couple days," she said. "No strenuous activity. Limited screen time, and take this when you feel a headache coming on." She tipped the pain pill onto my palm. "Your blank spots will fill in now that you're home and in familiar surroundings, but if you feel yourself getting worse instead of better, or you're not back to your old self within a few weeks, I want you to call me immediately."

I agreed. "Thank you, Doctor."

"And, you three." She turned on Micah, Rhodes, and Alex, ending their argument with Davis. "I want you to monitor her, keep her hydrated, and all-around be at her beck and call."

The four of them traded chuckles.

"Now, if that's all"—Dr. Martin pinned Davis with a look—"she needs to rest."

"Yes, of course," he replied, finally peeling himself off the door. "I'm glad to see you're in good hands, Mrs. Kim. The tow company should be in touch with you directly, but if you don't hear from them within the week, call me personally and I'll take care of it." He crossed the room and laid his business card on my nightstand. "If you need to discuss anything with me," he murmured, meeting my eyes. "Just call."

"Uhh, right. Okay."

Tipping a nod, he left—following Dr. Martin out the door.

It closed shut, leaving me alone with Sue's family.

"Lily, baby." Micah came over and lifted Nari up. "Why don't you go and get Mommy some water, so she can take her medicine?"

"Okay!" She shot off and out the door, racing to obey.

"So," I spoke up when I found my voice. "I know you guys will want me to go to the hospital for the MRI, but I really feel fine—"

"What the fuck do we care if you get the MRI?"

I blinked. *What did he say?*

Rhodes scoffed, lips curling. "Damn, you always did put on a good fucking show. Making up some shit about losing your memory just so you and everyone in the room can hear us say that you own us, and have done for seven years."

"Was that your favorite part of the performance?" Alex asked, snapping my eyes to him. The expression on his face actually made me scoot back against the headboard. "'Cause I was fighting to keep down my breakfast when she was playing and tickling Nari like she hasn't been leaving every room our daughter enters since she was fucking born."

"Wha...? What—?"

"Save it, Sue," Alex snapped. "When we all woke up this morning and your bed was empty, we actually let ourselves hope that you fucked off and weren't coming back."

The three of them turned away, heading out the door.

"We should've known that was too good to be true."

They left, leaving me sitting there with my jaw literally hanging. At that second it finally hit me that Sue had three husbands, but I had her phone... and it didn't ring once the entire night.

They didn't call asking where she was.

They didn't text to see if she was okay.

They didn't say *I love you* or *I'm so glad you're safe* when I walked through the door.

Micah, Rhodes, and Alex truly were my soulmates.

Because they hated Sue just as much as me.

***

I crept out of Sue's room the next morning, tiptoeing through my own house like I didn't belong there. I certainly didn't feel welcome since Micah, Rhodes, and Alex didn't come back after walking out the day before. They really didn't give a shit about my recovery.

Not even Nari came back with the water, I had a feeling that was because one of the guys intervened, and redirected her to another activity that had nothing to do with her terrible "mother."

I did leave the room a few times to get food, water, and twice, to check on Omma. Both times I poked my head in my mother's room, she was sleeping and her live-in hospice nurse asked me to poke my head right back out and let her rest.

The presence of Reynard Agassi, the nurse, wasn't too much of a surprise. Sue did tell me Omma was ill and didn't have long, and since Sue was in no way the nurturing type, of course, she'd hire someone to look after her.

What did surprise me was the notable lack of any other staff. If Sue didn't nurse, she for damn sure didn't cook, clean, garden, or mow, so where were the housekeepers, cooks, and groundspeople that we grew up depending on?

I passed through the dimly lit hall, straining to see thanks to the many burnt-out bulbs. Not that I needed more light shone on the dingy walls, dusty furniture, and dirty carpets. Every room I wandered into the day before was in desperate need of a good dust-sweep-mop combo, and the kitchen didn't have anything in it other than a few dusty old cans in the pantry, and a mountain of takeout containers in the trash.

Did Omma and Sue fire all the staff?

My mother didn't like to be seen in any way other than her best, so it was possible she dismissed the staff when she fell ill.

It was also possible that they all straight up quit and left when Sue bought Omma out of the house.

Sue wasn't kind or respectful to the staff when we were kids. I very much doubt that changed when she became their boss.

Stepping out onto the landing, I gazed down on the bottom floor—listening to voices filtering out of the dining room.

"—gotta hurry, baby girl, or you'll be late for school."

"Daddy, I did all my homework," Nari proudly announced. "It was so easy."

"Well, naturally, it was easy for you—the smartest, most talented Lilybug in the whole world." Even after all these years, I knew Micah's voice when I heard it. And I knew there wasn't a trace of disdain in it when he talked to Lily.

Not like there was when he spoke to the woman he thought was her mother.

"I bet you could do Daddy's homework too, right? How does that sound?" I heard the strange plasticky squeak of Styrofoam. "Want to go to Daddy's work and boss everyone around for me?"

"Yes," she cried, giggling away.

"You got it, but first, school."

"Is Mommy picking me up today?"

I straightened, ears perking up.

"Mom can't pick you up today, sweetie. Remember, she's not feeling well. That's why she couldn't tuck you in last night or have breakfast with you."

I choked, indignation welling up in me fast. I would've happily done all of those things! He only had to ask!

As fast as that fury flared up, that's how quickly it dissipated.

It wasn't me he didn't invite to bedtime or breakfast, it was Sue. And she probably gave him good reason.

I shook my head, turning away and continuing on.

I couldn't imagine Sue as a mother. We hated each other's fucking guts, so growing up, there weren't any late nights spent giggling under the covers as we talked about our dreams and wishes for the future. Meaning that I genuinely never knew her stance on children or if she wanted them, but I know that I'd never witnessed Sue care for a single being on this planet that wasn't herself.

Every pet she was gifted she neglected. Every friend she made she gaslit and tormented with her stupid drama and mind games. And every member of her family she played, lied to, or tortured.

You didn't tend to find those actions listed on the résumé of a good future mother.

Which makes me wonder what past experiences were on Omma's life résumé before she had us. My steps slowed carrying me to my mother's door. *Was she cold, rigid, and exacting with everyone in her life? Or did she save those qualities for her only daughters?*

"Hello?" I knocked, then pushed in. "Omma, are you awake—? Oh!"

Click.

A blur crossed the carpet—moving from the head of the bed to the foot so fast, they made my still concussed brain dizzy.

"Alex?"

The thirty-two-year-old man spun on me, lips curling and eyes flashing like I was a swarm of dung beetles that stormed the room. "What are you doing in here!?"

I jerked back. "Excuse me? What do you think I'm doing in here? I'm here for my sick mother? What are *you* doing in here? And why are you yelling at me?"

"I—I didn't—" Alex tossed his head, his cheeks reddening. "I... apologize for raising my voice. You just startled me."

I cocked a brow, no less confused by that explanation. I called from the other side of the door and knocked before entering. What was he doing that he didn't realize I was coming in until I jump-scared him?

Stepping further in, I noted the corner nook where Reynard set up his chair, books, and medical items was vacant. "Where's Mr. Agassi?"

"I know you long for the days of slave labor, Sue, but he's on his breakfast break. Where the fuck else would he be?"

Wow, is that what I sounded like whenever I talked to Sue?
Like a moody bitch.

"Fair enough." I slowly closed the distance between us, even though his entire demeanor screamed, *fuck off!* so loudly, it was deafening.

Let it deafen me. The last time I was this close to him, and he wasn't putting on a show for a cop, was ten years ago.

It was crazy how one look at my old crushes activated that deep longing in my soul like no time had passed at all.

Alexander Montgomery used to walk the halls of Titan Prep with a smile for everyone, and a kind word for everyone else. He was just one of those people you couldn't help but like. And it wasn't just because he was pretty.

Which he very much still is.

I raked him up and down, unable to stop myself. The years had been good to him—again Alex went from a handsome young man to a gorgeous grown one. All of the parts of him that still needed filling out took to the task with his valedictorian gusto.

His shoulders were wider and thicker. His youthful plumpness shed away, leaving behind a hard, ropey body. And the bulge straining his running shorts was *bulgier.*

He even smelled more delicious than that time in high school when I *pretended* to accidentally bump into him. Back then he smelled like apples and erasers. Now, he smelled like cinnamon, pine, and the salty spray of the ocean—a combination that didn't make sense, but scrambled my head all the same.

"So..." I ran a finger down his chest, tensing him up tighter than a bowstring. "Do you take over his nursing duties when he's off on break? Or are you some kind of pervert with a geriatric kink that gets off on watching old ladies sleep?"

"What the hell did you just—!" Alex caught sight of my grin. Slicing his rant off, he sighed—flicking his shiny, brown locks out of his eyes. "Fucking hell, all right. You caught me. I decided to end our six-month dry spell by climbing atop the drooling, nearly vegetative woman who called me a wet, limp sock of a man."

I choked on a laugh, slapping my hand over my mouth. "Oh my gosh, Omma said that? Wow. She was never nice to any guy I brought home, but that's particularly cutting. And incredibly untrue." I dropped my hand, folding it safely behind my back. "Only have to look at you to know there's nothing limp about you."

A ghost of a smile tugged at his lips. "Hmm. Well, that's Ha-eun Kim. She's the master of reducing a man down to nothing in seven words or less."

"Or at least she was"—Alex sidestepped me and walked out—"until you took over."

I let him go. What would I even say to stop him? His words were for Sue, not me. The marriage between the four of them had clearly gone sour, and the last place I should be is in the middle of it... right?

I mean, my fourteen-year-old crushes couldn't compete with my sister's marriage to these men, or the very real child she had with them.

"No," I whispered, silently closing the door. The only thing for me to do was make peace with my mother, find a way to keep her happy and comfortable for the rest of her short time, and then leave with the inheritance Sue stole from me, and the one my mother wanted to give me.

Micah, Rhodes, and Alex straight up told me to my face that they wanted Sue gone. It's not like they'll miss her.

But Nari will, another voice whispered through my mind. *And she'll spend every day of the rest of her life believing her mother ran out on her.*

Her mother did leave her, sense returned. *For better or worse, the true Sue is gone, and I don't have the right to trick that poor child into believing anything else.*

Shaking my head, I tossed all the whispering voices out of it—focusing on my mother. Somehow, she was still asleep. The mother I knew never went to bed before me, or woke up after me. If I ever wanted to catch her asleep, I lurked around in the wee hours like I was stalking Santa Claus.

"Omma?" I perched on the edge of the mattress and took her hand. "Omma, can you hear me?"

Looking upon her then, still and frail in sleep, one truth struck me through the chest.

Sue did not lie to me. My mother was dying.

Her thick, salt-and-pepper strands were gone, leaving only a silk bonnet wrapped around her scalp where her hair used to be. Everyone I knew used to remark on how young Omma looked for her age. That they couldn't believe she gave birth to us at forty.

I doubt she'd heard such platitudes in a while.

The cancer leeched away the deceptive smoothness and natural color to her complexion, leaving a washed-out, wrinkled version of my mother. Her eyebrows were gone. Lips dry and chapped. Eyes sunken in, and her frame bereft of nearly twenty pounds at least.

"Omma?"

She stirred, one eye peeling open.

"Good morning, Omma."

When we were little, our parents adopted the "one language for each" method to make sure we grew up fluent in both English and Korean. Up until around ten, our father only spoke to us in English, and our mother only spoke to us in Korean. And if we wanted to speak to her, we'd better respond in Korean.

As a result, I'd spent the first ten years of my life addressing this woman as Omma. Even after she relaxed the rule and allowed us to speak to her in English, calling her Mom, or Hera forbid *Mommy*, was just weird.

"S... S..." She strained to turn over.

"No, don't." I sprung forward, taking her hand. "Please, don't strain yourself. I didn't want to stress you out first thing, I just had to let you know I was here—"

"Sarang."

Direct and clear as a bell, Omma saw through the clothes I dug out of Sue's wardrobe, and straight to me. Of course, she did. No mother would ever confuse their child with someone else. Not even their biological copy.

"Sarang, dear, is... that you?"

"It's me." I moved closer, the hand in hers trembling.

I replayed this moment over and over in my head almost every day for ten years. All the things I would say to her—*scream at her*. How many apologies I'd extract from her in exchange for my forgiveness. All the crow I'd shove down Sue's throat as Omma finally saw through to who my sister was. I built the fantasy up so much in my head—

—and now I didn't care about any of it.

She's dying in a broken-down manor with no money, no friends, no husband, and no Sue. Omma took my life, and life took her daughter.

I'd say we've both suffered enough.

"You look well," she whispered. Her eyes were barely open. She looked seconds away from drifting back to sleep. "Have you... been eating?"

I cracked a smile. "Yes, I have been eating. Turns out that's a requirement for living."

A soft chuckle reached my ears, blowing my eyes wide. My mother did not laugh easily. I'd seen her sit through countless romantic comedies and not summon so much as a twitch of the lips.

Emboldened, I scooted closer, laying my other hand over hers. "I've even been making japchae the way you like. I can't believe I ever said Korean food was yucky. That's why you can't trust the culinary opinion of a kid who thinks boogers are a delicacy."

Omma laughed out loud—or the closest thing to it. A rough, whispery sound coughed up her lungs—weak and soft, but still, a laugh.

"Oh, my silly girl, what do you mean you made japchae? You know you're not allowed in the kitchen."

My brows snapped together. "What?"

"It's not nice to take credit for Mrs. Prado's work."

"Mrs. Prado?"

Mrs. Prado was the manor's head chef when I was a kid, and going by the current state of the kitchen, she hadn't been around for a long time.

"Promise me you'll stay out of the kitchen and out of Mrs. Prado's way." Omma closed her eyes, giving up the battle with her heavy lids. "Say it, Sarang."

"I promise," I blurted—surprised even at myself for how quickly I fell into old patterns with her.

"Sarang?"

I jumped, snapping up as Reynard pushed into the room.

"Did she just call you sarang?"

I seized up—wide eyes darting left to right for somewhere to hide. "I— I— She— She—"

"That means love, doesn't it? That's so sweet."

"Um... sweet?"

"I've never heard her call you, or anyone, by a pet name before." He came in the rest of the way, carrying an empty water bottle and his lunch bag. "Although, to be fair, she could be saying all sorts of things in Korean that would zip right over my head." He laughed. "That's why I've started taking lessons."

"Lessons?" I couldn't seem to stop repeating him like a moronic parrot.

"Yes," he sighed. "You know how rough it's been. How confused she's getting. More and more she's going whole days where she doesn't say anything, and if she does, it's all in Korean. I figured that's my cue to fire up the language-learning apps."

Reynard stopped his packing away to smile at me. "But I'm very glad I learned enough to hear you two make up. Last week, she screamed such awful things at you— Things she didn't mean," he rushed to say. "But today she calls you love because that's what you are, and how she truly feels. She loves you, Mrs. Kim. Never forget it."

"Oh... uh... Thank you," I finally got out. "That's really nice of you to say." I got to my feet. "And it's nice of you to go above and beyond in caring for my mother. Makes me feel like less of a horrible daughter for hiring someone to do it for me."

He busted up. "I hear that a lot, and I tell those families the same thing I'm telling you. Even your parents relied on teachers, babysitters, nannies, and relatives for help when they were raising you. So why should you feel guilty about needing help to care for them?"

"Huh." I rocked back, blinking at him. "I never thought of it like that, but that's an amazing point. I wish I had that comeback ready when I was fourteen and Omma told me if I ever dared put her in a home, she'd write me out of the will. I should've been like, *this from the woman who never met a nanny she didn't like!*"

Reynard laughed so hard he doubled over.

I liked him. He was a jovial man and he thought I was much funnier than most people did.

"She needs to rest," I said. "I'll be back later."

Making for the door, I flicked to the opposite side of Omma's bed to her nightstand—wondering what made the click that Alex was so desperate for me not to notice, he evaporated from the spot as quickly as he could.

Chapter Six

"Mrs. Kim?"

I raised my head, setting down the magazine. A prim and proper gentleman in a brown suit and large glasses flashed me his best professional smile.

"Right this way, ma'am, the manager can see you now."

Standing up, I smoothed down the vintage designer dress I found at the back of Sue's walk-in dream closet. It was an old-school, off-the-shoulder, little-black-dress Chanel. A gorgeous piece, but I was surprised Sue owned it. I was the one into cute, funky, vintage clothes.

Sue was into turning up her nose at *pre-owned* clothes. When we were teens, she wouldn't be caught dead clothed in something some random had farted and sweated in.

But I guess even my sister is allowed to change. I followed behind the gentleman, passing under the tinkling, gold chandelier. *Although, not that much. She still settled for nothing less than the finer things.*

After leaving Omma to rest and have her breakfast, I showered, changed, then found myself in the back of a stranger's car, paying them to take me to the bank whose logo I read on all the financial documents I found in Sue's desk.

Swanky was the first word that came to mind when I walked into Lantana Private Bank.

No one had to tell me this bank catered to the ultra-rich of Lantana. I figured that out myself when the attendant looked me up and down at the door, clocked my designer dress and purse, made me produce ID before taking another step inside, and then guided me to a gold-and-blue waiting area with plush leather seats, financial magazines, and a selection of herbal teas for me to drink while I waited for the manager to *receive me in the personal client room.*

He swept open the door for me, actually bowing and gesturing for me to enter.

I wasn't sure if he bowed to all the clients, or just the Asian ones, but I doubt that added layer of deference made the huge account minimums, and even huger account fees, worth banking here.

I'd have done just fine with the rinky-dink, two-manned credit union down the street.

"Good morning, Mrs. Kim." The manager rounded the desk and pulled the chair out for me. When he bowed to me too, I knew it was an Asian thing. "Lovely to see you again. What can I do for you today?"

I relaxed in the armchair, fighting not to gape at the extravagance around me. Ten years of poverty made me forget what it was like to sit in rooms with expensive artwork on the wall, custom mahogany antique Victorian desks, stained glass windows depicting the life and laughter of dancing mermaids, and a desktop computer I couldn't afford even if I sold my eggs.

"Good morning," I greeted. He didn't tell me his name, and I didn't ask for it. He obviously knew Sue, and giving away that I didn't know him would be a major red flag. But he did look exactly like how I pictured the guy who managed a bank for the uber-rich.

Like the Monopoly man.

"I don't want to take too much of your time," I said. "I'm here for a complete financial review of all of my accounts, and then I want the total of all of those accounts to be transferred to another bank."

"Very well," he replied, not blinking twice at the request. "We can certainly take care of that today. First, if I may, I'll need to take you through the security questions and reconfirm your identification."

I replied yes also without blinking twice.

Mother's maiden name? Knew that.

Street I grew up on? Check.

Name of first pet? The hamster was named Henri until Sue went days without feeding him, and I saved the poor thing from her and named him Mister Fuzzybutt.

"And your account pin?"

"Five-eight-two-three," I rattled off. That I didn't know off the top of my head, until I found it scribbled on the back of her account papers in her desk. Honestly, it amazed me that more siblings didn't rob each other blind.

Not that they should, of course.

"Thank you for that information, Mrs. Kim." *Tip-tap-tap* he went on the keyboard. "Now, the financial review is rather simple. You only have one personal account with us now, after choosing to close your investment and business accounts. The total in your remaining account is..." He flipped the screen around, letting me see the number.

$42,176

"Forty-two thousand dollars," I whispered.

It didn't come near enough to pay back the money Sue cost me from my college and trust fund, but that was enough to pay for IVF, and put first month's rent and a security deposit down on a better apartment in a good neighborhood. It wasn't everything... but it was a start.

"Okay, what about the marital accounts?" I asked.

"Your husband and partners removed your access to those accounts three months ago," the manager said without inflection. "As of today, they have not reversed that decision."

I didn't say any more on the topic. I didn't want the guy questioning why I didn't already know that.

"Very well. Let's get started on the transfer." I riffled through Sue's bag, taking out the folder I brought. I brushed against my phone screen doing so, and the home screen came to life—reminding me that I had seven missed calls from Satan.

No doubt, Dan was trying to get ahold of the police so that he could get more information on the accident that killed me, but I was still amazed that I faked him out the first time. I wasn't going to test my luck. I just had to hope he'd give up and go away.

Sue's phone rang at that moment, and I flicked my eyes to the— *MENTARY SCHOOL* flashing on the screen.

"One moment, please." I got up and crossed the room, answering on the third ring. "Hello?"

"Hello? Hello, Mrs. Kim, is that you?"

I glanced back at the manager. "I am Ms. Kim," I replied, slipping in the slight correction. "Is something wrong?"

"Yes, I'm sorry to interrupt your day, but Lily is in the nurse's office. She's been throwing up for the past half an hour, and she wants to go home.

I tried all three of your husbands first, but didn't get an answer. What time will you be by to pick her up?"

"Throwing up?" I cried, snapping up. "Why? What—?"

Stop! a voice snapped in my head. *Just because you want to be a mother, doesn't mean you can pretend to be someone else's. Her teacher is looking for Lily's parent, and that's not you.*

Hang up the phone.

I swallowed hard, chest tightening. "I'm sorry, I can't help. Please continue trying to get a hold of her fathers until you reach one of them."

"But, Mrs. K—"

I hit *end*, and then nearly pitched across the room and threw up in the toilet. Everything about leaving a little girl crying and throwing up in a sterile nurse's office felt wrong, but everything had changed. When I thought it would just be me and Omma hiding out in the manor in her final days, I didn't care about any lies I had to tell.

But now there were three men and a young child involved, and keeping up the deception was both way too dangerous, and way too creepy. The only thing to do now was take the money, and leave. There was no life left for me to live in Lantana.

Clearing my throat, I put away Sue's phone. "Okay," I rasped. "Let's get started on that transfer."

***

"—why didn't you pick up?!"

"I had a meeting! What the fuck's your excuse?!"

"You know I have to turn my phone off at work. That's why *your* phone is always supposed to be on!"

"I told you, I had a meeting!"

"Lily?!"

"Lily!"

The door flew open and three men fell through it, nearly colliding and ending up as a pile on the carpet.

We stared at them.

"Uhhh... what are you guys doing?" I asked.

Nari opened her mouth for another spoonful of broth. She was tucked up tight in her ladybug bed, kicking her little feet under the covers.

And by ladybug, I meant ladybug. The circular bed had little bug feet for legs, antennae on the headboard, and red-and-black polka-dot sheets. It all paired nice with the green, shaggy carpet masquerading as grass, the beautiful meadow painted on the walls, and the clouds and sun on the ceiling.

"What are we doing?" Rhodes snapped, untangling himself from his fellow brothers in matrimony. "What are *you* doing? Why did you take Lily out of school?"

"Why?" I fed her more soup. "What do you mean why? I left all three of you a voicemail, telling you Lily was sick and needed to be picked up from school. Didn't you listen to it?"

They slowly approached, surrounding the bed and the two of us like we were suspicious packages left at the airport—

No. I saw the looks on their faces. *All of their suspicions are for me.*

"Yeah, we got it..." Alex said slowly. "But it didn't make any sense..."

I cocked a brow. "What didn't make sense? They had a carnival at school for student appreciation day, and the little lady here overdid it on the cotton candy, funnel cake, and lollipops."

Micah bit off a swear as Lily ducked her head under the covers. "Overdid it? How does that happen?" They were still talking much louder than they needed to. "Why weren't those idiots watching her? Who lets a six-year-old eat that much sugar unchecked!"

I shrugged. "Lily puked on her teacher's shoes, so I'm sure he learned his lesson. Anyway, why are you all here? I also said in the message that I'd bring her home and take care of her." I set down the broth and picked up the bag at my feet. "The pharmacist said this is a really good anti-nausea medicine, and it's safe for kids.

"Lily took some an hour ago, but she said if she's not better by the afternoon, to give her another dose. Or if she's not better by *tomorrow*, to call her doctor. But I don't think that will be necessary," I said to their unsettling, wide-eyed stares. "She's already feeling much better, right, Nariboo?"

A giggle floated out of the sheets. "No!"

I gasped. "Huh? No? But you know what happens to little girls who are sick?" I dove under the covers. "They get their toes eaten!"

Nari flipped out, kicking and squealing when I grabbed her foot, nibbling on her toes.

Hands suddenly grabbed and pulled me out. The world spun as I was tossed over Micah's shoulder and carried out.

"Lilybug, finish your soup," Alex called over his shoulder—standing side by side with Rhodes and Micah. "Daddies will be back in a bit to check on you."

"Okay," she chirped, not in the least bit concerned that her auntie was in for it.

"Guys? Micah!" I wiggled in his hold. "Okay, short people don't like to be picked up! It's one of our top five fears and dislikes!"

"Want to know what my top fear and dislike is?" Micah plopped me on my feet. In a blink he had me up against the wall, slamming his hands on either side of my face.

Before I could get a word out, Rhodes and Alex were right there—boxing me in on the left and right.

I wasn't going anywhere.

"My worst fear is that my twisted and duplicitous wife will con our daughter into believing she's the cool, fun parent, all so she can get full custody of her in the divorce—but plot twist that everyone saw coming—she only wants to use our child to drain us of every cent she can get in child support."

My eyes bugged. "Child support? Divorce?! What the hell are you talking about?"

"What the hell are *you* talking about!" Micah roared, blowing me back. "Enough with the doe-eyed, innocent act, Sue! For once, fucking enough!"

I shrunk back, eyes huge in face of his fury. My heart pounded a mile a minute, racing faster than the chill crawling up my spine—because I knew this rage.

This was the rage born from being played and manipulated by an evil, gleeful psycho who got off on fucking with your life, and making you look like the crazy one. It was the kind of rage that filled me just before the thought entered my mind that I could do it.

I could kill my sister, and not feel an ounce of guilt over it.

"Okay, okay, just slow down," I breathed, putting my hands up in surrender. "Listen, I know I've done awful things to you. I've lied, I've messed you around, I blamed you for all of it, and I never took responsibility. Whatever resentment you have toward me, I've earned it."

Rhodes's lips peeled back from his teeth. "Oh, nice. We get Insincere Apologies and Fake Accountability Sue today. You haven't brought this personality out in a while."

I weathered his sarcasm with a hard face. "No, Rhodes. I'm not being insincere. I'm not being fake. This is the one hundred percent truth: I don't want a divorce."

Of course I didn't want a fucking divorce! I can't divorce men I'm not married to, and widowed men don't get divorced in the first place!

"And I'm not going to fight you for custody, or demand child support, or anything like that," I heard myself say. "I've got more than a sense that Soo Min Kim hasn't been the world's greatest mother."

The three of them exchanged looks, trading disbelieving expressions.

"My point being," I continued, "that if you've been her primary caregivers all this time, then you're the ones who know what's best for her. I'm not going to even think about getting in the way."

Micah dropped his arms, stepping back. "Sue, what the hell is this? What are you saying? You're the one who demanded the divorce. You're the one who said you wanted all *four* of us out by the end of next month. You're the one who said we were a couple of dickless wonders who couldn't find your G-spot even if we put our empty heads together, and you were replacing us with a man who could get the job done."

I blew out a hard breath, stifling a scream. *Hera's sake! Even in death, I'm cleaning up after Sue's cruelty! Why couldn't that woman ever, for once, spare the jugular?*

"I lied," I dropped. "I didn't mean any of that. I just said that to hurt you because I'm a childish, spiteful bitch that gets off on tormenting people for my own amusement."

Three pairs of brows bounced up to their hairlines.

"There's no affair. There's no other man. I don't want a divorce," I said forcefully. "But... but I will tell you what I do want."

Their expressions hardened.

"Here it is," Alex scoffed. "Knew it was too good to be true."

"Let me guess," Rhodes added. "The cost of this *amicable* split will be a cool eight figures and—"

"I want you to take the manor," I sliced in. "I'll be the one to leave, and you three can stay here—live here—and raise Nari in her home."

"I— Excuse me?" Micah blurted.

"The only thing I ask is that you buy me out of my share of the manor. Whatever the cost would've been if we sold it, give me a fourth of it and that'll be more than fair." A thought occurred to me. "Well, also Omma's personal things, her books, photo albums, and the rest. But otherwise, I don't need anything else."

If I thought I shocked them before, it was nothing compared to the thrice astonishment looking back at me now.

"Buy you... out of your share of the manor?" Rhodes slowly repeated. "But it's yours already. Why would you just give it to us for a fraction of the price?"

"Because you have to raise Nari here."

"But why—"

"Because no mother should ever throw their child out of their home!" I shrieked, blowing them back. "This is her home! It's her *home*! And Nari will leave when she's ready, and not a minute sooner! Got it?"

"Yikes, we got it," Micah grumbled—though his tone was ten times milder than when he tossed me against the wall.

"Okay." My chest heaved, breaths coming hard. "Good. Then, just two more things. First, I know that things aren't great between us and it'll be awkward but, please, don't ask me to move out until... until Omma..."

For the first time since I walked through the door, something approaching a real and kind emotion toward me crossed Rhodes's face. "Sue, come on, of course you can stay with your mother until the end. We're not monsters."

I blinked rapidly, swallowing hard around the lump in my throat. "Okay... thank you." Ducking my head, I dug in Sue's bag. Lucky for me I was already holding it when they carried me out like a sack of potatoes.

"Now, for my last request." I took out the folder and handed it to them. "Here."

Alex looked at the folder like it might bite him. He made no move to take it. "What's that?"

"It's the trust documents. I opened it today, transferred all of my money into it, and put you three in charge of it. It's for Lily."

Still cautious, Alex took it from me. Surprise sprouted color in his cheeks, drawing my eyes to those glass-cutter cheekbones. "The Silly Lily Fund? What the hell's this?"

"What it is is nothing more than what Lily is owed. From her mother to her—that's how it's supposed to be."

Yes, it was true. Like the big, dense, stupid softie I was, I transferred all of Sue's money into an account for Lily. I had no problem stealing from that evil succubus, but I did have a big problem with stealing from her daughter. Now that Sue was gone, everything she had rightfully belonged to the child she left behind—and no amount of righteous rage could justify doing otherwise.

There you go, big sis. The last and only kind thing I'm owed you. Now you can continue frying in hell.

"Listen," I rasped, "I know you don't have to respect my wishes, but I called it the Silly Lily Fund because I hope you'll use the money for all those silly, impractical things that young girls want growing up, but are always told are a waste of time and money.

"This house was always such a mausoleum," I heard myself say. "The only time there was ever laughter or joy in these halls was when I was running around, playing with the staff's kids, and even that ended at five o'clock.

"Did you know Omma made u—me justify every single item on my birthday and Christmas lists? Every single club or camp I wanted to join?" I burst out. "Everything that wasn't food, clothes, or academics had to be defended and justified. *Why do you need a kid's salon set? Are you planning on being a hairdresser? If you're not going to be a hairdresser, why do you want to play around with fake hair when you should be studying to achieve your true goals?*"

I huffed a frustrated groan like I did all those times before. "Just don't do that to her, okay? Don't make her beg to have fun, or be a kid. Tell her she's got forty thousand dollars' worth of silliness to take advantage of in the next twelve years, so don't use that money wisely."

"We're not going to tell her that," Micah deadpanned, his lips quirked up into something resembling a smile. "But what we're also not going to do, and you can trust this, is raise Lily the way your mother raised you. She's going to be much happier than you were, Sue." His gaze pinned me through. "Because we've seen the result of what happens if she's not."

I flinched, jerking back like he hit me. Micah meant that comment to hit Sue, but it struck me just as squarely. I grew up in the same house with the same parents, and I was a failure.

I was what you got when a family like mine chewed you up and spat you out.

"But," Micah continued, tipping my chin up. "Why are you talking like this? Like you're never going to see her again? Is that what you want?" he asked. "To walk out the door and out of her life, and never come bac—"

"No," I barked, blurting it out before sense could stop me. "Of course, I don't want that. I want to see her as often and as much as you'll let me. I love her."

The words were out of my mouth, and I knew they were true. Frankly, I was always one of those people who made silly faces at babies in the grocery store, and volunteered at children's homes during the holidays just to see their little faces light up when they opened their presents. I loved every kid and baby I came across, but Lily was special from the moment I laid eyes on her.

This was the baby with my hair, my face, my unique eyes, and my last name. The one I'd been waiting twenty-eight years to meet. The one I so desperately wanted to have one day. And I had already decided at our very first meeting that I'd be the best auntie this girl ever had—it wouldn't even matter that I was her only one.

"I want to see her after everything is said and done," I told them in a calmer tone. "But I understand that you three need to trust me with her first."

Rhodes sighed, scrubbing his face. "Sue, come on, we're not going to keep her—"

"You're right," Alex broke in, clamping a hand on Rhodes's shoulder. "You do need to earn our trust before there's any thought of you having further contact with Lily after you leave. You've treated our daughter like a nuisance since the first bout of morning sickness, and nothing's changed since. You've almost got her believing that it's normal, or even right, for a child to beg and plead for her mother's attention.

"You're done fucking with her, Sue, and you're done fucking with us. You want trust, earn it," he gritted. "And you start by putting everything you just said into writing. No divorce, no child support, no alimony, and no staying here past the funeral. Write it, sign it, and make eight copies for all of us, and our lawyers.

"Do it today, or we've got nothing more to talk about."

I tipped my head. "I can do this today." Pulling out Sue's phone, I showed them the screen, and the recorder app. "Everything we said and all of my conditions, loud and clear for the lawyers to hear. I'll send you guys a copy now.

"I want this to work," I said. "I want us to live peacefully in this house until the end, and I want that for my mother. Omma was cold, strict, and unforgiving. She cared too much what outsiders thought and concerned herself more with looking like the perfect family than actually being one, but she was the mother I needed when it counted. So I'll be here for her... when it counts."

Micah, Rhodes, and Alex didn't seem to know what to say to that, so they didn't reply.

"I told work that Lily's sick and I won't be back," Micah said as all three of them turned their back on me. "I've got her from here. You can go back to whatever you were doing, Sue."

Dismissals didn't get much clearer than that.

The three of them went toward Lily's room, so I went the other way—heading for the east wing staircase that spilled out into the front room, and therefore the hallway that would take me to Omma. If I was staying here and keeping up this charade for my mother, then I should be with my mother—spending as much time with her as time allowed.

My fingers glided along the railing, leading the way across the landing. I passed by the east wing hallway—the only part of the manor I'd yet to revisit since coming home.

I did not return to the corridor, but the corridor returned to me. Fractured memories of my bare feet on the red-carpeted floor. The lone flickering bulb with the dead bug stuck to it, flickering its shadowy little corpse on the wall like an omen. And the screams.

Always... the screams.

So many things were done in this house...

I turned away.

...but that was the only thing done right.

Chapter Seven

If I thought putting an end to an inevitably nasty divorce and custody battle would end the tension in the Kim Manor, I was laughably mistaken.

A week passed since that day Micah, Rhodes, and Alex cornered me in the hall. The day that, despite all the evidence debunking their existence, I became a ghost.

The guys didn't talk to me, they didn't look at me, they didn't even sneeze in my direction. The only three people in the house who had a kind word to say to me were Lily, Nurse Reynard, and Omma—the kindness from the last person on that list being the most shocking.

Maybe it was the meds, maybe it was the morphine, maybe it was her final days ticking down faster and quicker than she was ready for, but in all the years I'd known this woman, I'd never heard her laugh or joke this much in my life. Even though she spent pretty much every day stuck in another time—alternating between telling me to put my dolls away, or break up with my worthless tenth-grade boyfriend that I hadn't seen in years—she still had a smile on her face for most of the day, and that smile was for me.

"Do you remember Mrs. Park? The one with the grandson she was constantly bragging about? Going on and on about how he was going to be a doctor saving lives, and not a silly little lawyer playing with briefs." I divvied up the cards for me and Omma, laying them on her lap desk.

She dipped her chin in a slight nod, and just the strain from those slight muscle movements made her cringe.

"I saw her and said grandson in town yesterday morning, and guess who lost his medical license for selling his scripts, and is now living in Grandmammy's basement growing and selling shitty weed?"

"You... don't say?" she rasped. "But, shitty or not, I wouldn't mind... a little of that weed right now."

"Omma!" I cried, setting off another bout of her whispery, rattling laughs. "Very naughty, young lady, I'm surprised at you."

"Excuse you..." She raised a shaky finger, tapping the card she wanted me to flip. "I lived many lives... before you two came along. By the way, Sarang... where is Soo Min?"

I stilled, seeing Reynard's reflection in the lacquered headboard.

The nurse was humming to himself—sorting Omma's pills into her caddy, and logging her meds into his chart.

"Nurse Agassi?"

"Hmm, yes?" He raised his head, then frowned. "Wait, Nurse Agassi? What's with the formality? I told you you can call me Reynard."

"Reynard," I corrected. "And you can call me Sue, but would you mind giving us a minute in private?"

"No problem." He left without an issue, shutting the door behind him.

I waited until his footsteps retreated down the hallway before responding. "Sue's on a boat trip, Omma, and she's loving it. She's spending every day deep-sea fishing."

"Fish?" She pulled a slight frown that smoothed away with her drooping eyes. "Soo Min hates... fish."

"She'll be back soon. Until then"—I laid my hand over hers—"I'm here."

She smiled, her fingers slipping out from under mine to fall on the duvet. "Sweet girl. I... missed you."

I let her drift off to sleep, only staying long enough to put away the cards and lap tray.

That was the first time she asked for Sue. I knew it was coming, but still the lie felt strange on my tongue. It felt stranger that it had taken me a whole week to tell it. Those drugs Reynard had her on were something magic, letting Omma live in all her happy, carefree, time-traveling memories awake and asleep.

I left Omma's room and almost ran into Alex coming down the hall.

He sidestepped me and strode on without a glance in my direction.

I sighed. "Wouldn't mind some of those happy, time-traveling pills right now. If I did, I'd go back to the last time I saw you happy," I whispered after Alex. "Strangely enough, it was the last day I was truly happy too."

Shaking my head, I put my morose thoughts aside long enough to head to Sue's room, get changed, then slip through the drafty halls to the old servants' back-door entrance.

Rhodes lifted his head when I stepped out, fingers paused holding his laces.

A sinfully gorgeous morning peeked out from under the porch, casting warm, cheering sunlight on the tips of my running shoes. A cool, but not bracing, breeze whipped up the trees—challenging them to a dance that stole their leaves and carried them along the muddy path, inviting us to join.

"What are you doing?" he asked, bending back over his sneakers. "Making content for both of your followers?"

I snorted, smothering a giggle. "That's a good one, but no. I'm out of the influencer game for good," I confessed. "Including all that SueNation nonsense. Right now, I'm looking forward to the next big thing for me. I'm even thinking of going back—"

Rhodes laced up and jogged off the porch, leaving me and the rest of my sentence hanging there.

"—to school," I finished.

Taking off, I raced after him—easily falling in step and keeping pace. "Well, that was really fucking rude," I said mildly. "You're an ass."

He tripped. "Excuse me? I'm the ass?!" He whipped around and got in front of me so fast, I collided headfirst into his chest. "You once stuck your phone in my shower while you were live, just to increase your follower count! I had to report the video to get it taken down, because you refused to!"

Anger was coming off him in waves, but all my jangled mind was thinking about was how good he smelled, and how hard his pecs were. This guy was not letting domestic unbliss slow him down.

Get it together, woman! Stop fantasizing while he's trying to explode your head with his mind!

"That's awful, obviously," I said, lingering too close to him for too long. "Absolutely no excuse for violating your privacy that way, but I thought we called a truce last week? That we were—all four of us—were trying to get on better, amicable terms so that we could still be a family for Nari, even after I move out.

"Did I get that wrong? Am I the only one who wants to start over?"

His eyes flashed. Taking hold of my shoulders, he gently—but firmly—moved me out of his personal space. "You did get it wrong if you believed you get to lie to me, cheat on me, neglect our daughter, and then turn around and decide when a truce is called, and I have to get over it.

"Being a good father to Nari doesn't mean sitting around listening to you prattle on about yourself—as if you ever do anything else. Some days it'll mean walking away from you. And one day it might even mean not letting Nari have any contact with you.

"Get this through your head, Sue. *I* will tell *you* when we have a truce."

He made to turn away. I grasped his chin, turning him gently and firmly back to me.

"I have never, would never, and will never cheat on you, Rhodes Newbury," I whispered. "Because I know... Seeing you—truly seeing you again after all this time. I know... that it's always been you." I rested my palm against his cheek, making his eyes widen. "Now, I want you to look in my eyes, and tell me if I'm lying."

Rhodes gazed at me. For a split second, I thought his lips parted to reply, but then he pulled away and jogged off, and I decided I imagined it.

I watched him for a second, wondering what the hell I was doing, and why I gave him a hard time about hating the woman he thought I was.

This would all be solved by telling him I'm actually Sarang. The long-lost twin sister that Sue and Omma erased from existence, who's popping in after illegally disposing of the true Sue's body—all to ensure Omma doesn't rip my inheritance from me for the second time, because resentment doesn't make my hovel livable, or my cheap eats go down easier. And, oh yeah, please keep up the lie and let my mother go on believing Sue's still alive out there, even though there is absolutely nothing in it for you.

I blew out a rough groan, picking up my feet to start my run. Every ten minutes I got it in my head to come clean to Micah, Alex, and Rhodes, and every eleven minutes I ran through how that conversation would go—and concluded it would be a complete disaster.

The fact is I knew these guys in high school. At least as much as any freshman knows a couple of seniors who don't acknowledge their existence.

I didn't know these guys now. I didn't know how they'd react to the truth of what happened that night. I didn't know what I could possibly say to convince them I was a safe person to have around their daughter, when my own mother didn't believe I was a safe enough person for Nari to know existed.

Why gamble my chance to get out of my hellish life on a couple of wild cards, when all I had to do was be patient, spend these final days with Omma, and then quietly leave after the funeral?

No, I thought, picking up the pace. *It's just not worth it. Let them think I'm Sue, because this way, we both get what we want. I get a new life, and they get a life free of Sue.*

Rhodes ran a few yards out in front of me. Sprinting the cracked and overgrown stone path, he headed straight for the forest—escaping into the trees.

I followed after him. Not to be a nuisance, but because his path was my path. Back in high school, I ran our manmade forest trail night and day. There was something about running that made you feel like you were moving forward, even if you always ended up in the same place.

Catching up to Rhodes, I ran out in front of him, fell back on his right side, crossed to the other, and ran out in front of him again.

Okay, now I was being a nuisance.

Three more times of that, he snapped, "What the hell are you doing!"

"What I'm doing is literally running circles around you," I called as I shot around him again. "Is this what became of the great rugby captain of Titan Prep? Fourteen years later, he's beaten in a race by a flat-ass girl."

"Nothing flat about your ass, girl—" Rhodes clamped his jaw shut, growling like he couldn't believe he aimed any kind of suggestive, flirty comment in my direction. "We're not in a race," he barked. "I'm warming up and you're getting in the fucking way.

"Run in the opposite direction, Sue. I don't have time for your—"

A huge, lumbering black mass tumbled out in front of us. "Gaargh!"

We pulled up so fast we collided with each other, limbs tangling, and faces smashing into hard, damp chests—nearly bringing us both down before the bear.

"Holy fuck! Holy fucking fuck!" Rhodes bellowed, ripping another grunt out of the bear. He grabbed my arm—running and trying to take me with him.

"Rhodes, no!" Untangling myself from him, I spun to face the animal—throwing my legs out and arms high.

I didn't know much about black bears or how big they should or could be, but I did know the hefty fellow in front of me could bat my car aside like a gnat... so what could he do to me?

A thick, black coat did nothing to disguise his girth, or the lethal claws sinking into the hardened, packed earth. Dark, beady eyes beheld us—fixing all his attention on the new creatures in his path. All of a sudden, wherever he was going, he didn't need to get there as quickly anymore.

"Don't scream," I hissed through gritted teeth—desperately trying to obey the command myself. "Don't run. Don't act like prey, or he'll *treat* us like prey. Just do what I do—"

The bear rose on his hindlegs, shotgunning my heart into my throat and making Rhodes break the first rule. I shook—my throat-heart thudding so hard it made every word out of my mouth vibrate.

"Hello, Mr. Bear," I said in as calm a voice as I could muster. "We're very sorry we disturbed you on your morning stroll." I waved my arms above my head as slowly as I crab-walked sideways.

I swear the bear cocked his head like he was wondering what the hell this strange human was doing.

"We're no threat or harm to you," I rasped. "We—uh—we love bears. Black bears most of all. Clearly, you're the best of all bears. The polar dicks can go fuck themselves."

He woofed, snapping a growl that loosened my bladder.

"No, no, no, I really mean it," I said quickly. "You're much prettier and more elegant than those bleached bastards. That's why you're the state animal of four states"—tears leaked out of my eyes when the bear stepped closer, sniffing the air—"and the polar bear is the state animal of nothing—"

"Sue, what in the bleeding, bloody, fucking hell are you babbling about!" A waving hand caught mine, lacing our fingers together.

The shock of his touch reverberated through my bones harder than the thud of the bear dropping down on all fours.

"Stay with me," he hissed. "We need to back away—"

"Garrgh!" Roaring, the bear charged.

"Sue!"

The world tumbled in a whirlwind of greens, browns, and fur. Rhodes pulled me behind him, snapping his arms back and around me to ensure I couldn't escape from my human shield. Bending forward, he roared—bellowing so hard at the charging bear my neck hairs stood on end.

Ears snapping back, the bear whipped around at the last possible second and bounded off into the woods.

We stood there gaping after it for so long, my stiff and aching legs gave out from under me.

"Oh my gods," I croaked—shaking from head to toe. "I can't believe that just happened." Slowly, I tipped my chin up. "I can't believe you protected me."

"Well... I... Of course, I—" He took a step back and stumbled. "I wasn't going to just—just let it— Shit." Rhodes's eyes rolled up his head.

He collapsed on the ground.

"Rhodes!"

***

"Can't believe I passed out," grumbled into my ear.

I stifled a laugh, holding tight to Rhodes's arm. He leaned heavily on me, letting me help his still unsteady self back to the house.

"You're entitled to pass out when you gallantly defend a lady from a charging bear."

"You're making fun of me," he deadpanned, making a giggle slip out.

"I'm not, I swear." I pulled him a little closer. "With as much as you hate me, the first thing you did in that situation was risk your life for mine. That was the most amazing and selfless thing I've ever seen anyone do in my life."

If his melanin didn't prevent it, I swear I'd be looking at the biggest, pinkish honking blush two sculpted cheeks ever conjured.

"It... uh..." Rhodes roughly cleared his throat. "It wasn't a big deal."

"It most certainly was a big deal. So much so that I'm going to return the favor. As a token of my appreciation, when I tell the world of this story, I'm leaving out the part where you shat your pants."

Rhodes burst out laughing, almost bringing me down when he doubled over. "That's your pants you're smelling, sweetheart, not mine. And at least I didn't try to stop that bear by hitting on him."

"Hey, that was a perfectly valid tactic!" The manor came into view, peeking through the trees. "The sites say to be calm and talk to the bear, let it know you're human. *But*," I stressed, "humans suck. We cut down their forests, hunt their food, then kill and stuff them.

"I had to let him know that, yes, we're humans, but we're the bear-*loving* kind. We're his friends. And I know it got through," I said, sticking my nose in the air. "That's why he didn't eat us. Because flattery really does get you everywhere."

"Yeah, so does bullshitting."

"I'm telling you, all the shit you're sniffing on is directly below your nose."

We couldn't hold it in—guffawing and stumbling our way to the back porch.

"So, how do you want to do this?" I asked, climbing step to step with him. "Should I keep going with the payback, and let you hide out in the stables while I run up and get you a change of pants?"

"Wow. That's funny because *I* was about to cash in more gallant points by letting *you* hide out in the stables while I grab you a change of clothes."

"Well, that's going to make it really hard for me to keep pretending I didn't crap myself too," I muttered.

Rhodes's eyes shone—dancing with mirth and sending my throat-heart flipping.

"Why don't we go back-to-back?" I squeaked out. "Keep the crab-walk going until we both get out of this looking good?"

"I do desperately need to see that walk again, but this time with a camera in my—"

"Isn't this cute?"

We sprung apart like colliding ball bearings—my throat-heart almost ejecting out of my butt. I clamped my hand over my pounding chest, the jump-scare fading as Alex emerged out of the shadows of the screen door.

"Looks like you two had a great run, and an even better time. Sorry I missed it." The expression on his face did not match his words. "Even sorry to interrupt your giggling now."

Rhodes straightened, sobering quickly. "It's not like that, Alex. Just some leftover nervous energy after narrowly escaping a bear attack."

Alex's face crumpled. "What the fuck you just say? A bear?"

"Never mind all that. We're fine and I've got to get ready for work."

It physically pained me seeing all the lightness, humor, and kindness leak out of Rhodes's face.

I shrunk back against the handrail, cringing as the claustrophobic fog of Sue-created resentment rolled over us. Even after she was gone, I was still suffering the effects of her biting cruelty.

"We're supposed to call the Lantana Wildlife Agency when these things happen," I spoke up. "They'll make sure the bear is really gone, and then check the property to see if something attracted him.

"I'll make the call," I offered. "And I'll keep Nari inside until they give us the all clear."

Rhodes inclined his head. "Thanks—"

"You're not keeping Nari anywhere," Alex sliced in. "If there's really a bear wandering around our backyard, I'm getting us a hotel and keeping her far away from this place until they give the all clear. Fuck's sake, Sue, use your head and stop putting your laziness ahead of our daughter's safety."

I bristled, opening my mouth to snap back—

"Cut it out, Alex," Rhodes barked. "It's a bear, not a wrecking ball. Nari will be perfectly safe inside. The woman just faced down a three-hundred-pound killing machine. Maybe give her a break."

I could only gape at Rhodes, genuinely shocked that he rose to my defense not once, but twice in the same hour.

Rhodes threw open the screen door and brushed past Alex, storming through the back hall and through the kitchen. The door slammed shut and Alex swooped down and locked it before my fingers touched the handle.

"Excuse me?" I rattled the door. "What are you doing? Open the door. Let me in."

Alex stared at me—the strangest glint in his eyes. Slowly, his gaze drifted up and over my shoulder.

I turned around, and landed on the bear.

Large and unmoving on the entrance to the forest path, the bear watched me like it had been waiting, scenting, and stalking to see where its prey would lead, and his patience paid off.

A chill climbed my spine, feeling those beady eyes see through to my very soul.

"I can't open the door," Alex murmured, snapping me back around. "There's a bear on the loose."

"Alex—!"

He slammed the main door shut—the click of the lock ringing in my ears.

Chapter Eight

The bell chimed overhead, welcoming me into the vanilla-scented haven. I spotted her immediately—standing behind the counter, frosting a tray of the cupcakes responsible for that mouth-watering scent.

"Welcome to CCC," she called, not looking up. "Feel free to browse, I'll be with you in a moment. But a little tip, we've got a sale going on everything chocolate from chocolate chip cookies to chocolate ganache cupcakes."

"Sounds delicious."

Courtney's head snapped up, her hand jerking and squirting the frosting all across the counter like jizz.

"You always knew the way to a girl's heart."

I couldn't have pictured Courtney's jaw-hanging, bugged-out expression if I planned it.

I took the first step. "Okay, I know this is weird, but the first thing you need to know is that I'm not So—"

"Sarah!?" Courtney threw down the piping bag and launched over the counter. "We're closed," she shouted at the other two milling customers before tackling me.

I shrieked—suddenly finding myself with one hundred twenty pounds' worth of baker while wobbling in Sue's impractical high heels. I lost the battle.

Screaming, we both went down like Jenga.

***

Twenty minutes later, two angry customers were out on the street, the closed sign was hanging in the window, and we were sitting at one of her cute, tiny little café-style tables with that same tray of cupcakes between us.

"I can't believe you knew it was me," I mumbled around a mouthful of confectionary.

Courtney gave me a look. "You think I don't know my best friend when she's standing right in front of me? Honestly, it always baffled me that people couldn't tell you and Sue apart. Never had there ever been two people who were more different."

I just nodded.

Courtney looked great. It had been ten years since I saw her, but no one told her velvety smooth skin, blemish-free cheeks, killer figure, and long, flour-dusted locks.

"I... erm... Can I take it as a good sign that you said best friend, and not former best friend?" I tried for a smile. "Meaning that our best-friends-forever, never-tell-a-soul-our-secrets pact is still in effect?"

She gave me another look. "Sarah, of course we're still friends, and of course you can still tell me anything and I'll keep my mouth shut but..." Her brows crumpled. "We're not in high school anymore, so if you're invoking the pact, I'm guessing what you have to say is pretty bad."

I swallowed around the lump in my throat. "Yeah, it's pretty bad. It's as bad as it gets."

I told her everything. Everything from Sue showing up at my apartment in Willingsworth, to the accident that killed her, to lying to Dan, to lying to the police, to lying to Sue's husbands and child, and all the lies in between.

When I finished, I had to pat myself on the back—because I big-time got her to top her slack-jawed, bug-eyed shock from earlier with the crater-faced one before me.

"Sarah!"

"I know," I cried, clapping my hands over my face. "I know, I know, I know!"

"How— How— How?!" she settled on. "How could you just throw your twin sister off a fucking cliff?!"

"Trust me, that wasn't the hard part." I slammed my hand on the table. "I've been wanting to throw that bitch off a cliff since I was eight years old, and when I walked through the door and discovered she planned to surprise me with Micah, Rhodes, and Alex—jumping on another chance to hurt me while our mother lay upstairs dying?"

Hatred curled my hands into fists. "I wanted to throw her off twice."

"Okay... okay, yeah," she whispered. "That is brutally cruel—even for Sue. But how in the world are you passing yourself off as Sue to her husbands? They've been dating, living with, and raising a child with her for ten years!"

"I know! I have no idea how I'm doing it other than that those relationships are strained to snap, Court. They want Sue out of their lives for good, so they're not looking too hard at me or why I'm acting strange." I flicked away. "They're barely looking at me at all."

I felt her eyes on me. "And that hurts your feelings, doesn't it."

She said it like a question, but it wasn't one. Courtney was always able to see right through me.

"Yes, it does." My eyes stung. "You know what a massive crush I had on those guys my entire freshman year. And then after they graduated, I virtually stalked everything they did and everywhere they went. If there was anything I wanted as much as Yale, it was to be in Micah's, Rhodes's, and Alex's orbit," I said. "Now I finally am, and they look at me like bear shit on the welcome mat. And speaking of bears, Alex locked me outside with one this morning."

"Excuse me?!"

"Yep. No exaggeration. He saw the fucking bear behind me, locked the door, and walked away."

She gaped at me, speechless.

"I was fine," I quickly added. "The bear didn't try to come after me when I hurried my butt off the porch and to the front door, but the look in Alex's eyes when he did it..."

I tossed my head. "He truly despises Sue. The only thing I can't figure out is how she knew to go for them in the first place. I *never* told Sue how I felt about those guys. I wasn't an idiot."

"Uhhh...."

"Huh?" I raised my head, locking eyes with her cringe. "What? What is it?"

"Babe, I... I think I know how she figured those three were the perfect targets of your emotional annihilation."

"What?" I sat up straight. "How?"

Courtney sighed. Picking up her own cupcake, she chomped a big bite. "After that day in the auditorium—when you just suddenly disappeared and I didn't have a clue what happened other than that you were expelled.

After that day, I kept going to your house almost every day for weeks, trying to get in to see your mother to ask what happened to you.

"At first, the staff let me in but told me I had to wait in the front hall until your mother was ready to *receive* me," she mocked, putting on all the pompous airs that word deserved. "Hint: she never came down.

"Eventually, she must've told the staff to stop opening the door for me, because they started leaving me on the welcome mat—banging and shouting for someone to let me in." She blew out a breath. "Well, one day, the door flew open and your mother was there—looking down on me like I was the most disgusting, filthy piece of trash she'd ever seen."

Court's eyes glazed. "She told me she had no daughter by the name of Sarang Kim—"

The sentence cut me like a knife.

"—but if she was the mother of the person I was referring to, she must've lost said daughter to the influence of vulgar, insolent little sluts like me."

It was my turn for my jaw to drop. "She said that?! Oh, Court, I'm so sorry."

"It's fine," she said quickly.

It wasn't fine. All these years later, I could hear in her voice that it was not fine.

"Sarah, I'm telling you this because while your mom was eviscerating me on the welcome mat, I looked over her shoulder and saw your sister, Sue, crossing the hall with your journal in her hands." She tapped the table. "Remember the one you always used to carry in high school? The one—"

"—that had all my embarrassing, blubbering essays on my feelings for Micah, Rhodes, and Alex," I choked out. "Along with the business card Rhodes gave me when we promised to make a date for my eighteenth birthday.

"She took my journal." My voice was flat. Dead. "My private thoughts and feelings. She stole it and weaponized it—doing everything she could to hurt me even after I was gone."

A cold hand slipped into mine, squeezing tightly. "How did she even get it?"

"Omma didn't let me pack my things before she threw me out," I said to a pink-and-green-painted wall. "She didn't let me take anything but the car, and that was only because the car would get me the fuck out of her face quicker.

"The journal was still upstairs in my bedroom, but I had it hidden in the air vent to keep it from Sue's grubby, nosy hands. With me not there to stop her, she must've snooped around until she found it."

"I'm so sorry, babe."

I groaned, sinking down in the chair. "I don't want to talk about that monster anymore. I came because I needed to tell someone the truth... and because I need someone to tell me the truth." I leaned over, grasping both her hands. "Is what I'm doing insane? Should I just come clean to everyone and hope they'll understand?"

She was shaking her head before I finished. "No, Sarah. That is exactly what the fuck you don't do. If you come clean now, it'll spectacularly blow up in your face, and I'm not sitting on my ass without a clue while my best friend gets chased out of my life for the second time."

I blinked at her. Courtney was the wilder one of the two of us, but she was also the voice of reason. If anyone was going to give me the push to stop the lies, I thought it would be her. "But, how can you be sure telling the truth will blow up in my face?"

"Because you just told me that Sue's husbands hate her," she dropped. "They hate her for being the lying, scheming, manipulative bitch that we know she's been for the last ten years. So what happens when the sister that Sue and Omma hid pulls a *surprise, sucker!* on them?

"They're not going to give you the benefit of the doubt. They're just going to think Omma gave birth to two lying, scheming bitches, and how will you convince them they're wrong?" She gave me a wry look. "Upon meeting them again for the second time in ten years, the first thing you did... was lie. Not a ringing endorsement of your character."

"But I had to!" I threw out my hands. "I didn't want to lie to them, but Davis was standing right there. The fucker just wouldn't leave! How could I tell them the truth in front of a cop?"

"Sarah, I know that," she soothed. "I know you had good reason to lie, and I know that you're the best person ever, but *they don't*. You're nothing but a stranger to them. A stranger who threw their dead wife off a cliff, then moved into her bedroom."

I winced.

"How would you react if you were them?"

The words were pulled out of me. "I'd chase me out of town."

She dipped her head, nodding to the right answer. "And you know I'd want to move you in with me if they did, but your girl lives in a little shoebox apartment above this café with her kid, so there's no room."

I gasped, jumping up. "Kid?! Courtney Rose Thorne, have you been out here having babies that I don't know about?"

She grinned from ear to ear. "Yes, ma'am, I have, and that's because I was having all kinds of unprotected sex you didn't know about." She fished her phone out of her apron, and showed me the sweet, smiling kid waving on her home screen. "I caught this little munchkin from a one-night stand who blew through town one weekend and never came back.

"That's why I named her Chlamydia."

"What!"

She burst out laughing, falling off her chair. "I'm kidding," she shrieked. "Her name is Taylor, you freak."

I busted up so hard, I cried. Gods, did I need this. I couldn't remember the last time I full-blown belly-laughed. But Courtney was always the best person for that. Her wicked sense of humor would have me struggling to breathe in the back of class while the teacher shouted at us to be quiet or get out.

"Tell me everything about her."

Courtney beamed like the proud mama she was. "My Tay-Tay is five. She loves puppies, horses, and her kindergarten teacher. Loves him so much in fact, she's ordered me to marry him."

Courtney rolled her eyes, but I knew her too well too.

"And you want to," I said, blunt as a truck.

Her blush came on hot and fast. "I didn't say that. I mean, sure, Mr. Stevens is sweet, and kind, and amazing with children—especially Taylor—but I'm just starting to get back on my feet. The last thing I need right now is a messy relationship with my daughter's teacher."

I waited her out. "Tell me."

A hefty, whoosh-expelled breath tickled my hair. "Fine. You want the play-by-play? Here it is: After losing my best friend, I was forced to take off for Princeton without her right next door like we always planned.

"I want to say I still pulled it off without her, but not even close." Courtney scrubbed her face, suddenly looking ten years older. "Everything imploded during sophomore year. My parents were going through a messy divorce, and for some reason, the only person they could talk about it with was me.

"Do you have any idea what it was like being forced to listen to my mother ranting about my father losing interest in her sexually, and that every orgasm she had in the last ten years of their marriage was from a vibrator?"

"Urgh," I cried.

"That's right! Urgh!" she burst out. "It was so fucking gross and inappropriate, but when I told her that, she blew up on me and told me I needed to stop being so childish. That's how it was with the both of them. They wouldn't stop calling me up and pouring all this horrible and private stuff about their relationship in my ear—including that Mom cheated on Dad when I was three, had a baby, then they both secretly had him adopted—knowing that I'd never remember she was pregnant." She scoffed. "That is until Dad screamed the truth while in the middle of ranting that, of course, he lost interest in touching her. He never saw the 'cheating bitch' the same way after watching her give birth to another man's child."

"Oh my goodness." Horror laced my voice. "Court, I'm so sorry."

She wiped a tear from her cheek. "It was horrible, Sarah, and it just kept piling on. Between their nastiness, the discovery of a secret half brother, and all the classes I was failing, the only one I could talk to was Teo.

"I went to talk to him the night Dad told me about the adoption, and walked in on him fucking another girl."

"Oh, no..." I closed my eyes, hunching lower in my chair. *I can't believe Courtney was going through all of this while I was going through my own troubles.*

I guess the people we love choose an infinite number of ways to let us down when we need them the most.

"It was too much," she confessed. "I packed my stuff and dropped out of school the next day. The day after, I was on a flight to Paris."

That sat me up. "Paris?"

She nodded, shrugging. "I just wanted to be somewhere I could be happy, and you know those summers in Paris were my favorite vacations with Mom and Dad." She sighed. "Anyway, fast-forward to me faking like I was still at Princeton, pocketing Dad's tuition checks, and sleeping my way around the eighth arrondissement.

"Naturally, I couldn't fake not being in the country forever, so when my folks found out, they went ballistic. They both cut me off and disowned me—proving they could still agree on something." Courtney rolled her eyes. "Anyway, I was never too responsible with money, so I blew through every cent superfast.

"I needed a job, and at the time, I was dating a pastry chef. He said he'd give me a job in his café and let me learn under him so..." She fluttered her hands. "The rest was history."

"Not history," I reminded. "You came back to Lantana."

She tipped her chin. "Yes, I did, after being the one who went on and on about how I couldn't wait to leave this town. Well, after the pastry chef dumped and fired me, I was pretty sick of Paris.

"I came back home hoping to make up with Mom and Dad, but they weren't having it," she said, pulling a face. "I didn't know where to go, so I decided to stay until I figured out my next move and..."

"And then there was Taylor."

She smiled softly. "Yes, and then there was Taylor. As much as I bitched about this place, I wasn't complaining because I thought Lantana was a bad or an unsafe place to live. Just a boring one. But now that I'm a mom, I've come to appreciate how nice safe and boring is.

"I just want something stable for her. Something she can trust won't leave her when life gets tough."

"You're the something trusted and stable, Court." I grasped her hands. "You're that someone for me after ten long years, and you'll be that for her always."

She ducked her head, pulling a hand away to roughly wipe her face. "Don't make me cry."

"I won't if you say I can have another cupcake."

That got a little chuckle out of her. "It's all yours. You're paying for 'em."

After that we settled in, talking and catching up about how shit-miserable our lives got after our parents failed in their basic duty to not be massive assholes to their own children.

"I just don't understand why you disappeared on me of all people," Courtney said softly. We had moved from the table and were in the kitchen. I whipped the strawberry cheesecake filling while she prepped the graham cracker dough. "I've missed you like crazy. Every good and wonderful thing that happened, I wanted to tell you. Every horrible thing that happened, I wanted to talk to you first. I wanted you there."

"And you weren't."

My heart broke into pieces. "I'm sorry, Court. I wish I could say I didn't know why I never called you in all this time, but I do know why. I was afraid that you thought I could do it. That you believed what everyone else did—that I sabotaged the trapdoor and almost killed Colin—"

"But of course you didn't do it," she broke in. "You and Colin were friends. You both never took that competition stuff seriously. Plus, all you cared about was getting the grades to get into Yale, which you did. Why the hell would it matter that he became valedictorian over you when you'd already gotten everything you wanted?"

"Yes, thank you!" I shouted. "That's what I said over and over, and no one believed me."

She gave me a hard look. "I would've."

"I know that now, but I was a mess back then. I convinced myself that as long as I didn't know if you believed the lies, then we were still friends and nothing had changed. It was Schrödinger's friendship, Court, and it was really stupid and I'm sorry."

She held the look for a long spell, then let it go with a smile. "Well, all that matters is that you're here now. I love you, freak. Don't do that to me again."

"I won't. I love you too."

We lapsed into silence for a bit, working on our tasks.

I was first to break it.

"Have you thought about trying to find your brother? He'd be twenty-five now."

She shrugged both mouth and shoulders. "It's tough. After Dad let the secret slip, I went crying to Mom, then she went screaming to him. They both clammed up tight and haven't given me a single detail about the adoption since.

"I don't even know if they used an agency, or arranged a private adoption outside of the system. I don't know his name or birthday. I don't know if he's still in the state. Or the country," she cried. "I've got nothing to go on."

"I'm sorry. That is tough. But if it makes you feel better..." I reached out, putting my hand on her shoulder. "Siblings are the fucking worst."

Courtney barked a laugh, shaking her head at me. "Yours definitely was. Talk about a cautionary tale. But since you brought Sue back up on your own, I've got to ask, what the hell are you going to do now? Because you can't just sit around all day, lying and pretending while waiting for your mother to die." She flashed me an apologetic smile. "Sorry to phrase it that way, but I couldn't think of another way to put it."

"There isn't another way to put it because that's exactly what I'm doing." I clutched the mixing bowl to my chest, rocking back on my heels.

The kitchen of Courtney's Cookies and Cupcakes was as adorable and inviting as the rest of the café. She played up the Parisian theme that called back to her training, painting pink-and-green Eiffel Towers on the walls with little couples, families, and travelers painted in different poses beneath the towers. But as cutesy as it all was, I saw how serious Court took this business, and her goal to make it a success.

The kitchen was spotless. The work schedule posted on the wall had her slotted in at five a.m. almost every morning, and the internet search that brought me to this place, revealed a business that had hundreds of fabulous reviews.

No, she didn't become the journalist she always talked about being, but she was doing just fine to me.

"Your life imploded, but from the ashes you built something beautiful," I heard myself say. "That's what I want, but how and when to start? I want to go back to school, but obviously I'm not going to enroll as Soo Min. That's taking the fraud too far."

Courtney hummed. "I was never sure, but did you get your high school diploma, or did the expulsion snatch that from you?"

I shook my head. "I took on those extra classes and credits to get into Yale, so I was a semester ahead. All of my final grades and exams were in. All my credits were complete. I still got my diploma, but when the teachers who gave me recommendations called Yale to tell them why they were rescinding them..."

"They revoked your acceptance," she finished.

"Yep. And me being a dummy, I never applied for scholarships because Omma promised my college fund would cover wherever I wanted to go."

"Plus, I know Colin's mom sent letters to every college on the East Coast, telling them about the 'prank' gone wrong."

My whisk started beating the batter a little too hard. "Yes, she did. So, I had the grades and the diploma, but no money, no recommendations, and no college that would take me even if I had them. After three years of rejections, I gave up."

"Well, it's been ten years now. People don't hold the memory of others' tragedies for that long. Admissions staff don't stay in the same position or job for that long." She saved the batter from me, beginning the process of marrying it to their crusty, cookie husbands. "I bet you could apply—as you—and get in.

"Do you still want to be a lawyer?"

"You know, I don't think so." I leaned against the table, folding my arms. "Back then, I wanted to be a lawyer because..." Visions of the hallway floated through my mind, carrying the whisper of laughing children, stockinged feet, and unending screams. "Because I thought it was the best and most important job in the world for helping people in need. That's the kind of simplistic thinking you get from a kid.

"But now, after everything I've been through, I know you can help people in so many ways. And... uh... there's something I've been thinking about... wanting to do... maybe— But it's probably a terrible idea," I said quickly. "No one would go for it."

Courtney arched her brow at me. "Knowing you, it's a great idea, so spill it already."

I cracked a smile. "Okay, but promise to tell me if you hate it. Don't fluff me up."

She crossed her heart and threw away the key, getting another giggle out of me.

"Okay," I breathed, plucking up the shattered bits of my courage. "When Omma threw me out, I was two weeks away from my eighteenth birthday. Two weeks from being an adult, and not qualifying for any of the protections or help that would apply to abandoned minors—and that's exactly what the shelter workers told me.

"All the things that a youth shelter would've done for me or helped me with, would evaporate in only a few days, so there wasn't much point. That left me with only the adult shelters that weren't focused on mental health or education. It was all about helping me get a job, get a place to live, and then get out.

"Not that the staff weren't all nice and helpful people," I added. "But all of a sudden, I had to be completely independent immediately when a few weeks before, I couldn't be trusted to go to the bathroom without permission and a hall pass."

Courtney snorted, bobbing her head in agreement.

"To me, I was still a kid clinging to all my privileged dreams of Ivy League colleges, summering in Europe, and interning at a prestigious law firm. All I knew to do was to keep trying to make those dreams come true. I had no idea how to transition from all of that to sleeping in my car and trying to explain to managers why they should hire me and my lack of experience over dozens of qualified applicants. But," I cried, voice rising, "because my mother happened to expel me from her womb eighteen years prior, I was expected to just magically figure it all out!"

"Preach, baby."

"Now, after all this time, that idea just seems more and more ridiculous." I was gaining steam and nothing was slowing me down. "Society expects our parents to prepare for every possibility and every outcome. Putting aside the fact that literally no one can do that because some things just have to be lived—we've also got the parents that just flat-out refuse to.

"Omma and Appa did very little that amounted to actual parenting of me and Sue. The nannies raised us. The groundskeeper taught us how to ride bikes. Our friends played with us. Our teachers taught us. Our tutors helped us with homework. Our chef showed us how to make Korean food. And our Korean tutors and extended family taught us our culture and traditions! Can you even comprehend that, Court? Our parents outsourced teaching us their heritage!"

"I can believe that of your parents for sure," she mumbled. "Sorry if that's a bitchy thing to say."

"It's not bitchy if it's true! But how is being raised by people being paid to do a job, and don't give a shit about you outside of it, supposed to prepare you for the real world?"

"It doesn't."

"How do two cold and neglectful parents provide the stability a new adult can build their life on?"

"They don't," Courtney said.

"Exactly. That's why I've always felt we've needed something more. Something for the eighteen-year-old who gets thrown out onto the street because their sister is a psychopath who ripped her future away, but oh well, she's *an adult now and figure it the fuck out on her own*," I said. "Something for the college dropout who runs away because the emotional load got too heavy for their mental health to carry.

"Something for the foster kid who had to take a job working for a drug dealer because, even though his foster parents are good people, not even the money from the state is enough to pay for his care and the care of his sisters. And they certainly won't have enough to keep housing him after he ages out of the system.

"Who cares about those people? Who's helping them? Who still wants to see them make their dreams come true?"

"Well, that's easy." Courtney smiled at me. "Sarang Kim does."

A silly blush crept up my cheeks. "I told you, it probably won't work, but I'd like to offer something better for people who are lost and just need a little help. We've got all of these different programs run by all of these different organizations. The youth center run by the local high school. The food pantry run by the local church. The housing voucher program run by the government. The shelter run by the local charity. And *all* with different rules and requirements for who they'll help and how.

"Wouldn't it be great to have access to all of these resources in one place with all of it freely given without having to prove you deserve it?"

She paused in her baking to face me. "I mean… yeah, that would be great, but how would that work?"

"I want to build a community—a real one. With rent-free units, food pantries with fresh produce, tutors for wherever you are in your education, job assistance, language programs, on-site and free daycare, on-call doctors and psychiatrists, affordable medical care and prescriptions at a heavy discount, and community shuttles that'll get everyone around town for free.

"All of that, but no curfews that lock someone out into the cold just because the buses stopped running and they had to walk three miles from work. No stuffing thirty people into a tiny room with ten bunk beds. No living on canned food and ramen because it's too hard and expensive to source fresh, organic fruits and vegetables."

"All of that sounds amazing, Sarah, but how would you fund this paradise?"

"Annnd that's where the dream stops," I sang, slumping over the metal surface. "The money to make it happen. Maybe if I were more like Sue was, I could figure out how to take my dream from fantasy to reality. She was the creative one. She was the persuasive one. She was the ruthless one who could forge ahead without considering anyone else's thoughts or opinions. She was the one who could turn an idea into a successful business."

"Successful business?" Courtney picked up her tray of strawberry cheesecake cookies and carried them to the oven. "What are you talking about?"

"SueNation." I started picking up the whisk, mixing bowl, and cookie scoops. "She told me all about how she and her business were the headliners at last year's Lantana Street Fair. Took great pleasure in telling me about it, now that I mention it."

A strange noise sounded behind me.

I dropped the scoops in the sink, spinning to blink at a doubled-over, wheezing, knee-slapping, guffawing Courtney.

"She told you... she was... headliner!? Aha!" she cried, almost toppling into the oven. "Hera help her, Sarah, your sister wasn't just a liar. She was deranged! How can anyone sane rewrite history like that with a straight face!"

"Uhh..." I blinked. "What?"

"My love, SueNation was a bust. A disaster. A complete catastrophe!"

"Come again?"

"Oh my gods, come here. You have to sit down for this." Grabbing my hand, she led me back out to the café floor. "Okay, so get this," she whispered like we were back in our gossipy high-school-girl days. "After you disappeared, I didn't know how to find you or find out if you were okay, so I followed Sue on socials hoping eventually she'd drop a clue about you." She snorted. "And then I kept following her, because I just couldn't look away from that train wreck.

"It pretty much all started after your sister graduated from Columbia-Southern—"

I held up a hand. "Wait, what? Columbia-Southern?"

"Yeah, what about it?"

"Is that what they're calling Columbia U now?"

It was her turn to blink at me. "Columbia University? No, they're still calling that Columbia U. But Columbia-Southern Community College where your sister graduated is sometimes called Columbia-South."

"Oh. My. Goodness." I couldn't have been more blown away than if Sue walked in right then, sniffed, glared at me, and snapped that it wasn't a big deal that she lied about where she went to college. "She didn't get into the Ivy League."

Court snorted. "If she did, she made the wrong damn choice on admissions acceptance day."

"Okay," I cried, blowing back in my seat. "So, Sue attending and graduating from Columbia University—lie."

"Lie," Courtney confirmed. "The only thing those two colleges have in common is they're both in New York. What wasn't a lie was Sue's big, fat, trust fund. After graduating, she tried to launch her influencer career by backpacking all over the world, and flaunting all her favorite tips, tricks, products, and sex adventures as a solo polyamorous female traveler. She was dating Alex, Rhodes, and Micah during all this, but non-exclusively.

"Things were going pretty well by this point," she admitted. "Her followers seemed to really love her whole independent, sex-positive, Asian-women-centered brand. But—"

"I felt that *but* coming in my soul."

She laughed. "*But* then it all went wrong. One day, a video taken by a café customer hit the internet, and it went viral within the hour. It showed another customer clearly bumping into the waitress and making her spill her tray. The problem was… that whole tray of frozen ice mocha lattes spilled on Sue."

"Oh, no."

"Oh, no is right! Sue flipped the fuck out. She jumped up, screaming and ranting at the woman—who was apologizing profusely," she cried. "Sue picked up her cup of coffee—her scalding, hot coffee!—flung it at the waitress's face, and called her a stupid, Black bitch."

My jaw dropped, eyes popping wider than the Yellowstone caldera. "Tell me you're joking. Please, tell me she didn't do or say that."

"I wish I was joking, babe. When I tell you your twin sissy was dragged across the internet superhighway, I'm putting it lightly. And you know she did not handle it gracefully."

I groaned, never more ashamed to share a face with a person than I was right then. "Let me guess, she didn't apologize in any shape or form."

"Nope. Not even when it got out that she gave that innocent woman second-degree burns," Courtney said. "Sue just hopped on socials, crying and bawling that she was the real victim. She was the one forever being stalked, recorded, and harassed by strangers who couldn't understand that 'everyone has a human moment.'"

"A human moment?! She called that a human moment?!"

"You know she did." Court rolled her eyes. "As you can imagine, her complete lack of accountability made the backlash worse—which turned the river she was crying into an ocean. She was the one *being bullied* and *felt unsafe*. Her *mental health was suffering* and the rest of the world were the real monsters because we *wouldn't accept her apology and move on.*"

"The apology she never gave?" I clarified.

"Yep, that's the one."

I shook my head. All of that was typical Sue behavior every time she got caught in a lie or terrible act she couldn't wiggle her way out of, but still, it would never stop surprising me that anyone could live an entire life without ever saying sorry.

"As you can imagine," she continued, "your sister was canceled hard. All of her sponsors dropped her. None of her followers would support her. Did you really never hear about any of this?"

"I had no idea," I confessed. "For one, I for damn sure did not follow Sue on socials. I avoided anything to do with her. I didn't even like looking in the mirror for a full two years after she ruined my life. Besides, you don't have a lot of time to mess around on social media when you're trying to survive into the next day."

"Very true," she said, falling back against her seat. "Well, if it makes you feel better, after the café incident, Sue's world tour adventure was done. She ended up moving back to New York, officially marrying Rhodes, and commitment ceremonying Alex and Micah. Their baby was born pretty quickly after that, and they settled into domestic bliss."

I nodded slow. "Do you know when they all moved to Lantana and into the manor?"

"I want to say it was a little before Taylor was born," Courtney drew out, her gaze drifting over my head and into the past. "Mom and Dad still aren't big fans of mine, but they love their grandbaby, and have since I told them I was pregnant. Mom even threw a huge party for my baby shower and invited your mom. What's even wilder is that your mom actually came."

"She came?" My brows hit my hairline. "The same woman who called you an insolent slut went to a baby shower for a kid named Chlamydia?"

Courtney giggled even as she swatted me. "She absolutely did, and she brought Sue. *Your mom*," she stressed, "was very polite and courteous the entire time. She congratulated me and gifted Taylor the cutest pair of purple baby booties. But *your sister* spent my entire baby shower hitting up my family, friends, and all the other moms to invest in her new organic skincare line—SueNaturals. *The flagship product of SueNation*," she mocked.

"Yikes."

"Yeah, yikes, and now we get to the good part."

"No," I groaned, massaging my temple. "Please, don't tell me there's more. There can't be more after my sister went full psycho racist bitch on an innocent waitress."

She gave me an amused smirk. "Oh, there's more all right. Sue clearly believed all she had to do was wait for the heat to die down, and then everyone would be willing to forgive and forget. But she was wrong. No one wanted a thing to do with SueNaturals, or the lifestyle brand she was trying to resurrect.

"She claimed she invented the formula for an all-in-one, all-natural and organic face cream that was a moisturizer, anti-wrinkler, and blemish-eraser. She hawked it like mad, but she clearly couldn't get the buzz going, because suddenly an ad went up on the Lantana Business Bureau website saying she was taking on affiliates.

"For every jar an affiliate sold, they'd get a seventy percent cut of the sticker price."

I whistled. "Wow. That was generous of her."

"Wasn't it?" Her smirk went nowhere. "All of a sudden, SueNaturals was the talk of Lantana. People were holding parties and inviting all of their friends to hear about this amazing, revolutionary new face cream. They were getting their own followers all whipped up.

"Sue was making money again, and she was loving it. All of a sudden, she was back on the hashtag-femboss scene, going on about expanding into fashion with SueThreads and money management with SueMoola."

"But..." I drew out.

"But—" Courtney cut herself off giggling. "All of a sudden, the first batch of SueNaturals customers started reporting rashes, breakouts, hives, and skin infections in the places where they applied her cream. Sue swore up, down, and sideways that it had nothing to do with her product, and she wasn't responsible, so one of them took it to a lab to be analyzed."

She was laughing so hard she could barely get it out. "The report came back and—and—it turned out there was no special, all-natural super formula at all! It was just a bunch of other popular face cream brands all mixed together with the special ingredient! Poop!"

I jerked in my seat. "What! Did you just say poop?"

"Poop, Sarah! Bird poooooopp! Shit! Excrement!" She was crying, she was laughing so hard. "Sue scooped the crap out of the bottom of Tweety's cage, plopped it in a jar, and charged two hundred dollars for it! And when the wives of Lantana found out, they sued her ass so hard and fast, she couldn't sit down for a month."

My jaw worked for a full minute. "They... sued her?"

"You bet they did. Not only that, but she was slapped with a huge fine by the FDA and ordered to stop selling immediately," she said. "Sue settled all the lawsuits out of court and made them all sign NDAs as a condition for payment. I guess she thought that would be enough to make it all go away because, yes, she did attend the Lantana Street Fair last year with her SueNaturals booth.

"But she wasn't the fucking h-headliner." Court caught another case of the giggles. "Sarah, they chased her out of there—screaming and pelting her with anything they could get their hands on. Someone actually stole a tray of my cupcakes just to throw at her!"

If there was something to say in response to all of that, I didn't know what it was. For eight hours, my sister blathered on and on about her perfect life and successful business, and it was all a lie.

"Wow," I whispered. "Just wow."

She squeezed my wrist. "Look, I told you all of that not only because it brought me great joy, but because I need you to know that Sue wasn't the smart one, or the creative one, or the successful one. The only thing she had on you was being a better liar and bully. You're the best twin, Sarah. Doesn't matter that you had a ten-year delay, you will make all of your dreams come true."

My eyes swam. "Now you're making me cry."

A knock sounded on the glass, drawing our attention to the figure in the window.

An older woman with thick-framed glasses, wispy red hair, and a worn, threadbare brown coat knocked on the glass again, and then pointed to the stack of papers in her hand.

"One sec." Courtney went to the door. Flipping the lock, she stuck her head out. "Yes? Can I help you?"

"Hello," floated to my ear. "You won't know who I am, but my name is Collette Williams. My daughter, Tracy Williams, has been m-missing for two w-weeks." I saw her eyes well through the glass. "She was last seen leaving her job at the post office on the night of the fourteenth"—Mrs. Williams turned and pointed to the post office right at the end of the street—"and I haven't heard from her since.

"My daughter wouldn't leave without telling me. She just wouldn't." A shaky hand peeled a piece of paper off her stack. "This is my girl. Have you ever seen her before? Maybe— Maybe she came in one afternoon for a cupcake or...?" She trailed off at Courtney's headshake.

"I'm so sorry, but no," my friend said. "She's not familiar to me, but I spend most of my time in the back. My assistant mans the shop. I'll ask if she recognizes her," Courtney offered before she asked, taking the flyer. "And I'll put this up in the window."

"Th-thank you," Mrs. Williams rasped. "Bless you, and thank you."

"I hope she comes home safe and sound soon."

Mrs. Williams just nodded, smile wobbling as she turned to go.

Courtney came back in—stricken. "That poor woman. I can't imagine what she's going through right now. One time Mom and I got our wires crossed, and she picked Taylor up from school on the wrong day. When I got there and they told me Taylor wasn't there, I had a straight fucking heart attack in the ten seconds it took for Mr. Stevens to finish his sentence and say her grandmother already picked her up. Worst feeling in the world," she whispered, gazing at Mrs. Williams who was across the street, speaking to the owner of the dry cleaners. "I wouldn't wish it on anyone."

She tossed her head. "Okay, now we both need cheering up. Come with me to pick up Taylor. It's long past time she met her favorite auntie Sarah."

I was up, out the door, and in the car before the woman got her keys.

***

That night, I bustled around the kitchen—putting away groceries, tidying up, and prepping dinner while the music blasted from Sue's laptop.

After a shit-my-pants terrifying morning, I ended up having the best afternoon with Courtney and Taylor. Together, the three of us went to the park, the farmer's market, and then the mall because Taylor informed me that I wanted to buy her a present. So, naturally, I bought her the biggest stuffed bear in the place.

I danced across the hardwood. "Shake that ass, shake that ass, shake—"

"Mommy?"

"Shit! I mean, shoot!" I bleated, spinning around and slamming the laptop closed.

Lily stood in the entrance to the kitchen, smiling innocently at me. "What are you doing?"

"I was... uh... I was just dancing, sweet girl. Dancing and cooking." I clutched my racing chest. "I didn't know you were home. Daddy Alex said you were having a hotel sleepover."

She shrugged. Skipping inside, she hopped on the barstool. "We were, but the bear people called and said they took the bear away. So we came home."

"Well, that's lucky. I would've missed you if you were away all night."

Lily giggled behind her hands, her bright eyes dancing.

"Where's Daddy Alex?" I asked.

"Bathtime."

"Okay," I said simply. Thanks to Courtney, I got all the info I couldn't get directly from the source, because they'd have me committed.

She told me that after selling GloryBoi, the guys stopped working together, and split up and did their own things. Rhodes started an investment firm-slash-hedge fund. Micah became a corporate consultant, and Alex was planning to go to med school when Lily arrived. Instead, he became a stay-at-home dad, and was now beginning to look at schools again since Lily was in school herself.

Courtney got all of that from their socials, proving that people really do put their entire life story online. I tried myself to hit up their pages through Sue's account, but nothing came up.

Every single one of them blocked her.

"What are you making, Mommy?" Lily asked, snapping me out of it. "Can I have some?"

"Yes, ma'am. I'm making bulgogi. Have you ever had that before?"

She shook her head, making me grit my teeth.

Dammit, Sue. Talk about outsourcing passing down your heritage. What had you been teaching your daughter about her culture for the past six years?

"Well, it's very yummy. Every time Omma and Appa took us—me," I quickly corrected, "to Korea, the first thing I'd make them do is take me to the nearest convenience store for a bulgogi roll."

Nari stared at me like she didn't understand a single word I just said.

I laughed. "Don't worry, baby girl. I'm going to teach you everything you need to know before your first trip to the ROK."

"We're going on a trip?"

"Yes, we are," I told her, and who the hell knew why. It was all just tumbling out of my mouth. "We're going to visit Korea, and you're going to meet all the family you have there. I'm even going to teach you Korean."

She nodded, her two pigtails bouncing against her cheeks. "Is it hard to learn?"

"Not if you start when you're young."

"Am I young?"

I chuckled. "Yep, afraid so."

"Did you learn when you were young?"

"I did." Pulling out the cutting board, I started chopping the onions and green peppers.

"Did your mommy teach you?"

I shook my head. "I had a Korean tutor who taught me."

"Were they nice?"

Smiling, I flicked her cute little nose. "You know, they were very nice. I think that's why I liked learning Korean so much. It's so much more fun when you have a nice teacher."

"My teacher is nice," she mused. "He let me have *allll* the cotton candy I wanted."

"Mmh, yes, I know. That's why I got *all* the cotton candy you wanted all over the backseat."

That set off another round of giggling.

"So, I was thinking," I began. My knife blurred across the cutting board. "I can't deliver on that brother or sister, but what do you think about a cousin?"

She cocked her head. "Cousin?"

"That's right. What do you think about an adorable little cousin named Taylor? She's five years old, loves puppies and horses, and she can't wait to play with you. Interested?"

"Hmm." Lily scrunched up her face, looking up to the ceiling. "I'm not sure. I'll think about it."

I almost choked stifling a laugh. "Yes, ma'am. Take all the time you need."

Onion fumes stung my eyes. I turned, rubbed away the tears, then turned back. "But what— Ah!" I shrieked, startling Lily, but only raising Alex's brow.

He appeared out of nowhere, strolling into the kitchen to fall in beside Lily. The sweet, woodsy scent of his body wash filled the kitchen—tickling my nose. He was dressed simply in a plain black tee and shorts, and still my heart skipped a beat like the silly mare I was. Why did this guy have to look good in everything?

Even a sneer.

"Who is Taylor?" he demanded. He put his arm around Lily like I was a threat to her. "She's not Lily's cousin, so who the hell is she?"

Lily giggled at the slight swear.

"Why do you want her to meet this kid so badly?"

I met that guy's eyes and sneered right back. He may be hot, but this was the same jerk who locked me outside with a bear. I wasn't too fond of him right then either. "Not for whatever nefarious reason you're inventing in your head.

"Taylor is Courtney's daughter. My friend from high school," I admitted. "I met up with them both today, and Courtney mentioned that she'd love for the girls to have a playdate." I winked at Lily. "Queen Nari is considering it."

"She doesn't do the considering, Sue. She's six," he said slowly, like he was speaking to an idiot. "You're supposed to discuss these things with me before getting Lily's hopes up. If you had, I would've told you straight out that the answer is no. We don't let our daughter have playdates with strangers."

"She—!" I amended my tone, not wanting to yell in front of Lily. "She's not a stranger. I just told you Courtney is my best friend."

He crooked a brow. "Your best friend who you haven't mentioned once in ten years? I don't know what your scam is, but go run it on someone else. You're obviously trying to get something from whoever this Courtney is—money most likely—so you're playing doting mom to get close to her."

"It's not happening."

I blew a hard breath out of my nostrils, seriously fighting against the no-yelling rule I just enacted. I knew all of this animosity and suspicion was for Sue—the woman who used someone else's baby shower as a personal marketing opportunity—but it was seriously annoying being treated like I couldn't be trusted.

You took over his dead wife's life, and now you're making plans for his child, even though you're a virtual stranger to both of them. Would you trust you?

My anger faded, falling back in the face of plain sense. Alex was a jerk, but I was still in the wrong.

"You're right," I said, catching a flicker of surprise on his face. "I should've asked you first. More than that, I should've introduced you to Courtney and Taylor before I ever thought about a playdate. You have every right to want to know who's spending time with your daughter."

"I... Thank you. I appreciate..." His eyes narrowed to slits. "What is this? Why are you being so agreeable?"

"I don't know what you mean." I twisted away, turning back to the food. "We said we'd do our best to live in harmony during Omma's final days, so that's what I'm doing." I peeked at him through my lashes. "Do you want me to fuss, fight, and argue with you?"

"No, but..." He glanced at Lily. "No, I don't want to fight. Harmony sounds nice for once."

"Good." I clapped, making him jump like I was about to attack. "Then, stop standing around and help. I'm making the bulgogi and the cucumber salad. You're on rice and drinks," I said. "I was in the mood for some strawberry-ade, so I got all the ingredients. If you don't know how to make ade, the recipe is right here." I plucked the sheet off the counter and held it out to him.

Alex took it from me with two pinched fingers—as though it was used tissue paper and not the recipe to deliciousness.

"I'm making enough for everyone, so make sure you do too," I told him. "Tonight, we're having a family dinner."

Alex slowly moved to the fridge. Opening the door, he glared at the suddenly full shelves like they personally offended him. A sideways step and he was glaring into the pantry.

"Nariboo," I sang. "Is all of your homework done?"

She shook her head.

"Go finish it in the dining room—"

"Bring your homework into the dining room," Alex sliced in. "Daddy will be right here if you need help."

"Okay!" Hopping off the counter, Nari was out and up the back stairs like a bolt.

I watched her go with a smile. "She is just the cutest—"

"I changed my mind." Alex slammed the pantry door. "I want to fight with you."

"Excuse me?"

"You heard me," he hissed, bearing down on me so fast, my grip tightened on the knife hilt automatically. "What the hell game are you playing, Sue? What is this domestic goddess routine, and who are you performing it for!" His head whipped this way and that. "You got secret cameras set up in here, or something? Is this the next chapter of your failing business? Sue-Homemaker?"

"What— I— I have no idea what you're talking about!" I tossed the knife down. "There aren't any cameras, and I'm not playing any games! How many times do I have to tell you that I just don't want to fight anymore!" I screamed that last sentence pretty loud for someone who didn't want this fight.

"Because this"—he gestured around the kitchen—"isn't what you do when you don't want to fight. When *you* don't want to fight over the latest, twisted, shitty thing you did, you just withdraw into a sulky lump of wounded pride and victimhood—withholding even the slightest glance in our direction until we give in and apologize to you for what *you* did."

Yeah, that sounded like standard Soo Min protocol.

"What you don't do," he flung, "is buy groceries, cook family dinners, and get on Lily about her homework. You didn't even do this shit during the good times in our marriage—all two weeks of it."

"What if I know that, Alex? What if that's the fucking reason I'm trying to do things differently now?"

"Why in the fuck would now be any different!"

"Because I almost died!" I screamed, blowing him back. "Because I woke up in the dirt and the dark with a bleeding head and a phone that didn't have one *single* message from anyone I loved asking if I'm okay, where I was, or if I needed help.

"Not one, Alex!" Tears sprung to my eyes. "Do you know what that's like? To wake up on the worst morning of your life, completely lost in every way, and discover that no one was looking for you.

"Maybe I want to change because I realized I've lived a life that no one cares about. That no one... would miss."

Alex's shoulders drew down. Dropping his head, the haggard lines on his face disappeared behind his big, calloused hand. "Sue..."

"I want to start over with all of you. You, Micah, Rhodes, Omma, and Lily. No bullshit," I whispered, cutting the air. "No tricks. No games. This is a real and honest fresh start. But if you can't let it be," I said, raising his head. "Then, let me know now and I'll go."

"You'll... go," he said slowly. "Just like that."

"Yeah, just like that. I'll move into a hotel and visit Omma while the guys are at work, Lily is at school, and you're out... doing whatever it is you do."

He flared up quick. "I'm out applying to med schools—as it happens. I don't just sit around all day, Sue. I'm moving forward with my life."

"Hmm. You mean, like I'm trying to do?"

He clamped his jaw shut, jewel eyes glittering with emotions—but none of them that I could read.

"What will it be?" I asked. "Can I go one day without you accusing my pan of sauteed beef of being evidence of a nefarious plot? Or not?"

Alex stared at me for a long time. So long, the warming oil on the stove hit smoke-point—filling the air and stinging my eyes.

And then he stood there even longer, watching me as Lily came trotting through the kitchen and into the dining room.

"Al—"

He turned away and left—walking out the door with the shock left on my hanging lips.

Closing my mouth, I swallowed hard around the lump in my throat. *Don't make an offer if you don't want the outcome, Sarah. You learned that lesson hard.*

There wasn't anything to do about it. I told him I'd leave if it meant Lily didn't have to live in a home full of shouting and resentment for another minute, and I meant it. Time to go.

Taking off my apron, I turned off the stove and—

"—will be right in here," Alex called over his shoulder. "Shout if you need help."

"Okay, Daddy."

Alex took the spare apron off the hook under my huge eyes. "So what's this strawberry-ade stuff?" he threw in my general direction. "Is it just lemonade but strawberries?"

"Uhh... it's... it's a little different?" I confessed, slowly approaching. "More like a sweet fruit syrup mixed with sparkling water."

He hummed. "Doesn't sound too bad," he replied, bending over the recipe. "But you know Rhodes doesn't do sugar when he's training, so he'll only want the sparkling water."

I picked up my slotted spoon like he might reach over and snatch it from me at any second. "I got some extra bottles of sparkling water for that reason."

Alex tipped a nod. "Did you also print out the other recipe?"

"The other recipe for what?"

He was really not looking at me then. "The recipe for... how to make rice."

I snorted.

"Don't you fucking start."

"Don't start on what, rich boy." The snort became a full-blown laugh. "On how you need directions for boiling water? Or is it the part where you throw in the rice and turn the stove off after fifteen minutes that stumps you? Aww." I pouted. "Counting to fifteen is so hward, but baby Alex can do it if he weally tries."

"You know, my name isn't on your marriage license." He snapped his apron putting it on. I could've been imagining it, but I thought I heard amusement in his voice. "I don't have to put up with this shit. I can just walk out the door."

"Sure, if you can find it." I patted his shoulder, oozing sympathy. "Do you need directions to that too?"

Alex made a sound—moving away and out of my reach. "Fuck you twice," he replied, but I didn't imagine that time.

That sound... was a laugh.

Chapter Nine

Utensils clinked. Glass thudded on wood. Chewing filled the air. The air conditioner rattled and hummed.

If I thought a family dinner would defuse the tension and clear the space for conversation, my delusions were soundly and thoroughly popped.

Every attempt at conversation I made was only picked up by Lily—the only person in the room who wanted to talk to me. Thirty minutes into the awkward silences, I was on the edge of giving up.

"So—" How in the hell did I become Davis 2.0? "What does everyone think of bulgogi? Yea or nay?"

Micah rolled his eyes. He picked up his wineglass—filled with the merlot he pointedly stood up and rescued after being told I chose to serve the strawberry-ade. "We've had bulgogi before, Sue. We're not the uncultured swine you think we are."

"Oh."

I thought he'd say more. Nothing came.

I turned my smile on Lily. The five of us were sitting at a dining table built to hold twenty. I sat at the head of the table with Lily sitting directly to my right. All three of the guys sat at the opposite end, making the distance between us literal. "What do you think, baby girl?"

"Mmmm." She tipped her head to the ceiling—little face scrunched up in thought. "It's okay."

"Okay enough that you'll take leftovers to school tomorrow for lunch?"

That got another ponder. "Mmm, no, thanks, Mommy. Tomorrow is pizza day."

"Course it is," I muttered. "My cooking doesn't beat out microwaved pizza, but I bet you don't have these mixed feelings about boogers."

"Ewwww!" she squealed.

"You ewwww! I know you're a booger-eater just like your mama!"

"Nooo!" she carried on, nearly pitching over and laughing herself out of her seat.

Eeee!

Three chairs scraped across the hardwood.

"Time for bed, Lilybug." Micah set his empty glass down next to his full plate. "Daddies will race you."

"Okay!"

"Wait," I cried, jumping up. "I can do Lily's bedtime routine tonight if you want—"

"No need." Rhodes scooped up a giggling Lily mid-run. "You did the cooking, so you just relax. We'll get Lily down and then clean the kitchen."

"But—"

They were already gone.

Blowing out a breath, I turned my attention to clearing the table and washing the dishes despite Rhodes's offer. Truth was, both Courtney and Alex got me thinking I was spending too much time playing homemaker and hiding in the house because I didn't know how to move forward from here.

I knew I wanted my chance to graduate from college, and that I wanted a degree that would help me serve lost and abandoned people who had to watch all of their dreams get stolen from them, but knowing wasn't the first step to doing like so many thought.

Money was the first step to doing. And that was one thing I had none of.

Giving everything in Sue's bank account to Lily was the right thing to do, and I'd do the same thing again, but it didn't leave me with any of that steal-my-life-back-from-that-treacherous-bitch money I was counting on.

All I had to my name was the one hundred and twelve dollars sitting in my real bank account. Getting a job under my real name in the same town where I was pretending I was Sue, and the real Sarah was still away, was stupid to the extreme. On top of that, asking Micah, Rhodes, or Alex for money was out of the question. Once again, that was taking the fraud too far. Improper disposal of a body was enough of a charge. Didn't need Sue's widowers to tack theft to the docket.

My hands slipped in and out of the soapy water, working on autopilot as my mind ran a mile a minute. *There's got to be something I can do for money that doesn't involve stealing it from innocent people...*

My mind crashed into a wall—it's run over.

The fact was, if I were overflowing with marketable skills, I wouldn't have been in the bleak situation Sue pulled me out of. That was the downside of having a mother who shamed you out of having interests or exploring hobbies outside of academia. Even with drama camp! I was only able to convince her to let me go with Courtney because I spun some yarn about it being good practice for when I had to stand in front of a jury and give a defense I didn't morally believe in.

"Those drama camps were fun," I muttered to myself. "And I already have experience working with kids after years of volunteering at the children's home. I could—"

—get laughed out the door when the face of the person who threw scalding hot coffee on a woman, then called her a Black bitch, walks in. And that's before they ask me if I'm there to sell more bird shit face cream.

I tossed my head back, groaning. I was carrying around Sue's baggage now, and that shit was heavy.

"Okay, so I need to do something solo," I concluded. "As my own boss. Something that fulfills a need in a wealthy community that can already afford to buy whatever they want. Something that I won't need to put my face on, because I can't have that bastard finding out I'm still alive." Thinking of Daniel reminded me that the number of missed calls from him had hit the double digits. "And something that people will still buy from me even though this is the same face that sold them bird shit."

I threw my sponge down. "Yep. This is hopeless."

Giving up in every single way, I claimed the bottle of merlot Micah left on the counter and headed upstairs. What was needed then was a hot bubble bath, and me drunk in it.

I headed for the east wing, leaving through the dining room into the informal sitting room that would take me to the back staircase—that spilled out onto the landing that overlooked the east wing. So much room for only seven people, but to a little kid, it all felt like living in a storybook.

Or at least it does until the day you discover monsters do lurk in the shadows.

I halted, spun on my heels, and went back the way I came—making for the west wing instead.

I'll just check on Lily and say goodnight. It's not too late. She should still be up.

I reached the top of the landing, took a left, then slipped through the shadows shrouding the damp and dusty hallway.

Speaking of storybooks, I might as well be living in Beast's castle right now. Hera knows why furniture that could dance and sing couldn't clean itself too, but I know why you can't. My fingers skated over the peeling wallpaper. *I need to contact Mrs. Prado. Find out why all the staff up and quit, and after she tells me Sue was the reason, I can beg her to come back and help me return the manor to its former glory.*

"...think she's for real?"

I slowed—my feet sinking into the carpet that muffled me.

"I don't know." Alex's voice floated into my ear. "You should've heard her in the kitchen, face leaking as she told me how much it hurt to wake up from a near-death experience and discover no one even noticed she was gone."

The hallway split into three—one way carrying me back the way I came. The other leading to the wing with their rooms, and the final being where they stood in the shaft of light from Lily's bedroom... speaking about me in hushed tones.

"She wouldn't be the first person who got scared straight after nearly flying through a windshield," Micah grudged. "Even Scrooge heeded his wake-up call."

"I don't know. I don't know, man," Alex kept repeating. "We've been down this road before. You both know that as well as I. Sue makes these grand declarations about wanting us all to start over and be happy, makes us out to be the jerks if we don't give in, and then two weeks later, she's back again going out to the spa instead of picking up Nari from school, sneaking Rhodes's phone to hit up his confidential clients to sell them on an *investment opportunity*, and shouting at Micah for sending his mother money when *we've already got one poisonous prune draining our bank account.*"

I winced, pressing tighter to the wall. That did sound like Sue.

"We can't get sucked back into her spinning, swirling vortex of psycho. Not when we're so close to being rid of her for good."

Rid of her for good?

I heard the soft footfalls of someone pacing. "Guys, I..." Rhodes began. "I'm sorry, but I think I believe her."

"What!" someone whisper-shouted.

"Look, you weren't with her out there when we faced down that bear," Rhodes said. "The old Sue would've taken off and left me to be that animal's breakfast without blinking twice." He scoffed. "Then, she would've soaked up all the sympathy and attention she'd have gotten as a bear-attack widow, while patenting her new, organic line of bear spray.

"But she didn't do any of that. Guys..." His voice fell, straining my ears to hear. "She didn't just refuse to abandon me. She... stepped in front of me—standing between a three-hundred-pound killing machine, and a guy that just told her it'd be a cold day in hell before he ever forgave her.

"Yes, okay. Every chance Sue had to show us she changed, she spat on it before flipping us off. But not this time. Maybe this time... is real."

My heart soared, sending a smile rising unbidden to my lips. *They're going to do it. They're finally going to give me a real—*

"No."

My heart caught fire and crashed into the dirt.

"No," Micah repeated. "Alex is right. Something doesn't add up. Only a couple of weeks ago, she declared she was dumping us for the piece of shit she's secretly been fucking, and she wanted us all out of the house. And now out of nowhere, she's sorry, she doesn't want the divorce, and she's just giving us the manor for a fraction of what it costs? Not to mention that Silly Lily Fund thing," he hissed. "This is the same woman who wouldn't let Lily have paint, Play-Doh, kinetic sand, markers, or a single toy that might make a mess. But now all of a sudden, she's pulled forty thousand dollars out of her ass for Lily to *have fun*."

"That was weird," Rhodes confessed.

No, Rhodes, no! Not you too. Not after everything you just said.

"Where did that money come from?" he continued. "We removed her access to all of our accounts."

"You know Sue's got her ways," Alex replied. "She probably ran another SueNaturals scam on the last pack of dumbasses who haven't heard of her."

"But if that's what she did, why would she turn around and give all the money to Lily?"

A heavy silence fell on the group.

"Rhodes, you did have legal look over those trust documents, right?" Micah asked.

"You know I did. I told you, Erik said it was clean. A straightforward trust managed by us, for Lily. Sue gave up her access to it as soon as she signed the bottom line."

"But just because the trust is clean, doesn't mean the money is clean," Alex reminded. "Have him, and your IT guy, look into all of it again."

"Fine." Rhodes sounded the music of resigned. "But what are we saying right now? We're not giving Sue a chance? We're just going to make her keep begging and pleading for another chance while she ticks down the days until her mother dies and we throw her out? Because even with all she's put us through, we'll be the evil bastards if we do that."

"That's why we won't," Alex put forth. "You're right, man. If she's willing to hold to a truce, then there's no reason for us to make life in the manor unpleasant just to be a couple of resentful bitches. Let Sue make all the dinners and buy all the vomit medicine she wants because"—his voice changed—"it's not like we're actually waiting until the old prune croaks it."

My lips turned down, heat leaking from my face.

"That's right." Micah laughed. "We've only got to make it to the anniversary party."

Anniversary... party?

"About the party," Rhodes started. His tone did not match their satisfied ones. "I was thinking that maybe we should cancel that after—"

"No." Alex's voice was clear. Final. "It's too late to cancel. The party is going ahead like we planned, and when it's over, we'll finally be rid of her for good. Agreed?"

"Agreed," Micah returned without hesitation.

Seconds passed.

Then minutes.

The clock ticked down as they waited for—

"Agreed," said Rhodes.

I stood there, silent in the shadows, long after they walked right past me into their rooms.

***

Carnival music filtered through the speakers, inviting one and all to a freakishly fantastic adventure.

I darted behind the clown, curling my legs and arms in tight around me—shrinking away from the spinning, technicolor lights.

Footsteps thudded over the music. Heavy, loud, and coming closer.

"Now, where did you run off to, little girl? Huh-hyuck," he laughed—that strange, hiccupping laugh. "There's no need to be scared of Captain Chucklepants. He just wants to play."

I clapped my hands over my ears, desperately trying to drown out his voice, his laugh, the music, the lights, the colors, that awful smell.

A shadow fell over me.

"There you are. Hide-and-seek is over."

I screamed as he reached for me.

"It's time to play."

"Ahh!" I shouted, ripping out of the dream.

Shooting up in the bed, the sweat-soaked sheets clung to my neck and shoulders. I fought to kick them off but not in time. Pitching over the side, I vomited right on the carpet.

"Ugghh." I crawled off the bed—stomach flipping and heaving.

I knew with my return to the manor, the nightmares would sneak back into my sleep. Honestly, I was surprised they had taken this long.

I lay there on the carpet for a spell, willing my stomach to settle. Only when I trusted myself did I push up on my hands and knees and crawl out of Sue's room. I didn't force myself onto my feet until I reached the staircase.

The kitchen light beckoned me the rest of the way. Either I forgot to turn it off, or the guys did after they finished up their secret meeting in the hall and came down to clean up after dinner.

My already aching jaw clenched. As much as I told myself it shouldn't bother me while I polished off the merlot in the bath, it fucking bothered me. I knew how hard it was to forgive Sue. Twenty-eight fucking years and I never accomplished it.

But what I also knew was how much it sucked to be blamed for Sue. To have to carry the weight of her actions, her callousness, her lies, and her manipulations. I did it the day she paralyzed Colin. And now I was doing it again.

Sighing, I trudged over the threshold, heading straight for the cabinet over the sink. *I'm sure I put Lily's nausea medicine in this cabinet. Hopefully, it works just as fast on adults—*

"Guess it's my turn now."

"Zeus in heaven!" I belted, spinning around. "What the flipping fucking fuck are you doing!"

Micah grinned at me from his seat on the kitchen island. "Same as you. Couldn't sleep." He shook the container of my bulgogi at me. "That's what I get for going to bed hungry."

"That's what you get for being a jerk." I snatched the medicine off the shelf. "Next time, don't cut off your nose to spite your stomach."

Micah cocked his head. He was wearing nothing but a pair of boxers, and my eyes didn't know where to look. His long, raven locks swept the top of the warring tigers tattoo that claimed the whole of his hard, bulging pecs. The man was a father and husband in his thirties, and still he looked like just seconds before he was getting up to some illegal shit with his buddies under the bleachers.

"Hmm. I'm not sure that analogy works," he said. "Cutting off your nose doesn't affect your stomach in any way. What you should've said is—" He cut himself off, laughing heartily at the two birds I flipped in his face.

"Seems that's a no, then," he said, chuckling. "You didn't come here to corner me and seduce me with your new sweet-Sue act."

"My dude, I'm down here because I vomited all over the carpet," I grouched out—my body as wrung out and tired as I sounded. "This is all the seduction I've got for you." Just like that, I tugged my camisole down and flashed my itty-bitty left titty for his viewing pleasure. "Oontz, oontz, oontz," I sounded off—bouncing up and down in place.

Micah choked on his fork. He fell off the island, hacking the fork and a chunk of beef on the floor. Wheezing, he clutched his inky chest—laughing so hard that if he wasn't already on the floor, he would've fallen.

"Hope you got everything you needed from that." Popping my top back up, I made to leave with my medicine.

A hand on the ankle stopped me.

"What if I didn't?"

I blinked down at him... and the smirk flashing up at me. "Uhh... what?"

"It's been a long time, baby. Seven months, two weeks, and five days." He smiled. "But who's counting?"

"Who, indeed."

"You want to work out a truce between us so badly, let's do it the fun way. I'll trade you." A warm, stroking finger glided up my ankle—popping goose bumps on my flesh. "Each orgasm I give you also comes with a day of no fighting, no sniping, and no passive-aggressive digs. I'll be something I've never been before." He winked. "A good boy."

My jaw worked for a full minute. "This is a joke, right? You're joking."

"Why would I joke about having sex with my hot-ass wife?"

Because not five hours ago you were telling Rhodes and Alex that you would never trust your hot-ass wife!

"Because you just got done hearing me say that I threw up. I even have some on my pants."

"My plan involves ditching the pants, so this works out just fine for me."

I gaped at him, then my eyes narrowed. "Hold on, is this a trick? Are you planning to lure me to the east wing where Alex is waiting in the shadows with a pee-filled balloon?"

"A what?" He laughed. "You're watching too much TV before bed, babe. That's what's making you nauseous."

"I—" My stomach heaved, doubling me over and pitching me sideways against the kitchen counter. *I wish it were jumbled comedy reruns haunting my dreams. At least those aren't real.*

"All right." Hands encircled my back and knees. "Guess I'm initiating this time."

"Wha— Micah!"

He scooped me up, squishing me against his hard, tattooed chest, and carried me away.

I struggled weakly in his hold. If there was ever a time in my life when I was not in the romantic mood, it'd definitely be when I was covered in my own vomit!

"Micah, please," I rasped as he carried me up the stairs and down the same hallway where I listened to them count the days until they'd be rid of me. "I don't think this is a good idea—"

He kicked the door open, carrying me over the threshold.

"I can't keep up with this hot-and-cold thing you're doing," I said. He rested me on a bed I could barely see in the dark. "You might think it's sexy, but it very much isn't."

"Then, I'll stick with one." His hands slid out from under me, then he did too—moving away in the dark. "Just hot."

Before I could reply, the lights flicked on—flooding every corner of the plain guest room.

I say plain guest room because that's exactly what it was when I was growing up—with nothing to say for itself except for a calming cream-and-blue color palette, four-poster bed, two dressers big and small, and an armchair and end table by the window. I didn't know how long Micah had been living in this room, but however long that time was, he didn't spend it redecorating.

The only new addition was the mini-fridge he was currently standing over.

"Even if you don't take me up on my deal, I'll take you up on yours." Micah took a water bottle out of the fridge, and then crossed to the bathroom. His voice floated through the open door. "The truce. A ceasefire. For as long as you're playing the part of doting, loving wife, I'll play the role of attentive, loving husband."

I saw his smirk first, then I drifted down to the water bottle in one hand, and the spit cup in the other.

"I won't break... until you do." He handed me both. "Here. Rinse out your mouth, and then drink. Finish half that bottle, then the medicine."

"You won't break until I do?" I repeated slowly even as I complied with his order. "What's that supposed to mean?"

"It's just a little incentive for you to keep up the act—and we both know it's an act—longer than you were planning to. Nari loves you like this." He accepted the gross spit cup from me, setting it down on the end table and then tapping the water bottle to remind me to drink. "For her sake, I want you to keep the real Sue down for as long as you can."

Silence fell while I drank. "And how is the deal you're offering me any different from the deal you think I'm offering you?"

"Aww, yes," he breezed, falling back and laying his head on my lap. "You see, the one I'm offering you comes with a guarantee. Whatever your orgasm tally is, I'll be a good little husband for that number of days no matter what you do or don't do."

I nodded slow. "And if I break the truce without taking you up on your offer?"

Dark, piercing eyes stuck me through. "Then it's war. Bloody, brutal war with casualties on all sides."

Setting down the water bottle, I picked up the medicine, measured it out, and downed the lot. Only when I recapped and put it back, did I say, "Well, that's something to think about."

I poked his chest. "I should get back to my room."

"No, you shouldn't." He heaved himself off. "What you should do is relax and get some rest while I clean up in there."

"What? No, Micah. Come on, you don't have to do that."

"Course I do." He winked his way out the door. "It's what any good husband would do."

He was gone before I could argue some more, leaving me with my flipping stomach and spinning head.

What was I supposed to make of his offer? Unlike what he assumed, I wasn't putting on an act, so if he was really willing to hold out as long as I did, he'd be holding out forever.

Or until the anniversary party. Whenever the hell that was, and whatever the hell the three of them meant by getting rid of me for good.

Could they have been talking about serving Sue with divorce papers? a voice asked.

I shook the question away. Why would they want to put themselves and Nari through a potentially messy divorce when I already said on tape that I would take a far smaller price to walk out of their lives for good?

That's a deal any scorned husband would jump on. It doesn't make sense for them to escalate a situation I already defused.

Then, what did the three of them mean when they were speaking in the hall, and what does Micah mean by this strange offer only a few hours later? And then the even bigger question, what are the ethical, and mostly legal, ramifications of sleeping with a man who believed I was someone else?

I tossed those questions back and forth in my mind for so long, I passed out before I got an answer.

Chapter Ten

"Hello? Hello, is this Mrs. Prado?"

Crackling came through the speakers, followed by a thin, weedy voice. "... is this?"

I checked the screen, clicking my tongue at the weak signal. Reception wasn't so great deep in the trees—which is where the founders of Lantana Little Learners Day School insisted on building the elementary school.

I climbed out of the passenger seat, waving around the phone and moving farther and farther away from the car trying to catch a signal.

"Hello? Can you hear me?" I asked. "This is Ms. Kim of Kim Manor. I'm calling to speak to Mrs. Prado."

"Mrs. Eleanor Prado?" came back clearly. "Is that who you need?"

"Yes, it is. Are you her?"

"I'm her daughter," replied a smoky voice. "Mom's out walking the dogs, but she should be back soon. Do you want to wait, or call her back?"

"I'll wait. Thank you."

I strolled the length of two parking spaces, eyeing Micah out of the corner of my eye. He loitered outside the school entrance with the other pick-up parents, chatting up three attractive, well-dressed moms who were hanging on his every word.

That they were fawning over him, despite all boasting wedding rings, did not surprise me. What did surprise me was actually being there to watch.

I woke up that morning with the surprise of my life—Micah's arm thrown over me, and his chest warm and steady at my back. I ended up slipping out from under him to sneak back to my room—which was clean and vomit-free just like he promised.

After showering and getting dressed, I went downstairs into the dining room and discovered Lily munching on buttered toast and cinnamon oatmeal. Micah set a bowl and plate down on the table for me before I even asked.

Together the three of us ate with the conversation focused on Lily and the activities they had planned for her at school. When we were done, Micah invited me to join them for drop-off, but I was so weirded out by his sudden and complete turnaround, I mumbled something about needing to spend time with Omma while she was up and semi-alert enough to eat her breakfast.

He accepted this, but then several hours later, he found me in Omma's disused office, searching her papers for Mrs. Prado's number. His consulting client rescheduled on him and he was free to pick Lily up from school. He invited me to join him, and thus was the story of how I ended up in the Lantana Little Learners parking lot watching married women flirt with my sister's widower.

You'd have thought I'd have spent that time crafting the very clear and direct speech I'd give to him, Rhodes, and Alex on how it was best they consider their physical relationship with Sue terminated, just like they considered their marriage to her terminated. There would be no sex with her—or anyone who may happen to look like her—at all. Ever.

Yes, you'd have thought I'd have that speech ready to go...

One of the women said something, and Micah threw his head back laughing. His long, thick hair caught the wind, which tried to carry it away—taking it only so far as the strong, warm hands that captured, then smoothed it down, would let it. Without his hair hiding his cheeks, they revealed the deep, teasing dimple above his chiseled jaw.

...but you'd be wrong.

Did normal women turn down a wild romp from a hot *single* man when it was offered up on a silver platter? Because I had a feeling that answer was no, and they'd say as much in the jury room when they're deliberating over my fraud case.

"That's just too much damn fucking fine to say no to."

"Excuse me?"

I jumped. "What! Hello?"

"Hello?"

"Mrs. Prado?" I asked, recovering quick. "Hi, this is Ms. Kim—"

"I know who this is."

I blinked, wondering if I mistook the chill in her tone. "Yes... uh... thank you for taking my call. Do you have a few minutes to talk?"

"About?"

"About possibly coming back to work for—"

"Excuse me? Coming back to work? For you? You must be joking. This is a joke, and not one that has the decency to be funny."

Okay, I didn't imagine the chill.

"How dare you waste my time with this non—?"

"I'm sorry," I blurted. "I'm so sorry for everything I've done and said. Sorry for mistreating you and pretending for even a second that you're not the best chef and house manager that anyone could ask for."

"I... What?" The wind whooshed out of her rant. "Who is this?"

"You know who this is," I replied, skirting around the question. "And you know I don't give apologies easily."

She snorted.

"Or at all," I rushed to say. "But this one I owe you. I'm sorry, Mrs. Prado, please, hear me out."

"Hmm." Only she could infuse a hum with suspicion. "Five minutes."

"That's all I need." I clapped my hands, waving them at the sky and sending my thanks to Hera. "Because I'm going to get straight to the point. The manor's become a shitpit and I need your help restoring it to its former glory."

Another hum. "A shitpit sounds about right," said the fifty-eight-year-old woman. "And needing my help is accurate too, but why in the world would I come back?"

"I—" I halted, cringing. "I want to say for a substantial raise, but I... I don't have any money to pay you."

She scoffed. "What else is new? Since when have you ever had, or been willing to part, with a single cent?"

I deflated like an old balloon. I was forced to learn how to cook and clean after being kicked out of my fancy life, but that didn't mean I was prepared to cook for an entire family three times a day, or clean a manor bigger than my old apartment building. And that didn't begin to account for all the yardwork that needed to be done.

"But you didn't pay me before, so there's no need to start now."

"What?" My ears pricked up. "What do you mean I don't need to start paying you?"

"I will submit my pay stubs to the estate, Soo Min, obviously." Exasperation laced her tone. "As I did before. With the exception that these pay stubs will reflect a sixty percent rise in pay. Yes?" she snapped.

"Yes," I said instantly, tossing another thank-you to the heavens. "With a bonus thrown in if you handle the hiring and interviewing of the rest of the staff we'll need. Groundspeople, gardeners, housekeepers, painters, roofers, and an interior designer or two? Please," I threw in.

"Three thousand."

"Twenty-five hundred and I throw in a kitchen remodel."

"Deal," she pounced. "If you write up the contract with those terms and send it to me signed by your mother, the accountant, and the estate lawyer by the end of the week, I'll start the following Sunday."

"Absolutely. Not a problem."

"Then I'll see you Sunday."

Click.

I jumped up and down—doing my flat-ass dance right there in the parking lot. I was all prepared for a very awkward conversation with Rhodes, Alex, and Micah on their need to fund the household staff, but it never occurred to me that wasn't necessary because it was all handled by Appa's estate planning and lawyers. And that didn't occur to me because I never really understood how all of that worked in the first place.

What I did know was that my father, Jong Woo Kim, was the heir to a mini-fan empire based in Korea. As the second son, he didn't inherit the business from his father, but he did reap the rewards with a sizeable bank account gifted to him upon marriage. And therefore, Omma was gifted a sizeable prenuptial agreement on her wedding day.

Neither one of them shared the details of that prenup with me or Sue growing up, naturally, so we got the skinny from our cousins in Daegu one summer when we visited for a wedding.

Our older cousin, daughter of my father's sister, told us that Dad's older brother made his new wife sign a prenup too, but it wasn't "half as vicious as the one Omma signed."

We didn't know what she was talking about, but when we asked her, she just said, "If you don't know, I'm not going to be the one to tell you, but I will say this. If a guy handed me a prenup like that minutes before we were supposed to get married, and he told me to either sign it or walk out, I'd walk out... after kicking his ass."

Naturally, Sue and I were bursting with questions after being told that, but neither one of us was stupid enough to ask our parents about it.

We both wanted to live.

But the questions always hung in the air, especially after Appa died. Our standard of living didn't change at all. We still had nice clothes, expensive shoes, and a house full of staff, but after middle school, and the declaration that I would run away before I ever went to the same school as Sue again, I put the Titan Prep brochure in my mother's hands.

She agreed that it was a great school and I'd do very well there, but then she said something I didn't understand until that moment.

"I don't know if he'll approve the tuition cost when there are other private schools in the area that cost half this much," she had said, clearly forgetting I was in the room. *"I'm still paying back Halmeoni's surgery too."*

I asked her then what she was talking about, and she immediately shooed me away and told me to start on my homework.

Mrs. Prado's remark now put all of that in sharp focus. If my mother needed joint permission from an accountant and a lawyer just to hire a flipping house manager, it meant that my father locked his inheritance down so tight, my mother couldn't touch it even after he died.

Imagine how humiliating it must have been for my mother to have to go pleading and cajoling for the money to send her daughter to a better school? And then quadruple that humiliation when she begged him for money to care for her ailing mother, and he told her she could only have it as a loan.

From her father's control, to her husband's control, and now to a lawyer's control—my mother wasn't allowed independence a single day of her life... and now that life was ending.

"Fuck's sake, Appa," I whispered, shaking my head. "No wonder even your super conservative family members thought you were an ass."

"Sue?"

I turned as Micah crossed the asphalt holding tight to Lily's hand.

"Everything okay?"

"Yes," I replied, holding out my arms for Lily to jump in them. "Just wishing more men were feminists."

That got an eyebrow raise. "Didn't know you cared about that, but, if it helps my cause..." He flashed me that wicked, toe-curling grin. "I am."

I ducked my head, hiding a blush in Lily's hair. "Are you?" I shot back. "Because saying you are just to illicit the kind of favors you want to get from me, kind of proves you're not."

He laughed out loud—not in the least bit slighted.

I reached for the door handle and paused. Lily's teacher waved at us from the sidewalk. He waited for a car to pass, then jogged over.

"Yes?" I asked. "Is something wrong? Did Lily forget something?"

"No, not a thing." Charles Layton was a short, but handsome man with plump, round cheeks and a gangly frame. I didn't know how much chasing after kids in the hot sun he did day after day, but his pale skin was tan in some places, and red in the rest. I put him at around my age. "I just wanted to let you know that I have a faculty meeting tomorrow, so I'll be an hour late."

I stared at him. "Late to... what exactly?"

He laughed. "Very funny, Mrs. Kim. See you tomorrow."

I waved him off. "Nariboo, what's that strange man talking about?"

"Mommy, you know. My piano lesson."

"Oh, he's your piano teacher too?"

"Yes," she said with a hearty nod. "But I don't like it. Piano is boring. I want to play the drums."

Chuckling, I opened her door and helped her buckle in. I couldn't help but love her six-year-old straight talk. Honestly, I think the worst thing we do as a society is to stem a child's natural flow of truth and directness, and teach them they must run every word through a filter until the only thing they're left speaking is bullshit.

I climbed into the passenger seat and tossed a smile at Micah. "Good news," I told him. "I called Mrs. Prado and convinced her to come back and work at the manor. She's even going to take on hiring the rest of the staff that we need. Because for a *feminist*, you didn't take on too much of the cleaning and cooking, did you, Spencer?"

"Baby girl." He laced his fingers through mine and brought my palm to his lips before I could get out a squeak. "If you want me with a broom in my hands, you only have to say."

My face caught fire and exploded. "What kind of nonsense are you saying with a child in the car!"

That just set him off laughing at me. But he didn't let go of my hand...

...and I didn't make him.

***

I was a straight mess when we got back to the manor.

Micah spent the whole car ride rubbing tiny, mind-melting circles on my inner wrist that had me shivering up and down my spine so much, I would've vibrated out of the car if the door wasn't shut and locked.

As soon as he killed the engine, I hopped out, hurried upstairs, changed into my running gear, grabbed my phone, and then sprinted out the door.

My usual route was out of the question thanks to a certain clawed and fanged animal who might have aggrieved friends, so instead I turned right after climbing off the front step, and made for the cliff path.

The Kims owned miles and miles of prime Lantana land, except where Poseidon's trident cleaved the earth and forced it to give way to the sea. The cliff path was exactly what it sounded like. A running and hiking path that ran right alongside the cliffs.

The view was gorgeous. Nothing but the glittering, undulating waves stretched out to the horizon and beyond. I wished I could've run this path more often as a teenager, but back then I had a not-entirely-irrational fear that the last thing someone with a sister like mine should do... was get within pushing distance of a cliff's edge.

How ironic was it that I was the one who ended up throwing her into the sea?

But either way, Sue was the last of my concerns. She wasn't the problem chasing me across the coast.

"You can't sleep with him. You can't sleep with him. You can't sleep with any of them," I shouted into my phone, recording every word. "You can't sleep with Micah, Rhodes, or Alex, and you'll repeat this message to yourself every time you forget it!"

I shouted sense into myself and my phone for a good half an hour until my rubber legs demanded I go back inside.

Trudging through the mud and grass, I tried turning my thoughts to what I was making for dinner that night. Nari had eaten enough processed and takeout food to last a lifetime, and I didn't trust the three former rich boys inside not to go straight to all the packaged and microwaveables I bought at the store.

Corned beef and cabbage would be quick and easy, I thought, heading inside and climbing the great hall stairs. *I could throw in some white beans, and make an avocado side salad.*

My door loomed at the end of the hall, promising me a steaming hot shower on the other side.

I'll see if Nari wants to cook with me. I don't want her waking up at eighteen years old and finding out that without a cellphone and a delivery driver, she'd starve.

I threw open my door, and stopped dead.

There was a steamy, hot shower waiting for me all right, but it seemed someone else had gotten to it first.

I stood there blinking and gaping like an idiot, my sluggish brain fighting to connect how and why steam and singing were coming out of my open bathroom door.

"—that ass, shake that ass, shake that—"

"Hello?!"

"Oh, hey, Sue," called a completely nonchalant voice. "I forgot to grab it on the way in, but would you mind getting my shower gel from under the sink? No offense, but I'm not interested in smelling like a mocha sunrise. I don't even know what that means."

"I... uh..." I took a step, then found I couldn't go any further. "What are you doing in my shower?"

"Nothing but cold water is coming out of mine," he returned. "Speaking of, would you mind telling Mrs. Prado that if she's really coming back, we need her to bring a plumber with her. I can't stand this place," he grumbled. "Everything's falling the fuck apart."

"But why didn't you shower in Alex's or Rhodes's bathroom?"

Laughter carried out of the shower. "Why in the world would I?"

I heated up. Of course he wouldn't go in their space. He wasn't married to them. It was perfectly reasonable for a man to shower in the same tub as his wife. It wasn't his fault said wife was replaced by an impostor.

"Oh. Okay."

"Babe," he called, making me jump. "Shower gel?"

"Huh? Oh, yeah! Sorry." I willed movement back into my feet, making them carry me across the bathroom to the—

Micah stood under the warm spray butt naked with nary a shower curtain or murky glass partition to shield him from me. Under my wide, bulging eyes, his hands traveled down, down, down his chest to the wet and swollen member hanging between his legs.

I stopped breathing. Stopped moving. Stopped thinking as he grasped his cock, and started stroking.

"Hey, are you all right?" he asked with a laugh. "Why are you just standing there?"

My lips parted, but nothing came out. Nothing I ever experienced—sexually or otherwise—could've prepared me for seeing Micah Spencer naked.

Hera knew I imagined such a miraculous thing enough times in my teenage fantasies. And a few times in my adult fantasies when I was faking my way through sex with Dan, and a grown-up version of Micah, Rhodes, or Alexander would pop into my head—promising they'd satisfy me even if the stupid fool on top of me couldn't.

"It has been a while, hasn't it."

I jerked, heating the sweat on my body up for the second time.

"And now that I think about it..." Micah drawled, squeezing his length tighter the further down he went. "You never did give me an answer to my question. My deal or yours?" He tipped his chin, making those long, wet locks fall over his hooded eyes. "Join me and we'll work out all the... kinks."

Sense slapped me across the head, snapping me out of it in a blink. "Okay, that's it." I pointed at my feet. "Get out of my shower and get over here. We need to settle this right now."

"And I have to get out for this?"

"Move your ass."

Amusement etched into every line and water droplet on his face. Grabbing a towel, he climbed out of the shower and padded over to me. "What is it, Sue? I know you're committed to keeping up your act, but I promise not to hold it against you if you drop this blushing virgin routine."

"It's not a routine!" I was looking anywhere but down. Micah had a towel on... but it was around his shoulders. "You and I having sex is not a good idea! There are a thousand reasons why, and I can list them all for you right now," I said, whipping out my phone. "We need to be celibate. Can you agree to that, and stop trying to seduce me?"

"No."

"Very well," I said primly. "Then, I'm going to need you to speak very clearly into the mic, stating that you are willingly and soberly consenting to sexual intercourse with the knowledge that I am putting on an 'act' as you call it, but you're aware of and okay with this."

He blinked at the phone. "This is a new and strange form of foreplay. Did you learn it from your side piece?"

"Into the phone," I pressed, moving it closer. "Repeat after me: I am willingly and soberly—"

Laughing, Micah dropped the towel and draped me shrieking over his shoulder instead.

"I would much prefer a record of your consent before we—"

"You'd also prefer to drop that phone on the mat, or it's going in the shower with us."

"Micah—!"

Micah stepped in the tub—me and all.

I barely had enough time to toss my phone out of the bathroom before he dropped me on my feet, directly under the warm spray.

"If I could just get on the record that—"

Swooping down, Micah captured my lips—putting an end to my babbling for good.

So many days, and in so many ways, I imagined my first kiss with Micah Spencer, and not even in my most heated and vivid fantasies did it ever come close to this.

Lips steamy hot like the mocha sunrise he spurned, his moved against mine, melting my resolve like ice cubes on a Florida sidewalk.

I gasped, welcoming him in all too soon, and he stormed inside like the take-no-prisoners bad boy he was. Tongue tangling, moans mingling, fireworks exploding—my whole body came alive in his arms.

I had my fair share of first kisses. Some men were tentative as if they believed holding back was the sign of a gentleman. Others were too rough, too slobbery, or they tried to choke me with their tongue. Tongue Boy being Daniel.

Yes, there were all sorts of first kisses, but none of them were the best... because the best was happening to me right then. Sweeping me along into fluttery, flowery, drug-like euphoria that melted my bones—dropping me helplessly into his arms.

There was nothing gentlemanly about the hungry, punishing kiss that battled my tongue into surrendering, then sent my heart galloping away.

Micah tore my clothes off in a flurry, flinging the wet garments around the place with a chorus of wet slaps.

Panic seized me as he drew back, feasting on my naked body like he hadn't seen it in seven months—*when he actually hasn't seen it ever!*

What if Sue helped herself to a few new concealable tattoos and piercings I knew nothing about in the last ten years? Am I literally about to be caught with my pants down!?

"Damn, girl, I swear you only get more beautiful with every passing year. It's very unfair," he said, running his fingers down my wet cheeks. "Evil should age like a banana."

"Racist," I snapped, startling a laugh out of him. "And what happened to best behavior?"

"Why should I behave?"

The world spun—tossing me around and then depositing me blinking and bewildered on his shoulders.

"You haven't cum yet."

Heat beat against my neck, running down and around my shoulders—streaming down my stomach and hungrily splashing down on Micah's nose, cheeks, and forehead—as if there was no other place it wanted to be.

He pressed me against the cool tile. Kneeling down, Micah nuzzled my stomach in a way that wasn't even sexual, but still shot my blood pressure through the roof.

"Mi—"

He dove down, burying his head between my legs so fast, I hadn't finished gasping on his name before his tongue slipped between my lower lips. If I thought he wasn't shy about a kiss, that was nothing compared to how he approached giving head. The man ravaged my pussy like a starving man devoured a buffet.

Tongue plunging in and out of my well. Fingers digging into my thighs. Thick, wet hair rubbing against my clit. Growls and moans rumbled from his throat and crumbled my core to dust.

"Ah!" I cried out, doubling over and nearly pitching off his shoulders. "Ah, Micah, yes!"

He slipped down, resting me on the rim of the tub. I was a puppet in his hands, helpless to move let alone think of stopping him as he spread my knees, and lapped me up.

"W-wow," I choked, toes curling up into my bones. "That's— Hera, help me, that's good— Ah!"

Micah latched on to my clit and sucked like he was trying to take the thing off. My head flung back, colliding with the tile and ringing pain through my skull.

I didn't care.

Pleasure rocketed through my body, flooding every cell and nerve ending with fiery-hot flames.

It had been a long time, and I meant a long time, since I had even semi-decent sex. Even before things went sour with Daniel and we were *in love*, the sex was crap because the guy was such a selfish lover. Once he shot his top, he completely tapped out and left me to take care of myself.

That was a big part of why I suggested the sex tapes. I thought it'd give our sex life some much needed spice, and heat things up enough for me to stay interested. But that was Satan, and this was Micah.

Five minutes under his ministrations, and I knew our sex life wouldn't need any more extra spice. The man was a five-alarm fire with nothing but his hand, his dick, and a magazine, but the two of us together…?

Three fingers slid past my entrance, and spread—stretching my walls for the coming reckoning—and I swear I opened my eyes to see if true sparks were coming off my body, ready and willing to set us both alight.

"Oh, fuck, yes, right there," I moaned, eyes rolling up in my head. "Ah!"

"Oooh, I'm loving the soundtrack, baby." Pulling back, he positioned his hand, and started drilling my pussy like a jackhammer. "Did you become a screamer for your side piece?"

"Ahh!" I screamed, legs flying up and heels banging on the porcelain. "There is—no side piece!"

"Well, you would say that," he replied, amusement lacing his voice. "Because the prenup says you'll get nothing from divorcing Rhodes if you're caught cheating."

"No one is getting divorced," I forced through gritted teeth. I swear, men perfected the art of making women want to punch them in the head even in the midst of being brought to orgasm. "You want rid of me so badly, you can keep your money and I'll just go. How many times do I have to say it?"

"No more times, gorgeous. We already didn't believe you the first time."

"You—!"

He struck that spot, bending down to flick my clit with his tongue in rapid succession.

I came hard—jerking and shuddering on the rim until I popped off and took Micah down with me. Despite being a complete and total ass, he held me as I came down—running his fingers up and down my body, raising goose bumps on my flesh that scalding water couldn't keep down.

Micah put his finger in his mouth, popped his cheek, and held it up. "That's one down."

"That's your only one if you don't stop being a jerk!" My irritation came roaring back. "Has anyone ever told you that sometimes it's better *not* to talk?"

He smirked, folding his arms behind his head, and lying there like a freaking pinup model posing under a waterfall. It wasn't right for anyone to be this handsome!

"Nope, sorry. The same person who didn't tell you, never told me either."

I huffed. Rising up, I straddled him—poking his chest. "Wrong. I'll have you know, I'm well-versed in the proper decorum of when it's time to put my mouth to better use." With that, I stretched out against his hard, inked chest... and traveled down.

"Wait, what?" His smirk washed away. "Are you serious? You're really going to—?"

"Going to what?" I winked. "Blow you until you pop? I'm afraid I am, Spencer, so if you've got an objection, voice it n—"

"No," he blurted—going from hot model to eager horndog in the blink of an eye. "No objection. Matter of fact, I'm going to try out that shutting-my-mouth thing if it means you won't stop."

There was no chance of me stopping. I wanted this man's dick in my mouth more than I wanted a truckload of chocolate that would never hit my hips.

Palming his length, I had to stop just to marvel at it.

I didn't want to keep comparing every guy to Dan, but even before I realized he was crap in bed and it would never get better, I didn't remember ever having this kind of excitement for him.

Touching him, kissing him, pleasing him, and having him inside of me. None of that ever rose past the level of take-it-or-leave-it for me. Truth was, the spark was there with Dan, but never the passion. At that moment, I realized the passion wasn't there for any of the guys life threw my way after circumstances took me away from Micah, Rhodes, and Alex.

After all this time... it's still you.

I swallowed him to the hilt, filling every corner of my mouth with Micah, Micah, Micah.

Starting slow, I sucked till my cheeks caved in, drew up to the tip, swiped my tongue across the head, then sank back down—enveloping him down to my throat.

Micah choked. Every muscle beneath my body tensed like this little bit was enough to push him off the edge.

I didn't know what I'd get in exchange for making him cum, but I was very excited to find out.

Rising up, Micah got himself to his feet and me to my knees—giving me the better angle he sensed I was looking for.

I balanced on my toes, holding tight to his ass as I bobbed, sucked, and slurped his cock like a lollipop.

"Mmh hmh mgh!" Micah groaned, biting hard on his lips. Keeping his promise to shut up was likely a joke, and it was a good one because it was making me laugh.

I couldn't help but giggle every time I looked at his red-cheeked, constipated face—holding on to the filthy promises he wanted to pour on me.

It was wrong, and it was weird, and it was unearned, but I loved this. I loved that we blew past all that first-date/first-time fumbling, and were already at the point of being silly and comfortable with each other during sex.

"Mhh mmm gghh!" His muffled nonsense was quickly followed by his muscles tightening like bowstrings.

I got the message easily. Relaxing my throat, I opened up and accepted all he had to give me.

Groaning, Micah fell against the wall—howling behind his teeth while he came like a fire hose.

"Fluffy-backed tit-babbling booby!" he shouted, dropping to his knees and slipping out of my teeth with a pop. "Now I'm really fucking pissed at you!"

"What?" I cried, brows bouncing up to my hairline. "What are you talking about?"

"Ten years, Sue!" Micah glared fit to send me scurrying out the door. "Ten years you've refused to give me a blowjob because they're *degrading* and *disgusting*, and the whole time, that's what I was missing!

"Was this your plan?" he demanded, making me squeak. "To wait until you fucked up our marriage beyond recognition, so you could whip out your secret weapon and ruin me for the women who come after!"

"What the hell are you talking about?" I snapped. "See? This is why you should only speak with permission!"

"No, this is why I'm going to fuck you so hard, ten years of messing with me will become the best idea you ever had!"

"Wha—" That was all I had a chance to get out before strong, rough, calloused hands flipped me around and put me on my face.

Holding me down, Micah had my cheek on the porcelain and my ass in the air while I was still blinking the running water out of my eyes. A vague thought about condoms entered my mind, and then he was in, sinking so deep inside of me—a low, rumbling purr whispered through my lips, and he didn't give me a chance to breathe it back in.

Pulling out to the tip, Micah slammed back in—nailing that spot with scary precision.

My lower belly contracted in exquisite pain, squirting hot, slick juices from my core that coated his dick—telling him more, more, and more without a word needed from me.

The mouthy asshole set a brutal pace, pounding my hole with the promise of making me regret—or be thankful for—the ten years he went without my blowjobs.

Wouldn't have happened if you didn't go on a date with the wrong twin, asshole! I shouted in my mind, but with my mouth, I cried, "Fuck, yes, Micah! Right there! Harder! Ugh argh!" I screamed, devolving into unintelligible nonsense.

Everywhere he touched sent shockwaves through my body—warming me, chilling me, exciting me, and frightening me all at the same time. Like tumbling out of an airplane with nothing but an oversized nylon bag strapped to my back—every second of being in that steamy bath with him felt dangerous, thrilling, and addictive.

How could I give Micah up? How could I give them all up? This wasn't a failing marriage. It was a new relationship, and it was already off to an excellent start on the sexual compatibility front.

I bucked as he pumped, catching every one of his thrusts in perfect rhythm. My eyes were swimming. My moans gurgled through bathwater. My body was quivering down to the bones. I felt alive for the first time in my life, and never was I more thankful to be than when I walked away from the crash that almost killed me.

After shitting on me for nearly three decades, Hera finally rewarded my struggle with the third star of all of my naughty dreams—Micah Spencer.

He hit that spot and we both exploded, our cries mingling with the foggy air as pleasure and pain ripped through our bodies.

Micah collapsed on top of me, shielding me from the spray, but somehow filling me with more warmth and comfort. Just his skin on mine was enough to—

"Damn, that side piece has been teaching you a thing or three, baby. Are you sure he's not a hooker?"

My foot snapped up, wapping him on the ass. "Are you sure you don't want to look into getting that tongue surgically removed!"

Micah laughed unrepentantly. "I'm very sure about that, but the good news for you is, two orgasms earned you two days of me not bringing up your mister mistress—"

"Doesn't exist!"

"—but..." His grin filled my vision. "How about we go for a third?"

I gaped at him. Micah was still raring to go after blasting off twice? Daniel was always snoring five minutes after the first one, and here this guy was springing off for round three. Just what kind of delicious sex demon was I dealing with here? "That could be..." I roughly cleared my throat, teasing my voice to come back. "I mean... we did have a deal... after all."

His grin softened. Closing the distance, he kissed me. Not rough or punishing, but a slow, sweet kiss that both calmed my racing heart, and sped up my pulse. "Why are you so adorable? When did you get this cute?"

I might've said something, but my mind was squealing too loud to hear the words I needed to say.

Suddenly, Micah flipped me up and plopped me on his lap. Words didn't seem so necessary after all.

Chapter Eleven

"After we finally crawled out of the shower, I tried again to get him to record his consent, but he just kept laughing at me—saying he was starting to dig my new awkward-freak seduction play— And you can stop laughing at me too!"

Courtney howled, not sparing me a second's worth of sympathy.

The two of us were at the park, watching Taylor play with a couple of her friends from school. It was a half day for the kindergarteners, so a few of the parents decided to enjoy lunch at the park with their kids. And the strange, moaning weirdo who couldn't stop complaining about having hot sex with the man of her dreams—according to Courtney.

"Seriously, babe, it's not a big deal." Courtney flittered around the picnic table, setting out her buffet of baked goodies. "It's not like you did it with a married man. That contract breaks when the death does them part."

I groaned, dropping my head in my hands. "Promise me you'll say those exact words at my trial."

She busted up. I was clearly not going to get any sympathy from this source. "Anyway, what about Lily? I know first graders don't have a half day today, but she should be out here with us all the same." She leaned back, breathing in the crisp, autumn air. "She can finally meet Taylor while I ply her with cupcakes and cement my new title of favorite auntie."

"Uhh, first off, that title goes to me," I corrected. "And second, the guys freaked out when I took her out of school with the principal's permission and three heads-ups to all of them. I don't want to deal with the freakout when they find out I pulled her out for no other reason than just to hang out at the park. Alex— No, they *all* think I'm trying to pull something and being nice to Lily is part of the con." I huffed out a breath. "I want them to trust me with her, so I'm not going to push it."

"Okay, okay. I understand." She slid a maple bacon cupcake my way. "I guess that's one of the many good things about solo parenting. I don't have to ask a co-parent's permission for something I want to do with Taylor. I just do it. Whereas you've got three co-parents clocking your every move."

"Yeah," I said softly, "except I'm not a co-parent. I'm not her parent at all. So my moves should be clocked."

She paused her fussing to squeeze my hand. "No, you're not Lily's mother, but what you are is her family. And matter of fact, you're Rhodes's, Micah's, and Alex's family now too—and that word scares you. Family was never something safe for you. Something healthy."

I stiffened, throat tightening.

"And that's where all this fear, guilt, and hesitation is coming from now. You think they're right to protect Lily from you, because someone fucking should've protected you from your family. You can't let yourself accept that you and Micah were both adults who had a good time, because I stupidly said your keeping the truth from them makes you like Sue in their eyes, and the whole planet should've been protected from Sue.

"But you're not your father, you're not your mother, and you're for damn sure not your sister, so ignore what I said before and listen to what I'm saying now." She leaned over the table, taking both of my hands as she whispered, "You've got your family back—a real one. A better one. So don't fall into the trap of thinking they're better off without you, because that's not coming from you.

"It's coming from *them*."

I looked away, eyes stinging. There were downsides to having a best friend who can see right through you. And that was her ability to make you cry at the worst times.

I roughly cleared my throat. "I'm not sure your advice applies to a family that's already breaking up, but thanks for saying it anyway. It was nice to imagine, even for a second, that I'm already where I belong."

"But you are—"

Sue's purse buzzed, giving me an excuse to pull away from Courtney and go digging inside it. *Sue's designer purse. Sue's Chanel dress. That I took from Sue's room after waking up in Sue's bed next to Sue's family. How am I ever supposed to feel like I belong here with this family when her ghost carved her initials into all of them?*

I picked up Sue's phone, dropped it, then fished around until I found the true source of the buzzing. *Satan* flashed on the screen.

"Ugh," I groaned, flinging my head back. "He will not quit! He's calling like five times a day now, and it's bullshit. He doesn't get to play the dutiful, loving boyfriend after torturing and blackmailing me for months."

"Gimme that."

"Wha— Wait! No! What are you—!"

Courtney put her finger to her lips, silencing me better than a shout. She answered the call without so much as a by your leave—leaving me internally screaming for her to hang up. "Hello, who am I speaking to?"

"Who the fuck do you think!" Yes, Dan shouted that so loud, I heard it loud and clear without her putting it on speaker. "I've been calling for almost two weeks, so you better tell me who the fuck you are because I'm reporting you to whichever flea-ridden hick calls himself the sheriff of your town!"

I rubbed my temples, irritation cracking my jaw. I still couldn't believe I ever thought I was in love with this guy.

"I'm sorry you feel that way, sir," Courtney replied, putting on a deep, serious voice for reasons unknown. "Our priority these last couple weeks has been to find, notify, and release Ms. Kim's body to her immediate family, so that she may be given the peaceful goodbye she deserves. I'm sure you understand that we could not release any information to *any* other party before those priorities were taken care of."

Daniel quieted enough that I didn't hear his response.

"You're Ms. Kim's fiancé?" Courtney glanced at me and got bug-eyed shock in return. "Then, I apologize. Her mother did not inform us of a fiancé. And what might your name be?"

"Daniel Mills," she repeated, voice changing. "Would that be the same Daniel Mills found to be the subject of a number of recordings recovered from Ms. Kim's cellphone?" Grinning at me, she shot around the table—sitting down and pressing the phone to my ear so I could hear too.

"—that's not—those recordings aren't what you think," Dan sputtered. "They—"

"Is that so? Because what I believe they are is evidence that Ms. Kim tried multiple times to convey to you that your romantic relationship was over, and to prevent this, you threatened and blackmailed her with the release of her private videos."

"Hold on, I—"

"Mr. Mills, are you aware that soliciting sex under threat or coercion meets the legal standard of rape?"

"Rape?!" he screeched. "What the fuck are you talking about rape!? I didn't rape Sarah! She was my girlfriend!"

"She was not your girlfriend," Courtney said—voice hard. "She made that very clear to you in language I, and a jury, can understand. And that same jury will have serious doubts that you couldn't."

"Jury?! No, wait, stop." The man was hyperventilating into the speakers. "You have this all wrong. Those recordings were just a joke between Sarah and I. A kinky—kink-play—thing!" he burst out. "It wasn't serious, and I *never* forced her."

"Hmm. I'm afraid it's not up to me to decide if you're telling the truth. I'm going to have to refer this case to your local law enforcement authority and let them handle it," she said over his frantic blathering. "Please, confirm your address and the full spelling of your name—"

"No, please, it's not—!"

"And by no means, under any circumstances, are you to delete the sexual video content you're keeping of Ms. Kim. It is now key evidence in a rape investigation and—"

Click.

Daniel hung up.

Courtney beamed at my slack-jawed expression. "Done," she chirped, slapping the phone on my palm. "Not only are you never going to hear from that asshole again, but as we speak, he's deleting all traces that he ever knew you from his phone, his laptop, and his life.

"You are finally free of Daniel Satan Mills."

"Oh... my... gosh," I whispered. "It's you. You're my guardian angel sent from heaven. The whole time, it was you." I cupped her cheeks. "What is your true name, sweet angel?"

Courtney tickled my sides, sending me squealing and squirming away. She hopped up laughing. "Angel sounds right, but I would've done that if I was your guardian demon. That fucker'll be lucky if I don't track him down and throw him off a cliff."

I bit my lip, seriously so happy and relieved I really was going to cry. Courtney was right. This is what I've been missing for so long—

Family.

"Thank you, Court. Just... thank you."

She winked, but then her smile turned down—fading away.

"What's wrong?"

"Huh? Oh, no, it's..." She sighed. "All this talk of evil brutes and the things they do to women just reminded me of the news this morning," Court said. "Do you remember that lady who came to the shop, asking us if we'd seen her missing daughter?"

I nodded.

"Well, tragically, she's not missing anymore. The cops found the body of Tracy Williams on Bonsai Beach this morning," she explained over my gasp. "She was murdered."

"Oh no, that's terrible. That poor woman. Not to mention her mom." I clutched my chest, my heart breaking in two. "Who would do something like this?"

Courtney resumed setting out the food, her lips pressed tight. "I don't know, but if I was a supernatural creature, I'd swoop down on the evil shit-stain that killed some poor, sweet girl from the post office and left her in the sand like driftwood—and I'd split his skull open."

"This is so awful, Court." I glanced behind her to all the kids happily laughing and playing. None of them knew the true ugliness that existed beneath the surface of the world, and gods how I wished they'd never find out. "There must be something we can do for Mrs. Williams. Even if it's just reaching out and letting her know that she's not alone."

"I still have the flyer she gave me with her number on it," she confessed. "I'll call her as soon as we get back home but..." She shook her head. "What can anyone say or do right now that'll make her feel better?"

I didn't give her an answer, because we already knew there was only one.

Sue's phone went off, stealing my attention.

"Hello?"

"Hey, Sue?" Ringing bells and voices stacked on louder voices crowded Micah out. "Hey, can you hear me?"

"Yeah, what's up?"

"It's my pickup day for Lily, but it's looking like I'm going to be late coming back," he said. "This meeting is running long, but I can't lose this potential client. Would you mind picking Lily up from—"

"Yes, I can do it," I blurted. "I'll pick her up and—and actually, I'm going to pull her out a few hours early." I flashed Courtney my resolved face. "We're enjoying a picnic at the park, and I want Lily to join us."

"Yeah, whatever," he breezed, springing a smile to my lips. "Just make sure you're both back at the house by four, and that's four o'clock our time, and not four o'clock Sue-time. Layton's giving Lily these piano lessons for free, so don't jerk him around."

"Why don't we just cancel the piano lessons?" I asked, slipping into the use of *we* quicker than I knew what to do with. "Nari said she'd rather learn the drums."

"—right, yeah. Just a sec— Sue? Sue," he called. If possible, it was getting even louder on his end. It sounded like someone was straight up screaming. "Look, I've got to go, but it's a hard no on switching instruments again. The deal was Lily would stick with the piano for three months, and then if she wasn't into it, she could try another instrument. It hasn't even been three weeks.

"Stop letting her play you, Sue, and *start* knowing what the hell's going on with our kid."

"Yes," I said easily. "That's exactly what I'm going to do."

"All right, I'll see you and that tasty pussy tonight. Keep it sweet, wet, and ready for me."

My face caught fire. "Micah!"

"Buh-bye," he signed off, laughing himself off the phone.

I rolled my eyes even as a giggle escaped my lips. Keep my pussy ready for him? That was something else I was going to do.

***

"Did you have fun today?"

"Yeah!" Lily shrieked, throwing her hands up. "Auntie Courtney is the best, Mommy! She said I get free cupcakes from her shop whenever I want them!"

"Yes, she did say that, and it's the best news you've gotten all day because you're a sugar fiend!"

"No!"

"It's true," I carried on. We turned down the final street leading to home. "You're the sugar bandit! The sugar swindler! The sugar master. The Sugar Claus," I belted. "You better be nice, not naughty, or the Sugar Claus is coming for your cookies! And those elves better watch out too."

"Ahhh!" Lily squealed, laughing so hard she tipped over in her booster seat. "Mommy, you're silly!"

"No, you're the silly one."

"No, you're the silly one!"

This kicked off a repetitive, but hilarious, back-and-forth that had both our sides in stitches. I only stopped when we rumbled through the gates and I saw Mr. Layton standing on the front steps, waving at us.

A glance at the clock told me it was fifteen minutes before four, so we weren't late. "Even so, we've got to put our sillies away now, Lily," I told her. "Your teacher is being very nice and giving you free lessons on his own time, so we've got to be serious."

"Aww, okay." She sat up, a pout stealing away her smile. "But can we be silly after?"

I reached back and tickled her, teasing out another squealing giggle. "We can absolutely be silly after. Tell you what, when you're done with your lesson, we can have a spa afternoon with nail polish, face masks, and big, fluffy robes."

"Okay!"

I stopped the car, then twisted around in my seat to unbuckle her.

"I like you. You're much better than my old mommy."

My grin vanished like a dewdrop in the desert. "Wha—"

Lily wiggled free and shot out of the car. "Hi, Mr. C! Mommy took me to the park!"

"Lily, wait!" I yanked and struggled with the seat belt, fighting to get out. *She couldn't have said— No, she said it! She said old mommy, but that couldn't be what she meant. I have to—*

"—talk to you." I tumbled out of the car. "Lily, come back, please. I—"

The front door flew open.

Lily waved hello to Alex on her way inside. Mr. Layton followed, with me just as quick on her heels.

A hand flew out and smacked the doorjamb, blocking my path. "You took Lily out of school early." It wasn't a question.

"I did after running it by Micah." I rocked from foot to foot—eager to get past. "Courtney and a bunch of the moms were having a picnic in the park with their kids, so I—"

"Couldn't let them go without giving them a chance to invest in a new and exciting SueNation investment opportunity," he finished. Alex had an odd smirk on his lips that was really creeping me out. "Can't blame ya."

I bristled. "It wasn't like that. The only thing we invested in were a couple of new breakouts and several new pounds from a whole tray of maple bacon cupcakes. I'm not running some con with Lily as the closer," I said. "If you must know, I'm done with SueNation for good. I've even got some job interviews lined up, so as long as one of them pans out, I'll be able to work from home and bring in some income while still being here for Lily and Omma."

The smirk vanished. "You...? You, Soo Min Kim, have job interviews lined up? Real ones?"

"Yes, real ones," I returned hotly. "I was banging my head against the wall trying to think of something I could do from home without drawing a lot of lawsuits-and-bird-poop hate, when the answer hit me over the head.

"Captioning."

Alex stared at me. "Caption... ing."

"Exactly." Excitement bled into my voice. "K-Pop and Korean dramas are getting more and more popular every day, and what do all of these production and music companies need? People fluent in English, Spanish, French, and so on to caption their videos. Seriously, I don't know why I didn't think of this before. Everything I read online says I can bring in an extra fifteen hundred dollars a month."

"And you'd really work for that little?" His brows crumpled. "You spend two thousand a month just on makeup."

"Not anymore. It's time we both start tightening up around here—be a better example for Lily." I pointed. "Starting with rehiring the groundspeople, housekeepers, gardeners, and cooks. I am very much done with the haunted house vibe. Time for the manor to be a home for *living* people again."

Amusement etched into the lines of his face, flicking my eyes to the early morning stubble still lingering on his jaw. Only Alex could make bike shorts, rumpled sweatshirts, and jaw scruff sexy. "I agree, but the last time I brought it up, you said you weren't going to waste any more money on this overgrown outhouse, because you were just going to throw all of us out, sell it, and buy yourself a chateau in France with your new lover."

I cocked a brow. "Alexander Montgomery, we've been married for seven years. When are you going to learn to ignore the stupid shit that comes out of my mouth?" I asked, startling a laugh out of him. "You want to know why this place is an outhouse? You're looking at her."

He doubled over—cracking up and clearly surprised to be doing so. "That was a good one," Alex wheezed, straightening up. "But self-deprecating humor doesn't make up for lying straight to my face. You see?" His laugh lines melted away. "I knew this new nice-Sue routine was all bullshit."

"What? Lying? When did I lie?"

Alex's eyes narrowed to slits. "Two fucking days ago, I told you we don't allow Lily to have playdates with people we don't *all* know. Not after that whackjob invited Lily to his daughter's birthday party, and then tried to grab and drag her into the bathroom while everyone else was distracted by the cake."

"Whackjob?" My eyes bugged. "I had no idea—"

"What the fuck are you talking about?" he exploded, blowing my eyes wide. "You were the one distracted in a corner, messing around on your phone when Lily's screams brought everyone else running! But no, that wasn't you," he mocked, putting on a voice. "It was her other mother who failed to keep an eye on her then. Just like it was her other mother that stood in that kitchen and promised she'd respect my boundaries with Lily, and then turned around and did whatever the fuck she wanted anyway."

I quieted, shrinking lower and lower in Sue's gold-lace wedges.

"Not only did you take her out to a picnic with some *best friend* who you've never mentioned or spoken of in ten years, but you pulled her out of school to do it. It's like I asked you not to do the most irresponsible thing ever, and you went and said, *now I'm going to do it even harder.*"

"Alex, please," I whispered. "I didn't see it that way. I didn't mean to—"

"You'll never change." The words pierced my heart. "No matter how much I want to believe it. No matter how many times I convince myself to give you another chance. It's always going to be nothing but lies to my face, deception behind my back, and fake tears and amnesia when you're caught. I'm done, Sue." Turning around, Alex walked away. "I'm just done."

I stood there for a beat, then I cleared my throat, picked up my feet, and walked past the receiving room and the strangled piano chords floating out of it.

I made it all the way to the bathroom door before I started crying.

***

Clang! Clung! Clang!

Emerging from the bathroom, I made my way to the receiving room and stuck my head through the doorjamb.

Alex sat in the armchair beside the window, tapping away on his laptop while Lily banged away on the ancient piano that was here when Omma and Appa bought the place.

"That's very good, Lily, now let's try to do one smooth movement. A, C, F-sharp. A, C, F-sharp."

Lily played the correct notes, but there was nothing smooth about it. The girl was, in a word, terrible.

No wonder she wants to switch to the drums. At least it's fun banging on those. Banging on piano keys just makes your ears bleed.

I chuckled at the joke and three heads snapped around. Alex's glare sent me shooting back with a mumbled apology on my lips.

Courtney said I needed to stop tiptoeing around and accept that this was my family, and I belonged here. But the look in Alex's eyes whenever they landed on me screamed unwanted intruder so loud, I wanted to scurry back to Willingsworth and hide.

The front door swung open.

"—get the invite?"

"Got all five of them," Rhodes replied, pushing in and holding the door open for Micah. "They keep saying it's just a mixer for promising business students to meet and connect with the top alumni, but we both know all the dean wants is to tap us for a check."

"No question." Micah shrugged off his coat and hung it on the rack. "But still, a weekend in the city on Columbia's dime doesn't sound so bad. We'll bring the Lilybug and make a whole thing of it."

Rhodes hummed, nodding. "She would love that." He noticed me by the door and gave me a real, stomach-fluttering smile. "Evening, Sue. Everything okay?"

"E-everything's fine," I croaked. *Hera, help me, will the day ever come that I stop getting tongue-tied around Rhodes Newbury?* "I was just about to make Lily's pre-dinner snack. Interested?"

"Might be." Micah came over and smooched me right on the lips, staining my cheeks red. "What's on the menu?"

"I found a healthy nacho recipe online. Lots of whole grains and veggies to make up for stuffing her full of cake and cookies at lunch."

Micah laughed. "Cake and cookies for lunch? I respect how hard you're trying to win the favorite-parent award, but I'm always going to be number one."

Rhodes snorted, shrugging off his own coat and tossing it in the direction of the rack. "If I've told you once, I've told you a hundred times, Spencer, you've got to stop dreaming when you're awake." He brushed past us. "I'll help you make her snack. Just tell me what to chop."

"I—"

"No nachos for me, but I will have some of that beer you snuck in the fridge," Micah tossed over his shoulder—following behind Rhodes.

"Uh…" I blinked after him, rooted to the spot. After getting my ass chewed off by Alex, I wasn't sure what to make of Rhodes's and Micah's pleasantness. I'd never been in a relationship with more than one guy at a time, so I had no idea what the play was when one of them was pissed at you? Was I supposed to act like nothing was wrong with Rhodes and Micah, and just ignore Alex's elephant-sized resentment in the room? Or did I have to fix things with Alex before playing happy families with Rhodes and Micah?

It took me so long to decide, I was still standing outside the door when Alex and Lily came out.

"Did you like my song, Daddy?"

"I loved your song." Alex's smile lit up his whole face as easily as it stole my breath. "You're getting very good, baby girl. Soon, I'm going to have to clear two shelves for all of your piano trophies."

Giggling, she clapped—jumping up and down to her father's sweet, but blatant lies.

"Go upstairs and take your bath," Alex continued. "When you're done, Daddy will bring your snack into the living room, then you can have one hour of screen time." That smile vanished when he flicked to me. "Mr. Layton is being very nice by not having you do the assignments you missed today, so you don't have homework."

"Yay!" Lily took off running.

"No running on the stairs," Alex and I both blurted at the same time.

His glare intensified. "I'm sure you want to get back to your job hunt, Sue. Don't let us keep you."

"Oh, actually, I was just about to make Lily's snack—"

"No need." He blew past me. "I've got it."

"Alex!"

He left without a glance back.

Is this how it's going to be with him? Every day spent shouting at his retreating back?

"Excuse me? Mrs. Kim?" Mr. Layton filled my vision. "Do you have a moment?"

I dragged my attention off Alex and focused on him. "Yes?"

"It occurred to me that it's rather silly for you and your husbands to have to go all the way to Lantana Day, pick up Lily, and drive behind me to your house, when I'm going to the same place anyway."

My brows crumpled. "What? What are you talking about?"

"I'm saying," he replied with a laugh. "I can drive Lily home from school on the days we have piano lessons." Layton held up a pen and piece of paper. "All the administration office needs is for you to sign this permission and liability form."

And why should I spend every day apologizing and chasing after Alex? He wants to talk about safety when he's the psycho jerk who locked me outside with a bear? A fucking bear!

"Huh? What?" I was barely listening. "Oh, no, that's okay. We don't mind driving Lily home. Besides, if we stopped, all the married moms will lose their chance to ogle my husbands in the pickup line."

"Are you sure? Because I don't mind—"

I'll admit, it wasn't right for me to tell him one thing, and then turn around and do something else, but I am not Sue. My apologies aren't for show, so I'll say sorry for what I did, and he can damn well do the same in return.

"Let me get your coat." I snatched his coat up and tossed open the door, running through everything *I* was going to shout in *Alex's* face. "Thanks for coming by. We'll see you next week."

"But I—"

I closed the door on his sentence, then marched through the drafty, dusty halls into the kitchen.

Alex's, Micah's, and Rhodes's shadows moved across the hardwood, signaling me to start my rant.

"Al—!"

"Was that a kiss hello I saw?" Rhodes asked.

"Yep. Sue and I came up with a little side truce of our own, and now we're fucking again."

I tripped on air. Scream trapped in my throat, I pitched sideways and barely caught the handrail before my clumsy feet dumped me hard on the back stairs.

"What side truce?"

"Orgasms for good behavior. I got her to cum three times last night," he said over my dropping jaw. "So that's three days I'm matching her fake-nice act with one of my own. An act I won't break even if she does."

Rhodes's voice was dry. "I see what she gets out of that, but not what you do?"

"Hey, we both know she's got an ulterior motive for this happy-family scam she's pushing on us."

It's not a scam!

"But if I'm going to play along, I want something for my trouble. And that something is pussy."

Rhodes chuckled. "Wasn't it two weeks ago you were saying you'd fuck a deflated blow-up doll from the dumpster before you fucked Sue again?"

"Might've said something like that." Drawers banged open and shut. "But, I don't know, something's different. Guess it's all part of the scam, but she's being all sweet and innocent and doofy, and it's just working for me."

No one had ever blushed harder than I was in that moment.

"You should've seen her bouncing around the kitchen with her tits out and vomit on her pants."

"Well, that explains it," Rhodes deadpanned. "Bouncing tits and vomit was the soundtrack to your college years. Of course you can't resist."

"Now you're getting it." Micah had no shame. "Plus, she's picked up a shit-ton in the last seven months. No more lying there like a tranquilized mattress. She was bucking on my cock like a bronco rider. And—"

My voice came roaring back up my throat. "Micah!"

I burst into the kitchen and charged Micah.

Putting down his beer, he caught me, spun me around, and settled me blinking and dizzy against his chest. Rhodes went back to checking out the pantry, and Alex returned to cutting apple slices, like nothing even happened.

"Anyway, like I was saying, Sue's sucking dick now," Micah dropped like he was talking about the weather. "You've got to get on these blowjobs, boys. Last night, she did this thing with her tongue that about killed and sent me to heaven."

I choked—embarrassment welling up in my body, exploding, and opening the hole beneath my feet that I was desperate to fall into, but Micah had too tight a hold on me.

"All right, sure," Rhodes said. "I haven't had a blowjob in seven years, so I'm down."

"D-down?" I eeked out.

He shrugged. "Yeah, why not. One day for one orgasm. I can handle that." Rhodes emerged from the pantry with pasta, garlic, pine nuts, and a jar of sun-dried tomatoes all tucked under his arms. "Tonight good?"

What. Is. Happening?

"Nah. I'm booked in for tonight," Micah replied, dropping a kiss on my temple.

"Tomorrow night, then," Rhodes confirmed. "Alex, you getting down on this?"

"Nah, I'm good." Alex didn't even look up from his apples.

"Cool. Then, you and me, Sue?" he probed, meeting my eyes. "Tomorrow night, yeah?"

My jaw worked for a full ten seconds. "Y-yes."

"Sweet." Rhodes bent, opened the island cabinets, then stood up holding a pot and strainer. "You made dinner the other night—and set us up with all these ingredients—so I'll make dinner tonight. Sun-dried tomato pasta good with everyone?"

"Sure."

"Fine," Alex agreed. "But I promised Lily an hour of screen time, so let's do dinner at six."

"Good with me," Rhodes said. "That gives me an hour and a half to learn how to make sun-dried tomato pasta."

The guys cracked up, leaving me alone in my complete state of befuddlement.

Was this how it worked when married to three men? They talked about sharing your pussy over garlic and apple slices, and then ribbed and joked around in the next breath like it was all no big deal?

I guess if I'm doing this, then I'm really doing this. I've got to get used to these new sexual dynam—

"Wait, who were you calling doofy!"

"Don't worry, it's a compliment. It's so exhausting being with someone who has to be perfect all the time. Seven years, and that doofy seduction dance was the first time you've ever really made me laugh." Micah's phone went off. He scooted out from behind me, picking up the phone as he winked and said, "Even with vomit on your pants, you had never been hotter."

If I thought I was speechless before, it was nothing compared to the silence that just struck me dumb.

"Where's Lily?" I heard Rhodes ask.

"Taking a bath," said Alex.

"I'll go check on her. Make sure she's not playing swamp monster again."

By the time I caught my breath, and my mortification, I realized Alex and I were alone—and there was something I needed to say to him.

"Alex?" I closed the distance, not stopping until the island stopped me. "Can you put the knife down? There's something I need to say to you."

"There's nothing you have to say that I need to hear."

"Wrong, bitch!"

Alex almost cut his finger off. "Excuse me?" he blared, knife shooting away. "What did you just—"

"You heard me!" I rounded the island—coming at him so fast he backed up into the fridge. "I'm getting real fucking sick of your attitude, Montgomery. I messed up, I know that. It wasn't right for me to say one thing, and then do another. But co-parenting is hard for every parent—even the ones who get along.

"If you don't want me to do something with Nari, you need to talk to me and explain why. Don't just bark orders at me, and then treat me like a monster for using my own judgment instead of blindly following yours." The words shot from my mouth one after the other—pelting Alexander from all sides.

Even more wonderful than that... I was actually making sense.

"I completely understand your caution with Nari after she was grabbed by that piece of shit, but you need to hear me when I say that I love that kid," I shouted at him. Yes, shouted. I was on a roll and couldn't seem to slow down or lower my voice. "I love her, and I would never willingly or knowingly put her in danger.

"Courtney *is* my best friend. I trust her with my life and I trust her with Lily, but if you don't, why don't you stop being an ass for two seconds and just *meet her*! Get to know her and Taylor, and give Lily a chance to make a friend who isn't her teacher!"

"Sue—"

"And another fucking thing," I screeched, slapping the fridge door just to the right of his wide eyes. "How flip flipping fucking dare you lock me outside with a bear! A bear, Alex! What kind of vindictive psychopath does something like that, and then turns around and acts like I'm the dangerous one!" I shoved my face in his, swallowing his eyes in my narrowed ones. "If you ever do anything like that to me again, you're going to wish that car crash finished me off, because I'll never stop coming for you, bitch!"

A growl ripped from his throat. "What? Is that supposed to scare me? Is that supposed to be a threat?" He knocked his forehead against mine, shoving me back with his head alone. "I already fucking wish that car crash finished you off!"

"No, you wish you weren't a lonely, pathetic, unemployed bitch baby with a shriveled-up, unsucked dick!"

"No more than you wish you weren't a shit-peddling failure that the internet chewed up and spat out! I'm lonely and pathetic? Ha!" he barked, making me jump. "You're the one with no friends, no job, no husbands, and no life! The only one who can stand you is our kid, and even that biological imperative is wearing off fast! Not even your own mother wants you around!" Spittle showered my face. "Lord fucking knows why you're hanging around until she croaks, because if my mother told me I was a worthless leech and her worst mistake that many times in a five-minute conversation, the only thing I'd be sticking around to do is piss on her grave!"

"Make sure you pull down your pants and squat for that piss, bitch boy, otherwise that little guy will never reach!"

His face turned a dangerous puce. "You're so fucking—! Argggggh!!!"

I blew back, then returned his bellow with my own. "Ahhhhh!"

Footsteps thundered down the stairs. Micah and Rhodes burst into the kitchen.

"What the fuck?!"

"What's going on!"

"I'm done with him!" "I'm done with her!" we shouted at the same time.

"Can you be done with each other a little fucking quieter!" Rhodes blared. "Lily can hear you!"

That silenced me better than anything else could.

Alex and I flung away from each other, glaring at opposite corners of the kitchen.

"Look, guys." Resignation laced Micah's voice. "If you can't get along for Lily's sake, then—"

Sue's phone went off, cutting off whatever Micah was going to say. I answered it rather than listen to another word about that asshole.

"Hello?"

"Good evening," a light, cheery voice replied. "Am I speaking to Mrs. Kim?"

"Yes. Who is this?"

"This is Christie Baudelaire, owner of Baudelaire Blasts and Celebrations." I never understood calling a voice chirpy until I heard hers. "I'm calling to confirm our nine o'clock on Sunday morning?"

"Nine o'clock?" I repeated, my galloping heart still pounding on a heady cocktail of rage and adrenaline. "I'm sorry, what is this in reference to?"

She giggled. "Your wedding anniversary party, of course. In two weeks," she added when I didn't say anything. "I am very excited, Mrs. Kim, as I'm sure you are. No expense has been spared—just as you requested. I've flown in five crates of Conti Grand Cru wine. The linens are hand-spun silk. The aerialists arrive next week, and your dress— Ah!" she screamed. "Your dress! Mrs. Kim, it is a work of art.

"Now, as you know, I need to get my crew into your lovely house with not a minute's delay. They need to begin setting up the ballroom, double-checking the integrity of the beams, and of course, your final fitting!" She squealed again, clearly crushing on this dress hard. "So, can we confirm for—"

"No," I sliced in. "There's not going to be a party. This marriage ain't anything worth celebrating. Cancel it. Cancel it all."

"But— But, Mrs. Kim," she cried. "I beg of you to reconsider. The invitations have gone out and several outstanding bills are still to be paid. Not to mention the refundable deposits you won't get back, on top of the last-minute cancellation fee. If you cancel now, you'll have spent over sixteen million with nothing to show for—"

"Sixteen million who now?!" I shrieked. "Tell me that's won. Please, tell me that's sixteen million won and not dollars!"

"Um, Mrs. Kim... I don't understand—"

The phone disappeared from my grip.

"Hello?" Alex said. "Hello, Christie, it's me, Mr. Montgomery. Yes... No, ma'am, we're not canceling." He laughed a light, buoyant laugh that didn't match the glower directed at me. "My wife was just kidding, you know she has a dark sense of humor.

"We absolutely want to celebrate seven wonderful and loving years together," he said, his eyes pinning me to the spot. "We wouldn't cancel this party for the world."

Christie's relief poured out of the speakers.

"Sunday at nine o'clock," he confirmed. "Actually, come at eight if you want. *We* will be here."

Click.

Ending the call, Alex took my hand and placed the cell on my shaking palm.

I looked from it, to Alex, to a silent Micah and Rhodes. "I... I don't get it. You just got done telling me how much you hate me," I said to Alex, "and how much you two are only interested in me for my blowjobs," I threw at Rhodes and Micah. "So why would you want to throw a lavish and obscenely expensive party to celebrate a marriage that's dead?"

Alex looked in my eyes, and smirked. "Dead? It's not dead yet, baby."

"Hell no," Micah breezed. "The old girl's still got some kick in her."

"That's right," Rhodes threw in, sharing a grin with his fellow brother-husbands that stood my neck hairs on end. "Can't tap out before they call T.O.D. That would be wrong."

"But when it is dead," Alex whispered, his smile widening as he turned away. "That'll really be something to celebrate. I promise you, my dear wife, that's going to be the party you care about."

My lips parted—I thought to ask what they meant, but they were gone before I found the words.

Chapter Twelve

"Please, no, I don't want to go to sleep! The clown will come!" Tears and snot soaked my face. "He hurts me! Make him stop, please!"

"No!" I bolted upright, kicking and flailing in the tangled sheets.

Morning light streamed through the curtain, casting a single glowing beam across my pale, shaking hands. My stomach gurgled and heaved, threatening to bring up my half-eaten dinner of minestrone.

Tipping over, I scrambled for my phone. "It's okay, you're okay," I rasped into the mic. "The clown was real. What happened to you—what he did to you—was real. But what's also real is that he's gone. The clown can't hurt you anymore.

"You're safe."

I repeated that over and over again until my heart stopped racing, and then I played back the recording for even longer. Only when I trusted my stomach to hold on to its bile, and my legs to hold me up, did I slowly untangle from the sheets and trudge into the closet.

I emerged a bit later in my running clothes. Glancing at the clock, it flashed just past seven in the morning. That gave me two hours to run, shower, and be back downstairs to meet with our party planner, Christie.

My teeth gritted. I wanted no part of that meeting, that sham of a party, or that strange, unsettling grin the guys gave each other when they spoke about it, but I didn't see what choice I had but to attend. Mrs. Prado was officially starting her second first day of work at ten o'clock, and I had to be there to run her through our and Lily's new routines. Not to mention she had a stack of employment profiles she needed my final approval on before hiring. As much as I wanted to hide from the strange and sudden thickening of the atmosphere in the manor, Lily had been living in a busted-up haunted house on a steady diet of takeout for long enough.

Either way, I was going to be in and out of every room in the manor that day, explaining to Mrs. Prado what we needed, so that would make hiding from Christie and Alex impossible.

I headed out of the east wing to the west, making for the back door. Rhodes looked up from the same spot I found him in the first time—sitting on the patio bench lacing up his sneakers.

"Sue—"

I took off running without a warm-up or backward glance. It was my turn to leave him there with his mouth hanging open.

"Wait, Sue!"

Rapid footfalls chased after me, so I picked up the pace—tearing through the trees and running off the path. I knew these woods. I didn't need a manmade path to tell me where to go.

"Whoa, where are you going—? Sue, will you wait a minute, please?" Fingers grasped at my sleeve. "I don't understand what happened! Things were good for three days, and then all of a sudden you're giving us the silent treatment," he huffed. "We were supposed to have sex the other night, and you just blew me off."

I skidded to a halt. Whipping around, I gaped at him. "*That* is what you're mad about? That you didn't get your dick sucked? Are you for real right now, Rhodes!"

He stared at me. "I mean... I'm not mad, but it seems like you are. I just kinda want an explanation for why you're sleeping with Micah, but not with me."

My jaw dropped lower, deepening his confusion.

"What?"

"You have to be kidding," I hissed. "You're chasing after me, demanding an explanation *from me*, after you three acted like the creepiest freak triplets that ever walked out of a horror movie!"

"What the hell are you talking about?"

"What was all of that with the anniversary party?" I cried, hands waving about. "Why is it so important to you three that we have this eye-wateringly expensive bash when all of you want to be rid of me, and none of you believe I want to start over and give our relationship a real chance—?" I clamped down hard on my tongue, shock rocking me to my core.

What did I just say?

"What did you just say?" Rhodes echoed. Confusion battled with the surprise on his face, and both were winning. "You want to stay together? Since when?"

"I— I— I— That's not the point," I snapped. "The point is that you, Micah, and Alex *don't* want to stay with me, so why are we spending sixteen million dollars celebrating a seven-year failure? Huh? Huh!" I cried, getting in his face. "You know, I heard you three in the hall that night. Saying that my truce is just an act, but you have no choice but to go along with it until the anniversary party, because after that, you'll finally be rid of me."

"Ooh," he drew out, understanding dawning. "You heard that and you thought—" Breaking off, he snickered.

"Hey! Don't laugh at me!"

"I— I can't help it," he replied, cracking up. "You have it so cutely and adorably wrong. Sue..." He grasped my shoulders, gently rubbing them with a shockingly tender touch. "We were talking about you, and how hard it is to trust this new persona of yours, but we *were not* talking about you when the topic of the party came up."

"You... weren't?"

"No," he pressed, laughing. "Why would we be planning and plotting to get rid of you? You already offered to leave amicably with only a fraction of the money you'd be owed in the divorce. The other guys don't have to worry about that last bit, but I'm the one who's legally married to you. You could have—and still could—completely cleaned me out. I, of all of us, am very happy about this truce and your willingness to agree to a peaceful separation. Trust me when I say I have no interest in provoking you into changing your mind."

I stared at him—his words slowly penetrating my brain... and staining my cheeks. "Oh."

"Yeah." He smirked, flicking my nose. "Oh."

I ducked my head, looking anywhere but at him. "But if you weren't talking about me, who were you talking about?"

"The truth?" Sighing, his hands fell from my shoulders. "It's been a rough... decade. After GloryBoi, everyone kept after us about our next big thing. We were geniuses. Wunderkinds! The college boys who became billionaires at twenty couldn't possibly be one-hit wonders." He fell back, leaning against a vibrant red maple. "What a joke."

"What happened?" I asked, voice soft.

He scoffed under his breath. "I guess we never did tell you the full story." He flicked up, his obsidian eyes piercing. "I guess you never asked."

"I'm asking now."

Rhodes nodded, his gaze trailing up and getting lost in the leaves. He didn't speak for so long, I turned to go.

"We weren't geniuses." Rhodes's voice stopped me in my tracks. "I wasn't a genius. I was just the son of a gambling addict whose mother handed him over to his grandmother. She let Nana raise me because anything was better than being woken up in the night from the shouting and banging of the bookie's goons chasing down my father for what he owes. Anything was better than having to hide my birthday and Christmas money, because they'd end up on a poker table faster than I could cry, 'Daddy, give it back.'"

"Oh, Rhodes..." I laid my hand over his, my heart breaking like it could hear that little boy's cries. "I'm so sorry."

"It's fine," he ground out. "I don't have anything to complain about. I told you, my mother got me out of that environment. Because of her, I grew up in a safe and stable home with grandparents who loved me, and a mother who spent time with me every day. But for most children of addicts, it's a very different story, and a different outcome." He folded his arms, breaking free of my touch. "And that's what I told Micah and Alex that day in our dorm.

"For other addictions, they're not easier battles, but at least there are more tools to fight. There are people and programs that want to help you fight. But when it comes to gambling addiction? This country just feeds on it. It preys on gambling addicts," he said. "Did you know in Vegas, you're allowed to smoke in the casinos? Everywhere else it's banned because—fucking hello, smoking kills—but it's not banned in Vegas because they don't want you to leave the tables for any reason. Not even to go outside and smoke."

I rocked back. "Wow. I never thought of it like that but, yeah, that makes a grim amount of sense."

"It is grim. It's dark as fuck, Sue. From Vegas to Atlantic City to game night with the boys to the millions of poker and betting apps on our phones, why wouldn't it be hard for a gambling addict to say no, when society makes it so easy for them to place just one more bet."

"Rhodes, I understand what you're saying, and I agree with you, but if you've always felt that way, why did you sign on to GloryBoi? Why make your own betting app?"

He tossed his head, groaning. "It's going to sound so stupid now, but I was going off all those new theories of harm reduction. You know what that is?"

I nodded. "It's like with drug addiction. They say if they're going to use anyway, then we as a society have a duty to make sure they have access to clean needles, safe injection sites, and medical staff present to stop an overdose. If we can't stop the harm, at least we can reduce it."

Rhodes nodded along with every word. "And that's where my mind went. My parents were from wealthy families, and there were still months we didn't eat or couldn't pay the rent because Dad pissed away everything in our bank account on a sure hand," he said. "That night, drunk on beers, I got to blathering about how that wouldn't have happened if my dad could've placed those bets without losing any money. All the high without the cost."

Understanding knocked me over the head. "And so you came up with GloryBoi," I cried. "An app that lets people place bets, make real money, but only lose seven dollars a month."

"Exactly. That was by design, Sue," he said. "Seven dollars, and seven dollars only. That was the most a sub could ever spend in a month. We didn't allow early re-subs to get more credits, and we banned subscribers from signing up through multiple accounts. A safe gambling site. The first safe gambling site." His eyes grew unfocused, gazing at the brilliant cardinal leaves. "Because if you can get your fix for only seven dollars, then you can afford to get your son that Transformer you've been promising him for two birthdays in a row."

History tumbled through my mind. "But it went wrong," I whispered. "You were bought out, and GloryBoi is nothing like that now. I know for a fact they allow early re-subs and multiple accounts. Plus, before you could get almost three hundred credits for a dollar. Now it's a dollar for one measly credit."

"Yep," he clipped, expression hardening. "Those shithead, corporate bastards completely gutted our app—ruining everything we tried to do. Turning it into all that I fucking hate!"

His anger didn't scare me. The opposite. It drew me closer to him. "But, then why?" Gently, I cupped his cheek. "Why did you sell?"

His jaw tensed against my touch. "Sue, believe me, you've never met a more dangerous enemy than a bunch of rich, soulless shitbags fighting to protect their money. GloryBoi was popular. Ten thousand times more popular than we were expecting, and it was costing all those app owners and casinos big," he said. "Turns out, it's not just the sons of gambling addicts that like the idea of betting big and winning big without losing their rent money. Pretty much everyone wants that.

"When the conglomerate first came at us with a buyout offer, we said no." His eyes darkened. "And that was a mistake."

"They came after you." It wasn't a question.

"They went after *everyone*. My mom, my dad, my grandparents, and my family," he said, widening my eyes. "They went after Micah's and Alex's families. They went after our friends and girlfriends at the time. They sicced private investigators on us, digging up every dirty secret in our closets. And that was the stuff that was true.

"We also came under attack from a deluge of internet trolls and bots spreading nasty, sick stuff about us, and lies about the app. It was relentless," he said. "Our girlfriends dumped us. Our parents begged us to just sell and make it stop. And then, it got even worse."

"It got worse?" I blurted. "How could it have gotten worse?"

"Neither Micah, me, nor Alex are coders," he said. "Creating GloryBoi itself was way beyond our capabilities, so we hired some kid from the computer engineering college. We gave him a flat fee of a quarter of a million dollars and a contract we printed off the internet, and he gave us everything we asked for."

"The cuntglomerate targeted him next, didn't they."

Rhodes cracked the slightest grin. "Cuntglomerate? I like that. I've called them lots of choice shit over the years, and never came up with that gem. Nice." His smile faded fast. "But to answer your question, yes. They pounced on Dereon fast. They claimed the contract he signed was nothing—worthless. Their lawyers would shred it in court, then Dereon would be named the true owner and creator of GloryBoi. And so, we had a choice. We either sold to them right there and took their *generous* offer of twenty billion, or we watched them steal our app and leave us with nothing."

I hissed, lips peeling back from my teeth. A few choice phrases for those greedy corporate bastards were going through my head right then.

"We sold."

My eyes fluttered closed—my lids as heavy as my heart. I could picture the three of them then. Only twenty years old, and terrified. Pressure bearing down on them from all sides. Threats coming at them from everywhere. When all they wanted to do was make the world a fairer place.

"I'm so sorry."

"You don't have to be sorry, baby." Warm fingers brushed my lips, popping my eyes open. "Not about this. This one was all me," he said softly. "I was the chickenshit bitch boy that let a few cunts in suits scare me into selling out. I was the one who had a billion people counting on me to provide a safe place to gamble... and I just gave it away."

"Don't say that," I cried, eyes welling. "You weren't any of those things, Rhodes. You were only twenty years old. Barely an adult. You weren't even old enough to gamble on your own app!" That got a wry chuckle out of him. "You were put in a terrible position of having to choose between protecting your family and friends... and protecting your father."

He swallowed hard, turning away, but somehow leaning firmer into my touch.

"Those shitheads never should've put you in that position, but they did, and you made the best choice you could. You have to know that."

"What I know is I was the one who called up my dad, telling him to join GloryBoi. I told him that if he gambled on the app, and only the app, it could be his version of harm reduction, and eventually, when he saw that he could control his addiction, he'd see that he could beat it too." His expression was blank—dead. "And I also know the name of the divorce attorney I drove my mother to meet after the cuntglomerate changed my app, and

Dad gambled away all the money Mom had saved to throw Nana's seventieth birthday party.

"All of that money," he rasped. "He stole from her and spent it all… on GloryBoi."

"That's not—"

"Don't say it's not my fault," he sliced off. "Please."

I fell quiet.

We both did. For a long time.

"Anyway," he breathed, shaking himself. "You asked why all of this means we have to throw an eye-wateringly expensive celebration for our failed marriage. Well, after we were bought out and I had to watch them destroy GloryBoi, their money felt dirty to me. I didn't want to spend a cent of it, so I gave it away."

I blinked. "I beg your pardon? Did you just say you *gave away* almost seven billion dollars?"

"That's right."

"I see," I repeated, tone calm. "And have you always been stupid?"

Rhodes started, body jerking as a surprise laugh ripped from his lips, and then kept coming. He howled, eyes watering and head falling on my shoulder. "Ouch, baby. No sugarcoating or nothing. Would it help if I told you I spread the money out among various addiction support groups, rehabs, and charities?"

"That just pisses me off more," I snapped. "Because now all I'm thinking is how sweet and generous you are when I'm trying to be pissed."

A lopsided grin teased the dimple from his left cheek. Eyes shining with mirth, I heated up to be on the receiving end of it.

Gods, Rhodes is sinfully gorgeous when he smiles.

"It was the right thing to do," he affirmed, taking my hands in his. "But then, I ended up being another business graduate with no app, no money, and no one who wanted anything from me other than my next billion-dollar idea.

"And, I mean, the three of us did try," he said, expelling a deep sigh. "We tried for years to come up with something in the same spirit of helping people, but part of the terms of the buyout was that we couldn't launch another competing gambling, games, or sport-related app or business so…"

"And so, there wasn't anything else you were passionate about," I finished. "Not in the way that you were passionate about helping people like your dad."

He just nodded. "Starting the investment firm was a last-ditch effort to do something worthwhile with my life while still making enough to support my new wife and the baby we had on the way. I refused to let Micah or Alex invest their buyout money into the business, and my grandparents were done investing in me after my last idea outed that Grandpa had a whole second family he was hiding in Long Island—"

"What?!"

"Oh yeah," he drew out. "Apparently, he'd been with this woman as long as he's been with Grandma. We're talking two other adult children and six other grandchildren out in the burbs that no one in the family knew about." He whistled. "You ever seen a sixty-nine-year-old woman beat a seventy-one-year-old man half to death? It's not pretty. Funny," Rhodes admitted. "But not pretty."

"Wow. And I thought my family drama was explosive."

He snorted. "Yep. But like I said, no money was coming from that source, so I had to shop around for investors, and that's how I ended up in business with the *her* you heard us speaking about last night."

"What's wrong with her?" I asked. "Why do you need to get rid of your investor?"

"You always want to be the one in the strong position when you're negotiating, and unfortunately, I wasn't. I had to give her controlling interest and a say in every business decision—no matter how small. For the first few years, I held free financial literacy classes online and in-person all over New York. I even managed investment accounts free of charge for clients who made less than one hundred thousand dollars a year. It wasn't much," he said, "but it felt good to help people and families in some small way.

"But when the firm hit a pandemic-sized speed bump, she shut down the classes and kicked out every free client who didn't agree to pay a minimum of five hundred a month to stay on."

"Well, she sounds fucking awful."

"She's ruthless," he gritted. "If our yearly earnings slip even a dollar below her mandated minimum, there's a clause in the contract that says she can fire me and demand her investment back. Doing that would only leave me without a job, but destroy my business and leave my employees with nothing. What I need to do is buy her out completely, but the firm is in bad shape after paying to settle someone's lawsuits." He crooked a brow at me, making me once again wish I didn't share a face with that shit-peddling fraud. "Say what I would about you, you throw an A-list party, Sue.

"In two weeks, I'm going to be in a room with dozens of potential high-value clients. The kind of clients that can drag our bottom line above the minimum—"

"—before the yearly financial report comes out," I finished. "And maybe even inject you with enough capital so you can finally get *rid of her*."

He tapped his nose, winking at me. "See? We weren't talking about you. For once, you're not the woman who's causing the most grief in my life."

I rolled my eyes, smiling slightly. "But what does any of this have to do with Micah or Alex? Because they were grinning just as creepily and twirling their mustaches over the thought of being free of your investor."

Rhodes frowned. "Sue, you know this."

Oops, I do? That's not good.

"Remember what happened to Micah's parents?"

"I—uh—yeah," I squeaked. "Of course, I do. Sorry, I got mixed up for a second. Don't like to think about it."

His frown deepened, then smoothed out. "Yeah, that's fair. None of us like to think about a greedy piece of shit scamming a sweet, elderly couple, but since the cops were never able to recover the money, Micah sends every cent he makes to his folks. And since Alex stays home with Lily and you're not working, we *all* depend on the investment firm," he said. "Last thing we need in the new year is my severance package."

It was my turn to frown. "I get all of that, but I still don't understand why we're spending sixteen million dollars for you to schmooze. Why not use that money to buy out the investor?"

"The buyout price is fifty million."

"Flip flipping fuck!" I cried, eyes bugging. "So you have always been stupid! Why would you sign that contract?"

Rhodes busted up, his whole aura lighting up and making his eyes dance. "Ease up on me here. I'm not the only one in these woods who makes unwise business decisions." His smile took the sting out of his words. "In my defense, I was starting a high-end investment firm in New York City. No one worth billions would've signed with a guy working in a one-room shitpit above a restaurant. I needed money to attract money."

"*You* needed a financial literacy class," I shot back, "which is hella ironic. I don't even know what to do with you right now. Do you have a backup plan in case you can't get anyone from the party to sign with you? You know, people generally don't like being hit up for money when they're in the middle of getting shit-faced."

"Trust me." A hand slinked around my waist, pulling me closer and widening my eyes for another reason. "I've got that part handled. But..." I blinked at his growing, wolfish grin. "If you really want to know what to do with me, I've got an idea."

"Um... what's happening right now?"

"What's happening," Rhodes whispered, tracing the shell of my ear with his lips, "is that we never did get to go on that date Friday night."

My pulse picked up fast, running away as Rhodes's hand traveled lower... and lower. "Pretty sure it wasn't a date. It was an appointment for me to suck your dick."

"And I'm deeply interested in rescheduling that appointment." He kissed the sensitive spot just beneath my ear—once, then twice. My nipples sprung up like Rhodes-seeking missiles. "Now a good time for you?"

"Um, sure, I guess—"

That was all the confirmation of consent he needed.

Hands grabbed me and the world spun. I was left blinking and still trying to catch up as Rhodes pushed me up against the tree. "Our sex life has been stale for years. If you decided it's time to spice it up, that's a thing you've got to let a guy know."

"Oh?" I hopped up, wrapping my arms and legs around him. "Consider my sudden need for spice a post-accident-related new lease on life. The last thing I'm going to do is die without ever having your cock in my mouth."

Said cock snapped to attention, poking my middle.

"I completely agree," he gruffed hoarsely. "That would be a terrible way to go, so we'd better not waste a second. There are bears in these woods after all."

The man had abandoned all shame and subtlety.

Giggling, I nipped his nose. "I'd better get to it, then."

I slid down his hard, strong, ropey body... taking his running shorts with me.

Rhodes had his shirt up and off in an instant, tossing it somewhere over his shoulder.

I ran my hands up his chest—splaying my fingers across his abs, and soaking in the rising heat burning through his body. Somehow, some way, this man was all mine, and I wasn't going to waste a minute of this miracle. "Any preference, or does it not matter what I do because you're so wound up, you're going to burst from the first lick?"

"I'll let the answer to that be the jack you spring from the box."

Matching wolfish grins connected across his tall and sexy landscape.

Flicking down, I bit my lip—trying not to do something embarrassing like purr. Rhodes's cock stood erect and proud between his legs, demanding that I take it on. How could a cock be demanding? You'd only have to switch places with me to discover the answer to that question.

Palming him, I licked his tip, then made a show of reeling back—ducking side to side like I was avoiding the coming explosion.

Rhodes laughed so hard he fell against the tree, and over me. A tender smile graced his lips as he stroked my cheek, brushing the hair from my eyes. "It's just so impossible not to want you. You're so adorable, my heart can't take it."

I heated up body and soul. "I— Uh— We—" Diving forward, I swallowed him to the hilt, literally putting a stop to my nonsensical rambling.

Rhodes choked on a sharp hiss, thighs tensing.

I went wild. My head bobbed between his legs—licking, sucking, and nipping his length to my heart's content. Filthy promises and sweet nothings poured from his lips, telling me all the things he was going to do to my pussy when it was his turn.

Rhodes rocked back and forth on his running shoes, thrusting in and out, in and out of my mouth—picking up speed the harder I sucked.

My cheeks caved in. My head banged against his stomach. My nails pierced his thighs—leaving my mark for me and only me to see.

Rhodes Newbury was mine.

"Ugh, fuck," he gruffed, eyes pinned shut and head digging into the bark like the exquisite torture of my mouth on him would kill him—but if it did, he'd die happy. "Holy fucking fuck!"

I never thought I was that good at giving blowjobs, but Micah and Rhodes sure knew how to make a girl feel great about her skills. I was starting to expect an award.

Rhodes suddenly drew back—slipping out of my mouth with a pop. I didn't get a lick of warning before hot ropes of cum painted my lips, chin, and chest.

"Fuck, that was so much better than I remember." Legs giving out, he fell on me—grasping the back of my head, he tipped me up and kissed the crap out of me.

I had a second to gasp, and then I gave in to it *hard*—pushing him over and rolling around on the grass and leaves—making out like a couple of horny college students. Which I knew without a doubt we would've been if I could've gone back in time and gone on that eighteenth-birthday date with Rhodes, Micah, and Alex.

So much would've been different if that demon who called herself my sister hadn't made it her life's mission to take everything good away from me.

I would've been a successful attorney who committed my life to helping people the way Rhodes wished to—and I would've gone after the double-dealing, shitty corporate bastards that took that dream away from him.

I would've listened when they were vulnerable. Supported them when they felt like failures. Took the slack when they needed rest. And gave them mine when life came for me too.

We would've made something big, amazing, and wonderful out of our lives living in New York, traveling the world, and loving each other in all the places between. It would've been perfect—

But then, there would have been no Nari. A small smile tugged at my mouth. *So maybe everything worked out the way it should after all.*

"Uh-oh." Rhodes flipped us both—dropping me wide-eyed and blinking on his lap as he stretched out on the grass. "You haven't taken a hard enough pounding yet if you've still got time to smirk."

I blushed like the silly girl with a crush I was. "I cannot disagree with you there."

I squealed when he practically ripped my shirt off me, freeing my breasts from their confines. My pants were next to go. I was up and balancing on the balls of my feet in a blink. I grasped the bark beside me as firmly as he grasped my thighs—positioning me over his mouth.

Rhodes buried his head between my legs, devouring my pussy like a starving man. There wasn't another way to describe it, and I loved that. Rhodes was never one to do a thing halfway... and making my pussy sit up and beg was no different.

My fingers tugged on his thick, coiled hair. Head thrown back, I moaned from a deep, primal part of me when his tongue slipped past my folds and plundered the treasure trove. Large, warm hands were soft, cupping my breasts while rough, calloused fingers tweaked my nipples mercilessly. The man was undoing my sanity right there in the dirt, and he'd just gotten started.

His tongue darted in and out, tongue-fucking me to distraction. I writhed on top of him, not even trying to hold back my cries. Every point of contact from him to me was water thrown on live wires. The current surged and exploded out of control—building and building—until it overwhelmed and shorted out my senses.

I was hot and tingling and hoarse. My vision blurred, and my hips rocked, moving back and forth on his mouth—riding the fuck out of that beautiful face. I couldn't believe I ever wasted a sweaty, unsatisfying second with any man who wasn't Rhodes or Micah. All those guys were the stingy appetizer. The ground-up, under-seasoned beef on a piece of stale bread.

Rhodes was the main course, the dessert, and the sweet, fruity cocktail that washed it all down. He was good, caring, and generous. He seemed so serious and buttoned up when we were in school, but the whole time that *was* because he was serious—serious about making the world a kinder place. The sexy, quiet confidence made me want him in high school. But the quivering in his voice when he talked about creating GloryBoi for his family, and then had to watch that creation destroy them... it was that open, naked vulnerability that made me love him.

"You're everything I want, Rhodes," I rasped. "You always have been and always will be... everything."

Our eyes connected, communicating so many things we'd never say out loud—because we didn't have to.

Rhodes latched on to that bundle of nerves and sucked *hard*.

"Yes!" I bucked, flinging my head back. Fireworks exploded in my mind, sparking bright spots dancing in the air like I stared into the sun. He flicked and teased my helpless clit—giving it no escape and me no chance to catch my breath.

I came so hard I doubled over, almost tumbling over his head.

Rhodes held me fast—steady and strong as wave after wave rocked me, spreading pleasure to every corner of my soul.

Chest heaving, I collapsed on his chest. Rhodes caught and kissed me deeply, sharing the taste of me on his tongue.

"You're everything too," he whispered. "You weren't always... until you were."

My heart compacted, and then burst into confetti. The man couldn't just say something like that and then walk out of these woods without my pussy juices on his dick.

I slid down, grasping his length and pressing it against my entrance.

My eyes rolled up in my head as I took all of him—a deep, satisfied moan escaping from my chest.

I let myself adjust, steadying myself on his chest, and then I was off.

I saw why they called this riding because I was bouncing, bucking, heaving, and hopping on Rhodes's dick like a bronco rider.

Rhodes held tight to my hips, meeting me dip for thrust. We were throwing up leaves with our wild, frantic lovemaking—plunging us both in a warm, woodsy, natural world where nothing existed but the leaves, the trees, the quiet, and us.

My lower belly tightened—core melting like wax over the flame. We were both at our limits. This was never going to be anything but hard, quick, and dirty.

I screamed, legs snapping together and anchoring me to Rhodes—connecting us for now and ever.

We both came hard, exploding on and in each other to a chorus of gasps and moans.

Pitching forward, I dropped into his waiting arms, snuggling my forehead in the crook of his neck. "Wow," I breathed. "That was incredible."

"Whew, baby." I was very proud of myself that Rhodes was just as breathless as me. "That topped our record by miles. Best fucking sex we've ever had by far."

"Yeah?" I flipped onto my back, taking him shocked and blinking with me. I grinned, draping my arms around his shoulders. "Well, let's see if we can go higher than number one. But first..." I reached over his head and rescued my phone. Turning on the recorder, I held it to his chin. "If you wouldn't mind repeating after me: I, Rhodes Newbury, am willingly and knowingly..."

***

We stumbled back to the manor in a light and giggly mood.

"Well," Rhodes drawled, throwing his arm around my waist. "We didn't run anywhere but we got in quite the workout. I definitely felt those calories burning, baby, how about you?"

I giggled, hiding my face in his shoulder. "My kind of early morning workout, for sure. I especially loved how it's turned you into a horny teenager."

He laughed, tickling my side until I squealed and ran around to his other side. "Blowjobs have that effect on a man. You should see how badly I devolve after anal."

Grinning, I winked at him. "Okay."

"Wait, wha—?" His slack-jawed gaping got another giggle out of me. "Are you serious?"

"Sure," I said, throwing my arms around him in turn. "I mean, what's the point of being married to three hot guys if we're just going to have vanilla sex. That's all the judgment of the alternative lifestyle without all the deviant fun."

"Uh, that's the fucking spirit," he cried, scooping me up and into his arms. "Deviant fun!" Rhodes straight took off running. "Here we come!"

"Right now?" I was laughing my head off. "But we just had deviant fun in bear-infested woods! Seriously, what is the rebound time on your jack-in-the-box penis?"

"You obviously wanted to find out, or you wouldn't have dangled the promise of anal sex over my head." He leaped over a fallen branch, sprinting a shrieking me back to the manor and a waiting bed. "No chance I'm giving you time to change your mind."

Rhodes burst through the trees, and skidded to an abrupt halt. Both our mouths dropped open.

"Okay," he murmured, gently putting me back on my feet. "You may have been right about us going overboard on the party."

I would've agreed, but at that point it felt cruel to rub it in.

Christie had reconfirmed the appointment the night before—with me and Alex so I couldn't get away with canceling—and she promised that it would just be a quick catch-up to go over the details, show the caterer the kitchen she'd be working in, and the flyers' manager the ceiling they'd be swinging on. I expected to meet with three people for said quick catch-up before sitting down with Mrs. Prado.

What I didn't expect was a fleet of white vans camped out on my brown lawn like the funny farm attendants had finally come to take me away, and they had the place surrounded.

I counted fifteen vans with Baudelaire Blasts on the side, and I didn't even try to count the dozens of people loading things out and into them.

"Woo-hoo!" A tiny figure in pink waved from the front steps. "There you are, Mrs. Kim. So sorry, we had to start without you, but I know you'll love what we've accomplished so far." She climbed down the steps and came at me pretty fast for someone in six-inch heels.

I felt my naughty post-romp romp with Rhodes slip away as she hooked through my arm and dragged me away. "I'm sure you're going to want to take a quick shower before the fitting. Absolutely no sweat stains on the masterpiece." She laughed to lighten the sentence, but it didn't work. I knew a command when I heard one. "While you're washing up, I'd like to get started on the security scheduling and placement."

Christie was a short, slim, young woman with a bright smile, severe nose, and shining chestnut curls teased into a fashionable updo. She was also deceptively strong.

I was putting an embarrassing amount of effort into freeing my arm from her, but the woman had a grip of steel.

"Did you decide on local law enforcement for the party, or will we be providing bodyguards?" she asked. "I should let you know, there is an extra fee if we provide the bodyguards."

"Bodyguards?" I gave her an insane look. "Why would we need bodyguards? I know my husbands are hot as hell, but those rich bitches won't literally try to steal them, will they?"

Christie's laugh was surprisingly loud and honking for such a tiny person. "Mrs. Kim, you are a scream. Absolutely, my favorite client—but don't let the others know," she added with a wink.

"Uh, okay, but—"

"No to the bodyguards," Rhodes sliced in, keeping pace with us easily. "We've already spoken to the chief. He can spare three officers on the night to cover all three exits in and out of the ballroom."

"Hmm." Christie worried her lip, weaving me through the parade of vans. "I'm not certain that three will be enough. Ideally, I'd like fourteen more officers stationed at the front doors, back doors, and in the hallways."

"That's a bit excessive," Rhodes remarked.

"Unfortunately, it's not. The jewels Mrs. Kim is renting for the night are priceless. Sanders and Sanderson will want to see we've made every effort to protect their property from theft, or they won't let it out of their sight."

I opened my mouth to say I didn't need jewels that came with a side of seventeen cops when something near the front gate caught my eyes—distinct in the fact that it wasn't a white van, but instead a small, modest blue car that hadn't changed in ten years.

"Mrs. Prado." I paused a few feet from the fountain, rising on tiptoe to see. "Is that her? Must be. But is she here early, or am I that late? Is it ten o'clock already?"

Rhodes checked his smartwatch, then shook his head. "It's barely nine thirty. She's early."

"I don't see her," I murmured, straining harder to see through the tinted windows. "She must be inside."

"I'll meet with her while you and Ms. Baudelaire talk final details," Rhodes offered. "I've still got an hour before I've got to get ready for work. Shouldn't take much longer than that to reorientate a woman who's lived here longer than me."

"Are you sure?" Christie was dragging me again, leading me inside. "It's not just reorientation. She also has a stack of employee profiles she'll need you to go through."

"It'll be fine." His smile made my stomach do flips. "Mrs. Prado helped me, Micah, and Alex survive Lily's toddler years."

I didn't miss that Sue wasn't mentioned.

"I learned to shut up and do what she says a long time ago. Just like I'll shut up and hire whoever she tells me."

I cracked a smile, remembering all the times growing up that Mrs. Prado chased me from her kitchen, but then always came back and found me later to sneak me a meringue and hot cocoa. Omma never did figure out how I kept getting cavities when she never let us have sugar.

Stumbling up the stairs, I was twisted around talking to Rhodes when light pierced my eyes, making me wince.

What is that? Something white? silver? glinted in the fountain basin—catching the light and beaming it directly into my eyeball.

I put my hand up, squinting to see. *Did one of the workers drop something? A watch maybe?*

Twisting free, I broke out of Christie's hold and descended the stairs—brushing past Rhodes and two gentlemen carrying in chairs.

"Mrs. Kim? Mrs. Kim, we really can't delay your fitting any longer."

My brows crumpled—feet carrying me closer of their own accord.

When I arrived at the manor those weeks ago, the fountain was nothing but mud and trash. In the following days, autumn stole the greens, reds, and golds from the trees—sprinkling them in the waterless pool and providing a slightly more pleasing sight.

"Greens, reds, and golds," I whispered, following the glint. "But that red..."

...is different from the rest.

Reaching into the fountain, I brushed aside the leaves, and screamed.

"Sue? Sue!" Rhodes came running.

Christie let out her own scream, jumping half out of her skin when my cries startled the staff into dropping the chairs at her feet.

"Sue, what's wrong—!" Rhodes skidded to my side, eyes popping when he shared the gruesome sight.

Lying face down in the muddy basin was Mrs. Prado... with a glinting, shining knife sticking out of her back.

Chapter Thirteen

"I don't know about any of this. It just feels wrong." Beauticians fluttered around me—touching up this, fluffing that, painting this, and pulling that. "A woman was murdered here two weeks ago. The fountain is still roped off with crime scene tape. Having a party amidst a murder investigation is just ghoulish."

Courtney reclined on my bed, perusing the menu with one eye, and sweeping Sue's palace of narcissism with the other. "I agree, babe, but what else could you do? This party is too expensive to cancel," she said. "At least the cops agreed that the killer most likely followed Mrs. Prado here, blended in with all the vans and workers, then killed her and slipped away."

"But that makes even less sense," I burst out. "Why would anyone stalk and kill Mrs. Prado? She was just a cook and house manager, not a mafia boss. Why would anyone want to hurt her, let alone be so desperate to do it that they'd risk being seen by dozens of people?"

"But they weren't seen by dozens of people," she said softly. "That's what really freaks me out. How do you stab and murder someone, and then bury them under a pile of leaves amid a mass of chaos, and no one sees a thing?"

I shuddered, and was scolded for my trouble.

"Mrs. Kim, please, stay still." Elin grasped my chin and snapped my head around. I was already cringing before her tweezers descended on my eyebrows.

There were still hours before the anniversary party started, but Christie assured me hours would barely be enough time. That's why I invited Courtney to join me in primping hell. I snagged her an invitation the second I could. I was also going to get one for her mom, but she offered to take Taylor on a grandmama-grandbaby vacation so that Courtney could get her first adult-only weekend in five years.

Her hair and makeup were already done, so that left her chilling in a fluffy bathrobe on my borrowed bed. "I saw the LPD outside," she continued. "Why? Are they worried the killer will come back?"

"They can't say if he will or he won't since they have no idea why this happened," I forced through my smooshed-up mouth. Freya got ahold of my jaw while Elin had me distracted with the burning fire above my eyes. "But no. They're here to protect shiny rocks tonight, not the rest of us."

"Are you worried?" She reached over and brushed the back of my hand. "What am I saying? Of course you're worried."

"I don't know what to think," I admitted. "I haven't been around for—I mean, I haven't been in Mrs. Prado's life for a while. Maybe she did have enemies, and one caught up to her when her back was turned, but remember, Court? It's not just her. Tracy Williams from the post office was murdered too."

"I remember," she replied, voice grim. "You're thinking there could be a psychopath running around Lantana."

"And if there is, he literally came to my doorstep."

Courtney shuddered—suddenly feeling the same unease I was. "Do the police have any leads? Any evidence that the two deaths could be related?"

I would've shaken my head, but Elin and Freya had moved to my hair and were screeching at me for the slightest head tilt. "Davis said no, and I did ask him exactly that. The *investigations are ongoing*, so he won't give any details. All he would say was that Mrs. Prado and Tracy Williams had less than nothing in common. Different age groups, different friend groups, different neighbors, different income brackets, different causes of death.

"I guess the good news is he said the same for all the potential suspects we had running around the manor that day. Christie's business is based in New York. She and all of her staff drove in that morning from over three hours away. Not a single one of them has been to Lantana before, and Mrs. Prado has never been to New York. There's just no connection there," I said. "The only connection is—"

"—to you, Micah, Rhodes, Alex, and your omma," she finished. She flashed me a look I only half saw out of the corner of my eye. "Did he grill you guys?"

"Only some of us," I mumbled, face heating up. "Obviously, he knew my mother didn't crawl out of her deathbed just to murder her old cook. Micah had already left for work. And Alex was with Christie and her staff during the time of the murder. There were only two people—according to Davis—who had opportunity to commit the murder, and alibiing each other out is pointless, since a wife would easily lie for her husband, and vice versa."

"But you can alibi each other out," she said, grinning away. "You two were too busy banging each other's brains out in the dirt to be going around murdering cooks."

"Yes, thank you," I cried over Elin's, Freya's, Natalie's, Rose's, and Marcus's snickering. "I know what we were doing—didn't need the reminder."

She laughed at me without a lick of shame. "The point is that the murder had nothing to do with you, or your family. What happened to Mrs. Prado was horribly tragic for her and her family, but you've offered to pay for her funeral, and you petitioned the estate lawyer to convert the salary you were going to pay Mrs. Prado into a college fund for her grandkids. What you're doing is very generous, Sue," she said, slipping into the wrong name easily. "And it's your best. The best you can do, so please, don't sit here torturing yourself. Let's just enjoy celebrating you and your husbands tonight, especially since you guys have something to celebrate these days."

It was wrong to smirk and grin on the heels of discussing the brutal murder of someone who took part in raising me, so I bit hard on my lip—fighting back the rising smile that grew from thoughts of Micah and Rhodes.

After a rocky, and I mean mountainous, bad start, I finally figured out the key to true peace in this house—

Sex.

Micah and I were rolling around in the sheets nearly every minute of every day except for all the minutes of the day that Rhodes and I were banging away. To say the spark ignited into passion that grew into a towering inferno of raging lust is putting it mildly. The three of us were far from fighting these days. Just the opposite. We'd fallen into a nice routine of eating breakfast together before work and school, laughing and being silly with Nari while cooking dinner, and burning up the sheets all the free minutes in between.

The only one who wasn't in on the new terms of the truce... was Alex.

If anything, my relationship with him had gotten even worse. Alex's cold shoulder morphed into an Arctic chill. He left every room I walked into. He attended meals with me for Lily's sake, but afterward he'd hustle her away for the next activity in her routine, and left the three of us sitting in the awkward.

I did try once the week before to talk to him, but he just stopped me and said—surprisingly politely—that he'd prefer we maintain strict boundaries and only speak when it had something to do with caring for Lily.

I let him go without a word, swallowing my hurt, because what right did I have to push and harass him? *We* didn't have a relationship to fight for. We didn't even have a co-parenting relationship to fight for.

I wasn't his wife. I wasn't Lily's mother. I was nothing to him at all.

At least I'm something to Micah and Rhodes, I reminded myself. *The next time I leave this house, I'll be packing some good memories with me. The memories of my first, third, twelfth, and thirty-third screaming orgasm. Plus, the memory of waking up the next morning after those orgasms with their arms around me, and no nightmares retracting their claws from my mind.*

And even though Rhodes and Micah claimed all they wanted out of the last days of their marriage was lots of hot sex, I could feel things changing between us. Micah was joking, teasing, and laughing with me now—instead of jabbing, taunting, and laughing at me. Some nights, we didn't even have sex. We'd just curl up in bed laughing at old-school comedy reruns and bemoaning the current state of comedy television.

As for Rhodes, we never touched on what I blurted out in the woods about wanting to stay together and work on the marriage he didn't know we didn't have, but things seemed to change with him all the same. Sex really seemed to mellow the guy out the way early morning runs never could. Over the last couple weeks, he'd been opening up to me about the pressure he was under—having to run a business based in two states and support a family of five. Even though the manor and Omma's care were paid for by the estate, Latana was still an expensive town to live in—as ultra-rich communities tend to be. Just one semester at Lantana Day School costs fifteen thousand dollars.

I wish I could've freaked out over those numbers, but Omma spent twice that a semester to send me to Titan Prep. Competition was fierce in a community that can afford to send their kids to any college they want. If you wanted your kid to have the edge, you had to pay for it.

Even though there wasn't much my thirty dollars an hour and I could do to relieve his financial pressure, it seemed to help him just having me listen and hear him out without judgment. So much so that over the last week, he'd been opening up to me about growing up under the weight of being Rhodes Newbury of the Chicago Newburys.

He had to be perfect at all times—never letting the public see a crack in the façade. And most importantly, never sharing family business with an outsider. Meaning that his whole childhood, his parents and grandparents refused to have any kind of conversation with him about his father's addiction, while also forbidding him to talk about it with anyone else. He was forced to keep all of it—his dad stealing from him, the nights he went hungry in a penthouse with the lights shut off, the move to his grandparents' when he was ten, and the slow destruction of his parents' marriage—pushed down deep inside.

So deep, he didn't tell his two best friends anything about it until they all got drunk one night in their dorm room. And he never told Sue at all for reasons I didn't have to guess.

I knew from our first real conversation what a big deal it was for Rhodes to open up to someone—which just made my stupid, lovesick heart squeal that he chose me.

"Look at you grinning away," Courtney teased, lighting my cheeks on fire. "You're so cute when you're in love."

"Not love," I rebutted immediately—almost harshly, but I couldn't help it as thoughts of Dan floated through my head. "Love requires truth and transparency on both sides. We aren't in love. But I... I guess I'd be comfortable saying we're in lust. Possibly in friendship some days."

"Uhhh-huh," she teased, hiding her smirk behind the menu.

I ignored her, and the shared strange looks between the beauticians. They were obviously wondering why a woman getting ready for her blowout anniversary bash was denying she loved her husbands.

"So, who all is invited to this thing?" Courtney asked.

Again I wanted to shrug but Freya's immediate, mind-reading glare kept my shoulders where they were. "Rhodes's mom and grandmother. Micah's parents, and Alex's cousins," I rattled off. "Also, pretty much every bachelor, bachelorette, and couple in Lantana with the highest net worth—including Charles Layton," I mentioned. "Did you know Lily's first-grade teacher was heir to the Lantana Lakes Lager fortune?"

"Whoa." She whistled. "I didn't know that, but good for him. That's some tasty beer right there."

I had to agree. Micah and I had taken to splitting a can while we curled up watching reruns of *The I.T. Crowd*. And by that I meant, he poured it down my chest and licked the lager off my nipples while the show played in the background.

"Not just the Lantana VIP list, but New York too," I continued. "Almost all of Rhodes's clients got the invite, and a bunch of the guys' friends from college."

"I see, and has it occurred to you yet that you'll be in a room with dozens upon dozens of people who've known the happy quadruple for seven years or more, and will definitely want to catch up on old times and all the things they missed in the life of Soo Min Kim...?" Her knowing eyes met my paling face. "...or is that just occurring to you now?"

"Oh my—!" I whipped around, snagging the eyeliner across my temple and cheek.

"Mrs. Kim!" Elin, Freya, and Marcus shrieked.

***

Hours later, the manor was booming. And I meant, walls-shaking, chandeliers-rattling, floor-thrumming booming. The party was in full swing, and the only one missing was the wife of honor.

"Mrs. Kim, you're a vision," Christie gushed—eyes misting. "Madame Lavigne outdid herself!"

I blinked at the spectacle in the mirror, truly at a loss for words. "She really... let her muse off the leash."

"But of course she did," Christie cried. She jumped up and down, clapping in her white pumps and glitteringly white strapless gown. Elin, Freya, and the others were behind her doing much the same. After throwing Courtney out for distracting me, they'd finally gotten the chance to finish their masterpiece to satisfaction. "Nothing but the best for you."

I pushed a smile onto my lips. "Thank you, Christie, Elin, Marcus, and everyone. You've not only brought life back to this haunted mansion, you've also brought me to my optimal hotness. I will never look better than I do right now."

The ladies giggled, patting their cheeks like they were about to blush.

"I mean it," Christie said, wiping her eyes. "My favorite client. Why can't they all be like you?"

And by that I was sure she mostly meant, why couldn't all of her clients write her a check for one point six million dollars? I was also sure that's why she kept tearing up. I would too if I cleared seven figures on one job.

"Elin, would you mind handing me my cellphone? I need Court to help me to Omma's room. I want to check on her and say goodnight before she goes to bed."

"We can help you with that." Elin and Freya had their hands on my wrists and elbows before I could politely decline.

Giving in, I let them help me out of the room and down the hall. Davis was behind me in a blink.

"Good evening, Mrs. Kim, you're a vision."

"As compared to the mess I was when you peeled me off the steering wheel?" I floated over my shoulder. "I'm still working on my come-hither smile, Officer, but don't worry. I promise to have it ready the next time I almost die."

"Mrs. Kim, please," he hissed. I could practically hear the blood filling his cheeks. "I deeply apologize for the misunderstanding, but I've explained to you that wasn't what I meant."

I smothered a laugh. If I believed in hell, I had a feeling that's where I'd be going for constantly flustering the poor man for my own enjoyment. "Thank you for being here tonight," I said in a more serious tone. "I realize it's way below your pay grade to follow me and a bunch of sparkling rocks around when you could be catching criminals, or spending time with your own family, but I appreciate it all the same."

"It's... This certainly is an unusual assignment. To be honest, I don't approve of law enforcement being used as personal bodyguards. We serve the entire community—not any one individual or family. But," he grudged. "I was told every officer who signed up for the assignment would be sent home with the chef's prepared meal and a guest gift bag that includes an MT tablet, so... it's fine."

I hummed. "So, what you're saying is, you took the assignment... for a bribe."

"What! Bribe?! No," he blared at my back. "That isn't— That's not—!"

I bit hard on my lip, penning in a laugh. Oh yeah, I was definitely on my way to a fiery pit.

Omma's door loomed in front of us. Christie broke free from the pack, scurrying ahead to open the door and ease me inside.

Reynard glanced up from his charting. Decked out in tight, expensive jeans and a formfitting tee, I tried not to ask myself what this man was doing as a hospice nurse when he was clearly meant for the runway.

Okay, I asked the question in my head, but sense kept it from leaving my mouth. Being handsome didn't mean a man couldn't be caring, nurturing, or have other interests and pursuits that didn't involve flexing his muscles.

Reynard took one look at me and dropped the clipboard. "Wow," he breathed. "You look... wow." He jerked, panic seizing his expression. He meant to keep that in his head too. "I mean— I didn't mean—! Shit, Mrs. Kim, I'm so sorry. That was completely inappropriate of me. Please, forgive—"

Giggling, I interrupted him. "Reynard, it's okay. Trust me, you never have to apologize for making a lady feel beautiful."

He flushed. Spinning away, he turned his back to me, reaching down to pick up the chart. "Your timing is good," he told the wall. "I just gave Mrs. Kim her nighttime meds, including her sleeping pill. You can say goodnight before she retires."

I closed the distance to the bed. Crouching down as much as the dress would let me, I took Omma's hand—gently murmuring to her.

Her left eye fluttered open.

"Hey, Omma." I wished I could have some privacy, but I really did need help staying upright in the dress, and the insurance company needed an officer on my tail at all times. "I don't want to disturb you. I just wanted to say goodnight."

"Sa...rang," she whispered. "Is that... you?"

"Yes, it's me." I squeezed her fingers with both hands, rubbing warmth into them. "Of course, it's me. I'm not going anywhere, Omma. I'll be here until... I'll be here."

"Beautiful," she murmured, her eye drifting closed. "My baby... an angel."

My throat tightened, squeezing around the lump forming in my throat. Why? Why after all the horrible things this cold and withholding woman had done to me over the years, did a rare kind word from her still reduce me to that little girl who wanted nothing more than her mommy's love?

"Goodnight." I pressed a soft kiss to her forehead, then I let my entourage pick me back up and practically carry me out.

Reynard joined us, shutting the door behind him. The live-in part of the live-in-nurse description meant that he never really clocked off and went home. He had the adjoining bedroom right next to her, and an alarm set during the night to wake him every three hours to go in and check on my mother.

Since a peek at his meticulous charts proved my mother never actually needed anything in the night—thanks to a heavy-duty sleeping pill that allowed her to rest in peace—I asked him if he'd like the night off to join the party. After all, we were giving out obscenely expensive Maverick Tech tablets that retailed for two thousand dollars on sale, to a bunch of rich people who could afford to buy twelve of their own. Why not spread the generosity around to the people who were actually in Sue's life?

Because one thing I knew for sure was that I'd had Sue's phone for almost a month, and not a single one of the *friends* she invited to the anniversary party had called or texted her once—not even to confirm they were coming.

But, in Reynard's case, he jumped on the chance for a night off and decided he'd rather meet up with some friends and spend the night with people he did know, instead of partying with a bunch of strangers that he didn't.

Our group traveled through the shabby east wing and out onto the circular landing, bypassing the second, third, and fourth officer stationed on the second floor.

Music streamed through the vents, doorjambs, and cracks of the drafty manor—welcoming one and all to a good time, and I made sure of it. Christie wanted the classical music and band that Sue and she agreed to, but I was in charge now, and I wanted to party like a woman in my late twenties, not like a woman in my late eighties.

"We're about to blow this shit up," I crowed, head bobbing and body bouncing down the stairs. "Christie, I better see you on the dance floor shaking it with the rest of the rich and gorgeous."

"Mrs. Kim, please," she cried, blushing away. "I couldn't possibly. I'm here as a member of staff, not as a guest."

"Well, between you and me," I started, dropping my voice. "I won't rat you out to the boss."

She giggled, swatting my arm like we were conspiring to get away with something.

My party brought me to the doors of the ballroom, and then melted away. Whispering, giggling, and throwing me thumbs-up—the makeup artists escaped down the hallway toward the second sitting room where a nice dinner was waiting for them before they made the long drive back to the city.

That left me, Christie, Davis, and the two tuxedoed gentlemen—yes, tuxedos, gloves, and hair slicked back in the full pomp and circumstance. The men bowed to me, then to each other, before grasping the door handles and welcoming me inside.

Time stopped. Slowing to one awe-filled moment.

Soft, ivory flakes fell from the rafters, blanketing the snowy-white world in a dusting of magic. High above, aerialist angels wrapped in silk spun, soared, and danced through the air—transporting us to a world unknown.

Every detail down to the patterns on the forks was deliberate. The cream platform placed over the worn hardwood. The cream linens. The white rose centerpieces, and the white gowns, heels, tuxes, and bowties on all the laughing, flirting guests. Christie promised me she'd take the simple of simplest themes—*white*—and give me something that had never been done before. And the statement piece to her creation—

—was me.

The music stopped—a hush fell—as my dress and I swept into the room.

My wings crested overhead, catching the light from the chandeliers in its diamonds and thanking them with dancing rainbows. A pitch-black sheer bodice hugged my frame like a lover, delicately preserving my modesty with a swirling pattern of rubies that flowed down to my voluminous layered skirt—lining the hem of each tier with more rubies. And that's where the effort to preserve modesty ended.

The skirt barely covered the apex of my thighs, and that's because it was too busy parting down the middle and fanning out to reveal my black, ruby-encrusted stockings and black stiletto heels—those same, gorgeous satin heels stubbed with the citrine gems that graced my train.

Midnight gown, diamonds on my wings, rubies on my body, and citrines on my hem—I was the red admiral butterfly. A tiny, beautiful delicate creature that carried their multicolored bands and spots like I carried the loves of my life with me always: Micah, Rhodes, and Alexander.

Or at least that was the flowery shit Soo Min poured in Christie's ear when she told her to find a dressmaker who could bring this spectacle to life. But if I knew my sister, the real reason she wanted a dress decked out in real diamonds, rubies, and citrines was so she'd get worldwide attention from wearing one of the most expensive gowns that ever existed—and with the dress coming at a cool eight million, she put herself at number seven on the list.

That is until the party was over and Sanders and Sanderson's Jewelers ripped the thing off my back and pried every rented gem off of it—along with the ruby choker, earrings, and tiara. That was why we had to endure armed cops at every entrance and exit, and one following me at all times. The jewelers would make sure they collected the publicity coming their way, and their stones—before the night was over.

The hush gripped the room, stealing the speech of almost a hundred perfect and near strangers.

It broke in a blink.

"Aaahh," an orgasmic cry broke through the silence. "Amazing. Magnificent! Bravo, bravo!"

The tide unleashed. Cheers, claps, and shouts of praise trumpeted my entrance, and put a silly smile on my face. Okay—maybe Sue did have a point about this dress.

The crowd parted, making way for three men more gorgeous than my gown ever could be.

Micah reached me first. Taking my hand, he dropped on one knee as he bowed over my hand—pressing soft, dusky lips to my knuckles. "Gods above, you're the most contrary woman I've ever met, Soo Min." His wicked grin thumped my heart hard in my chest. "I tell you that you couldn't possibly get any more beautiful, so you had to go and prove me wrong."

Rhodes leaned in. Taking my chin softly between his fingertips, he kissed me slow and sweet over the aahs from our audience. "Perfection," he whispered against my lips. "Simple and absolute perfection."

I was fluttering. I was on such a high, my wings truly could've lifted me into the air and carried me to the heavens. Why not? I was already there. Of course I was... because there was Alex.

Dusky-brown tousled hair was slicked back, showcasing his hazel eyes with no impertinent obstruction. The white tux he chose fit his form in all the right ways—doing nothing to conceal the rippling of his muscled thighs as he closed the distance. Gazing at me then, he did something I hadn't seen him do since I walked through the door.

Smile.

"Wow, Sue, you look..." he breathed. Leaning in, his nose tickled my cheek—drawing a line in goose bumps from the corner of my mouth to the soft, sensitive spot beneath my ear. "...like the winged specter of death."

Illusion shattered.

"For eight million dollars, you rented—*rented*—this ridiculous eyesore." He drew back, still smiling away, but now I knew it was for the dozens of cameras and eyes on us. "You should be studied, because for fuck sure there's something wrong with you that medical science has yet to diagnose."

My jaw clamped down hard. Again, I knew his words were for Soo Min—the person who admittedly did throw away an astonishing amount of money for a dress she'd only be wearing for a few hours—but nonetheless, it was Sarang who was about to punch him in the face.

"This from the guy who wouldn't let me cancel the party," I gritted. "Can we just be civil, please? Can you manage that? Or is your unemployed ass secretly getting paid to be an unsucked dick, and you've got to commit to the only work you can get?"

"Guys," Micah hissed.

But Alex just chuckled. "No, dear, I'm not being paid to be a dick, so if it's your request, my love, I will take the night off."

My eyes narrowed. I knew I shouldn't have said that. Alex wasn't unemployed. He devoted himself full-time to raising Lily, and considering that she was the best kid in the world, he was doing a great job. But being attacked, insulted, and punished for a crime Sue committed was a big-time trigger for me. Every time he did it, I lashed out thoughtlessly—

—and he never responded like this.

"What's this?" I demanded. "What are you doing?"

"I'm doing as you ask. And to kick off this perfect night with my perfect wife..." He held out his hand. "May I have the first dance?"

I flicked from him, to the hand, then to our watching audience. "No," I dropped, stealing surprise across his face. "But you can walk me to our table and signal the start of dinner. Not only did the beauticians refuse to let me eat, but it turns out eight million dollars' worth of rocks is *heavy*." I took his hand in a firm and steady grip. "Thank you, dear."

A tight smile stole across his face. "Of course."

"A ceasefire. I like it." Rhodes kissed my cheek. "Alex, you help her to the table and I'll tell the chef it's time to serve."

Micah pecked another quick kiss on my lips. "I'll tell the deejay to turn down the music, so we can start the toasts."

They went their separate ways, leaving me with Alex.

"Lean on me," he said simply.

I did as he asked even though it quickened my pulse to do so. At some point in the last couple weeks I accepted that it didn't matter how much of a jerk Alex was—my body would never stop responding to his nearness.

Together we walked through a sea of white, collecting greetings and well-wishes, but exchanging no words.

I broke first. Turning my head, I spoke into his ear. "I'm sorry. I shouldn't have said that shit about you being unemployed the first or second time. I respect what you're doing as a stay-at-home dad." I saw his brows pop out of the corner of my eye. "You're doing the most important job in the world, and you're crushing it like you crush everything else because Nari is the best kid there will ever be. I'm sorry," I said clearly, "and I make no excuses for lashing out like an immature baby, but, Alex, you have to know you're not being fair.

"I agreed the party was too over the top and expensive, and I tried to cancel it. *You* were the one who wouldn't let me, and now you're turning around and insulting me and calling me wasteful for wearing the dress you wanted me to get. I just can't win with you," I cried, emotion leaking into my voice. "Everything I say and do is wrong in your eyes, and it hurts. It really hurts, Alex. Do you truly not see that I'm trying?"

"I—" Alex spun around and pulled me up so fast, I tripped into his arms. Hands around my waist, he held me strong and steady against him. "I do see that," he whispered, stealing my breath. "I see that you're trying, Sue, and you're right. I shouldn't have said you looked like a winged specter because it's not true." Torment lit his eyes aflame. "You're beautiful, baby. You're always so fucking beautiful it makes my chest hurt... and that's why this is so hard."

My lips parted, eyes blowing wide. Of all things I wanted him to say, I never expected this. "But—"

"Excuse me?" Davis's voice snapped our heads around. "I apologize, Mrs. Kim, Mr. Montgomery. I understand it's your anniversary, but we are under strict orders to stop anyone other than Mrs. Kim from touching the gems. You must limit your interaction to skin on skin only, and maintain a distance of at least two feet."

I goggled at him. "Officer Davis, seriously, he's not going to—"

"It's fine," Alex sliced in, putting me back on my feet and pulling away in the same breath. "These are the terms we agreed to. I'll respect them." He stepped to the side, then offered his elbow—ever the polite and unfeeling gentleman. "Shall we?"

I hesitated, searching for something—anything—in his eyes like the inscrutable emotion that shone in them when he held me. "Yes," I finally said, resting a hand on his elbow. "Thank you."

Alex helped me the rest of the way, guiding me to the platform at the head of the ballroom. Sitting atop that platform a head above the party was a dining table for four, and four throne-like chairs. Two of the waitstaff immediately peeled off the wall to help me onto my throne, bowing over me as they pushed my chair in.

Really overdid it with the queen for the night, Sue, but again... I get it.

As a former waitress who once had a customer bump into me, knock an entire ice-cold milkshake down my shirt, and keep walking like they didn't even see me, I was low-key loving all the awe-filled eyes being on me for a change. From the bodyguards on my tail, to the twelve videographers posted up around the room, to the real and actual celebrity sitting at the table in front of me—a queen was exactly what I felt like.

Soon, everyone was seated and the waitstaff was placing the first course. Courtney waved to me from her table as they set down her salmon tartare with shallots and lemon dressing, then she pointed to the guy seated next to her, and drew a line across her neck—baring her teeth at me.

"You're dead."

I smirked like the crafty bitch I was. Yes, I invited Taylor's teacher, the infamous Mr. Stevens, to the party. Yes, I purposely arranged the seating chart so they'd sit together. And yes, I felt no shame about it.

Courtney basically stopped dating after giving birth to Taylor—too busy raising her daughter and running a successful business. She deserved to spend one night talking, dining, and dancing with the only man she's been interested in in a long time.

Rhodes got to his feet, fixing all eyes and all lenses on him.

Turning down the music, the deejay handed a mic to Christie, who brought it over to Rhodes.

"Good evening, everyone, and thank you for joining us on this special night. Now, the three of us could stand here and tell you all the things we love about Sue, but eventually you'd be forced to have these officers arrest us for holding you hostage for weeks." Laughter filled the room. "So, with the honor of speaking for the three of us, I will condense down to this..." Rhodes reached for me, taking my hand in his. "Most of us here know that marriage is a cross-country journey. Most days you're hiking, other days you're flying, and some days you're crawling over dirt and gravel with shredded knees and broken fingernails."

Descriptive.

"Not every couple, or quadruple"—more laughter—"finish the journey together. Not everyone is meant to, and I can admit to you here today that there were times in the past seven years that I didn't think we'd go the distance, but over these last few weeks with you," he said softly—his thumb stroking slow, tickling circles against my palm. "Laughing with you, talking with you, facing down bears with you, and counting your hairs on my pillow as you snore and snort in your sleep—"

Hades, now would be a good time for that sudden and abrupt trip to Tartarus that we talked about.

"I've never been more sure that I'll crawl on bloody knees over rocks and glass forever... as long as on the other side is you."

I covered my mouth, hiding the trembling smile on my lips.

"I love you," Rhodes said.

"I love you," chimed Micah.

Alex drew my hand away from my lips and pressed them to his. Gazing into my eyes, he said, "I love you.

"Happy anniversary."

I choked up as oohs, aahs, hoots, hollers, and applause echoed through the ballroom.

Rhodes handed back the mic and the party kicked off anew.

Knowing my evil twin as well as I did, I knew Sue chose an all-white theme and dress code just so she could be the black butterfly belle of the ball with all eyes on her. I also had a feeling she was going for a classy, elegant, snooty party to impress all the high-society friends she *didn't* have in New York City.

Good thing baby sis was here to screw that all up.

"Whoo!" I shrieked—bouncing up and down the dance floor, shaking my ass like the song demanded. Courtney bounced after me, leading a very happy and very tipsy Mr. Stevens around by the tie. "Come on, Mama Spencer!"

I grasped Micah's mother's forearms. She was hiding on the edge of the dance floor, acting like she didn't want to dance, but I could see her toes tapping from across the room.

"Don't get all shy on me. I know there's a wild woman in you," I said to the slight terror on her face. "You didn't make a son as fine as yours by being all innocent and demure."

"Sue!" Micah cried over his mother's giggling. "Can you not? I was conceived by immaculate conception, and I will not be told otherwise."

Marsha Spencer only laughed louder. "Well, I was known to get a little naughty back in my day." She winked at me. "Truth is, Micah gets it from me."

"Yeah, he does." I put my hands on my hips, jutting them this way and that. "Now show everyone the real meaning of the phrase birthing hips."

Chortling like a schoolgirl, Mama Spencer got *down*—wining, wiggling, and twerking to put everyone to shame.

That was until Micah promptly grabbed and led her away. "Time to rest, Mother. You're drunk and my wife is clearly a terrible influence on you."

"Terrible or not, she's fun," I heard Marsha say. "Was she always like this? Why have I never seen this side of...?"

I didn't let the loss of my dance partner stop me—not when I had no shortage of them. The nineteen-thousand-dollar bottles of wine were flowing, our bellies were full of delicious food, and the bass was thumping. Everyone was either on the dance floor, or hooking up in shadowy corners. I wasn't about to be the wet blanket sitting around when my flat ass needed shaking.

"Wow. You're having fun."

Three women came up on me so fast, I almost tripped over my heels bouncing to a stop.

Naturally, they were all wearing elegant white gowns, but that wasn't the matching that concerned me. For some reason, they were all looking at me with identical nasty smirks.

"Uh, do I kn—?" I cut the question off at the knees—Courtney's words ringing in my head. Very likely, the real Sue did know these women, so asking that question would be the stupidest thing I could do. "Is something wrong?" I asked instead.

The woman in the middle flattened her grin into a thinner, blander smile. She had long, bronze hair and a little button nose. "What could be wrong, Sue Bear? It looks like you're doing very well for yourself. Seems like just yesterday the four of us were hanging out outside Hamilton Hall, watching the guys playing football on the south field. You said then that you'd bag the richest and handsomest of the bunch"—she looked around—"and you did."

"Uh… huh," I drew out. *Old college friends from New York. This is bad.* "It's true, I have been very lucky in love. Three amazing, smart, talented men are in love with me, and we're raising a beautiful little girl. I've got nothing to complain about." *Good. Just keep it generic. Don't offer any details.*

Her grin widened. "I bet."

"Good for you," the woman on her right agreed. She was just as glamorous, but she opted for a short red pixie cut and purple contacts that made me wonder if she copied the eye color after her first meeting with Sue. Our naturally purple eyes were always our most talked about, and envied, feature.

"But, you know, it's funny," Pixie continued. "I'm on the Columbia alumni committee. I'm sure your lovely husbands told you that the CAC has a little fundraiser coming up, but the weird thing is," she said, sharing a look with her friends, "you weren't on any of the alumna contact lists. In fact, Sue, you're not in the database at all."

"Weird, right?" breezed the woman on the left. Her ivory gown matched her shockingly white hair. Why a young woman would choose to dye her hair all white, I didn't know, but I did know it strangely suited her. "Because you graduated from Columbia too, Sue? Didn't you?"

Oh. They're those kinds of friends.

"Nope," I dropped. "I actually graduated from Columbia-Southern Community College. Still in the city, but definitely not Ivy League."

Their smirks melted away.

"I only hung around Columbia to chill with my besties"—I wiggled my fingers at them—"and sell the lie. A bit pathetic, for sure, but when you're young, you think appearances are everything." I beamed at them. "Thank goodness we're above all of that now. Right, ladies?"

Button Nose's jaw worked. She clearly wasn't expecting me to come right out with it. "Well, yeah, of course we are," she snapped. "We don't have to worry about our appearance, especially since we've never been a customer of SueNaturals."

"Oh my gods, thank goodness," I cried, laughing my butt off. "Can you imagine telling people that you smeared bird shit all over your face? Super embarrassing."

"*We* have nothing to be embarrassed about," Pixie shrieked. "We're not the ones who got caught selling the stuff. We heard you lost everything in the lawsuit— Sorry, make that *lawsuits* plural."

I sighed, shaking my head. "I got my just desserts for sure. What a stupid, awful thing to do that was. I don't even know what I was thinking, except that I let my obsession with becoming a super-successful girlboss get the best of me.

"But what matters to me now is my family and my friends, and remembering to never take advantage of either of them." I lurched forward, making Button Nose squeak when I grasped her hands. "I was deeply pathetic and insecure back in college, but you guys didn't care. Despite the fact that you likely saw right through me, you were amazing friends then, and you're amazing friends now—coming here tonight to support and celebrate me even after all my legal trouble. Thank you, girls," I gushed. "I literally could not survive without you."

Button Nose, Pixie, and the Chic Ghost exchanged another look—this one shocked with a tinge of baffled.

"I... uh..." Button Nose started. "We... uh... I mean, of course we did know the whole time that you were pretending," she blustered, nose hitting the air. "We just didn't say anything because we wanted you to trust us enough to tell us yourself, Sue."

"Yeah, that's right," Chic Ghost put in. "You never had to keep it from us, honestly, Sue, what kind of snobs did you think we were? We love you, babe. We're always here for you."

Just like that, we were exchanging air kisses and promises to keep in touch.

I was waving goodbye when someone sidled up to me.

"Nicely done." Courtney handed me a glass of wine. "Defused that whole situation without even knowing their names."

"Yes," I replied, keeping my voice low. "I am that good."

Giggling, we downed our drinks, and got back to wiggling, jiggling, and dancing like it'd save the world.

"Mrs. Kim, please!" Sanders of Sanders and Sanderson blared. He wasn't a guest of the party, but it seemed he only made it as far as the main road before he turned back—not able to be parted from his eight-million-dollar investment. "The gems aren't welded on! All that jumping and shaking could knock them loose!"

"You better follow me around with a net, then, baby!" I threw my hands in the air, riding the beat like I was as drunk as I looked. "Whoo!"

"Are you actually trying to take off?" a dry voice asked. "Because those aren't real wings, wife of mine."

I twirled around, whipping said wings through the air and tearing distressed cries from Sanders and Davis. "Can't know for sure unless I try." I leaped into the air, flapping and waving my arms around.

"My goodness, woman," Alex hissed. "So many people are looking at you. *All* of the people are looking at you!"

"Uh-oh," I teased, shimmying closer. "I'm not embarrassing you, am I?"

"Please, don't."

"Don't what?" I smirked like a loon. "Do... this!"

I burst into the chicken dance and just about made Sanders faint.

"Or... this!" I got my macarena on, unscrewing Alex's jaw. "Or th—!"

"Enough."

The world spun. The next thing I knew... my world was Alex.

Hands sliding around my waist, Alex held me tight to his chest—chasing all the giggles and sillies right out of me.

"If you want to dance so badly," he gruffed, lips brushing the tip of my nose. "Dance with me."

"Just a minute, Mr. Montgomery," Davis and Sanders called over the music. "You have to maintain a distance of two feet at all times."

"Can't." Alex trapped me in his shimmering, glacial pools. "Guess you'll have to arrest me."

Sanders looked at Davis like he expected him to do just that. And Davis tipped his head back, pleading with a deity above to explain how in the world he went from keeping the streets safe to preventing a man from dancing with his wife.

Alex spun me—not waiting around for either of them to decide.

"What's this?" I whispered, body thrumming as he laced his fingers through mine. "Do you really want to dance with me, or do you just want me to stop?"

"Can't it be both?"

We both chuckled, but I sobered quickly.

"You're a hard man to figure out, Alexander Montgomery."

"Am I?" Alex spun me, gliding me across the dance floor in a beautiful, elegant waltz that was wildly out of tune with the reggae-pop streaming from the speakers. "I wouldn't say so."

he said enigmatically. I soaked him in, wishing I could see inside his mind.

Alex was a mystery to me in all ways. Rhodes told me why he donated every last cent he got from the buyout, and he also hinted that something catastrophic happened to Micah's parents and family. Something that wiped out every generation's wealth, and that's why he was now sending every penny he made home.

But Alex...?

Why did he spend every day typing away on his laptop, researching med schools when he had the billions to *buy* the medical school of his dreams—let alone get accepted into it? And if he didn't have the money anymore... what happened to it?

Rhodes and Sue were the ones legally married, and the investment firm was listed as a joint asset, so it was that asset that got raided when she had to pay to settle all of those lawsuits.

Alex was under no such legal obligation to fund Sue's shit-in-a-jar fraud. He could've still helped out, but not to the tune of seven billion dollars. If a judge ordered her to pay back that much, it would've made the news and I would've heard about it. *Everyone* would have heard about it—NDAs or no.

Which meant... it was something else.

Sometime in the last ten years since we met, something happened—or a series of something happened—that resulted in the Titan Prep valedictorian, Columbia grad, and co-founder of GloryBoi having nothing to do between the hours of eight and four besides resenting his wife and working to start his life over.

"I haven't been someone you can talk to for a long time, have I?"

Alex stopped—just the slightest hitch in his step, and then his grip was firm on me again—his body molded to mine as he dipped me.

"I know it's too late to say *I've changed* and *everything's going to be different now* but... I've changed," I said softly. "And everything's going to be different now. For me, for Lily... and for you."

Our eyes locked—trapping us both in a void of all the things we wanted to say. Ten years of lies and abuse. Ten years of struggle and loneliness. I could see it all in his eyes and for the first time, as his brows softened and his lips closed the distance, I knew... that Alex saw me.

Someone stepped on my wings, almost ripping me out of Alex's arms.

"Heavens," Sanders bellowed. "Enough! That is enough!"

I blinked at the small, dangerously red man. I didn't know he could emit such a booming sound.

"Mrs. Kim, we have a contract," he bellowed. "You will abide by it, or you'll change out of that dress—now!"

"All right, all right," I soothed, letting Alex put me back on my feet. "I apologize, Mr. Sanders, I got carried away. Christie did order a backup dress for me, so I'll go up now and change."

"You will?" I thought the man might pass out from the relief. "Thank you, Mrs. Kim, I, uh, I believe that's for the best. This is a dress for a party, but not a party dress."

"Well put." I tried not to let the disappointment show on my face when Alex's arms fell away from my waist. "I'll go put on one that is."

Davis swept his hand, gesturing for me to go first. "I'll radio for a female officer to help you out of the dress. Until they arrive, I'll escort you to the door."

I just nodded, picking up my feet to go.

Alex turned in the other direction.

"Alex, wait—"

He slipped between two gyrating couples, disappearing in the crowd.

I blew out a sharp breath, disappointment tinged with sadness warring in my chest. I didn't know what my life would look like after I moved out from the manor for good, but I knew I wanted nothing to do with another life that didn't have Micah, Rhodes, Alex, and Lily in it.

It was like Courtney said. They were my family. The only family I'd have left after Omma leaves me, so of course, I wanted to be on good terms with Alex—even if those terms were only platonic and not romantic.

But how do I get through to him? I thought, ascending the staircase with Sanders at the front and Davis at my back. *His walls are up high, and I can't begin to see the top.*

My thoughts twisted and spun as we passed the officer guarding the entrance to the east wing. What's the right way to get close to someone when you're pretending to be someone else?

I took Ethics as an elective when I attended Titan Prep, but nothing we discussed in that class could've prepared me for this moral quandary.

As promised, a female officer arrived shortly after we reached my bedroom—along with Christie and Elin. I let them in and they changed me out of Sue's over-the-top, show-off dress and into a sleek, black number wrapped in shimmering tulle.

Taking off the dress meant I also had to give up the tiara, choker, and diamond waterfall earrings. My time as a queen was over, but thankfully, Elin was there to restyle my hair into a classy bun with pearl clips to match my new pearl earrings and necklace. I still looked like a queen getting ready to grace my subjects, and for the first time since the accident, I felt a twinge of regret that Sue wasn't here for this.

She organized this whole thing because she knew it would be their last night as a family. I mean, of course it was, because she told the guys they had to be packed up and out the door ten minutes after the party ended. Which kind of made the idea of a big, multimillion-dollar anniversary a bit psychotic, but for once, I don't think it was about any of that. Sue must've just wanted one more night of being loved and adored before she *tore* her world apart, and weird as that was... it was also desperately sad.

Sue was sad, I thought, gazing at her and me in the mirror. *Looking back, she was the saddest, loneliest person I've ever known.*

"Mrs. Kim?" Christie tapped my shoulder. "Are you alright?"

I tried for a smile. "I'm fine. Just spacing out. All that fancy wine is going right to my head."

"Then, some food in your belly is exactly what you need, and lucky us, it's time for cake," she cried, bouncing in her heels. "I know you wanted to wait until you cut into the cake to find out what it is, but I can't wait another moment! It's a crème brûlée cake with caramel custard and a rum-soaked graham cracker crust. Your whole life will change after the first bite!"

She expected enthusiasm, so I gave it to her—letting out a little squeal and dance that she returned tenfold.

I had to laugh. Some people search their whole lives, and other people discover their calling straight away. Christie Baudelaire was the latter. She was meant to be an event planner. Life was a nonstop fun-filled celebration for her, and to be a part of bringing that fun and joy to others was what she lived for.

"Let's go eat this cake," I cried.

"Yay!" Grabbing my hand, Christie ran off with me.

She threw open the door, letting Sanders in and leaving him, Davis, and Elin to handle returning the dress.

"Wait." I pulled up short. "I should check on my mother while I'm up here. Her nurse only agreed to a night off by making us promise we'd take over the three-hour checks. Might as well do the first one now."

"Absolutely," she chirped, spinning us both around the other way. "I'll come with you."

Together we clomped down the hall, then rounded the corner to Omma's room.

I frowned. "Her light's on. Did we forget to turn it off when I said goodnight?"

"No," she replied. "I remember Mr. Agassi turned off the light on his way out the door."

"She must've woken up." I picked up the pace, reaching for the doorknob. "I hope she hasn't been up all this time, calling for someone and none of us—" I pushed inside.

Red.

Red everywhere. On the carpets. On the wall.

Is it paint? Who splashed paint everywhere? Omma will be so mad when she— Sense crowded in, smothering that mindless, chattering voice.

Not paint. Blood.

I stepped inside the room, my heels squiging on the blood-soaked carpet—and met my mother's wide, unseeing eyes.

I was wrong about Christie only living to share in others' joy. When she saw my mother's body. She screamed just as loud as me.

Chapter Fourteen

"... no one leaves..."

"...separate rooms..."

Voices were going in and out. Sounds were going in and out. My breaths were going in, but barely out.

I couldn't move. I couldn't breathe. I couldn't think. But I could see... her face... the blood... clear as day... over and over again.

"...turn over all phones, cameras, and recording devices—"

"Come now, man," Captain Roberts gruffed—popping the cone of silence that descended on me. "There are very important and influential people here. Celebrities! None of them walked up here and murdered some old woman in her bed!"

"Respectfully, sir, we cannot rule anyone out at this point. There is enough food and beds in this mansion that no one can claim cruel or unlawful treatment. On the contrary, I'm sure all of those important and influential celebrities would rather spend the night in a mansion than in our holding cells."

"Holding cells?" he sputtered. Captain Roberts was a stout, hefty man with red cheeks getting dangerously redder, and a weak quivering jaw that was shaking like Jell-O right then. "Look here, Davis, there won't be any talk of holding cells. I will not allow LPD to be the top news story—blasting the brutish, heavy-handed cops who rounded innocent people up and treated them like cattle without cause. I—"

"Sir," Davis cut in, tone calm. "May I request that you let me lead this investigation from this point on? You've had more than a little to drink... sir."

I don't know if it was what he said, the way he said it, or the obvious delay in address, but Roberts went from red to puce so fast, it could've been a health event.

But Davis didn't waver in his stiff-backed resolve. He had taken control of the scene from the minute our screams brought him running. In an instant, he was on the radio alerting the other officers, locking down the party, and tackling me when I tried to throw myself on my mother.

He dragged me bodily from the room, and no doubt would've tried to get me farther than one foot outside the door, but he had to drop me and protect his face because I was doing too good a job clawing it to ribbons.

The man probably would've booked me for assault if he didn't have other things on his mind.

"This is horrible," Christie cried. Crying into my hair, she crushed me to her chest. "This is so horrible. How could this happen? How!"

"You are under my command," Roberts roared. "You will do what I say."

"Without question, sir." Bleeding from a dozen cuts on his face and a head shorter than his captain, and somehow Davis still looked like the bigger man. "The media will inevitably pick up this story, and my fears are yours, sir. What will they say of the Lantana PD if they discover we compromised the investigation into the murder of a prominent and influential member of our community, because we kowtowed to a bunch of arrogant and entitled cityfolk?

"You are absolutely right, sir, that we cannot allow that to happen. The reputation of our community and those of us who serve it faithfully are at stake. The last thing you will allow, sir, is for the LPD to be called anything less than fair, diligent, and by the book."

"That— That—" Roberts blinked, wobbling on his feet. Davis was right, the man was completely skunked. "That's correct, Davis, well said. The men and women who serve me are complete professionals. I won't have some grubby journalist claim we let the rich play by a different set of rules."

Clearing his throat, he backed away—looking around at all the officers, event planners, and grieving daughters like he didn't know what he was doing there. "Davis, you have this in hand. Secure the crime scene until the detectives arrive."

"Yes, sir."

When he finally left, Davis turned to the five officers awaiting his instructions. "Secure the scene— No, secure the entire wing. No one except law enforcement comes anywhere near this area," he said. "Begin confiscating all the phones, cameras, and recording devices.

"Separate the main suspects from the rest, and keep watch over them at all times. We had officers on all floors and at every staircase, so it shouldn't be a problem identifying every individual who left the party and came upstairs for whatever reason they gave. But your focus is to be on the staff..." Davis shifted, his gaze penetrating through to my soul. "And the homeowners.

"It is not a coincidence that two elderly women were brutally stabbed and killed only two weeks apart on the same property. Everyone," he gritted, "and I mean everyone who was in the proximity of those events will speak to us now.

"This never should've happened." Davis's voice shook. "Twice this killer has struck while surrounded by people, but this time they did it in a manor full of cops—taunting us for being so stupid, arrogant, and slow that we let this happen not once, but twice. The fact is that we have failed the people of this community, and we started with Eleanor Prado. But on my badge, we will not fail Madame Kim as well."

"Yes, sir," the officers belted, even though I was fairly sure they were all ranked at the same level as him.

They snapped to it—following his orders of securing the scene, herding the partygoers, and separating the most likely suspects from the least.

Davis approached me.

"Mrs. Kim," he began, not unkindly. "I am deeply sorry for your loss, and I'm not just parroting what I've been told to say. No one should ever have to see their mother that way. No one should lose their mother in such a terrible way. But—"

"But?" Christie cried, holding me tighter. I was a silent, dead-eyed doll in her hands. All I could do was stare at my feet, and the drops of blood on the carpet between my shoes. "What but?"

"But," Davis pressed. "While it is undeniable that you didn't kill your mother while I was at your side all night, that fact does not rule you out as a suspect."

"What on earth are you talking about!" Christie shrieked, summoning all the rage I should be feeling. "How could you even think such a monstrous thing! Did you see—did you see—what was done to—" Christie gagged, nearly throwing up for the second time. "You s-saw what that beast did to that poor, helpless woman. No *sane* person had any part of that!"

"I did see what was done to Madame Kim." Davis was the picture of calm. "And *that* was rage, Ms. Baudelaire. No one stabs a bedridden woman that many times for fun. Only someone who hated Madame Kim could do that, and"—that same look pinned me to the spot—"Madame Kim had twenty-eight years to fill Mrs. Kim with resentment—in the ways only a mother can."

"Heaven help me," Christie breathed. "What a foul way to see the world. You're talking about a mother and her child, Officer. Do you even hear yourself!"

"I do hear myself." Davis knelt, looking me in the eyes. "And now I need you to hear me, Mrs. Kim. Take a minute, find your strength, and then get up. You have a few hours—possibly even until the morning—before the detectives arrive. Take that time to rest, eat, call a lawyer—I don't care. But when they come, you'd better be ready to answer all of our questions, because this time, I'm not leaving until I catch the miserable fucker that did this."

***

I don't know what it was. If I actually found my strength, or if hearing the straitlaced Davis cursing did it, but somehow, I got off the floor and let Christie lead me down to the kitchen for some water, and a too-big slice of crème brûlée cake.

She said that sugar would help with the shock, but I don't think I was in shock. What's shock supposed to feel like? How did anyone know for sure if they were experiencing it?

Christie was sure I was though, because I saw the third most horrific thing I'd ever seen in my life... but I hadn't shed one tear.

"It's okay, Mrs. Kim, don't feel any shame over letting it out." She pushed a cup of sweet chamomile tea at me in between squeezing the stuffing out of me. "You cry if you need to cry. I'm right here. I won't leave you for a second."

That was a really nice thing for her to say. Despite knowing me for only a couple weeks, she was being so supportive—making space for me and my trauma, even though I was no more than another client.

Christie was good people, but she didn't have to go through the trouble.

No tears were coming.

I touched my cheeks, staring uncomprehendingly at my dry fingertips. *I cried when Sue died accidentally, and I hated that bitch with every fiber of my soul. Why could I cry for her, but I can't cry for my own mother after she's brutally murdered?*

No answer was forthcoming.

"Where are Micah, Rhodes, and Alex?" I asked the countertop.

"Your husbands have been invited to retire to their rooms for the night. We didn't want you four to— What I mean is, there's nothing for you or them to do at this stage except to let us do our jobs while we wait for the detectives to arrive," she said. "You too should get some rest, Mrs. Kim."

I heard the real end of her sentence loud and clear. *We didn't want you four to compare your matricide notes and get your stories straight.*

"What about my guests?" I heard myself say. "Courtney? My in-laws? I have to make sure they're okay and—"

"*We* will take care of everything, Mrs. Kim. No one is so heartless that they'd ask anything of you right now. Just get some sleep." She held out her hand. "Let me take you up."

I didn't know what else to do, so I gave in—allowing her to take me to the bedroom currently being stripped of its laptop, computer, and even its television. Seeing as smart TVs got the capability to connect to the internet years ago, I understood the precaution. Apparently they couldn't chance me contacting whoever I was "working with."

"Your phone too, ma'am."

Saying nothing, I crossed to the nightstand, stuck my hand inside, and pulled out Sue's phone without hesitation. It disappeared into an evidence bag and was almost out the door when I said—

"Of course, I'm certain you won't attempt to access my phone, laptop, or even my television without a warrant." My tone was flat. Dead. "Because, just so this is clear, you do not have my permission to do otherwise."

Two of the officers paused at the threshold—one of them the woman who'd been assigned to me by Davis.

"I see," she said.

"And," I went on, "of course you must secure the crime scene and make sure the suspect doesn't slip away, but you do not have my permission to conduct a search of any room in this manor that isn't my mother's."

"How unfortunate, Mrs. Kim." Her tone matched mine. "We assumed you'd want to do everything to help us find your mother's killer. Were we mistaken?"

"You were if you thought emotional manipulation would work on me." I tugged on my hair, undoing the stupid bun, and taking out the clips and earrings. "I won't let you treat me or my family like suspects. Davis suspects the same person who—who k-killed"—my voice broke—"my mother, also killed Mrs. Prado. And he ruled me and my husbands out as suspects in that crime weeks ago, so the last thing I'm going to let you do is waste time going after us while the real killer slips out the front door—if he hasn't already.

"Because your captain is right. Right now, the manor is full of wealthy, entitled townies and cityfolk who've seen enough crime shows to know that they *don't* have to speak to you, and they *don't* have to stay here longer than they want to.

"So every fucking second you spend fiddling with the phone of the woman who was downstairs with a cop shadow all night, is an unforgivable insult to my mother—who deserves competent officers who don't need it explained that a person can't be in two places at once."

She stiffened, eyes flashing.

"You better spend every fucking second of every fucking minute from now until the detectives arrive comparing notes with each other and identifying who came upstairs and into the east wing when they had no reason to be there, and then you turn the heat up on those fuckers until they fry!" I burst out, finally unleashing an emotion—but it wasn't sorrow. "And if you don't have that list ready and in my hands by sunup, I promise you— I swear on my life! That I will sue you and your whole department for negligence!"

"Mrs. Kim—"

"How dare you!" I screamed, throat shredding. "How dare you question my desire to see that filthy fucking psychopath in the electric chair!"

"Mrs. Kim, I—"

"You don't need my help to find him. You don't want it!" I roared. "Because if I go searching for that bastard, I won't stop until I stab him so many times in the fucking face HIS EYEBALLS BURST!"

She gaped at me—truly stunned like she didn't know if the five-foot-one, hundred-and-ten-pound woman was about to attack.

Chest heaving, I felt that tight, writhing, festering, flaming pit that appeared after finding my mother, harden into something heavier, sharper—deadlier.

"So, trust me," I rasped—my sore throat lacing the words sinister. "I want you to be the ones to find him. *He* wants you to be the ones to find him. Because if I get to him first... I'll be the one going to prison for murder."

Both officers stared at me, their poker faces blown. Her partner opened his mouth like he was going to say something. And then she opened her mouth.

Thinking better of it, their lips resealed, and they left.

***

Hours later, we were all back in the ballroom—spread out among the tables and chairs as three individuals stepped up onto the platform.

The full table was mine. Rhodes, Micah, Alex, and Courtney huddled around me—all of them touching at least one body part. My hand, shoulders, my thighs. All of them trying to will comfort into my bones.

But none of it touched the pit.

A woman in silk gray pants and a matching gray vest broke from the pack and stepped forward on the platform. "Hello, everyone, I am Detective Balogun," she began. "I won't say good morning, because it's far from that. I'm deeply sorry for what has happened here, and I extend my sincerest sympathies to Madame Kim's family." She nodded in my direction. "I know you're all tired and scared. You want to go home, and for those of you who are home, you want to know who came into it and violated it in the worst way.

"I swear to you that I, and my partner, Detective Kaplan, will do everything in our power to achieve those ends, but we'll need your help," she said.

"My officers have been very thorough in pooling their recollections for the creation of this list."

Micah brushed his hand across my thigh and slipped under my palm, lacing his fingers through mine.

Even with everything happening, my body responded to his touch—leaving a tide of goose bumps in his hand's wake. Surrounded by him, Alex, Rhodes, and my best friend, the pit didn't shrink, but it didn't grow either.

"This list," Balogun continued, "is you. With the exception of Mrs. Soo Min Kim, you are the people who left the party and went upstairs for reasons unknown before the time of death. And we will be speaking to you all now—one at a time—to discover why."

"No, you won't," a voice spoke up, turning all eyes to Pixie. She was sandwiched between Button Nose and Chic Ghost like she had been all night. At the table next to her was Mr. Layton—Lily's teacher. "This is an outrage. I certainly didn't drive all this way to murder a woman I've never even met. I demand you release us," she said, nodding to her friends. "Now."

"Happily," Balogun said smoothly. "As soon as we ascertain why you left the designated party area to wander around the home of a woman you've never even met."

"I'm not answering any questions without my lawyer present," she snapped.

"As is your right, Mrs. de la Fountaine." She nodded to Davis, who nodded to an officer posted at the ballroom door, who stuck her head out the door to speak to someone. "We are returning all phones and devices at this time, so feel free to call said lawyer now, and then get comfortable. I hear the three-hour-drive becomes four hours thanks to the New York morning rush hour."

Mrs. de la Fountaine bristled, clearly hearing the edge that snuck into Balogun's tone.

"Are you also electing to wait until your lawyer arrives, Mrs. Kim?"

"What?" My head snapped up. "Me? But you just said—"

"You may not be on the list," she sliced in, "but you did know the victim best. We need to interview you." She gestured to the door. "After you."

"Hold on a minute," Rhodes cried, getting to his feet. "Anything you need to know about our mother-in-law, we can tell you. The last thing we're going to let you do is interrogate our wife less than twelve hours after she lost her mother. Fuck's sake, you can see for yourself that she's in shock."

What was written on my face that they all could see but I couldn't?

"Have some compassion," Micah barked.

Balogun didn't twitch. "I do have compassion… for Madame Ha-eun Kim." She pointed again. "After you, Mrs. Kim."

"She—!"

"It's okay," I croaked, stopping Courtney with a hand on her knee. "I'll talk to them. I won't be the reason the investigation is held up."

"Okay, if you're sure." Micah helped me up, and then he just held me. Pressing his forehead to mine, he dropped a light kiss on my nose. "I'm so sorry, baby, but we're here for you. We're not going anywhere—you're not going anywhere—until we find the bastard who did this."

A deal made what seemed like years ago, floated through my mind. "Just until we find him?" fell from my lips unbidden.

Micah rocked slightly back, brows rising. He tossed a glance at Rhodes and Alex, who looked back at him with the same surprise.

The surprise fell away from Rhodes's eyes, and something else took hold. "And after."

"And after," Micah agreed.

"And…" Alex met my eyes. "After. If that's what you want."

"I—"

"Mrs. Kim?" Davis appeared at my side. "With me, if you please."

I certainly didn't feel like making any love confessions in front of the man who all but accused me of hiring a hitman to kill my mother, so I let him lead me away—leaving my reply unsaid.

That's how I found myself in the front room, sitting on the couch as the detectives pulled over two armchairs and placed them directly before me.

The proximity allowed me to get a proper look at the two of them, and they were opposites in almost every way.

Balogun was tall, slim, bald, and severe from the way she dressed to her angular features and sharp cheekbones. She was also young. She didn't appear to be much older than me, but she was already a homicide detective with the LPD.

Whereas her partner, Kaplan, was short, thick, sported a full head of silver hair, and had round red cheeks to go with the almost jolly smile he gave me when he sat down.

A click behind me turned my head.

Davis stepped into the room, shut the door, and leaned against the wood.

"Morning, Mrs. Kim," Balogun said. "Before we begin, we'd like to warn you that we are recording this interview." She slipped the recorder out of her pocket and tapped it on before I got a chance to object.

"Go ahead. It's fine with me." It really was fine with me. My own phone was on and recording since Davis knocked on my door an hour before and told me to go downstairs.

"We're sorry for your loss, Mrs. Kim," Kaplan spoke up. "We know this is difficult, and if you need a minute, please tell us."

"I will," I replied. "But I can do this. I want to help."

"Good," Balogun said. She whipped out a notepad and pen. "With that said, let's cut straight to the heart of the matter. There was a lot of rage poured into the attack that killed your mother. Do you know anyone who held such a grudge against her? Did Madame Kim have any enemies?"

I was shaking my head before she finished. "My mother was a hard woman. Strict, judgmental, humorless. But she also minded her own business. She didn't work, so when she wasn't hanging out with the Ajumma Gossip Network, she was home—gardening, reading, doing jigsaw puzzles, and keeping herself to herself. She—"

"I'm sorry, excuse me." Balogun paused in her notetaking. "Ajuman gossip network? Is that what you said? What is that exactly?"

I tossed my head. "Oh, sorry. Of course you don't know what that is. Ajumma means like middle-aged woman, or married woman, or both in Korean," I confessed. "Part of the reason my parents chose Lantana is because there's a thriving Korean American community here. Whenever Mrs. Park, Mrs. Choi, and Mrs. Jeong came over for tea, the four would sit... here," I whispered, "and gossip about everyone in town. That's why I called them that."

Balogun wrote something down. "Had your mother been in contact with her friends recently?"

I shook my head. "Omma stopped seeing all of her friends and pretty much shut the world out when she started losing her hair," I said bluntly. I wasn't making that up. Mrs. Park told me as much when I ran into her and her grandson in town that morning. "My mother was a proud woman. She didn't want anyone seeing her like that."

"Understandable, but are you sure that was the only reason?" she asked. "There could've been a falling out. Maybe the real reason she stopped seeing her friends is because—"

"—because she committed a crime against them so terrible, they waited almost a year after she stopped inviting them over to sneak into her house and stab her in the face?" I sliced off. "And apparently getting this revenge was suddenly so urgent, they had to do it while the manor was full of cops and my mother was already on her deathbed? Because waiting for nature to take its course is such a poor option compared to life in prison."

My gaze hardened. "Detective, I invited all of my mother's friends to the party, but *you and your officers* didn't invite them to stay this morning—meaning, none of them went upstairs around the time my mother was killed, and therefore, aren't suspects. So why don't we both stop wasting each other's time and you just ask me what you want to ask me."

Kaplan leaned back in the armchair, blown back by that response.

But Balogun didn't. A smile stretched her lips. "I'm sorry if you think I'm wasting your time, Mrs. Kim, but you certainly aren't wasting mine. You can tell a lot—almost everything—about a person by the way their own child describes them. And you describe her as hard, judgmental, gossipy, strict"—my own words shot like bullets from her lips—"humorless, exclusionary, distrusting—"

"I didn't say she was exclus—"

"You said she moved here because there were people that looked like her here," Balogun spoke over me. "And it was only those people she befriended and invited into her home, correct?"

"I— Yes, but that doesn't mean she was distrusting—"

"Doesn't it?" Balogun cocked her head. "These are the same friends she tossed aside when she needed them the most because she didn't trust them not to judge her for something as insignificant as a hairless head?" She gestured to her own. "You're her daughter, but you don't have a single kind word to say about her."

"I didn't—"

"No, that wasn't a question," Balogun said, flapping a hand at me. "There wasn't much love lost between you and your mother, Mrs. Kim, and your words told me so. But there was something else your words told me—that you're either innocent, or a sociopath."

"What?" I cried, shooting up. "What the hell are you talking about?"

"When I brought up your mother's friends and suggested they may have a motive, you immediately shut me down," she said. "In my experience, a guilty person *never* misses a chance to throw suspicion on someone else. *Anyone* else. They don't care who as long as we're not looking at them.

"But you didn't take that chance. Either because you don't have a guilty conscience, or because you have no conscience at all, and you really don't care if we suspect you. You don't care about anything. You just wanted your mother dead."

I stilled, thinking through my reply carefully. Balogun was smart—one conversation and I couldn't deny that. She was also tricky, laying traps for me that I couldn't see coming. I wasn't guilty of my mother's murder, but I was guilty of something.

And the last thing I needed was for her to follow that trail and discover what happened to the real Soo Min Kim.

"Well, then, you know the answer to that question too," I finally said. "You can't say I'm an emotionless sociopath today, but a raging psychopath last night. Whoever killed my mother was in a rage, and I felt a lot of things toward Omma, but rage wasn't one of them. The opposite, actually.

"I don't know what it was. Maybe it was the morphine. Maybe it's because she felt time running out, but the last few weeks, my mother's been like another person," I confessed. "Laughing, joking, being kind to me—even in her lucid moments. The last thing she said to me was... that I was an angel." I swallowed hard. "I've waited a long time for my mother to look at me as anything other than a disappointment. Now that it's finally happened, why would I make it go away?"

A heavy, deep silence spread through the room.

"It's not that we believe you would," Kaplan put in. "But someone killed your mother and we need to know why. You and she may have made your peace in her final days... but someone else didn't. Who?"

"I can't tell you who, Detective. I don't know anyone so impatient to see my mother dead that they couldn't just... wait."

There was a pause as that sunk in.

"It's true," Balogun said, scribbling something in her notepad. "There isn't much sense in murdering a woman on hospice. But there also wasn't much sense in killing an innocent house manager and chef on her first day back to work, and yet, two women were killed on this very property only two weeks apart.

"Mrs. Prado worked for your family for twenty-five years," she continued. "Until, according to her daughter, she was fired three years ago, and then suddenly—out of the blue—you called and offered her a substantial raise to come back."

Was it a detective thing to make every little action sound suspect?

"Why is that?" she breezed. "Why was Mrs. Prado suddenly fit to work for you today when she wasn't fit for the job three years ago?"

"It had nothing to do with fitness. Three years ago, I was an ass," I dropped. "I took over supervising the household staff from Omma, but for reasons unknown, I convinced myself that staff meant slave. I treated them horribly and Mrs. Prado—who knew me since diapers—wouldn't take any of my shit.

"We butted heads too many times, and instead of admitting I was the problem, I fired her. Big mistake on my part because all the other staff quickly quit without Mrs. Prado there to be a buffer between me and them.

"It took me awhile, but I'm a different person now. I see now what a great, big, flaming asshole I've been to too many people in my life," I said, popping Kaplan's brows up. "But I don't want to be that way anymore. I reached out to Mrs. Prado and offered her a raise because I was wrong. Because she deserved an apology. Because she deserved the raise. And because she is—she was the best at her job. I was never going to ask anyone else."

Balogun looked down at her notepad, then flicked up—sharing a look with her partner.

"What?" I asked.

"Nothing, it's just..." Balogun turned that shrewd look on me. "Your description of the events that led to Mrs. Prado's termination matched her daughter's description to a tee. You don't hesitate to take full responsibility for the matter, and we don't see that often. Most people aren't as comfortable with accountability as you seem to be, Mrs. Kim."

"Thank you."

She bared her teeth at me in a semblance of a smile. "I didn't say that was a compliment."

I bared mine right back. "But I'm sure it was."

She chuckled. "You caught me. It was."

"Does this manor have any secret passageways?"

My smile wiped away. Head snapping around, I fixed on Davis—who was standing still and eyes shadowed against the door. "Excuse me?"

"Does this manor have any secret passageways, rooms, or staircases?" he repeated slowly.

I stared at him. "Why would you ask that?"

"To get straight to the point," he said, peeling himself off the door, "as you requested, Mrs. Kim. The facts are these: last night at 9:37 p.m. the killer slipped into your mother's room and stabbed her with what preliminary evidence says is a long, serrated blade. After a thorough search, that blade was not found in your mother's room."

My mind spun. *Not found in her room?* "But that means—"

"The killer took it with them," he finished.

I tossed my head, temples throbbing. "But you said 9:37? How could you know—?"

"Your mother's bedside table clock was knocked over in the... in the frenzy of the attack. The clock broke and the hands stopped at that exact time, allowing us to be precise. But that's not all the preliminary investigation told us," he continued. "There was blood absolutely everywhere in that room except for one spot—where the killer stood.

"You threw a white party, Mrs. Kim," he said, throwing my shoulders up at how fast he whipped the conversation back to me. "Everyone, including the party staff, was wearing all white. There is absolutely no hiding bloodstains on an all-white canvas. Even a few drops would've been noticed. But this wasn't a few drops.

"The killer would've had to leave the bedroom drenched in blood and holding a bloody knife, but even though ten people went upstairs and walked past my fellow officers last night, none of them came back in such a state.

"Which brings me to my original question," he said, voice more serious than I'd ever heard it. "Are there any secret ways in and throughout this manor? Because either one of those ten people planned the murder far enough in advance to have an identical white outfit stashed nearby along with a hiding spot for the weapon—allowing them to bypass the officer without raising suspicion.

"Or the murderer didn't need to worry about any of that—because they used a handy network of back staircases and hidden halls to move around freely and escape unseen." His gaze was like a lance through the chest. "Which is it, Mrs. Kim?"

My breaths came in rough, short pants. Memories flashed through my mind of the hallway with the flickering light bulb. The red carpet. The white gloved hand squeezing my fingers so tight the tips turned blue.

I saw it all, opened my mouth, and lied. "No," I replied—my voice reflecting a calm I didn't feel. "There are no secret rooms, stairs, or hallways in the manor."

"Are you certain?"

"Yes," I lied again. "I've lived here my whole life. Wandered in every room. Messed with all the things adults tell little kids not to touch. If there was some secret passage, I'd have found it by now."

"Because they were common for the time period this manor was built," he pressed. "During Prohibition, many wealthy people had secret rooms and passages built to hide the alcohol bootleggers were pirating up and down this coast. If this house was one of them, there'd be no reason to believe the estate agent would've known about it when they sold it to your parents. Therefore—"

"—that's a dead end," I broke in. "Because if the estate agent didn't know, then my parents couldn't know, and therefore they couldn't share with me what they didn't know. If we were all clueless about these hidden moonshine boltholes, the killer wouldn't know about them either."

His expression didn't change. "Not necessarily."

"Excuse me?"

"Well, it's as you said," he drawled, "when someone lives in a place for a long time, they... stumble over things."

It took me a second, but then his accusation smacked me over the head. My jaw snapped together. "No one who lives in this house murdered my mother."

"No?" Balogun's voice drew my attention back to her. "As Officer Davis clearly explained, we're operating under the theory that the killer either had an identical change of clothes nearby, or there was a nineteenth exit that allowed them to bypass the other eighteen guarded ones. How could someone who entered this house for the first time last night have such a plan in place? How could someone without regular access to this manor find a hidden passage that you didn't?" That strange, mirthless smile stretched her lips. "There's a reason we focus our attention on those closest to the victim. It's because it's rarely ever anyone else."

I looked from her, to Davis, to Kaplan, then back to Balogun. Any stereotype of schlubby detectives and incompetent officers blew out of my head. They clearly knew what they were doing, but I wouldn't open that door—literally. Only four people knew about the secret passages in Kim Manor—and three of them were dead.

This line of thought was a dead end, and the last thing Davis was going to do was drag me down it.

"I'm not sure that tracks," I heard myself say. "I mean, I'm not sure it's right that a first-time guest couldn't have stashed a change of clothes. Actually, the more I think about it, you're dead wrong."

A flicker of surprise flashed across her face. "Why do you say that?"

"Because I had guests coming in from all over—some of them from hours away. That's why I told everyone they were welcome to spend the night if they decided they didn't want to make the long drive back after the party," I said. "So anyone planning just that would've brought an overnight bag, and if in that bag they had an identical white suit or dress, why the hell would I know about it? I didn't have anyone searched on arrival.

"Also," I said in a louder voice when Balogun opened her mouth to interrupt me. "The officers arrived when the dress arrived, but none of them took up their posts until the party started. That left hours where my early guests were free to roam the manor—scoping out a room with a thick layer of dust that proved it wasn't in use because the person who was supposed to change that fact was murdered—"

Her brow twitched at the connection.

"If anyone asked them what they were doing in the room, they'd just say they were sleeping over. And, if for some reason, someone checked their bag and saw the identical outfit, they could claim they brought a backup just in case they spilled something on the main one," I said to their slightly slack-jawed expressions. "In fact, most of our guests likely did exactly everything I just said for innocent reasons—not murderous ones.

"So no," I said clearly, "you haven't narrowed your suspect pool down to my family. Not even close. And the fact that you think you have and that you walked me in here believing you were going to pull a gotcha, has me very concerned. I'm a twenty-eight-year-old former influencer and I blew holes through your best theory in two minutes. What does that say about your ability to find my mother's killer, or Mrs. Prado's?"

Balogun and Kaplan stiffened—their smirks and friendly smiles nowhere to be seen.

"If you two aren't the best detectives for the job, I need you to leave and bring him the ones who are."

Balogun roared up. "Mrs. Kim—!"

"And you," I snapped, whirling on Davis. "I take back what I said last night. If you really believe the bloody clothes and knife are stashed somewhere in the manor, you have my permission to search everywhere—search everyone! You don't need a warrant."

"Oh, I—" He made to move, then stopped. "Are you sure?"

"Of course, I'm sure. You can only hold my guests for twenty-four hours, so don't waste any more time. Find the bastard!" The shout made him jerk and twitch for his gun. "Because if you don't, I will!"

Davis didn't ask me again. Shooting out the door, I heard him address the other officers. "I want a full search of this manor starting with the rooms closest to Madame Kim's rooms and spreading out. Find the owner of every bag or case you find. Ask their permission before searching them, and bring the names of everyone who refuses."

I got to my feet. "I assume we're done here?"

"Yes, Mrs. Kim." A distinct and frigid chill blasted from Balogun's side of the room. "We're done."

I left the room, covertly shutting off my phone's recorder as I did, and nearly ran into Alex.

He threw his arms up to catch me. "Whoa, you okay?"

"I'm uh—" I glanced at the people who basically accused me of being the vicious, unhinged psychopath that wanted my mother dead. "I'm as okay as I can be right now."

"Shit—of course, you're not okay." He scrubbed his face, aging ten years before my eyes. "I'm so sorry, Sue, I just... I'm just sorry. I can't believe this happened."

I nodded, throat too tight to speak. Even then, the tears wouldn't come.

"I know this isn't much, but do you maybe want to come with me to pick up Lily?" Alex had changed out of his formfitting white suit into a pair of black slacks and a blue tee. Simple on a regular man, but on him, he was runway-ready.

It should be a sin for someone to be this brightly gorgeous on a dark and hellish morning.

"My aunt leaves on her cruise early tomorrow morning, so she can't keep her for another night." He sighed. "Even though I wish we could give Lily one more day before she walks into this."

By this, he meant the murder suspects in the ballroom, the irate rich snobs trapped upstairs, and cops and crime scene techs crawling over every inch of the manor.

"Are you sure it's okay?" I asked. "Don't you have to wait to be interviewed?"

He shook his head. "I've already been interviewed. It was quick. Apparently it means something that I didn't go upstairs until after nine forty. They just wanted to know if I saw or heard anything strange."

I glanced where he was looking, and it was then I noticed the two officers cross the front hall, escorting Courtney into the room where Lily usually did her piano lesson. Something flickered at the edge of my vision, drawing my eyes up.

The medical examiner's team hit the stairs. Collapsing the gurney, they readied to carry my mother down.

"Yes," I said, spinning around and walking straight out the door. "Let's go."

Alexander was right behind me. We were almost to the car when the gates rumbled open, letting in Reynard.

"What's this?" he called, rolling down the window. "Why is the medical examiner's van here? Did something happen?"

Alex turned to me. A surprisingly light touch caressed my cheek—momentarily catching my breath. "Wait for me in the car. I'll tell him."

I didn't fight him. Crossing the lawn, I climbed into the blue Mercedes-Benz SUV waiting beside the crime-scene-taped fountain. Why were so many horrible things happening? Whether I was Soo Min or Sarang, why couldn't either version be happy?

I got in the car as Reynard climbed out of his carrying a tote bag. He swung it up and on his shoulder, giving me a chance to read *My Other Bag's Full of Drugs* written across the face with syringes and bandages all around it.

The joke almost made me laugh—almost.

The hard, sharp pit in my stomach that was my new companion, would not be letting anything resembling a laugh leave my lips for a long time.

"What! That's not true! That can't be true!" Reynard shouted, throwing himself away from Alex. "How could—! How could that happen!"

It looked like Alex said something in response, but Reynard was already running—taking off for the house.

That's when I looked away. I didn't want to see his reaction when he ran into the gurney. How could I face his grief when I couldn't face my own?

Thankfully, Alex returned quickly and we were soon rumbling down the dirt road—leaving the nightmare behind.

"Do you want to talk?" he asked softly.

I rested my head against the cool glass, eyes squeezing shut. "I don't know what to say. I don't know what to think. Someone walked into our home and murdered my sick and dying mother in her bed. How do I make sense of that, Alex? If you know, please, tell me."

"I wish I could, Sue, I truly do. None of this makes sense to me either. Any more than I can understand why someone would want to harm Mrs. Prado," he said. "After you left the ballroom, Courtney was telling us that there was another young woman who worked in town who was murdered. For fuck's sake, are we dealing with a serial killer or something?"

My head was shaking before he finished. "Including Omma, all the victims were different ages, races, and from different backgrounds. According to the absurd amount of crime shows and books I've consumed, serial killers don't work like that. Their victims almost always have something in common.

"No," I said directly, "they don't think Mrs. Prado or Omma were murdered by a serial killer, and they don't think their deaths were random either. They're looking at us, Alex."

"What!" he cried, jerking the wheel and almost crashing into a tree. "Us? Who us?"

"Everyone who lived with Omma. Both murders happened in or in front of our home. Both women were connected to us. So why would they look anywhere else?"

He goggled at me. I didn't actually know Alex for as long as he thought I did, but I was one hundred percent sure no one had ever seen that dumbfounded look on his face.

"But—but that's insane," he blared. "If we didn't want you to rehire Mrs. Prado, we just would've *said* so. There wasn't any need to murder the woman! And as for your mom, if we wanted her dead, all we had to do was wait a week!" Alex said that, then immediately winced. "Sorry. I didn't mean for that... to come out that way."

"No, it's okay." I turned away, facing the window. "I pretty much said the same thing to Balogun, Kaplan, and Davis. There's nothing about killing a woman who was already dying that makes sense."

"But the officers I spoke to didn't give any hint that they suspected me, Rhodes, Micah, or you."

"That's called a false sense of security, pretty boy. They lured you right into it."

A deep sigh gusted out of him. "If we really are their main suspects, that means we won't be able to shake the cops until they find the real killer—and seeing as they're apparently dumbasses—that'll be awhile. That'll make it harder to keep all this from Lily. My heart broke the first time I told her about the cancer, and that Omma wasn't going to be with us for long. Now we have to explain why a horde of cops are crawling all over the manor for the second time. No one should have to tell a six-year-old that someone they love was murdered."

I stilled. Not for his last sentence, but for his third. Alex said *we*. He said we would have to explain to Lily what happened to Omma. Had something really changed between us? Was he starting to trust me?

It may have seemed wrong for me to be thinking about my relationship with Alex right then, but how could I think of anything else?

My mother—the last of my family on this continent—was gone. The only one left who shared my name was Lily, and if my perpetually empty bank account got its way, I'd never get the IVF money I needed to change that.

Lily was the closest thing I had to a daughter, and of course, I couldn't be in her life if Alex, Rhodes, and Micah didn't want me in theirs.

Courtney was right—these four were my family, and for once, I wanted my family to hold me close... not push me away.

"What if you didn't tell her?" I blurted. "I mean, not right away. Not today. Everyone's been telling me about the Columbia alumni reunion. When is that?"

"It's the weekend after next. Why?"

"Go now," I said firmly. "Take Lily. Make it a daddy-daughter trip, and spoil the mess out of her. But get her away from all of this. We don't know who is doing these terrible things, but we do know they have no problem strolling onto our property and murdering people. Honestly, I'd feel a lot better if Lily were miles away from this maniac."

He groaned, brushing his hair back from those enigmatic eyes. The car rumbled off the dirt road onto smooth pavement, and turned left away from town. "Sue, I hear you, but she can't miss two weeks of school."

"My dude, it's first grade, not NASA training. I think she'll be okay."

He cracked a smile, tossing me an amused look. "Okay, fine, if you're really going to make me say it, then here it is—I'm not leaving *you* for two weeks. Christie and three different officers all threw up after seeing what was done to your mother. I don't know what you saw when you went in there, but I know it would've been traumatic even if she had drifted away peacefully in her sleep.

"But that's not what happened," he said gently. "I can only imagine what's replaying over and over in your head right now, and the last thing I'm going to do is party it up in the city when you need me more than ever."

I blinked at him. "Since when do you care about me needing you? You don't even like me."

"No, I love you," he shot back—temper leaking into his voice. "That's why I can't stay away from you even when you're being a pain in the ass. Can you just let me be here for you without making me grovel for the privilege? Huh?" he barked. "Is that too much to ask?"

I cracked the tiniest smile, then marveled that he made me do that. "No, Alex." I slid my hand across the cupholder, slipping mine under his. "That's not too much to ask. Thank you, baby," I whispered. "I really do need you now more than ever. It means so much to me that you're here."

He mumbled something, shifting away. It wasn't until I glanced at the rearview mirror that I saw why.

"Oh my goodness, Alex Montgomery! You're blushing!"

"No," he said too quickly. "No, I am not!"

"You cute little blushing blusher." I rolled down the windows. "Hey, everyone," I shouted into the street. "Look at the pretty boy blush!"

"Fucking hell," he burst out, red cheeks deepening as he jammed my window switch. "What are you trying to do, woman? Get us pulled over? That's it. I want the divorce."

"Sorry," I teased, smirk tugging at my lips. "It's too late."

He dropped his head on his hand, eyeing me sideways with the same heart-melting smirk. "Yeah, I guess you're right. It's too late."

Chapter Fifteen

There was no such thing as feeling better so soon after losing your mother, but hours later when Lily, Alex, and I drove down the same dirt road for home—it felt like the pit had shrunk just the tiniest bit.

"How are you doing, Lilybug? Do you remember what Mommy and Daddy told you?"

"Yes," she said, putting down her ice cream cone. We took her to Bonsai Beach to tell her in the simplest non-murdery terms that Omma was gone. She cried for a while but stopped by the time we reached the ice cream parlor.

She'd been asking us innocent questions about heaven ever since, and if Omma was happy there.

"The police ofcers are back," she cutely mispronounced. "But they're nice and there to protect us."

"That's right, sweet girl," I spoke up. "They might ask you some questions about Halmeoni, but me or your daddies will be with you the whole time."

"You promise, Mommy?" She poked her head through the gap, staring up at me with those big, purple eyes. "You'll be with me forever now?"

"Lily, I..." Why was she asking only me that? Was it because of Sue's neglect, or because she knew I wasn't her old mommy?

Fact was I never did ask Lily what she meant that day. First, because Alex got in the way, and then because I wimped out like a big fat chicken.

Confirming that Lily knew I wasn't Sue meant opening the door to what happened to the real Sue, and I could lie to Alex, Rhodes, and Micah. But I didn't want to lie to her.

"Yes," I murmured, feeling Alex's eyes on me. "I promise I'll be with you forever. No matter what happens, I'll always be there for you."

"Okay," she chirped, dropping back to finish her ice cream.

Alex was still eyeing me as he slowed before the gate, waiting for it to open.

"Sue," he began, "about what we said this morning about you staying. We should—"

I shot forward, dropping my ice cream all down my shirt and lap. "Wait, what are they doing! Stop!" Throwing open the door, I fell out of the car. "Stop, let her go!"

Balogun and Kaplan held open the main doors, clearing the way for the two officers hauling Courtney out in handcuffs. With a goggling, nosy crowd trailing behind them—filming everything.

"Stay back," Kaplan bellowed, dropping the jolly, laid-back act quick. "Do not interfere, Mrs. Kim."

"My foot's about to interfere with your ass, bitch!"

He blew back, brows disappearing into his hairline. Pretty sure no one had ever said that to him before.

"Get off of her!" I threw myself at the officers holding Courtney, and found myself being thrown right back.

My obstruction caught and twisted my arm around my back, putting me in a screaming hold. "Calm down, Mrs. Kim," Davis ordered. "Don't get yourself arrested right along with her."

"Why is she being arrested?" I demanded. "What the hell's going on?"

"She's under arrest for the murder of your mother," Kaplan said. "Ha-eun Kim."

I dismissed that as soon as he said it. "Bullshit."

"It's not bullshit. She had every reason to want your mother dead... because of you."

"Who?" I whipped around looking for someone else, but Kaplan was definitely looking at me. "Me?"

"Yes, you," Balogun put in. "Years ago, when you ran into your friend in Paris and then told your mother all about your fun little weekend girls' trip, your mother turned around and told Ms. Thorne's parents all about it. It was because of your mother that your friend was disinherited."

I rocked back, jaw hanging. "That's insane! I've never been to—" I sliced off the sentence, sense rushing in and holding back my tongue.

Of course I'd never been to Paris, but the real Soo Min had. I had the photos of her in front of the Eiffel Tower to prove it.

What does this mean? Did cruel fate intervene and make Sue cross paths with Courtney when she was living in Paris, but pretending to be away at col-

lege? Was it really because of my sister and mother that Courtney's parents hit the nuclear button and cut her off?

"N-no," I croaked, tossing my head. "I don't care what happened *eight* years ago. Courtney would never hurt anyone, let alone my own mother."

"Exactly," my best friend cried. "This is nonsense. You've got it all wrong!"

"Do we?" Balogun drawled. "Because my officers are certain that you went upstairs shortly before nine thirty and you didn't come back down for a full half an hour. And you were packing a hell of a motive on the walk up. You went from an only child set to inherit millions to a broke and struggling single mom living in a one-bedroom shoebox above a bakery."

"Hey!" Courtney lunged at her, almost tearing her restrained arms from her sockets. "Don't you dare talk about my life that way! I love my daughter, my home, and my business. Plus, I made up with my parents years ago. *I* told *them* that I didn't want their money. I just wanted us to be a family again for Taylor's sake. If anything, Mrs. Kim did me a favor!"

"But that's not true, is it, Ms. Thorne?"

Courtney and I whipped around at the new voice. Officer Andrews—a short, thin woman who looked like she was swimming in her uniform even though it was her size—pushed past a pale-faced Mr. Stevens, and a phone-high-and-recording-everything Chic Ghost. "Around the same time last year, I was called to your bakery by Madame Kim herself," she said. "You threw her out of your shop—screaming, yelling, and pelting her with cupcakes. Half the street heard you shout that she was a miserable bitch that took everything from you." Gasps sounded behind her. Our ghoulish, gossipy audience loved every minute of it. "You didn't think she did you a favor then. No," she stated, eyes hard. "You still held a grudge about the money."

"But I didn't," Courtney half screamed. "It wasn't the money I was upset about losing! I was mad because she—because she drove away—" Eyes filling, Courtney cut herself off, and looked at me.

The truth hit me like a brick to the head. *Because of me. Courtney freaked out on my mom because she drove her best friend away, leaving her with absolutely no one on her side when her life imploded.*

But she can't say that here. Because how can she explain that she was angry with Omma for driving me away when "I" have been living in Lantana for over five years.

"This doesn't make any sense," Courtney cried, straining in their grip. "I didn't do anything!"

"If you didn't do anything, why was this"—Balogun snapped her fingers and an evidence bag was placed in her hand—"found in your overnight bag?"

I went slack in Davis's grip.

For the benefit of me, Courtney, the officers, Mr. Stevens, and all the gawkers, she held up the bloodstained evidence bag, and the long, serrated blade nestled within. "The murder weapon," she announced—as if there could be any doubt.

"If that was in my bag, you put it there," Courtney screamed. "Because I sure as fuck didn't! I'm the one who gave you permission to search my things. Why would I have done that if there was a bloody fucking knife in it?"

"Ms. Thorne—"

"They're framing me." Courtney whipped around, beseeching the cameras. "Help me, please! They're trying to frame me for murder!"

"Ms. Thorne!" Balogun barked, snapping the knife down. "That is enough— We are doing no such thing!"

"It's true," I seized. "Something isn't right. *You* told me yourself, Officer Davis, that whoever attacked and killed my mother would've been covered in blood, but Courtney didn't have a drop on her last night."

"That's true," Mr. Stevens blurted, color returning to his face. "That's right, she didn't have a drop of blood on her. She didn't even have a hair out of place. She's perfect— I mean, she was perfect. Last night."

"See?" Courtney said, hope rising. "That proves it. I left my bag in an unlocked guest room all night. Anyone could've put—"

"If someone put a bloody knife in your bag," Davis sliced in, "wouldn't you have seen it this morning when you changed your clothes?"

Courtney stiffened, flicking down to her flowy, brown maxi dress. "Well, then, someone put it in after I changed," she snapped. "I was forced to leave my bag unattended when *you* ordered me into the ballroom this morning," she told Davis. "It was you, wasn't it. You put the knife in there."

"I beg your pardon?" Davis sputtered.

"Yeah, my friend told me all about you." Courtney's nose twisted like she smelled something foul. "About how you were creeping on her seconds after peeling her out of a totaled car. You were grilling her on why she didn't have a boyfriend, if she lived alone, and why she wasn't wearing that *hot little miniskirt* you found in her trunk!"

"What!?"

"Even now, you're still feeling her up even though she stopped resisting ten minutes ago!"

Davis flung me away like I burned, only for me to spin on him.

"Everything she said is true," I flung. "Plus, just last night Davis told me he hates working security. He told me right to my face that he only did it because he was bribed"—Davis's eyes bugged out of his head—"if that's not corrupt, what is?"

"That's not true. None of that's true," Davis bellowed.

Hey, I knew I was twisting everything to make Davis look bad, but I didn't call myself Courtney's ride or die for the fun of it. She was my best friend who had my back even after ten years of radio silence. I'd sure as fuck have hers.

Besides, if there was one thing I learned after four years of high school mock trial, it was that the truth didn't win in court.

The best argument did.

"Oh my goodness." "This doesn't sound right." "Police corruption." "All you care about is your case-closure rate. Can't be bothered to conduct a real investigation."

Murmurs and not-so-whispered whispers rolled over the crowd. If these people were my jury, they were definitely voting not guilty.

"Hey, let her go," someone shouted. "Anyone can stick a knife in an unattended bag."

"Yeah," Mr. Stevens put in, stepping forth. "All you've got for motive is a year-old argument and a few thrown cupcakes? That's a joke."

"Yeah!" More than a few people were shouting now. "Uncuff that poor woman and find some real evidence."

"Stop—! Stay back!" Balogun shouted. "Officers? Officers, control this crowd!"

The order was warranted. They were pushing and shoving onto the front steps. The gawkers were quickly becoming a mob.

"Do not move, or you're all under arrest," Balogun carried on. "We have means, a multimillion-dollar motive, and opportunity! This is a lawful arrest; you will not interfere!"

"Where is the bloody dress?" I demanded, and the crowd immediately took up the chant.

"Where is the dress?" "Show us the dress!"

Balogun and Kaplan stumbled down a step, pushed back by the line of officers that pushed through the crowd and were forming a barrier between them and us.

"Ms. Thorne must've stashed the bloody dress somewhere—"

A raucous chorus of boos thundered over Kaplan.

"Bullshit," I chimed in. "You're saying Courtney found a hiding place for the bloody dress that was apparently so good you can't find it, but then went full idiot and put the murder weapon in her bag? The bag she gave you permission to search! Why wouldn't she have stashed the knife in the same place she put the dress?"

"That's right," Mr. Stevens blared at Kaplan's reddening face. "Explain that."

"I don't have to explain it," Kaplan replied. "That's for a jury to determine—"

"BOOO!"

"What kind of shitty reply is that? This is someone's life you're talking about!"

"Lazy," someone else shouted. "You're just lazy!"

Right then, I took back absolutely every snooty thing I thought about Sue's high-society posse. These were the best damn people in the world.

"Hello, everyone." The Chic Ghost shot her phone up above the heads of the officers. "You're live with me in Lantana where a horrible miscarriage of justice is happening right before my eyes. Detectives Lazy One and Lazy Two, along with Officer Pervert over there—!"

"Stop that!" Balogun bellowed. All of a sudden, she wasn't interested in hamming it up for the cameras. "Put that away!"

"—have framed an innocent single mother and arrested her for murder! They don't even care that the real killer is getting away free!"

"That's enough!" Kaplan roared, charging her. "Put that way! All of you, put your phones away or we're arresting you for obstruction!"

Kaplan grabbed her wrist. It probably wasn't even that hard, but she screamed like he tried to tear it from her body.

"Get off me! Help, help! Police brutality!"

"Let go of my wife, you brute!" A two-hundred-and-fifty-pound rocket rammed into Kaplan.

The problem was, there was an entire officer standing between him and Kaplan, and said officer was linked arm in arm with her colleagues—trying to form a blockade between the angry crowd and the detectives. When she went down... they all did.

"Ahhh!" One—three—five—eight officers pitched off the top step, tumbling head over ass down the stairs... and taking Balogun, Kaplan, Davis, Courtney, and me down with them.

***

Rhodes pressed the ice pack to my forehead while Micah tucked the blankets in tighter around us.

The five of us were in the family room—a room that didn't see much use before I came, if the thick layers of dirt and dust were anything to go by. But Micah, Rhodes, Lily, and I had taken to spending the evenings in the family room, taking advantage of Lily's short screen-time window to watch a movie together.

That night was the first night Alex joined us... but we weren't watching a movie.

"—riot broke out this morning at the residence of former lifestyle and travel influencer, Soo Min Kim," said a buttoned-up, conventionally attractive reporter. "Tragically, Mrs. Kim's mother, Ha-eun Kim, was found murdered last night, but when authorities attempted to make an arrest, it did not go well."

Cue the looping, stitched-together videos of me ranting, raving, and accusing an innocent man of perversion and bribe-taking all to keep my best friend out of jail... which didn't work.

After they peeled themselves off the dirt, Balogun and Kaplan rushed a crying Courtney to their car and took off.

No one was hurt, so no one else was arrested, but I showed up at the station anyway, and made enemies out of a dozen more officers and detectives. To be fair, I called them pretty cruel names when every single one of them refused to let me see Courtney. After two hours of getting nowhere, Rhodes led me away promising he'd get Courtney the best lawyer he could—assuming her parents weren't already on it.

That's how I ended up under a pile of blankets on the couch with Lily snuggled against my side while I broke the new takeout-only-once-a-week rule with a carton of Hunan chicken.

"Mommy, what are crazy eyes?"

"Hmm?" I peeled away two layers of blankets to find her. "What do you mean?"

She wiggled a purple phone at me. "Nicky says you have crazy eyes on TV. Like a witch. What's crazy eyes?"

"Uhh, I'd like to ask a question first. Where did you get that phone?"

Her beaming smile melted my heart. "Daddy Micah bought it for me."

Three pairs of eyes latched on to Micah, who was chilling on the opposite couch with a glass of wine. "I had to," he said with a shrug. "Sue was coming for my favorite-parent spot with all the skipping school for cupcakes and cookies, so I bought her the phone to defend my position."

"Micah, stop saying stupid things in front of the child!" I snapped over his guffawing and Lily's muffled giggling. "And, Lily, tell Nicky your mom doesn't have crazy eyes. She has the prettiest eyes in the world, and he's a stinky doo-doo head."

"Okay!"

"No," Alex sounded off. He reached over, stuck his hand in, and plucked the phone from Lily's hands. "Lily, since you have a phone now"—he glared at a grinning Micah—"there are going to be rules. Rule one: don't text mean things to people. Rule two: block anyone who texts mean things to you." He tapped on the screen and did just that, deleting and blocking that Nicky kid. "Rule three: I hold on to this. You can have it during screen time, and only screen time."

"Ugghhh," Lily whined, poking her head up. "But, Daddy, that's not fair. I didn't text the mean things, Nicky did."

"I know, baby girl, and you're not in trouble. But having a phone is a big deal, so we can't do too much too soon."

Lily pouted, her little face crumpling. "But we're having screen time right now."

Alex halted. "That's... that's true," he got out. Sighing, he handed it over. "But no more texting. Look at cute videos of koalas, or something."

"Okay, Daddy!" Wriggling free of the blankets, she took off with the phone like she didn't want to give Alex a chance to change his mind. As soon as she closed the door—

"What the hell, Micah?" Alex burst out.

"Agreed." Rhodes's voice was hard. "What the hell."

"We agreed she wouldn't get a phone for another four years—at least," Alex plowed on. "What's the fucking point of us setting boundaries if you're going to trample them for every stupid, insecure thought that—"

"Get serious, guys!" Micah dropped his grin fast. "I didn't get her the phone because of some damn cupcakes. I only said that because she was in the room. I got it for her because two women have been *murdered* in our daughter's home in the last two weeks! I don't know what the fuck is going on, but I do know I feel a lot safer knowing that Lily can reach us and we can reach her in case of an emergency."

The wind blew out of Rhodes's and Alex's rants like a popped balloon.

Alex slumped in his armchair, scrubbing his face. "Fuck, I wasn't thinking of it like that but... you're right. Things have gotten insane around here, and it doesn't help that all the cops are gone," he said, flinging out his arm. "They declared their case closed and cleared out, so if he or she really wasn't caught—"

"*She* wasn't," I stressed. "Courtney did not kill my mother. I'm as sure of that as I'm sure Lily didn't commit the murder. Courtney just didn't do it. The end."

"If you're sure," he agreed, but he sounded hesitant. "But that means not only did they arrest the wrong person, the true killer is still running around free. Now is a good time for Lily to have a cellphone."

I could feel how much the four of us hated it, making Lily grow up faster because of the dangers in the world, but that's just where we were now. How could any one of us feel safe when evil entered our home and walked right up the stairs?

"But, sorry, Sue, I've got to ask." Rhodes eyed the television. I was running at armed cops for the eightieth time. "Why are you so sure this woman didn't kill Omma? You barely know her. Plus, if what they said was true, your mother wrecked her relationship with her parents and robbed her of millions. People tend to get pretty murderous over things like that."

I was shaking my head the whole way through. "I do know her. Courtney was my best friend from middle school and all through high school. I never told you about her because she's ten times prettier than me, and you never bring your hot best friend around your three hot husbands. That's tempting fate in the worst way."

All three of them rolled their eyes at me.

"Now who needs to stop saying stupid things," Micah muttered. "But that does sound like some shit you'd do." Getting up, Micah came over and sat next to me, drawing my head down on his lap. My eyes fluttered shut as he softly rubbed my temples. "What now? Alex is right, the cops are done with their investigation. They've got means, motive, and opportunity. How will you get them to believe someone else killed your mother?"

"They didn't find a blood-soaked dress."

"That's a detail," Rhodes said gently. "A bloody knife in her bag is fact."

I blew out a hard breath, frustration strangling me. I knew there wasn't any point in them filling my head with fantasies, but right then, I needed someone to say Detective Balogun would call in ten seconds, apologizing for arresting the wrong best friend and announcing she caught, arrested, and was already giving the lethal injection to the real killer.

I waited—counting the seconds to ten... but no call came.

Fine, I thought, sitting up. *If that's how she wants to play it.*

"I have no choice," I rasped. "I told her to find the killer. I wanted her to find the killer. But she bungled it like the lazy dumbass everyone called her and her partner. She's left me no choice."

"Uhh, excuse me?" Alex drew out. "What does that mean?"

Red descended on my vision—exploding the white-hot heat of the bursting pit within my soul. "It means I'm going to find that fucker. I'm going to make him confess, and *I* am going to get Courtney out of jail and back with her daughter. And when I'm done," I forced through clenched and cracking teeth, "Balogun can have whatever's left of him."

The three of them traded looks.

"Sue?" Rhodes knelt in front of me. "I can't imagine what you're feeling right now. You want justice for your mother, and she deserves that, but you have to know that you can't go charging after a violent, psychopathic killer. It's too dangerous. Plus, where would you even start?"

The hard set to my chin didn't go away. "I'll start in the same place the detectives did—with the nine other people who were in the ballroom this morning."

"I was kinda hoping you'd say six," Micah deadpanned, pointing to himself and his fellow husbands. "Because we sure as fuck didn't do it."

"Those six might not have done it either," Alex spoke up, stealing our attention. "I was thinking about that this morning, but those six people weren't the only people upstairs during the time... it happened."

"What?" Rhodes stood up. "What are you talking about? Who else was there?"

Alex gave a long, serious look. "About half a dozen cops."

"You're not saying..." I trailed off, body chilling. "You think a cop... did that to my mother?"

"I'm not saying one of them did for sure, but just think about it." He leaned off the chair, his hands out to me. "They arranged their shifts and their placements among themselves. We just opened the door and let them in—we didn't even know who the fuck half of them were. If one of them did come here with a plan, and they put themselves in charge of guarding the hall to Omma's room, then who would've noticed them slipping away?"

I shuddered, bile rising up my throat. "That's horrible. That's so h-horrible, I can't— I can't even—" Rage squeezed my throat closed.

"I'm not saying that's what happened," Alex continued, finally coming over to me and taking my hands. "But if your friend is innocent, it means someone planted that knife in her bag. And who would've had the best opportunity to do that?"

"A cop." I know I spoke, but the voice sounded nothing like mine. "How do I prove it?"

"Sue," Rhodes began. "We don't know—"

"How do I prove it?" I barked.

The guys shared another fucking look.

"We need a reason," Micah finally said. "A motive. I mean, you know that Omma pretty much shut herself away from the world when she started losing her hair. This is an old grudge because she wasn't making any new ones while she was locked in her room ignoring everyone. Do you know who she may have gotten into it with before she started isolating? You got any other best friends who pelted her with cupcakes?"

I appreciated his attempt to make me smile, but my lips didn't move a millimeter. "I don't know, but I do know people who might," I replied. "I need the AGN."

***

That was how I ended up at the Bluebell Café two days later, sipping tea with Mrs. Choi.

Mrs. Choi was the first friend my mother made when she and my father moved to Lantana, and she was a good friend to have. Not only was she a member of one of the richest families in the whole town, she was also the leader of the Korean American clique.

I wish I could say Lantana's diversity was reflected in the friendships made and the groups formed, but that'd be a lie. There were four distinct charity cliques in Lantana, and the charity cliques were everything. Pretty much the entire social and networking calendar of the community revolved around them.

Stay-at-home moms or working moms, it was considered gauche in the extreme to flaunt the kind of wealth Lantanans did, but not give to charity. So almost everyone did so—which was good—but it was mostly so they'd have an excuse to throw huge, gaudy parties and flaunt more wealth—not so good.

Either way, instead of joining together, the middle-aged and elderly white, Hispanic, Black, and Korean members of the community split the four main causes: health, education, environment, and human services. One clique got one cause. Of course, everyone was invited to every party, but all the chatting, dining, befriending, and planning of said parties only happened with *their own kind*.

Balogun was right, I thought, sweeping the café and all the Asian patrons just like me and Choi. *This community is horribly exclusionary.*

Despite that, the Bluebell Café was a cute little spot with fresh flowers on every table, and all the specialty teas and coffees anyone could think of.

"Oh, Soo Min." Mrs. Choi took my hand across the table. "I'm so sorry, dear. I can't believe this happened. Ha-eun was one of my closest friends. I'm utterly devastated."

Mrs. Choi wasn't just saying that because it's what you're supposed to say. Her eyes were red-rimmed from crying, and not even the heavy makeup was hiding it. Like my mother, Mrs. Choi was pushing against her seventies, but you wouldn't know it from the expertly dyed black hair, and wrinkle-repelling eyes and cheeks.

"What can I do for you, sweetheart? Anything you ask, it's yours," she said. "Do you need help organizing the funeral? Contacting and flying your extended family over? Do—" She looked around, then leaned in. "Do you need me to track down Sarang again?"

I froze. *Again?*

"I don't care what was said and done in the past," she went on. "She must come back for her mother's funeral. Anything else would be obscene."

"I..." Everything I walked in here prepared to say flew out of my head. Of course, Mrs. Choi and the AGN had known my mother for over thirty years. They damn sure knew she had twins, but what they'd never known, was how to tell us apart.

She doesn't know she's already talking to Sarang. And I didn't know she was the reason Sue found me in Willingsworth. There's just no such thing as privacy or secrecy in the AGN—

—which is what I'm counting on.

"No, thank you, Mrs. Choi. This isn't about Sarang, and it's not about the funeral," I said. "It can't be when the investigation into my mother's murder isn't over."

She frowned. "Oh?"

"The person they've arrested, Courtney Thorne, didn't do it. The police have the wrong person, and I need to make them see that."

Her frown deepened. "But how can you say that, Soo? She was found with the murder weapon. Also, your mother told me all about that Courtney girl." She tsked. "Did you know she was a friend of Sarang's when she went to that fancy prep school on the other side of town? I say friend," she whispered, dropping her voice as gossip mode activated. "But her bad influence would be a more appropriate description.

"Your mother was certain that girl led your sister astray—dragging Sarang into parties, drugs, and boys until her grades fell."

Grades fell? I had a 4.2 GPA!

"She turned Sarang all the way around until when she finally tried to get on the right track, it was too late and that boy had already stolen the valedictorian spot from her. And then..." She trailed off, shaking her head. "Well, you know what she did to try to get it back."

My free hand tightened under the table, gripping my recording phone hard. So this was the lie my mother spread through the network? Blaming everything on my best friend in the world because she refused to believe the real monster was right under her roof.

"Well, it turned out it wasn't like that," I said when my anger cooled. "Courtney was and is a good person—"

"No, no, no," she hissed, leaning in and patting my hand with a *get this?* look on her face. "You know that Melinda Thorne—a complete gossip and whore till the bitter end. She was forever bragging about her *perfect, wonderful daughter,* Courtney, who got into Princeton while Sarang was expelled, and you went to community college. Heavens, she was so nasty with those '*where did your daughters go to school again? Oh, that's right, nowhere*' comments. All because your mother held the Coats for Kids charity dinner on the same night as her Save the Owls auction—and everyone went to our event instead of hers."

My brows popped. "Yikes. I had no idea things used to be so bad between Omma and Mrs. Thorne."

She scoffed. "Make that *Ms. Llewellyn*. The nerve of that slut—attacking your mother and her children while her own husband was divorcing her for sleeping around, and her daughter wasn't anywhere near Princeton. She was halfway around the world learning how to pick up STDs and surprise babies just like her mommy dearest. Did you know that Courtney girl has a daughter?" Mrs. Choi smiled that little, malicious smile shared by everyone who got sick enjoyment out of feeling superior over others. "Apparently, she's got no idea who the father is. Everyone was talking about it at the baby shower." She sniffed. "I tell you this, *Ms. Llewellyn* hasn't had a peep to say about you, Sarang, or your mother since then."

"That's... good," I forced out. What I really wanted to do was tell her off, but I couldn't. Opening up about the people who hated Omma was exactly what I needed her to do. I just wished she could do it without trashing my closest friend. "And I guess Ms. Llewellyn must've epically freaked out when I posted all over my socials that Courtney was in Paris, and then Omma told everyone else."

She whistled. "Epically freaked out is putting it lightly. She rammed your mother's car in the parking lot."

"What!"

"Shh," she hissed, flapping her hand—but that nasty smile widened. "Oh, yes, didn't you know? That's why your omma had to scrap the Ferrari. She totaled it and almost put your mother in the hospital. Didn't your mother tell you this?"

I shook my head. "There was a lot Omma didn't tell me. I guess kids never really know what's going on in their parents' lives."

"Dae Sung sure doesn't," she scoffed. "I swear that boy's fingers break every time he's supposed to call his mother. Even now, my best friend was murdered and my own son can't be bothered to pick up the phone."

"I'm sorry, Mrs. Choi."

"No, no, no," she gruffed, waving that away. "Don't you worry about comforting me. My loss is nothing compared to yours. It's you I'm here for."

"Thank you. I really appreciate that, and you really are helping me. Despite everything, I know Courtney didn't do it, and the four of us are terrified knowing a murderer walked right into our home and is still on the loose. I mean, we've got Nari to think about."

"Oh dear, I hadn't thought of that," she breathed, laying her hand over her heart. "If the police have got it wrong, you may still be in danger—not to mention that precious child. Oh, Sue, you must know how much we all love Nari. I swear the heavens gave us one of their own with that girl."

"Yes," I whispered, smiling soft. "They did. That's why I need to be sure. Now, you're saying that the feud between Courtney's mom and mine got so bad it resulted into road rage, but they must've buried the hatchet, right? Otherwise, why would she have invited Omma to the baby shower?"

"Hmm. It's true, she did." Mrs. Choi paused to sip her tea. "And ever since, they were both too busy showering their grandchildren with attention to worry about the other. It'd helped that Courtney's *predicament* humbled that nasty shrew. Llewellyn certainly wasn't bragging about her Ivy League–dropout daughter after she admitted she couldn't even remember her child's father's name."

I clamped down hard on my tongue, holding back the lashing. *You need her, you need her, you need her. For all her badmouthing Courtney, she's eventually going to say something that'll save Courtney's future.*

"Was there anyone else?" I asked. "Someone else who resented my mother so much, they couldn't get over it? Something they'd want to settle the score over, even though Omma was already dying."

Shaking her head, her gaze drifted out the window. "My dear, no. Of course not. It's as you say, any petty grievances were settled with the news that my friend didn't have long in this world. At this point, her death achieved nothing except satisfying the murderous lust of a monster. Because if it wasn't that Courtney girl, that's who it was—a monster," she spat.

"Some sick, soulless beast who's too much of a coward to face a woman head-on, so they strike from behind or when they're laid up in bed and couldn't hope to fight back. Just like they did with your mother, that woman who used to work for you, and that poor girl from the post office. Did you know that's how that young woman died?" she asked. "Struck on the back of the head. She was probably walking to her car, heading home from work, when that beast came up behind her. She wouldn't have seen a thing coming."

"I didn't know that was how she died," I admitted. "All I heard was that she was found on Bonsai Beach. Look, Mrs. Choi, I don't doubt the killer is a madman, but that doesn't mean he didn't have a motive to go after Omma specifically.

"The killer took a serious risk going after Omma in a house full of cops and witnesses. They planned a way to get in, out, and frame an innocent person all without being seen. That's a lot of premeditation for an opportunistic coward."

Mrs. Choi tipped her head, nodding. "Yes, I see what you mean."

"So, please, thinking back to everything my mother's said and done. Think about everything others may have done and said about my mother. Did anyone have a reason to want to silence her? One that couldn't wait."

She tossed her head, face crumpling. "Soo, I'm sorry, but there's nothing like that. Your mother shut herself away for months. No one had a reason to... to silence..." Trailing off, she stiffened. "Wait. Silence... Silence her..."

"What?" I pounced. "What is it?"

"It— No, it's probably nothing. Even the thought is ridiculous—"

"Please." My grip tightened on her hand. "She was my mother. Your friend. We have to do everything we can to find her killer—even if it's ridiculous."

She looked at me, eyes filling. "Sweet child, you say you want to know this... but I don't think you do."

"I do," I replied before she finished the sentence. "Tell me."

Sighing, she pressed her lips tight together—looking at me like she wasn't going to budge.

"Okay," she said, making me release a breath I didn't know I was holding. "First, you must understand that I was only doing what she asked of me. I even told her that she should talk to you and get your permission first, but she claimed a mother didn't need permission."

"Permission to do what?"

She trapped my gaze. "Permission to investigate her sons-in-law."

"Investigate?" I blew back, eyes darting around. "Investigate what?"

Mrs. Choi flapped her hand, gesturing for me to lean back in. Just because she loved telling everyone's business, didn't mean she wanted it shouted in public. "It was last year—around June," she said softly. "Apparently, you were in a bad spot in your marriages at the time, and it was looking like a divorce—or three—was inevitable. She said they'd already struck the first blow by canceling all of your credit cards and removing your access to the joint accounts." She gave me a look. "And you know what comes after that."

"Of course. Large cash withdrawals, secret Cayman bank accounts, opening trusts in your cousin's name, undervaluing assets, overvaluing debts, stashing money in the corporate accounts, and suddenly catching the urge to invest in gold and safe-deposit boxes," I rattled off easily. "All from the *Rich Douchebag's Guide to Cheating Your Spouse Out of Their Earned Divorce Settlement*."

"Precisely."

Hey, I grew up in the land of the rich with the rest of the Lantanans. I learned how to cheat taxes and hide assets before I learned fractions.

"You've devoted years of your life to not one, but three men. You have a child with them," she cried. "Your mother wasn't going to see you cheated out of a single cent that you deserve, so at the first sign, she asked me to put her in touch with a private investigator and forensic accountant.

"I'm entrusted with millions and millions of dollars meant for poor and needy people. Ha-eun knew I was fanatical about every dollar being accounted for," she said. "I gave her what she asked, but I made her promise that if they found something, she'd take it to you first. Let you take it to your attorney, so they'd be prepared to spring it on your husbands the minute they walked into the mediation room. If she tipped your hand to them, they'd be forearmed and ready, and it'd just drag out the fight that much longer."

I almost laughed. Of course, Mrs. Choi's only concern was to see Sue with all the weapons she needed to drain her rich husbands dry. She wasn't at all concerned about her and my mother poking their noses into someone else's marriages.

"And did the investigators find something?" I asked, and even as the question came out of my mouth, I hoped the answer wouldn't be—

"Yes," she stated. "Almost a month later, I was driving your mother to chemo when she just came right out with it. She told me they found out something about one of your husbands—something big. So big that it wouldn't just get you half, it'd get you everything and more. The money, the assets, the house, the cars, and Nari. You would even own his freedom."

My brows crumpled. "His freedom? That's what she said? That I'd own his freedom."

"That's correct."

"What does that mean? Like— Like— Like jail?" I screeched. "Was she saying she found something that would put one of my husbands in jail?"

"That was my assumption, yes."

I goggled at her. "What was it? What did they find?"

"She wouldn't say."

I was out of my seat and almost in hers, leaning over the flower centerpiece. "Did she at least tell you who it was?"

"She didn't name him, but"—discomfort crawled over her face—"she did tell me, rather inappropriately even I must say, that it was *the one you'd expect*." She gave me another meaningful look. "If you take my meaning."

"I do," I croaked, feeling that pit grow until it stole all the air from me. "Unfortunately, I do."

Chapter Sixteen

That night, I stood just outside the kitchen—watching Lily and Rhodes from the shadows.

"Do you think Mommy will like these?" Lily stood on the stepstool, frosting her batch of the cookies and her corner of the countertop to go with it.

"Course, she will," he exclaimed, swiping frosting on her nose. "Mommy loves ginger, cinnamon, and chocolate, so ginger cinnamon cookies with chocolate frosting will be like Christmas come early."

"Hmm, maybe. I don't know." She was so adorable with her chocolate nose all scrunched up in thought. "Mommy likes new stuff now, maybe she won't."

"Likes new stuff?" Rhodes said over my stiffening shoulders. "What do you mean?"

"New stuff," she repeated like it was obvious. "Like now she likes playing with me, and reading me stories, and dancing with me—even though she's really, really bad."

It'll always be your own kin that cuts you the deepest.

"She didn't like that stuff before," Lily said so matter-of-factly, it broke my heart. "So what if she doesn't like cinnamon and ginger anymore either?"

In fact, I hated cinnamon and ginger. Having both together would be like having a spice shop throw up in my mouth, but damned if I wouldn't scarf down every single one of those cookies like they were magic stay-young-and-beautiful-forever pills.

"She... uh... Mommy..." Even then, my stomach did a little flip at Rhodes's cute panicked expression. "Mommy is... different now," he confessed. "But it wasn't that she didn't like doing those things with you, baby girl, she just didn't know how to be silly and relaxed and have fun." Rhodes stopped icing and took her hand. "See, Lily, some parents don't let their kids be kids. They don't let them play, read fairy tales, or dance badly, so when they get older, they don't know how to do that stuff with their kids because they've never done it before."

"Is that what happened to Mommy?"

"Yes," Rhodes said clearly.

I wished I could deny a word of that, or even voice a word to defend my parents, but Rhodes was spot-on. Actually, he was putting it nicely.

"But how come she can play with me now?"

He paused, considering that. "Because of Halmeoni."

I frowned. *What?*

"Your grandmom only got to be Mommy's mom for twenty-eight years, and in that whole time, they never got to have any fun together."

"Really?" Lily whispered. "That's so sad."

Something broken and screaming in me went very, very quiet.

"It is sad. It's even more sad because they'll never get the chance to have fun together again."

Lily's mouth trembled—her little frosted nose wrinkling.

"But she doesn't want it to be that way with you and her," he said. "For as long as she's your mommy, she wants to have lots of fun with you." Rhodes wiped her cheek, catching a tear. "So, what do you say? Should we keep making the best frosted cinnamon ginger cookies ever?"

"Yeah."

"Yeah?!" he cried, tickling her.

Bursting into giggles, she belted out, "Yeah!"

"All right!"

They high-fived—tears abated as the two of them went back to working on their little cheer-Mommy-up surprise.

I stepped out of the gloom, clearing my throat. "Hey, guys. What's going on in here?"

"Mommy, no!" Lily dropped her spatula, dropping over the cookies to cover them. "Don't look. You're ruining the surprise."

"A surprise? I am?" I clapped my hands over my eyes. "Oh no, I can't ruin the surprise!" I ran into the fridge and bounced off. Spinning around, I ran the other way and bonked into the pantry.

If Lily wasn't already on the countertop, she would've fallen on it laughing.

"That's right. No peeking," Rhodes said. "We're going to hide these, because you don't get to see them until after dinner."

I tucked myself in the corner while Lily and Rhodes put the cookies back on the pan, and stuck them in the oven.

"Nicely done, Lilybug. Can you go and get your other daddies for me, please?" Rhodes asked.

"Okay." There was a clomp from her jumping off the stool.

Suddenly, little arms were around me. "I love you, Mommy."

My throat closed—my heart filling to burst. Three days since losing Omma, and it was her three little words that put the first crack in the dam of my tears.

"I love you too, Nari." Twisting around, I hugged her tight. "So much."

Leaning back, she popped a kiss on my cheek, and then took off—just a happy, sweet little girl who trusted and felt safe with her family.

Only after her footsteps faded did I turn to Rhodes.

I studied the back of his head, watching him flit through the kitchen finishing off what, from the smell of it, seemed to be one-pot chicken and potatoes.

Even the back of him was handsome. Rhodes Newbury was tall, fit, and a great dresser. Even when he went out for a run, he had the best running shoes and nice, tight running pants that motivated anyone running behind him to keep up... but never get ahead of him.

He was an amazing father. So sweet and patient with Lily, and he always made time for her no matter how tough a day he had at work. Yes, there were many things to love about Rhodes Newbury—

—but that didn't make him any less a complete stranger to me.

I've been an idiot. I crushed on him from afar for one year when I was fourteen, and then four years later, I made a date with him that I never got to go on—and I've acted like that's enough to know a person.

Ten years have separated me and Rhodes, no matter how much I wanted to ignore that fact. I wasn't here for the fights, the disappointments, the early growing pains of fatherhood, or the weight of his parents' failed marriage falling upon him.

I don't know this man at all, I thought as he turned to me, beaming away. *So how do I know he didn't kill my mother?*

"Hey, babe." He saw the look on my face. "Everything okay?"

"Um, no," I said slowly, moving closer to the island. "Not really."

"Is this about your friend?" Rhodes busied himself wiping the chocolate off the countertop. "How's she doing?"

"Not good." I was fixed on his face—studying his every twitch and tic. "Her father got her the best lawyer in a five-state radius, and she's poking all the same holes in their *investigation* that I did, but it's tough because she can't explain why she attacked Omma with confectionery if she didn't have a grudge against her."

"Why did she do that?" Rhodes didn't look up from his task. "I mean, it was so bad onlookers called the cops. Did she tell you at least why she flipped out on an old lady?"

"I already know why." My voice was measured—calm. "It was because Omma drove a wedge between us. Courtney is the sister I never had," I said—speaking truer than I ever had before. "And I'm hers.

"But, sadly, Omma didn't approve of her. And even more sadly, my self-worth was so tied to her approval, I gave up on my best friend when she needed me the most. It really sucks," I whispered, "when you wake up one day and realize you never had to be this lost and alone. The whole time, all you had to do is take the hand reaching out to you."

Rhodes slowed, staring down at the shining countertop. "I... Yeah," he said softly. "I know what you mean."

"So, Rhodes..." I slid my hand across the countertop, laying my palm over his fingers. My other hand slipped inside the pocket of my sheath dress and turned on the recorder. "This is me reaching out. Talk to me. Be honest with me. I'll listen."

He blinked at our hands. "Wait, what? What are you talking about? Be honest about what?"

"I spoke to a close friend of my mom's today, and she told me that last year, Omma hired private investigators to dig into your life, and they found something that would send you to jail." I could've gone for subtlety, but every single member of my immediate family died violently, and I was the cursed bitch who had to witness it all three times, so I was officially done beating around the fucking bush.

"Excuse me!" Eyes bugging, Rhodes shot up—his hand flying away. "Put me in jail? Sue, were you talking to this woman in a locked ward in a nursing home? Because that's the only way what you said makes sense."

I didn't back down. "What did my mother find out, Rhodes? What did she do with the information, because knowing her, she didn't toss it in the trash and forget about it? Was she blackmailing you?"

"Blackmailing me?" Rhodes straight goggled at me. "Blackmailing me to do what? To live rent-free in her house? To let her help cover our losses when we had to pay to settle *your* lawsuits? How in the hell did I lose in those situations?"

"I'm not saying you did, Rhodes, I'm just telling you what my mom told her, so please, stop answering my question with more questions and just answer me. Did my mother dig up dirt on you?"

He tossed his head, looking to the ceiling like he was beseeching a deity for help. "Okay, fine. You want a direct answer? The answer is no. Your mother did not dig up dirt on me, because there was no dirt to find. I haven't done anything illegal. I've never even double-parked."

"Did—"

"No," he sliced. "My turn. Did this woman really say that? She told you I broke the law, your mother found out when she *hired* people to dig into my life, and then apparently kept all of this from you—if you're really standing here asking me about it."

"All of the above," I dropped. "Except she looked into all three of you. She came back and told Mrs. Choi that the investigators hit the jackpot, but she wouldn't give her a name."

He cracked a brow. "Then why are you assuming it's me?"

"Because Omma said it was *the one you'd expect*," I told him. "My mother was many things, and a racist was one of them."

Rhodes snorted—not looking the least bit surprised. "Yeah, she was." Rhodes returned the same bluntness. "You always denied it or made excuses for her when I brought it up. Why are you seeing the light now?"

"Because I wasn't any better than her back then. Didn't you see me hit rock bottom and then punch through the floor to hell when I threw coffee on that waitress? I sucked," I said. "Honestly, why did you even marry me, weirdo?"

A startled laugh burst out of him, cracking the stern exterior. "Because I loved you, weirdo. And because..." He sighed. "I was making excuses for you too. Turns out I'm a hypocrite. There, Sue. You got me to admit it."

I gave him a long, serious look. "That's not the confession I'm looking for, Rhodes. Could my mother have been speaking about Micah or Alex—possibly. I doubt it, but it's possible, and I don't have any proof saying otherwise. But what can be proven is that you left the ballroom and went upstairs—"

"Whoa, wait—"

"—around the time she was killed. Around the time my racist, prying, digging-up-dirt-to-destroy-you-in-the-divorce mother—"

"Sue, stop," he cried, throwing his hands up. "Are you serious right now? Are you really asking me what I think you're asking me right now? How did we get from your mother hiring someone to dig up skeletons last year, to me killing her last week? That's insane! Why would I even bother? She was already dying."

"Maybe what she knew was still a threat to you—"

He flung away. "No."

"Maybe you had to silence her for good—"

"No!"

"—and you easily could've stashed a second pair of clothes and—"

"NO!" he roared, veins bulging in his face and neck.

I lurched back, eyes blowing wide—but not because he yelled at me. I stared at his right hand, the air trapped in my lungs.

Rhodes flicked down, looking where I was looking, and saw his hand on the cutting board—wrapped around the knife's hilt.

He threw it away like it burned. "Sue, I'm sorry. I'm sorry," he beseeched me. "I didn't mean to raise my voice, but you've got it so wrong, it's ridiculous. I did leave the party around nine thirty, but it wasn't to kill your mother." Just the way he said it made me feel a little ridiculous. "I went up, and kept going up, to the third floor. To my office."

It took me a minute for my heart rate to slow. "Your office?"

"My office. I told you that I'd be using the party as a chance to hook some new clients," he said. "Well, your man is good at what he does because one of them wanted to sign with me right then. He said if I'd had the kind of money to drape my wife in diamonds and throw parties like that, he wanted in.

"I wasn't going to give him a chance to change his mind, or sober up, so I ran upstairs to get a client contract. I was back down and watching you bounce around the dance floor like ten minutes later."

I hesitated. "R-really?"

"Really," he said gently, taking a step. Then another. "Baby, come on. You know me. That mugger came at us with a knife that night coming out of the subway, and all I did was punch him once in the face and disarm him. I didn't take the knife and stab him thirty-four times." Rhodes stepped closer, erasing the distance. "I could never kill anyone. Especially not my wife's mother.

"I love you." Rhodes gathered me in his arms, melting me with his warmth and steady, smooth baritone. "Even more than I did before. You're finally the woman and mother I married, so why would I ruin what we have now that we finally have something worth fighting for?"

I buried my face in his chest, shaking. His *I love you* wasn't for me, and yet... it was. "I love you too." I tipped my chin, lips parting just in time for his to crash on mine.

Fireworks exploded in my mind, their sparks lighting the fuses that burned and sizzled through my body—setting every nerve ending on fire. I gasped under the waves of crashing, rising heat, and Rhodes plunged inside—his tongue tangling with mine and wrangling it into submission.

I moaned into the kiss, losing myself in Rhodes, Rhodes, Rhodes.

No, I didn't have ten years of dating, living with, and raising a child with Rhodes to say I knew him. But I did have ten years of dating, living with, and thanking fate that I didn't have a child with the string of bastards in my past.

I knew a bad man when he was oozing his slime on me, and that wasn't Rhodes. Because he was here.

Rhodes endured the hell I knew my sister put him through and stuck by her until *she* told him she wanted out. He obviously had the patience of a saint, because if he was going to snap and kill anyone, I had a feeling it would've been my sister.

He broke away, resting his forehead against mine. We were quiet breathing each other in.

"Sorry," I whispered. "I shouldn't have accused you. I'm just in a weird headspace right now. I see now how lonely, isolated, and *despised* my mother was. First, she marries a misogynist who controlled her even after his death. Then she gets cancer, and instead of allowing her to pass away on a cloud of morphine, she's violently murdered in her bed.

"It feels like this house and everyone who lived in it is cursed," I rasped. "Cursed and haunted by evil everywhere we go until we lose the battle. It scares me, baby. I'm scared."

"Hey, don't talk like that." He stroked my hair—his hand heavy but comforting. "Our home isn't cursed and our family isn't cursed. It's not, because we have each other, and together we're going to get through this. I promise."

"Promise what?" Micah walked into the kitchen, turning our heads. "You guys okay?"

"We're cool. Sue was just grilling me on where I went when I left the party." He smiled at me to take the sting out of it. "Thankfully, I'm accounted for. All of the usual suspects—those closest to Omma—are. Even Reynard had a rock-solid alibi."

"Reynard?" I said to his back as he crossed to the stove, getting ready to plate dinner. "Why? Because he was out with his friends?"

"No, because he wasn't. When I was up in my office, I looked out the window and saw him in the garden—sneaking a cigarette. I remember thinking that boys' night couldn't have been that wild if it was over before ten o'clock," he said. "But the point is, if he was three floors down smoking a cigarette at nine forty, he definitely wasn't also upstairs hiding the evidence and cleaning up after committing murder at nine thirty-seven."

He gave me a sweet smile. "He didn't do it. I didn't do it. No one who lives in this home hurt your mother, baby, so there's no need to be scared. The evil is not in this house. It's not in your family, so don't push us away. We're here for you, and we're going to discover the truth together. That's the promise."

"Then it's one I'm one hundred percent on board with," Micah said. It was his turn to hug and kiss me. "Let us take care of you now. You and those sweet lager nipples are in safe hands."

I rolled my eyes, but he got a little smile out of me anyway. "Thank you, guys. I really needed to hear that."

"Of course."

"We mean it."

"We love you."

I just smiled, my gaze drifting up. *Yes, my lovely, hot borrowed husbands. I really did need to hear that on the night my mother was murdered, Reynard Agassi was not where he was supposed to be.*

Chapter Seventeen

The next morning, I caught Reynard coming out of his room. He turned the key in the lock and pocketed it before glancing up and noticing me.

"Oh, Sue. Good morning," he greeted. "Are you here to see me?"

It was a fair question. The only rooms in this particular hallway of the east wing were Reynard's room, my mother's office, and my mother's bedroom. Since I couldn't be there to eat breakfast with my mother as had become our little ritual, then I had to be there for him, but—

"No," I said lightly. "I need to look through Omma's office. Apparently, three days is long enough for a lawyer to wait before bugging a grieving daughter for the documents he needs to settle my mother's affairs."

"I'm sorry." He squeezed my shoulder. "If you need my help with anything, please let me know. It's the least I can do as thanks for you and your husbands letting me stay here until my next patient is ready for me."

"Of course. You were by my mother's side till the end." I studied him, and his constant steady smile, through my lashes. "Which is why I think I will take you up on your offer and ask for your help."

"Absolutely." He didn't hesitate. "Whatever you need. It's yours."

"Can we talk in her office?"

That was another yes. Reynard trailed behind me, following into the light, airy, never-used room.

My mother had always been a style-over-function person. So while the antique vases on every surface, six-foot-long glass desk, and shelves filled with first-edition classics were all nice to look at, it didn't make for a space anyone would feel comfortable working. You'd be too afraid to touch, dirty, or break something.

I went straight to the cabinets under the built-in shelves, making a show of rooting around for the papers. "My mother was murdered," I said without preamble, "and the police arrested the wrong person. I need your help to find the right one, Reynard, because no one spent more time with my mother in her final days than you."

"Whoa, whoa, whoa," he cried. "They arrested the wrong person? How could you know that?"

"Because I know Courtney, and she'd never kill anyone—let alone my mother." I pulled out an accordion folder—flipping through, taking papers out, and putting them back without paying attention to a single one.

I learned my lesson with Rhodes. Coming at him head-on would put his back up. I needed him to lower his defenses, then I'd come at him from the side, getting him to tell me what he was doing smoking cigarettes in my garden in the middle of the night when he was supposed to be out with friends he hadn't seen in months.

"Did she ever say anything to you about someone threatening her?" I asked.

"I would've told you if she had. You know I would've."

"Sure, but maybe it wasn't so direct. Of course you'd tell me if *she* told you someone threatened to sneak in and stab her. But maybe it was more like, 'Mrs. Jeong still hasn't forgiven me for getting drunk and making out with her husband at last year's Christmas party,'" I said. "Know what I mean? The slightest mention of a grudge or bad blood could point the cops in the right direction."

He hummed, tipping his gaze to the ceiling. "You're right. It would've had to have been something slipped into conversation like that, because your mother usually kept details about her personal life close to the vest. But even so..." He shook his head. "I've been here for six months, but it was in the last two that her pain became so unmanageable, I had to up the doses on several of her meds—leading to confusion, paranoia, and cognitive decline.

"These last few months, she's been in and out of time," he confessed. "She did speak of people, friends, and family every now and then, but I could never be sure of what year she was in. I remember once she said, 'that little slut showed up on my doorstep today, banging and screaming for me to come down. If it happens again, I'll call the police.'" He shrugged. "Or something like that. But when I asked who she was speaking of, she told me to mind my own business.

"She never gave me the kind of details that could be useful, and before she started slipping, she wouldn't say anything at all to me that wasn't expected of a professional nurse-patient relationship. She also never spoke of that Courtney Thorne woman," Reynard said, dropping his head to look at me. "If that means anything."

Actually, I'm pretty sure she did speak of Courtney to you. Who else could the little slut banging and screaming *be but my closest friend in the world?*

"I still think you should talk to the police." I pushed the accordion file back in and pulled out the one next to it. "Maybe you saw or heard something that night that could help them."

"Saw something?" Confusion laced his voice. "What do you mean? I couldn't have seen anything. I wasn't here."

And there it is. Your first fucking lie.

"No? My mistake— Or, I guess Rhodes's mistake. He said he saw you smoking in the garden a little after nine thirty." Getting up, I crossed to the window—looking out over the garden. "The garden lamp bulbs burned out a long time ago, and no one's replaced them. So if Rhodes saw you clear enough from the third floor, more light would've been shining on you than the light from a cigarette.

"That light must've been the light from my mother's bedroom."

A deep, heavy silence smothered us—smothered me.

"Mrs. Kim." Something in his voice changed, and it wasn't just the dropping of my first name. "Are you accusing me of something?"

Turning to him, I gave him a crazy look. "Accusing? What are you talking about? Of course I'm not accusing you. If you were downstairs smoking at nine forty, then you weren't up here wiping off the blood at nine forty. At this point, you're the only one I know it wasn't, and that's why"—I rushed him, making him cry out when I pounced and grabbed his hands—"I need you to tell me the truth, Reynard.

"You saw something, didn't you," I cried, blowing his brows up. "I remember every awful fucking second and every awful fucking detail of what I saw when I walked into that room. The shades were pulled down, but the drapes weren't drawn. As a kid, I spent enough nights reading in the garden to know you can see the outline of people moving around the room through the shades when the lights are on. So who did you see?" I shrieked.

"Sue—"

"Who was in this room that night? Who killed my mother!"

"I don't know— I don't know!" The man looked a little afraid of me. "I don't know what you're talking about!"

"Of course you do! You would've seen! Oh my—" My eyes narrowed to slits. "They're threatening you, aren't they."

"Threatening?!"

"The same disgusting, weaselly bastard that framed Courtney. They realized you saw something or—or maybe you're scared they'll do the same thing to you that they did to my mother and Mrs. Prado." I grabbed his shoulders, shaking him. "You don't have to be afraid. I swear, I'll protect you. I'll pay for you to live in a five-star, luxury safe house until the trial starts if that's what it takes! You just have to tell me who it—"

"Sue, stop!" he burst out, blowing me back. Reynard immediately pulled back and sucked in a deep breath. "Sorry. I'm sorry, but, please, just slow down, listen, and hear me. No one is threatening me. No one saw me in the garden that night—including your husband, because I wasn't there. He must've mistaken me for someone else, which would've been easy to do from the third floor. He would've been looking down on nothing more than a top of the head.

"No," he said clearly. "It wasn't me in the garden, and I can prove it." Reaching into his pocket, he pulled out his phone. Within a minute, I was looking at a grinning, tipsy Reynard sitting in a booth with five other tipsy, handsome gentlemen. "Look at the clock."

I squinted to see, but I didn't need to. He zoomed in, letting me read 9:21 p.m. clear as day on the bar clock over their heads. "This bar is an hour away. Not even if I sped all the way could I have been back here in twenty minutes to smoke in the garden. I also"—he gave me a soft smile—"don't smoke. I've watched enough people slowly die from lung cancer. I've no interest in being one of them."

"Oh." I deflated like a limp balloon, my hands falling off him. "So you didn't see anyone in here... and I'm right back where I started—with my mother gone and my best friend framed for her murder."

"Oh, Sue, I'm so sorry," he whispered, helping me down on the chaise by the window. "This is all just so fucked. I almost wish I was here—anything to help you and Madame Kim. Instead I'm this useless waste who was supposed to ease her peacefully into the next life, and couldn't even get that right!" Tears spilled down his cheeks.

Why could a man who has known my mother for six months cry for her, but I couldn't? That lone thought lodged the pit even deeper.

"And now you're asking me to help point you in the right direction, and I can't do that e-either," he choked. "I'm sorry, Sue. I'm just so fucking sorry."

"I'm sorry too," I whispered. "Only I could lose my mother right as I got her back."

"Don't say it like that." He crushed me to his chest. "Your mom was always here for you. In her own way, she was here."

No, she really wasn't. "But I need to be there for her now. She was never the mother I wanted, but she was the mother I needed when it counted. If I let her killer go free, then I really will be the disappointment she thought I was."

"Goodness, that's a lot of unfair pressure to put on yourself. If the police fail in catching the killer, that is on them—not you."

"Except there's a real woman involved with a real child who'll grow up only seeing her mother through wired glass." My voice was hard. "No one should sit by with their thumbs up their asses, singing at the breeze when an innocent person needs help, and another—*two* other innocent people lost their lives.

"I won't let this go, Reynard." I looked him dead in the eyes. "Ever. I will find him. If I've got to burn this whole town to the ground, I'll do it if it means I'll get to yank his corpse out of the ashes and burn him again!"

He blinked at my ferocity. "I understand how you feel, Sue, but the more I think about it, the more I'm certain it had to be some deranged sicko thief who heard about the party—because everyone heard about the party—and figured that if he showed up wearing white, he'd be allowed in with everyone else. When that worked, he came up here scoping out things to steal, happened on your mother, and... well, he silenced her."

"But nothing was taken, even though there was a jewelry box full of priceless gems on the dresser right next to her."

Reynard tossed his head, looking helpless. "Then maybe he panicked after the murder, and realized he had to get out of there quick. Or maybe he heard someone outside and got spooked— I don't know. I just know that your mother had limited to no contact with anyone outside of these walls for months," he said. "Even before she was plagued with confusion, she never used social media, and she only used her phone to keep in touch with her friends, and even though I don't understand Korean, shouting and harsh speech transcends language barriers. But I never heard any angry words pass between her and someone else."

"I hear you," I said, blowing out an angry breath. "No one my mother knew wanted to hurt her, so it had to be a stranger."

"It had to be." His voice was firm. "No question. No one who knew Madame Kim and how much she was already suffering would've had any hate left in their hearts after hearing she didn't have long. Even Mr. Spencer let go of his rage, and accepted that if she really stole all of his and his parents' money—"

I snapped up. "What?"

"—she would've come clean after learning she only had a few months left to live," he blazed on, unaware of my falling jaw. "I mean, it wasn't like she could take the money with her, and everything she had was about to be passed on to her only child, so if she did steal it—"

"Steal?!"

"—Micah was soon to know all," Reynard finished. "In my time, I've found that when faced with the option of confessing your sins when it counts, or waiting until you face the judgement of a deity—most people choose confession." He nodded to himself, convinced in the face of my astonishment. "Yeah, I'm sure of it. Either Micah finally believed your mother was telling the truth before she died, or he was waiting for the will to do that. But he didn't need to kill her for the latter. The cancer was doing that for him."

He flicked down to me. "What? Oh, shit, should I not have said that? I'm sorry, Sue, I know he's your husband, but I've lived here for half a year. I heard the knockdown, screaming fights between you and Micah, and Micah and your mother. I don't know why he was so convinced your mother was behind the scam that cost his parents everything, but if you'd have asked me four months ago who wanted her dead—I would've said Micah Spencer.

"But now that you're asking me today..." He shook his head, smiling. "No. Over these last few weeks, this cold, forgotten manor has become a home again. There was a happy family living here again, and no one in this family would've ruined that.

"No," he repeated, his gaze shifting away. "The monster you're looking for is out there."

Nodding, I stood up, breaking free of his grasp. "Thank you, Reynard. For being straight with me, and for saying so many nice things about me and my family—even though we've got to be the weirdest band of freaks you've ever come across."

He chuckled. "Not at all."

I moved to the door and pushed it open. "If you don't mind, I'd like a minute alone. I just need to process everything."

"Of course, of course. I understand."

I held my smile until I shut and locked the door behind him. Reaching into my pocket, I took out my phone and held the recorder to my lips. "A guilty person never misses a chance to throw suspicion on someone else. Anyone else. And Reynard was doing so good until he got to the end and not-so-subtly put Micah in the frame.

"But why?"

I crossed to the window, looking out over the dead and dying garden. "If he was really an hour away with his buddies, why did Rhodes say he saw him in the garden that night? Was Rhodes mistaken, or did he slip away and come back here just to pick up a new bad habit beneath the room where my mother was being murdered?

"And what about Micah?" I rasped. "Why in the flip flipping fuck did he think my mother stole from his? What could've possibly given him that idea? Because that's definitely the kind of grudge that sticks around. Ten years later, and I'm still plenty angry at the bitch who tricked and schemed to steal my college and trust fund from me.

"But," I continued—my mind twisting itself into shape. "How do I approach this with him? If Reynard heard us fight about it, then it's something *Sue* is already supposed to know about. I can't act like he hid it from me because I'm already supposed to know. Is there even a way to approach this with him without giving away that I'm not Sue?"

My phone had no answers for me, naturally.

"All right, I'm putting that aside for right now and focusing on where things stand," I said. "There were ten people who left the party and went upstairs during the time window. I'm going to exclude Pixie, Chic Ghost, and Button Nose. They lived their whole lives in New York, and Omma lived in Lantana. They had no reason to hurt her. No doubt they were upstairs snooping around like the nosy, catty frenemies they are.

"That leaves seven," I continued. "Courtney, Charles Layton, Nicolas Stevens, Christie Baudelaire, Rhodes Newbury, Micah Spencer, and Alexander Montgomery." My throat closed tighter and tighter until the final name was nothing but a strangled whisper. "Rhodes was upstairs on the third floor. Alex told me in the car that he left his phone in his bedroom, and went up to call his aunt and check on Lily.

"Christie cleared a cool seven figures that night, so what in the hell would she have been in a rage about? She had zero reason to pop upstairs and murder my mother. And if she did, she's the best actress in the world, because all that screaming, crying, and vomiting after we saw Omma looked pretty real to me.

"But," I forced out. "The fact is I don't really know Christie, and I haven't been the one she's been dealing with all these months that her and Sue were planning the party. Maybe something did happen between her and Omma, and she settled the score that night.

"Then there's Charles Layton. Why did he go upstairs that night? That's the first thing I need to ask him when he comes over for Lily's piano lesson tomorrow," I said. "It's not going to be as easy to corner Mr. Stevens, but if the cop that clocked Courtney going upstairs had seen her going up and then back down with Stevens by her side, wouldn't they have hauled them both in?

"They didn't, so Stevens went upstairs by himself. Why?" I asked. "Why?"

I dropped my hands to my side, shutting off the recorder.

Scoffing, I spun away from the bright, sunny morning—seething with hate. "I want to talk about how lonely and isolated Omma has become? Well, look at me. Talking to myself in an empty room, surrounded by murder suspects who think I'm someone else, all while my best friend sat in a jail cell. It's me who has no one and nothing real.

"It's me who's all alone."

If I thought someone would stick their head in right then to tell me I was wrong... no one came.

***

"That's right, Lily. Now C, C, D. C, C, D. One smooth motion."

Lily's banging was far from smooth, but I had to admit she sounded better than she did the week before.

I stood in the doorway holding a tray of lemonade and cookies while Alex read in his armchair in the corner, and Lily and Layton practiced.

My phone buzzed. Balancing the tray on my arm, I stuck my hand in my pocket and fished it out.

Alex: I want you so fucking bad.

I almost dropped the tray.

Snapping up, I latched on to Alex, who still had his nose in his book, but for some reason, had started tapping the pages.

Alex: I want you in my mouth, baby—sweet, dripping, and wet. I want every drop of you on my tongue until there's nothing left for anyone else.

My knees knocked together as my lower belly contracted painfully. A grown-ass woman, and my panties were dampening like a horny teenager.

Alex: And when you think I'm done— When you think you're done and you've got nothing else to give, I'm going to lay you out and devour you, eating you out until I'm fat and blissed on your sweet, tasty cookies.

What?

The next text dropped on the screen.

Alex: And I'll get on that as soon as this woman brings in the tray.

"You rat bastard!"

Alex burst out laughing. Giving up all pretense, the book he wasn't reading fell to the floor, then he tumbled after it—curled up on his side and wheezing until he couldn't breathe.

Lily and Mr. C stared at the two of us nonplussed.

"Are you okay, Mommy?"

I sniffed. "I'm perfect, sweet girl. I brought you a snack. Want to take it and your horrible daddy into the living room?" Alex laughed louder. "Have an hour of screen time before you start your homework."

"Okay!" Jumping up, she actually went over to Alex, gave him her hand, and then led the winking bastard out the door with the cookies and lemonade.

I just shook my head at his back. It was hard to know where I stood with Alex most days. His hostility toward me vanished after Omma was killed—pity tends to soften the heart. But he wasn't anywhere near as casually affectionate, or as horny, toward me as Micah and Rhodes.

He was basically as light and teasing as a friend would be, which was definitely better than it was before, but still...

I forced myself to look away and focus on Layton. His back was to me as he put away their sheet music and closed the piano.

"Mr. Layton—"

"Charles, please." He shone a bright smile on me. "Is this about Lily's assignments this week? Because I told Mr. Montgomery that she doesn't have to worry about turning those in. She just lost her grandmother. Allowances can be made."

"It's not about that, but thank you." I stepped inside, gesturing for him to sit in Alex's vacated chair. "It's about the party."

The smile melted away. "Oh."

"You were one of the ten who went upstairs during the time... it happened," I got out. "Did you see anything strange when you did?"

"Strange?"

I got straight to the point. "Someone killed my mother, and it wasn't Courtney. Did you see someone or something that might not have raised the alarm at the time, but looking back seems odd now?"

He was shaking his head before I finished. "I didn't see anything or anyone. If I did, I would've told the police."

"Why did you go upstairs?"

Charles winced. "Honestly, and no offense, Sue, but the party was a little rowdier than I was expecting. Half the guests were trashed in an hour. The other half were throwing themselves at me in an hour and one.

"I don't like telling people about the family business, because the second I do, they're wheeling out every young, single member of their family for me. It gets pretty old constantly being used for your money." He blew out a long-suffering sigh. "Anyway, I left the party and snuck upstairs to the library. I was there until a cop burst into the room and said all the guests had to gather downstairs to be accounted for because... you know."

I just nodded, my brain processing while my phone did the active listening.

"But, excuse me for asking this, but why does it matter where I was?" he asked. "I saw all that stuff on the news—claiming the police did a shitty job and arrested the wrong woman, but you don't really believe that, do you?"

"Of course I believe it," I said, crossing to the window. "I was right there in the video screaming that they did a shitty job and arrested the wrong woman."

"Oh." I sensed his presence at my side. "So, you don't think it's over? You think the police are going to come back, interview us all again, and search the manor?"

"I'm pretty sure a search would be pointless at this point," I confessed. "The cops stopped searching bags and rooms when they found the knife in Courtney's. Then, they sent everyone home—allowing the real killer to slip away with the bloody clothes. Unless the killer's an idiot, and they've proved so far they're not, they've already burned the clothes and tossed the ashes in the sea.

"No." Finality rang in my voice. "There's nothing left to physically find... except for a liar." I turned to him, my lips stretched in a mirthless, bloodless smile. "You say you were in the library, Charles? Well, I really hope that's true, because at this point, anyone who lies to me about that night goes right to the top of my list."

He lurched back, brows flying to his hairline. Then, he laughed. "Oh, wow, good one, Sue." He patted my shoulder. "You had me going there with the menacing voice and the crazy eyes. Obviously, I didn't kill your mother.

I didn't have a single interaction with her that lasted longer than *hello* and *goodbye*."

Said crazy eyes tracked him across the room.

"All right, I got to get going," he said, collecting his things, "but I hope you get to the bottom of all this stuff. See you Thursday."

"See you then."

I let him go.

Only when the door shut behind him did I take out my phone and dial his number.

"Hello, Mrs. Kim."

The chill wafting from his end of the call gave my ear frostbite. "Hello, Officer Davis. I know you're not too happy with me right now, so let me skip right ahead to the apologies. I'm sorry for insinuating that you take bribes, and I'm definitely sorry you got rushed by a mob."

"What about telling the world I was Officer Cop-A-Feel!" he burst out. "I've been put on review!"

I cringed. "I'm sorry about that too. First thing in the morning, I'll walk into the police station and tell your captain I made all that up."

"You—! Wait, what?" His voice lowered a decibel. "You will?"

"Of course I will," I said easily. "I want to foster open lines of communication between me, you, and the detectives. That can't happen if everyone sees me as a crazy-eyed, lying witch."

"Open communication? What on earth are you talking about?"

"I'm talking about seeing the chart or list or whatever it was that the other officers put together for that night," I said. "They came up with ten names and ten people who went upstairs and passed by the different officers at their stations—"

"Just a minute—"

"—but without context, it doesn't mean anything to you guys. You don't know what's where or which rooms are which. That's why I need to see it because I'm the one who'll know who's lying. For example." I raised my voice over Davis's second attempt to interrupt. "Charles Layton said he left the party and went to the library where he stayed until after my mother was killed. But the library dead-ends a short hallway in the east wing. The only way to get to it is by going through the hall two passages down from where my bedroom is. I need to know if the officer guarding that hallway is the one who saw him, because if they didn't, he's lying."

There was a pause.

"Are you finished?" he asked, voice flat.

"Yep."

"Good, then I can get straight to telling you no. All evidence collected is now material evidence in a murder trial. You're not getting anywhere near it."

I wasn't fazed. "You might want to rethink that since you're putting the wrong woman on trial."

"Ms. Thorne had means, motive, and the murder weapon in her purse. What more will it take to convince you?"

"She didn't have motive, and literally anyone could've put that knife in her purse—like the twenty-seven *other* people who also had opportunity."

"Twenty-seven? What are you—? Hold on," he cried. "You're not suggesting that—!"

"One of your fellow cop buddies who were just as free to wander around my home, had just as much opportunity to kill my mother, and were the obvious choices to plant their murder weapon in the first bag they *searched*."

"Where are you getting this shit from?" His shout made my ears ring. "The men and women I serve with are above reproach! They would never—!"

"Fuck's sake, Davis, you're not this dumb!" Just like that, I was shouting too. "You're smart, you're observant, and you actually care about this community and the people you swore to serve. Well, two of those people were murdered and another one is about to lose everything for a crime she didn't commit, so isn't it about time you did something about that!

"My mother and Mrs. Prado were killed by the same person, right? That's what you believe, isn't it!" I demanded. "But you know Courtney was nowhere near Mrs. Prado, don't you."

It wasn't a question, but I waited for him to answer anyway.

"Ms. Thorne... is not a suspect in that crime," he gritted out. "She had a rock-solid alibi. She was serving customers all morning."

"There the fuck you go."

"There the fuck I go nowhere," Davis flung back. "It's only conjecture that those crimes may be related, and conjecture isn't proof. We—"

"No, not we. *You.* You know they're connected. You know that two women don't up and get murdered in the same place two weeks apart, and it has nothing to do with each other. You know something's wrong, and you know that some sweet single mom who spends her days baking cookies has nothing to do with it. You know," I barked. "So stop parroting bullshit you don't even believe, and do something about it.

"Give me the list. I'll look into the people I know, and you can look into your cop buddies. Together we'll find the monster who did this to Mrs. Prado and my mother."

He was laughing before I finished my speech. "You've been watching too many cop shows, Mrs. Kim. This is the real world, and in the real world, beat cops don't investigate homicides, and they for damn sure don't team up with failed influencers.

"I'm not giving you a thing," he dropped. "Back off. If I find out you're playing amateur sleuth, I'll arrest you for interfering in a police investigation."

I scoffed. "Well done, Officer Cop-A-Feel. Once again, you've proven to be a shitstain embarrassment to your profession. Too bad no one was filming it this time. Pervert."

"Fuck you."

Click.

Groaning, I tossed my phone at the couch. "Welp, that bridge is burned."

Chapter Eighteen

That night, I sat at the vanity, putting my face cream on while Micah toweled off from his shower.

I'd been working up the courage since he came home to ask him about the money he apparently thought my mother stole from him, but after my shouting match with Davis, I knew I needed a better approach that didn't start with accusations and end with insults.

"Micah."

He parted the towel, peeking at me through the cotton. "Yeah?"

"You've been really sweet not to bring it up, but I think we should address the elephant in the room."

"Elephant? What elephant?"

My goodness, it was hard to keep my eyes on his face. This man firmly believed a towel was only meant to dry your bits, not cover them. *All* of him hung hard, hot, and free as he draped his towel around his shoulders.

Lips parting, I said the words I'd been scripting for half the day. "About the money you believe my mother stole from your family," I began. "I still don't believe she could've done that, but if she did and the lawyer finds it when he gets access to her accounts, I'll tell him he legally needs to give it all to you. No questions. No fighting. It's yours."

He stared at me, brows crumpling—and panic seized.

Oh no, did I say the wrong thing? Did I give myself away?

"Sue, uh… wow." He dropped down on my bed, reaching for his boxers. "Baby, that's… wow."

I swallowed hard. "Could I possibly get more than a wow?"

"If you want more words, don't be leaving me speechless." He tossed his head, sending those long, sweet-scented locks flying through the air. "We fought about this so many times. Every time you called me a twisted, paranoid piece of shit and refused to even entertain the thought of helping me get the money back. And now, just like that, you're saying you'll have it all returned? That's wow," he repeated, then smiled at me.

"That means a lot, Sue. It really does. It shows me that you're serious about a fresh start for our family, and for us," he said. "But it's completely unnecessary."

"What? What is?"

"Giving me any money from the charity clique's inheritance," he said, "because you were right the whole time. Your mother had nothing to do with the con. I blamed her the whole time because she was the one who introduced that man to my parents, but I see now that she was tricked and taken in by him just like we all were." The last few words were strangled as his jaw clenched and anger darkened his face. "Remember that day you called me asking if Lily could stop the piano lessons?"

"Yeah," I replied, turning to face him.

"Well, I lied," he told the floor, bending over to put on his pajama bottoms. "I wasn't out on a job. When you called, I was in a casino in Atlantic City."

"A casino? What were you doing there?"

"The conman piece of shit that robbed my parents is in the wind. By this point, he's changed identities fifty times, and the investigators we hired just can't find him," he said. "That's why the last one told us to stop trying. We needed to stop chasing the wind, and start looking at what it was leaving behind."

"Uhh," I drew out. "That explanation did nothing for me."

He chuckled. "What he meant was that we need to track down his other victims and figure out what we all have in common, and how he got to all of us. Once we know how he picks his marks, we can find his next target before he does, and finally get ahead of him. And that's why I'm an ass."

"Once again, you've lost me."

Micah dropped back on the bed, covering his face with his hands. "That day, the investigator tracked down another victim. I went to Atlantic City and found the poor drunk son of a bitch throwing the last of his dignity on the craps table. He told me everything.

"All about how he won forty-two million dollars in the lottery, but he wanted to be smart. He didn't want to go the way most of them do—broke in a year. So when his cousin introduced him to a financial advisor, he took the recommendation, because why wouldn't he? He trusted who his cousin trusted."

Micah groaned. "Everything he described was exactly what happened to my parents and the buyout money they tried to invest for me. I gave them all of the money because I didn't trust myself back then. I was partying too hard, drinking too much, smoking too much, and sleeping around too much. I really thought having all of that money would kill me. I'd be found dead in my mansion with vomit on my pillow and coke dust on my nose within a year. So I gave it all to the people I trusted most... and then that shit floated up.

"Apparently, this guy specifically targets new-money folks who suddenly get a massive windfall and don't know what to do with it. But unlike other preying scum, he's smart. He never approaches the person directly, instead he gets close to a family member or friend and happens to mention to them that he's a financial advisor and investor, so when his mark suddenly mentions that he's in the market for one, the friend will go, '*oh, hey, I actually know a great guy who can help you out. I'll give you his number.*'"

"Wow," I breathed, slumping against the vanity. "That's evil. It's smart, but it's evil. You automatically trust the guy a little more because you went to him. He didn't come to you."

"Exactly. Which is again why I'm an ass." Micah dropped his hands, sending me a sheepish smile. "That guy had never heard of your mother in his entire life, and neither has his cousin, for that matter. All this time, I blamed your mother for introducing that piece of shit to my parents when it was never her fault. He lied to her like he lied to so many others. The only one who was ever to blame was that thieving snake."

"Oh, baby." I went over and lay by his side, resting my head on his arm.

My heart did flips as he rolled to face me, resting his other arm across my hip. Micah was fresh from the shower—enveloping me in a cloud of apples and honey. I was less than in the mood to have sex five doors down from the room where I walked into a new and terrible nightmare, but damned if a part of me wasn't still wishing for a can of lager and Micah's naughty, searching tongue.

"I'm so sorry, but it sounds like that guy was right. Average people who suddenly come into massive windfalls have a hard time hiding it. If around them is where he'll be lurking around, your investigators can get there in time to take him down."

"That's the plan."

I stroked his cheek. "But why didn't you tell me any of this? The last few days, I've been low-key wondering if you killed my mother to settle the fight."

Micah laughed. "That's nuts, and wildly short-sighted on my part. Until literally right now, I had no way of knowing if your mother was packing a few extra billions in her bank account, and no way of knowing if you'd tell me if she did. For all I knew, that's why you suddenly had a change of heart about the divorce and wanted us to send you off with pocket change."

"So you didn't tell me because you didn't trust me?" I asked. "But at that point, you knew my mother had nothing to do with the scam? How did trust even come into it?"

Micah shook his head. "Trust absolutely came into it. I didn't tell you because I didn't trust you not to be nasty about it," he said to my shocked expression. "I could already hear you laughing at me, saying *I told you so*, and once again calling my parents a bunch of gullible dumbasses. Finding out that we were just one of many marks wasn't going to spark any sympathy in you... or so I thought. You've really changed, haven't you."

A tender, stroking finger caressed my forehead. "Amazing what a bump on the head can do."

My smile didn't reach my eyes. "I did walk away from that accident that morning believing I was meant for a new start. But now? Everything's just so fucked, Micah, and I don't know what to do."

"You can stop trying to do everything by yourself for one."

"What do you mean?" I propped up on my elbow. "Are you talking about settling Omma's estate? Because I don't want to do that by myself. You can absolutely help me."

"No, I'm talking about you trying to find Omma and Mrs. Prado's killer." He saw the look on my face. "Alex overheard you shouting at Davis. I know you're not going to stop until you get the truth—and I'm not telling you to," he rushed out when I opened my mouth. "But this doesn't work, Sue. You need information only the cops have, and you're not going to get it making an enemy out of every single one you come across."

"Argh!" I flung back, adopting the same hands-on-face position Micah did. "I know, I know. He just pissed me off so much because I *know* he agrees with me. He knows Courtney didn't do this and the missing bloody clothes are important, but he's not going to do anything about it, because he's a shit-his-pants coward. How is that not supposed to piss me off!"

"It pisses me off too. Especially because they were fucking lazy. After they found the knife in Thorne's bag, they stopped all the interviews and I never got to tell them that there was an eleventh person who went upstairs that night," he dropped on my head like a ton of bricks. "Someone who wasn't in the ballroom the next morning. Someone they missed."

"Excuse me?" I flipped over, jumping on him and tearing a grunt from his chest. "What are you talking about?"

"There was another person wandering around our house instead of at the party where they should've been," he said. "Dad's gout was flaring up but that didn't stop him sucking down the steak, and draining every glass of wine the waiters put in front of him. I went upstairs to get his medicine, and when I came out of their room, I saw a woman whip around the corner. I caught a glimpse of her face, but I did not see that face again the next morning when they gathered us in the ballroom."

"Meaning they missed someone." I rocked back on his lap, chest squeezing. "And you're just telling me this now. What. The. Fuck. Spencer! You and your damn secrets!"

"Whoa, whoa, easy," he said with a laugh. "It wasn't a secret, and I'm only bringing it up now to back you up." Micah grasped my hips. His thumbs slipped under my shirt, rubbing slow circles on my rising goose bumps. "You're right, they did a terrible job investigating both murders, and you have every right to be mad about it."

"But why bring it up now?"

He cringed. "I didn't want to say anything before because it's a sore subject. I recognized her immediately. It was Dana Finley, Colin Finley's mother."

A ringing sounded in my ears—drowning out Micah and my own shouting mind.

"C-Colin's mother?" I rasped.

"That's right." He was still smiling like it was no big deal. "I saw her upstairs but there's no way she attacked your mom. I mean, why would she? But it does bring up a good question—if she slipped by them unnoticed, who else did?"

I barely heard him, my eyes were searching every twitch of his muscles. My ears obsessed over the slightest inflection of his voice. "Micah." My voice came from far away. "You're asking why would she kill my mother? Seriously? How could you possibly believe Dana Finley doesn't have reason to hate this family?"

"Nah." He waved that away, widening my eyes. "I'm sure she doesn't hate your whole family, but that Sarang girl—"

I fell off his lap, stumbling away.

"—she must hate her... for sure..." Micah sat up, squinting at me. "You okay? What's wrong?"

"Sarang?" I was still breathing, but somehow air wasn't in my lungs. "You know... about Sarang?"

"What? Of course, I do." He laughed. "Well, I know what you told me. Sorry, babe, I still don't remember that year we were all at school together, but"—Micah hissed—"I do remember the day Colin went through the floor. Shit, that was horrible."

Micah reached his hand out to me. "I know you said the whole family cut her off after she was expelled, but I still don't think it's right. She should've gone to prison for what she did."

I stared at him, making no move to take his hand. One question and one question alone swirled through my mind.

Is this a trick?

"Micah," I whispered, taking a step back. "I really do want us to start over and make different choices this time. Become a stronger couple."

"Uh, okay?" His hand slowly returned to his side. "Did I say something wrong?"

"No, I did, and now I don't remember what lies I told you about Sarang and Colin."

"Lies?"

"Yeah, lies," I said firmly, falling back on the vanity seat. "Remind me what I told you, so I can tell you the truth now."

Alarm wrinkled his handsome features. "The hell? Sue, you told me Sarang was your cousin. She was messed up on drugs and a loser boyfriend, so her parents shipped her across the world to stay with you and your mom. But a bad pattern is called that for a reason. She came to Titan Prep and got mixed up with losers again. She was obsessed with looking good to her rich friends, so when they dared her to sabotage the stage, she did it." He scoffed. "I'm assuming she didn't see the pipe sticking out of the ground and wasn't planning for Colin to get impaled on it, but seriously.

"Rich jerks were always trying to get us scholarship kids to dance to their tune. But that doesn't mean it's not your fault when you don't fucking say no." He fixed on me. "But now you're saying none of that is true?"

I slowly shook my head, feeling the weight of the lies and manipulations Sue weaved falling on me. I wasn't sure, and I couldn't ask the guys without giving myself away, but now I knew how completely she and Omma erased me.

She, with Omma's help, convinced the guys that she was the one who got accepted into the prestigious Titan Prep, but unlike me, she sailed through with flying colors. Why wouldn't they believe it? Sue told them a lie about a girl named Sarang, but I never went by my real name in high school. Everyone called me Sarah. Sarah Kim was the name under my yearbook photo. And the last name Kim was one I shared with five other Kims in my graduating class—further muddying the pool if anyone ever brought up the *Kim* girl who almost murdered Colin. There were a lot of Kim girls at Titan Prep, and Sue stuck herself among them.

All Sue had to do was tell the boys she went by Sarah too in high school and switched to Sue to differentiate from the Sarah everyone hated, and if they ever asked why Sarang wasn't in the yearbook or why there were no photos of her anywhere, she'd say it was because Sarang Kim was her weirdo, loner freak cousin who never participated in anything or showed up for picture day.

Over the years, any rumors that swirled around she could easily gaslight away. Someone in town asks Sue about her sister in front of Alex? She'd just tell them the person got it wrong and meant her cousin. If anyone ever said twin, ditto on blaming it on the cousin-family resemblance. Everything gets blamed on a cousin that's long gone, and Omma and Sue got to continue living the fantasy that I never existed. And in a community like this where scandals are swept under the rug and only gossiped about in private homes over tea, the guys never had a reason to dig deeper into the lies my family told.

"It's not true." I clasped my hands to stop them from shaking. "Sarang didn't sabotage the trapdoor. She was framed."

His eyes bugged. "What? Are you serious?"

"As hemlock tea." *Be careful, Sarah. Think this through.* "The truth is that Sarang had an enemy during those years. Someone who hated her guts so much, they were willing to hurt an innocent kid to get rid of her," I said, choosing my words carefully. "But when she tried to tell the truth, no one believed her."

Understanding dawned. "Because all they saw was some troublemaker scholarship kid." He put his hand over his mouth. "Holy shit. She was expelled! Colin almost died! Who could hate anyone that much?"

"A truly sick and twisted person." Not a word was a lie. "But Omma didn't believe her. She was convinced Sarang was trying to shift the blame and weasel out of punishment by blaming someone else, so she kicked her out and..." I dropped my gaze. "And Sarang had no one."

"Holy shit. Holy shit!" Micah goggled at me. "But I don't get it, why would you lie to us about that? Why not just tell us your cousin was framed?"

"Because I was a part of it."

Micah's jaw fell open, but nothing came out.

"The truth is I hated Sarang too. I hated all the attention she got. I hated that Omma wouldn't stop comparing me to her. I hated that Sarang had friends, and fun, and a life—and all I had was a tutor with terrible halitosis. I hated her, so I helped the bitch that did it by getting her into the school. She didn't go to Titan Prep, so she needed someone to let her in—that was me."

And that wasn't a lie either. It was because of me that Sue was able to slip onto campus without raising an alarm. She did have my face after all.

"Oh, Sue..."

"I know." I could barely speak around the lump in my throat. "I'm a miserable, shit person. The only thing I can say in my defense is that I didn't know what she'd do. Never in a million years did I imagine she'd let her hatred of Sarang go that far. I didn't realize she was a monster with a human face mask until it was much too late."

Micah nodded slowly, feeling everything I told him sink in.

"After Colin was hospitalized, I kept quiet," I said. "I let Omma believe Sarang did it. I let everyone in town paint her as a psycho, even though I knew the truth. I was a coward." Anger bled into my voice. "A coward then, and every single day after that I went on lying and lying instead of telling everyone—most of all you, Alex, and Rhodes—the truth.

"I just didn't want you to see me differently." *Of course Sue didn't. She wanted you guys to go on believing she wasn't a snake in a human suit.* "But now I do," I whispered. "I want you to see the real me. All of me. It's the only way you can trust it when I say I love you."

"Oh, baby girl..." He opened his arms. "Come here."

I launched off the seat, falling into his arms.

He squeezed the mess out of me. "I'm not going to lie. What you did—letting that psychopath into the school, and then keeping quiet when you knew your cousin was framed—it was a terrible thing to do. A lot of people were hurt over some mean girl's vendetta, and that matters. Your cousin, your mother, Colin, and his family all deserved so much better."

This didn't hurt me. After all, I agreed with every single word.

"But all of that said," he murmured softly, "I'm really happy you told me. You're right, Sue. A marriage that's going to last can't be built on a mountain of resentment and lies. For the first time in seven years, I feel like I'm finally getting to know you—and this person is so much more wonderful than the woman I first met."

I buried my face in his chest, fighting a smile. It was wrong to be happy when we were discussing something so sad, but I couldn't help it. I felt it too.

The Micah I fell for was an illusion. A little teenage crush roasting on spit flamed by hormones. But the real Micah? The guy who loved dirty jokes, old British comedies, having tea parties with Lily, and snuggling with me even when I was covered in vomit? I loved that guy so much more now too.

We were quiet for a long time, just holding each other.

"I guess this means I'm a big flaming idiot who should've told the cops right away that I saw Mrs. Finley wandering around our home uninvited."

"Big-time on the uninvited," I mused, resting my chin on his shoulder. "None of us sent her an invitation."

"It's suspicious for sure, but do you really think she had something to do with your mother's murder? Or Mrs. Prado?" Micah drew back, capturing my gaze in his swirling pools. "If she was going to fly into a rage and kill someone, wouldn't she have done that ten years ago? And if she did want someone dead, why in the hell would she go after your mom? Omma had nothing to do with what happened to her son, and Mrs. Prado had even less than nothing to do with it."

I nodded slowly. "Those are very true statements."

"Could something have changed?" he asked. "Could she have found out the truth somehow? That Sarang was framed, and someone else put her son in a wheelchair for the rest of his life? Maybe Mrs. Finley thought there was a cover-up and Omma was involved." Micah's brows crumpled. "Who was it anyway? Who was really behind the prank?"

"She was a sad, broken bitch who died in a car accident. She's dead and Sarang's gone—leaving only me who knew the truth of what happened that day, and I certainly didn't tell Mrs. Finley anything different from what she was told," I said. "Which is why I'm just as curious as to what brought her to our home that night of all nights."

"We'll tell the police first thing in the morning—"

"No," I said instantly.

"No?" He gave me a wild look. "Why not? Whether or not she had murderous intentions, she never should've been here in the first place. At the very least the cops need to know that someone got past all the guards, and if Mrs. Finley did, the real killer could've too."

My head bobbed along to every word. "I agree with all of that, but I need to talk to Mrs. Finley before we sic Dumb, Dumber, and Dumbass on her. My family has caused hers enough pain. I'm not going to accuse her of murder without at least giving her a chance to explain what she was doing here."

"And I'm sure you also know that you're not going to talk to her alone. It's too dangerous," he added when he saw the look on my face. "We're dealing with a bold and violent killer. Don't think I won't give you a phone with a tracking app too, woman."

Cracking a smile, I nipped his nose. "No tracking devices needed for me. I'll ask Alex to go with me," I heard myself say. "We can drop Lily to school and then go straight to Mrs. Finley's house. Find out what she was doing here. After we settle all of that, I'll go straight to the police station and bail out Officer Cop-A-Feel. That fucking dick."

Micah busted up. "What is this beef you have with our local beat cops? At this rate, the next time we have an emergency, they're going to stop for coffee and donuts on the way over."

I scoffed. "That would not surprise me. I'm basically solving my mother's murder on my own to stop them putting my innocent best friend away for the rest of her life, so why not get used to doing their job for them?"

"Not on your own, baby." Micah kissed me sweet and slow until my toes curled. "Never on your own."

***

"Welcome, honored guests and esteemed alumni."

Bright blinding lights shone in the auditorium, blinding one and all—if there even was an all. I couldn't see anyone to the left or right of me. All I could see—standing at the podium—was the clown.

"We're happy to have you, Sarang Kim." The clown latched on me, grinning that grotesque grin. "And have you I will—always!"

"Omma," I screamed. "He's there! The clown's right there! Help me!" Chains lashed around my arms, chest, and legs—binding me to the seat. "Omma, help me!"

"Enough!" Omma's voice roared through the auditorium. "Enough of your lies! There is no clown! There never was a clown!"

"He's right there, please!" Tears soaked my face. "Please, believe me—"

The floor opened up beneath my feet, plunging me—chair and all into the darkness.

"Ahh!" I tumbled out of bed, hitting the floor with my face and shoulder.

Pulling my body in, I curled up on the floor—tears leaking from my eyes as the last traces of the dream faded away.

**

"Why are we here again?" Alex stopped the car in front of the house, parking on the street.

We eyed the pink one-story bungalow and the overgrown, brown lawn it sat on. I didn't know what I was expecting from the Finley house, but this wasn't it.

The lawn was dead. The porch was desperately in need of repainting. The wheelchair ramp was rusted and barely keeping it together. And one of the windows was boarded up like it was broken at some point, but no one got around to fixing it.

"I'm here to see an old school friend."

Titan Prep was a prestigious academy that welcomed elite and academically superior students from all over the East Coast and abroad. They were also known to give out one, and only one, scholarship per school year to a student who couldn't afford their obscenely expensive tuition.

The scholarship competition was extremely competitive, but Colin won. Thanks to that, he, me, and Courtney were the only students from Lantana who got into Titan Prep that year. Something the three of us bonded over, but the principal used as further "proof" that I pranked Colin. According to him, I was jealous of the scholarship kid who beat me out for everything, when in actuality, the only one who was jealous was Sue.

The main reason I chose Titan Prep was because it was so exclusive, it took a lot more than money to get you in. And that was what I wanted—to go to a high school full of strangers, and no Sue.

Surprise to no one, Sue made middle school a nightmare for me. She was constantly spreading false rumors about me, trying to turn my friends against me, or picking fights with me only to burst into tears and say I started it whenever a teacher broke us up. I wanted *away* from her, so I applied to Titan Prep.

The minute Sue heard about it, even though she knew exactly why I chose a different high school than her, she applied too—and got rejected.

Cue the sobbing and wails to our mother that it wasn't fair for me to go to a fancy prep school while she was stuck at our local one. She tried hard—and I mean *hard*—to get our mother to change her mind and stop me going to Titan Prep. The girl fired every manipulative weapon in her arsenal, but it didn't work.

So yes, it was true jealousy plagued me all four years that I attended Titan Prep, but it wasn't mine. That came from the monster my egg split into.

"Would you mind waiting here for me?" I unbuckled my seat belt and grabbed my things. "I don't want her to feel ganged up on. This is going to be a difficult enough conversation."

"Whoa, whoa." A hand on the arm stopped me. "What's going on? Does this have something to do with your mom or Mrs. Prado?"

"I'm not sure yet," I said honestly. "But whether it does or it doesn't, I realized last night that this conversation is long overdue. Mrs. Finley deserves to know the truth about what happened that day, and I was always going to be the only one who could've told her—that's why I should've done this a long time ago."

The man looked even more confused than before I opened my mouth. "Finley? Wait." His brows snapped together. "Why does that name sound familiar?"

"Don't be afraid to get out and stretch your legs." I hopped out of the car. "I might be a while."

"Sue, wait, who are you—? Hold up, is it Colin Finley?" Alex rolled down the window to call at my back. "Tell me this isn't Colin Finley's house!"

I could not tell him that, so I didn't bother trying. I came clean as much as possible to Micah the night before, but I hadn't had the chance to do so with Alex or Rhodes. All the same, something told me Alex would learn all during the car ride home, and Rhodes would be next that night.

I knocked on the door, psyching myself up. Did I think Mrs. Finley killed my mother? Of course not. Micah had a solid point. If Mrs. Finley was going to do any stabbing, she'd have done it ten years ago. Why wait until now, and why my mother?

Omma emptied out my trust and college fund and gave it to Colin's family. It didn't make up for what Sue did to him, but Omma literally paid for a crime she didn't commit. Why track her down a decade later and kill her when the person responsible had to be the one Mrs. Finley truly hated?

The door flew open, stopping my musing in its tracks.

Omma had us when she was forty, which meant the fellow mothers in the school pickup line were about ten to twenty years younger than her. Mrs. Finley was one such younger mother—in her early fifties compared to Omma, who was bumping up against seventy. But looking at the woman standing before me, no one would've guessed which one was younger.

Dry hair heavily streaked with white escaped the many clips haphazardly stuck on her scalp. Deep wrinkles competed with the stress and frown lines etched in her face—both trying and winning their mission to age her twenty years. She wore a large, purple muumuu that completely swallowed her figure, and ratty house slippers that were falling apart on her feet.

She wasn't smiling when she opened the door, but the minute our eyes met, I got the sense she'd never smile again.

"What the fuck do you want?"

A lump lodged in my throat. *Okay, not off to a promising start.*

"Hello, Mrs. Finley," I rasped. "I'm not sure if you know who I am—"

"Soo Min Kim." She spat the name. "I know exactly who you are. I repeat, what the fuck do you want?"

"To talk. We're long overdue for a conversation, Mrs. Finley."

"Oh?" She raised a brow that was darker than the hair on her head. "Are we?"

"We are," I said, voice firm but polite. "You believe so too, or you wouldn't have come to my house Friday night."

Her face shuttered closed. Of all the things she was prepared for me to say, I don't think she was ready for that one.

"Come in."

Looking back at Alex, I gave him a little thumbs-up, then stepped over the threshold.

The living room was small and cluttered. The couches, coffee table, end tables, and entertainment center were all too big for the space. A space made smaller by all the random gifts and knickknacks one accumulates over a long life.

I made to sit down but Mrs. Finley didn't stop. She passed through the entrance off the living room, so I followed her—winding up in the kitchen.

Just like the living room, the kitchen was cluttered. Dirty pots and pans covered the stove and filled the sinks. Stacks of letters covered the kitchen island, and all of the available counter space was taken up by appliances, and pills. So many pill bottles that I stopped counting at fifteen.

Mrs. Finley crossed to the kettle and flicked it on. Her back was to me as she busied herself getting cups, tea bags, sugar, and spoons. I took that chance to sit down at the island.

"Say what you came to say," she snapped.

"Oh, right." I sat up straight, sucking in a deep breath. "I'm actually not sure how to begin, but here goes… You may or may not know that something horrible happened last Friday night. My mother was murdered and—"

"What's so horrible about that?"

"Excuse me?"

"You heard me." She turned around, slapping me with a glare that almost knocked me off the seat. "What's so horrible about that rancid bitch getting exactly what she deserved?"

I gaped at her. "What the hell? Why would you say that? My mother wasn't responsible for what her daughter did."

"Yeah, and that's exactly what she said to the judge." She slammed the mug down, chipping the bottom. "Is that why you've come here? To tell me *once again* that since there's no proof of parental neglect or a documented pattern of behavior that said parent failed to address, parental liability cannot be proven, and therefore your mother wasn't at fault and had no obligation to pay."

"What?" My mind was in knots trying to follow this conversation. "What are you talking about?"

"What else would I be talking about!" she screamed, blowing me back. "What else is there to talk about! For ten years, it's been the same conversation, the same argument, the same fight, and a world that doesn't listen! That doesn't care! That doesn't help!" Her eyes bugged out of her head. "Lord knows, I wanted to talk about something else for once—for one day! Well, I got my wish!" She burst into a hysterical, shrieking laugh that chased a chill up my spine. "Now everyone can talk about something else, because Dana Finley is finally going to shut up!"

My eyes were huge. I was leaning back so far on my seat, one slight breeze and I'd topple off. "Mrs. Finley, I'm so sorry, but I truly don't understand. Are you— Are you talking about the lawsuit from ten years ago?"

Her glare intensified—lips peeling back from her teeth.

"But I don't understand," I repeated. "Why would you be upset about that? My mother paid you."

"Excuse me? Is that your new tactic?" she cried, disbelief coloring her tone. "Screaming at me that I was a worthless leech who wouldn't get a cent out of you or your family wasn't enough. Now you're pretending we live in your delusional fantasy land!"

I could only gape at her, horrible understanding dawning. "She... never paid you." My lips were numb. "My mother never paid the lawsuit. So, all this time..." I looked around the kitchen, then looked at her. "You've hated her."

If possible, her snarl became even more feral. "Why shouldn't I hate her? Why shouldn't I hate the woman who stood up in court and argued that plastic screws or no, the trapdoor wouldn't have given way if my son weren't *morbidly obese*! If I had done my job as a mother, kept him close and healthy, he wouldn't have almost died from being too heavy for the floor to carry him.

"Why shouldn't I hate the beast who claimed I was only using her to *profit* off my child's misery? Who claimed if my *vendetta* was truly about holding the guilty party responsible, I'd have sued your sister, Sarah Kim," she spat. "Well, fat chance of that when she disappeared! Shipped her back off to China—"

"Korea," I sliced in automatically.

"—where she could hide away in another McMansion, pretending nothing ever happened, while me and Colin had nothing!" She thumped her chest, the pound resounding like her booming voice. "Your mother blamed everything and everyone else except herself... for raising two spoiled cunts who should've been strangled by their umbilical cords and shat into a toilet upon birth."

I pressed my lips tightly together, breathing slow through my nose. She was trying to provoke me. If she really hated and wanted nothing to do with me, she wouldn't have let me through the door.

Was all of this deliberate? Was she trying to provoke me into striking first so that she'd have an excuse to kill me like she killed—

"Is that why you did it?" I asked. "Is that why you killed my mother?"

Her eyes glittered. "Why shouldn't I have killed her? She deserved to die. All of you—throwing that tacky, obscene party—celebrating while my Colin—my Colin—" Finley's lips trembled. "Dying peacefully on a cloud of morphine was too good for the whore who spat you out. Justice demanded she suffer, so I put it right."

I was shaking. My whole body rattled so hard my teeth chattered. "And Mrs. Prado?"

Mrs. Finley frowned. "What?"

"Why Mrs. Prado?" I demanded. "Why did you kill her?"

"Why— Why not?" She shrugged, lips twisting. "It was her own fault—that Prado woman. She shouldn't have gotten in my way."

I nodded slow. "How did you get into my home and upstairs unseen?"

"What the fuck does that matter?" she barked, eyes flashing. "I did it. Who cares how?"

"Okay, fine." My voice was nothing but a thin croak. "If I could ask just one more question then—why now? It sounds like you've hated my mother for ten years. Why kill her now?"

Mrs. Finley laughed. It was a terrible sound. "Why wait until she was a broken, wasted, shell of herself? Why wait until she was a leech and burden, relying on others to eat, wash, and shit? Why wait until she was scared and hopeless with nothing to look forward to?

"Why wait until I could stand over her, look her in the eyes, and see the moment she realizes I have all the power, and there's not a damn thing she could do about it?" She laughed that horrid laugh again. "I see why only your sister got into Titan Prep. You're definitely the stupid one."

I was quiet for a long time. So long, my bag started buzzing. It was likely Alex calling to check up on me and see what was taking so long.

I reached into my bag, pushed aside Sue's buzzing phone, and closed on mine. I turned the recorder off.

"You've been very honest with me, Mrs. Finley, and although you might not think this is sincere, I truly appreciate that."

Her eyes narrowed to slits. No, she did not think I was sincere.

"Honesty is everything," I heard myself say. "We all deserve it—you more than anyone."

"What the hell are you blathering about?"

"That's why I've come here," I went on like she hadn't spoken. "To do something I should've done a long time ago—tell you the truth. And it starts with this: Sarah never touched the trapdoor—"

"You—!"

"Sue did it," I sliced in, halting her mid-shout. "Sue snuck into the school, replaced the screws with cheap plastic destined to give way, and then she snuck away and let gravity and security cameras do the rest. *She* did this," I stressed, "and I know this because I'm not Soo Min. I'm Sarang. I'm Sarah."

Mrs. Finley didn't move. She didn't shout. She didn't blink. She didn't even look at me. Her eyes glazed out of focus like she couldn't see me anymore.

Starting from the beginning, I told her *almost* everything. How Sue and I started to hate each other by eight years old, and it only got worse from there. I shared the lies, the gaslighting, the sabotage, and her endless campaign to make my life hell. I told her about Sue's seething jealousy when I got into Titan Prep and then into Yale. Then I told her how it all culminated into Sue framing me for pranking Colin, which resulted in my mother throwing me out.

Towards the end is where I fudged it a bit.

"Sue ran off and abandoned her child and husbands, so I stepped up," I said. "I came back to be there for them and to be there... for my mother. I want to put right what went wrong." I climbed down off the stool, hitching my bag up my shoulder. "It's too late for you now. You're going to prison for what you did to Mrs. Prado and my mother, but I want you to know, Colin will be taken care of.

"Every cent my mother and sister should've given to him will go to him now. No matter how long it takes me, or what it costs—his care will be paid in full for the rest of his life." Gaze drifting, I fixed on the picture of the sweet, smiling little boy holding up his first-place ribbon for the science fair. "I'm sorry it took so long, Mrs. Finley. Sorry for you, for Colin, for me, for Mrs. Prado, and for my mother. The act of one jealous, mean girl shattered so many lives that day and for that... I'm just sorry."

Turning my back, I walked away.

"Sorry?" came a trembling voice. "You're... sorry?"

I didn't slow or turn back. There was nothing else to say and no more time to waste. I needed to get this recording to Officer Cop-A-Feel and get my best friend out of prison.

"You're SORRY!?"

Crash!

A mug hit the wall to the right of me, exploding in a shower of razor-tipped ceramic shards.

"Ahh!" I screamed, throwing my hands over my head and face.

Thunderous footsteps came up on me so fast, I didn't have time to turn around.

"What good is your sorry?" she shrieked. "What do your promises matter now! He's dead!"

Shock struck me through the chest. *What?*

"Because of you and your stupid sibling rivalry, my son lost everything!"

Something fell over my eyes, and wrapped around my throat.

"Eurgh!"

"His body, his future, his life—everything!" She wrenched the dishcloth tighter, popping my eyes and tongue out of my skull. "Where were you?! The whole time— The whole time!" she screamed, thrashing me around. "The person responsible was right there, and I didn't know *because of you!*"

Blood rushed to my face—trapping in bursting blood vessels as air trapped in my burning lungs. I clawed at the cloth, my nails bending and breaking under the assault.

"Because of you, we had nothing! No money to pay for Colin's care! Because of—!"

My fist flew up, striking something that crunched against my bones.

"Ah!"

Mrs. Finley flew back, loosening her grip.

I didn't waste a second.

"H-help!" I scrambled across the floor, crawling through the hall into the living room. The doorknob loomed only six feet from my grasping fingertips. "Hel—!"

A heavy mass dropped on me, bouncing my skull off the hardwood.

"Where were your promises last week, you narcissistic bitch!" Knees crunched my spine, pinning me to the floor as the dish towel found my neck again. "It's too late!"

I garbled and gasped, black spots popping in my vision. One of the shadows moved and I strained to look away—my hands pounding and slamming the floor trying to buck her off.

Alex?

Alex stood at the window, peering through the glass.

"Al— Ag!" I called for him, reaching through the bleeding darkness. *Alex, help me!*

"Just die!" Mrs. Finley wrenched my head back and forth, bouncing it off the floor—bloodying my forehead as my body desperately screamed for air.

And Alex didn't move.

HELP!

He didn't twitch. He didn't call for help. He didn't shout. He didn't tap the glass.

As consciousness fled, Alex stood there... and watched me die.

Chapter Nineteen

"...take her to the hospital..."

"...were you doing..."

"Your job!"

What... What's going on? A lone thought swirled in the darkness, tugging on my consciousness and demanding it leave the peace, quiet, and numb.

"She was doing your fucking job because she told you a million times Courtney Thorne didn't do it, and you wouldn't listen!"

My eyelid cracked open, sending searing light piercing through my brain.

"Look at my wife! Look at her!" shouted a familiar voice. "Is this what an innocent person does to a woman!?"

Through one eye, my vision slowly cleared. I was in something small and cluttered. The walls crowded me even as a firm surface kept me tethered.

Ambulance... my sluggish brain supplied.

I was in an ambulance—which meant the two figures standing at its entrance, shouting back and forth, were Alex and Officer Davis.

"This attack was unfortunate, but the fact remains that you and Mrs. Kim had no business here. You—"

I tried to speak. "Arggh." Nothing but a groan came out.

"Mrs. Kim?" An unfamiliar face bore over me. From the uniform I safely guessed she was a paramedic. "Don't try to speak, please. You're safe now and we're getting you to a hospital."

"O... O-omma..." I croaked. "O— Om...ma..."

"What's that? Uma?" Her freckled brow crumpled. "I'm sorry, I don't understand."

"She's saying Omma," Alex snapped. "It means mother—*her* mother, who *that woman* killed!"

"Mr. Montgomery, please calm down," Davis said. "There's no question an error was made. We have Mrs. Finley in custody, and she's already given a full confession." Davis fixed on me. "She's admitted that on the night of your party, she persuaded her nephew, Officer Callahan, to sneak her inside your home... where she killed your mother."

He swallowed hard, his Adam's apple bobbing in his stiff, tense throat. "Your reckless actions aside, I give you my sincerest apologies because it was my *lack* of action that drove you to it. You told me that it couldn't have been Ms. Thorne. You asked me to investigate my fellow officers for a traitor, and you said there were stronger motives we were ignoring—and you were right on all counts."

Davis looked back. "Last week, Mrs. Finley's son, Colin Finley, passed away from a stroke in the care facility he was living in. The facility was underfunded, mismanaged, and criminally negligent. It seems not only did the nurses neglect to give Colin his necessary meds that day, they also failed to perform their regular bed checks. If they had, there was every chance this tragedy could've been prevented."

My broken heart sank.

"Shocked and grieving, Mrs. Finley walked into your home to kill the person she blamed for Colin's death. If Madame Kim hadn't squashed her lawsuit, she would've had the money she needed to give Colin the best care." He sighed. "Or so she believed."

I tried to speak—my jaw working, but my voice had given all it was going to.

"That facility is now under investigation and Mrs. Finley will be charged for her crimes, but I know none of that makes up for your loss," he told me. "I am sorry, Mrs. Kim, but I hope now you can grieve in peace, knowing that you fought for your mother and for the truth."

No!

Davis tipped his head, then walked away.

"N—!" I tried to get out, my weak body not even trying to respond to my commands to move. *Come back!*

"She's getting a bit agitated," the paramedic lady said to someone. "I'm going to give her something to help her relax."

Alex climbed into the ambulance, taking a seat by my side. Nothing but love and concern shown in his eyes as he took my hand.

"Don't worry, baby," he said over my internal screaming. "I'm right here."

Darkness crowded in quickly, stealing me away.

"I'm not going anywhere."

***

That night, I sat in silence—watching my sleepy Lantana town pass by the window.

"Are you sure you're okay?" Alex reached over and stroked my arm. "They said you could stay overnight. Maybe we should've—just to be safe."

I shifted around, taking him in.

Alex Montgomery was handsome and wonderful in every way, as he always was every day. Every single minute since I woke up again in a hospital bed, he'd been at my side—loving and attentive as he got on the doctor's case, and assured Rhodes and Micah that they didn't need to come because he was taking care of me. Nothing about his actions after I woke up in the ambulance matched the dead-eyed apparition that stood there watching me die.

Did I imagine it?

"Alex..." My throttled throat still struggled to produce more than a whisper. "When Mrs. Finley— When she attacked me, I thought I saw... you."

He frowned out the window. "What do you mean?"

"Have you truly forgiven me for everything?" I narrowed on the side of his face I could see. "Are we okay now? For real?"

"Sue, baby, of course we are." Alex turned just to smile at me. "We are very much okay now. You know that."

"You're not still mad?" I pressed. "About the way I've treated you over the years? About the... suggestion that I was cheating?"

I got a flicker of bewilderment before he shifted back to the road. "Baby, I'm not mad anymore. I've put it all behind me so that we could start over." He squeezed my arm. "Why are you bringing this up now?"

"Because I saw you." I squinted at him. "In the window when Mrs. Finley was strangling me with a dish towel. You were just standing there watching like—like you wanted her to kill me."

"What?" he cried, slamming hard on the brake. He pulled off and stopped the car in a café parking lot before I knew what was happening. "Sue, what the hell are you talking about? Of course I didn't want her to kill you. I *stopped* her from killing you. It was me who broke down the door, pulled Finley off, and called 911. Of course it was," he beseeched me. "No one else was there."

That was undoubtedly true. It seemed unlikely that Mrs. Finley suddenly had a change of heart and up and let me go, then called the police on herself. Alex had to be the one who saved me, but did that mean my oxygen-deprived brain imagined him kicking back shooting the breeze while a middle-aged woman tried to pop my head off, or was what I saw real, and Alex just changed his mind?

If he did change his mind and choose me, do I just let it go? Or is watching someone kill you the kind of red flag you just don't ignore?

"I don't know, Alex," I rasped. "Maybe I imagined it, but I feel I need to say again that if being with me is too hard, it's okay. We can part on your terms with no hard feelings. You don't have to force yourself to stay with me—"

"Stop." Alex reached for me, taking my face in his hands. "I don't know what kind of horrible nightmare tortured you in those last moments, but say the word and I'll go back and kick Nightmare Boy's ass. No one fucks around in my woman's imagination—not even me."

The barest smile tugged at my lips. It tugged harder as he drew me in, kissing me soft and sweet.

"I told you," he whispered. "I'm not going anywhere. Yes, I admit, loving you was hard for a long time, but now... now it's the easiest thing in the world. I'm finally right where I'm supposed to be—next to you." Another soft peck graced my lips. "Don't ever doubt it."

"Okay." I pressed my forehead to him, my eyes drifting closed. "Thank you, baby. I really needed to hear that."

"It's been an awful fucking day. Let's go home. I'll bundle you up on the couch with the Lilybug and old comedy reruns while I'll make you some too-sweet strawberry-ade and burnt japchae."

A giggle escaped me—the very first one since Omma was killed. Of course it was Alex. It had to be Alex... who brought back my laugh.

"That sounds perfect." I meant it. "But I have to see Courtney. She's had the worst few days of her life. She needs her friend, and I'm not going to let her down again."

"They might not have released her yet." Alexander drew back and started the car. "Mrs. Finley was ranting her head off when they hauled her out of the car and stuck her in the back of the squad car, but she completely shut down when they got her to the station. Last I heard, she hasn't said a word."

"How did you hear that?"

He scoffed. "Balogun and her partner were trying to make up for being incompetent fools and save the LPD from a lawsuit by coming by the hospital personally to see how you were doing. You were still sleeping, but they told me that other than saying she killed Mrs. Prado and Omma, and then asking for a lawyer, she hasn't said another word.

"They said Courtney will be released once they get *the full picture of how Mrs. Finley committed these crimes and why she chose to frame Ms. Thorne*," he repeated. "No idea if they've got that picture yet."

"I need to call her," I cried, scrambling for my phone. "Finley's nephew let her into our house and helped her avoid the other guards. Not to mention she's clearly filled with murderous rage." I gestured to my bruised throat. "How much clearer does the picture get for these assholes?"

Another scoff. "It's ridiculous. At this point, they need to just shut up and listen to you, because you're the only one who had it right from the start." He stroked my cheek as we pulled out of the parking lot. "Look, for now, let's go home. Lily really needs a hug from her mom right now."

That swayed me better than anything else could.

"While you're relaxing, I'll get on the cops and make sure that poor woman doesn't spend another night in jail," he said. "I'll go down and break her out if I have to."

***

He didn't have to break her out, but he did drive down and pick her up the next morning—bringing her to stay with me for the day while Rhodes and

Micah were at work, Lily was at school, and Alex was upstate visiting his parents in New York.

"How are you, babe?" I snuggled into her side—the two of us buried under a mountain of blankets, chocolate, and funny movies in the second living room. "And I mean a real how are you?"

She gave me a trembling smile. "I'm okay. The detectives couldn't get me in front of a judge, so they kept me in the holding cell the whole time. Lantana isn't exactly a hotbed of crime, so except for the occasional drunken public nuisance that needed some time to sleep it off, I was in there by myself. Boring as shit," she dropped. "But not too traumatic.

"No, what freaked me out was knowing someone hated me so much they put a bloody knife in my bag and framed me for murder." She chomped a huge bite out of her white chocolate bar. "Why would Mrs. Finley do that to me? Did she blame me too for what happened to Colin? Did she think I helped you get away with it or something, so she wanted to take us all down?"

"No, but I bet she throws that lie on top of the rest to help sell that she's the killer."

She paused mid-chew. "Excuse me?"

"She didn't do it, Courtney," I announced, finally voicing the truth I tried to tell Davis the day before, and lost my nerve when I tried again with Alex. "She didn't kill Mrs. Prado or my mother, so it's highly unlikely she ever came anywhere near the murder weapon to put it in your bag."

Huge eyes swallowed me. "Sarah, what are you talking about? The woman confessed. She got her nephew to help her get inside. She tried to kill you!"

"All of those things are true." I climbed out from under the blankets. Crossing my legs, I sat up and faced her. "But when I asked her why she killed Mrs. Prado, I could see in her eyes that she didn't have a clue what I was talking about. Then, she made it worse by claiming Mrs. Prado *got in her way*.

"It's just vague enough that Detective Dumb and Dumbass might swallow it, but it doesn't make sense. Colin was still alive when Mrs. Prado was murdered," I said. "Mrs. Finley still had something to live for—someone to live for. She had a child who needed her, so why would she risk everything by knifing an innocent house manager in the back? With her in prison, Colin would have no one, and she just wouldn't have done that to him.

"And I know that because she's hated my mother and my family for ten years, but she never once tried to take revenge until—"

"Colin died," Courtney whispered, slowly bobbing her head. "You're right. Shit, Sarah, you're right. It doesn't make any sense that she'd just get up one day and kill Mrs. Prado for no reason, but are you sure?" She scooted closer, dropping her voice. "Are we sure that Mrs. Prado was killed by the same person? The police still don't have a motive for either murder, so how can you be sure?"

"I'm sure." My voice was firm. "My mother's murder was clearly premeditated. The party, the guards, the frame job, the escape—all of it was executed too perfectly to be random. I think the killer used Christie and the parade of staff she brought that morning to blend in and scope out the place. What they weren't planning on was Mrs. Prado being there—front and center to see them arrive.

"She must've recognized him," I insisted. "Knew that he wasn't some waiter for an event planner in New York, so what the hell was he doing strutting around my manor in a waitstaff uniform?"

Her head bobbed harder, following along with every word. "That makes sense! Mrs. Prado has been a house manager for forty years. She's worked for most of the rich families all up and down the coast. She'd definitely find it strange if she saw one of her former rich-boy young masters here pretending to be a waiter. So strange, she'd mention it to you."

"And just like that"—I clapped—"she had to be silenced."

"Wow," she breathed, leaning back. "It does sound less and less like Mrs. Finley had anything to do with this, but then why confess?"

"I have no doubt that Mrs. Finley came here that night with the goal of doing something final," I said, rubbing my neck. "But I also doubt she ever came close. What I think really happened is that Finley got lost."

Her brows rose up. "Lost?"

"Yep. My mother's room was in the east wing on the second floor, but Micah saw her skulking around the guest rooms on the third floor of the west wing—about as far from my mother as she could get. She was lost," I cried. "Stressed, grieving, breaking down, she didn't come here with any real plan, so of course, she got lost in this maze of a place—searching frantically while trying not to be seen.

"When my scream brought the rest of the cop guards to me, Officer Callahan rushed his aunt out the other way—getting her out unseen, but deeply dissatisfied," I told her. "She came here to get justice for her son, and instead left with nothing. She must see this confession as her second chance to fight for him.

"*Everyone* is going to want this story. Reporters are going to climb over each other to interview her. The trial will be televised. After a decade of being ignored and silenced, she gets to tell the world her and Colin's story. She gets to tell them all that the devil's name is Kim."

"Wow," she repeated, rocking back until she fell on the pillows—mind blown. "That's... that's just so sad. All of this—this whole miserable situation—breaks my heart."

"It breaks mine too, Court. I only went along, pretending like I believed her because I'd have done anything to get you out of jail, even if it meant handing the police a recorded fake confession, but honestly, sitting there listening to that devastated woman, all I wanted to do was something I haven't been able to do since this all started—cry."

We fell silent, thinking of all the lives destroyed, and the acts that couldn't be forgiven.

"So what now?" Courtney asked the ceiling. "The real killer is still out there, toasting his luck because someone else confessed to his crime. We've got to find them, and yes, I said *we*." She flashed me a stern look like she sensed an argument coming. "You're not searching for this guy alone. He's fucking nuts. He murdered a woman and tossed her in a dirty fountain just for recognizing him. If he gets his hands around your neck, he's not going to stop until he finishes the job, so don't argue with me. We're in this together."

I cracked a smile. "I wouldn't dream of doing this any other way. Together—let's bring this son of a bitch down."

We stared at each other.

"Uh, now seems like a good time to ask," Courtney drew out. "*How* do we bring this guy down? Where do we go from here? I'm sure your event planner vets her staff, but if the killer just stole a uniform and blended in with the chaos, she'd know nothing about them, so she's no help there. Ditto if some of the cops were being lax and weren't actually manning their posts. If someone else made it upstairs like Mrs. Finley did, they may not know about it—so ditto on being unhelpful."

I huffed out a groan. "I was thinking the same thing. Rhodes was in his office. Micah was in his parents' room. Alex went up after the murder to make a call. Layton was in the library. Mrs. Finley was lost on the third floor, and Reynard has a photo of himself out with his friends at the same time Rhodes says he saw him in the garden, but either way, he wasn't in my mother's room. So many people weren't where they were supposed to be, but they also weren't near my mother, so what does that leave other than a stranger who slipped in here unnoticed? How can I track him down if that's the case?"

"They can't be too strange," she murdered, chewing her lip. "It has to be someone who had a problem with your mother. Someone she knew. Someone we haven't thought of yet." She snapped her fingers. "Plus, they had to know the event planner and her fleet of minions would be arriving at the manor that morning. How many people could've known that?"

"That's the problem, Court. I don't know how many people could have known that, or who might've had a grudge against my mother. I haven't exactly been around for the last decade."

"True," she gave in, inclining her head. "Very true. So, basically... we're nowhere."

"Basically."

Courtney heaved herself up. "We'll keep brainstorming in the car. It's time to pick up the girls."

Surprised, I glanced at the clock, seeing that she was right. Afternoon snuck up on us quickly.

Quickly we cleaned up, then took off in Sue's car, first to pick up Taylor and then to pick up Lily.

"I'll see you there," Mr. Layton called, waving at us as he made for the car. "Short lesson today so Lily can play with her friend."

"Yay," Lily cried, jumping up and down and hugging Taylor like they were long-lost sisters reunited.

Seeing them made something broken and empty in my heart twinge. Not even at our best were Sue and I like this. We were always on opposite sides, and that war destroyed many lives—even got people killed. Even Courtney, the only real sister I ever had, got caught up in the poisonous miasma that seemed to follow the Kim family everywhere they went.

Makes me wonder if the real reason so many societies, cultures, and nations have a concept of curses... is because they're real.

Together we drove back to the manor. Courtney and I kept the conversation light while the girls chattered in the backseat. When we got home, Courtney took them into the kitchen for a quick snack while I prepped the sitting room for Lily's piano lesson.

Ding-ding.

I hurried out, rushing to the door to let Mr. Layton in.

"Hello, again," I said.

Layton stood on the welcome mat, his sheet music under one arm and his coat under the other.

He didn't move.

"Come in, come in." I swept aside, gesturing him in. "Lily's finishing up her snack but she'll be ready soon. I can get you something too while you wait—"

He dropped to his knees. Wide eyes swallowing me, Layton pitched forward—sprawling the welcome mat dead.

I took one look and clamped my hand over my mouth, screaming into my palm.

***

"Mrs. Kim." Balogun waited for me outside Lily's room with a serious expression that bordered more on disapproving. "We have to stop meeting like this."

"I agree," I rasped, stomach heaving. I was glad I couldn't see myself in Lily's wall mirror anymore, because I looked terrible. "Have any suggestions for how I make that happen? Because mine for you is that you catch the bastard who keeps killing everyone I know." It was a struggle not to scream.

Balogun seemed to feel the anger in my voice all the same. She pressed her lips tightly together as she gestured for me to follow her. "How is your daughter?"

"She's fine. My friend is looking after her right now, and my husbands are on the way home." I pressed my hand to my forehead, feeling flushed and sweaty. "Thankfully, she didn't see him like that, but now I have to explain to her that she'll never see her teacher again so soon after losing her grandmother. My goodness, who is doing these things, because you have to see that it's not Mrs. Finley," I cried, whirling on her. "You know that she's lying about killing my mother, don't you?"

She gazed at me steadily. "Mrs. Finley hasn't given us a chance to question her story because she refuses to tell us. She hasn't spoken a word since she was brought into custody except to say that she's the killer, and she'll give the full details to a reporter."

It was scary how right I was about that.

"Naturally," Balogun drawled, "that's never going to happen. We don't allow suspects to sensationalize their crimes for media attention. Even the thought of that is obscene and disrespectful to the victims."

"I completely agree—in most cases." I sighed, rubbing my temple. Together we tromped down the stairs. "But in this case, Mrs. Finley didn't kill my mother and she definitely didn't touch Mr. Layton. What she really wants is to give her son a voice. To speak up for him now that he's gone. If you promise her that she'll get plenty of coverage and attention for confessing to the crime, and strangling me, she'll give up the lie and tell you the truth of what really happened that night."

Her expression didn't change. "An interesting suggestion, Mrs. Kim, but not what we're here to discuss." Stepping off the bottom step, she pointed to the man dead in my doorway. "I'm here for him."

Seeing Layton like that again exploded bile up my throat. As dead bodies go, he didn't crack my top three of the most horrifying to witness, but still, the massive knife sticking out of his spine made me want to run and hide.

Her partner leaned over that knife, examining it while he jotted down notes in his pad. On either side of him were two crime scene technicians, and behind all of them, was Officer Davis.

"Walk me through what happened here." Balogun walked off, forcing me to follow—forcing me closer to the body.

"It's like I told the first officer who took my statement." I looked around for her but didn't see her. "I heard the doorbell, went to answer it, and found Mr. Layton on the doorstep. He didn't even get a chance to say anything. He just fell down dead with that knife in his back."

She hummed, her eagle eyes sweeping the doorframe. "And you didn't see or hear anyone else?"

"No."

"Why did you get rid of your security cameras?"

"I—" The question penetrated. "Wait, what?"

"Why," she asked slowly, "do you not have security cameras?" Stepping over the body, she crooked her finger for me to follow. "I noticed that the last time we were here when the mob you whipped up knocked me on my ass."

I sensed she was expecting me to throw an apology into that awkward pause, but I didn't. Scurrying around Kaplan, I went to see what she was pointing at.

"There, there, and there." Balogun's finger jabbed the air. "You have mounts for security cameras, but no cameras."

"We—"

"It's the same for your gate," she sliced in. "You have the booth for a guard, but instead of hiring one, you replaced the automatic opener."

"Replaced?"

"The sensor and gate opener are clearly new while that rusted-over gate is not." She gave me a smile that didn't reach her eyes. "You requested that my partner and I cease with the lazy investigating and pay attention to the details, and I assure you, Mrs. Kim, from this point on, I will not miss a trick.

"So again, I repeat, why are you missing the two things that could've prevented Mr. Layton's death, your mother's and possibly Mrs. Prado's as well? Why did you get rid of the guards and cameras?"

I blinked at the empty mount looming over my doorstep. I didn't notice them before she said something, and now they were all I could see. "I... don't know."

"You don't know?"

"I don't," I blurted. "I mean, the guard we... we probably let go of them because we couldn't justify the expense to the estate lawyer."

"Probably? You don't know for sure?"

Of course I don't know for fucking sure! I wasn't here when any of these decisions were made!

"My mother handled everything to do with the running of the estate, and then when she got ill, my husbands took over. I've never been involved with the day-to-day stuff."

"Even so." The tense lines around her mouth hadn't relaxed. "You would've noticed when the cameras disappeared. You didn't have a thing to say about that? You didn't ask why?"

"This is a safe town, Detective. We've never had a problem here until recently. My husbands were most likely tired of paying to film the leaves fall. None of us could've predicted all of these horrible things would happen."

"Hm."

That was it. Just a hum, and still that response filled me with dread.

"That will be all for now, Mrs. Kim. Please give us some space to do our work."

I didn't argue with her. Moving off toward the back entrance, I stared at those mounts until I couldn't anymore—her words banging around in my head.

Why did you get rid of the two things that could've prevented these murders?

***

That night, I burst into Alex's room, startling him so bad he spilled his beer.

"Goodness, woman," he cried, diving down to rescue the can. "You scared the mess out of me. You can't go around bursting into rooms when there's another freaking killer on the loose."

I stared him down, making him back up a step.

This was the first time I'd been in Alex's room. Unlike Micah who lived here for seven years but still barely moved in, Alex had made the space his home.

A massive big-screen television covered half the hideous wallpaper on the back wall while photos of Lily through the years covered all the rest. He got rid of the old four-poster bed that used to be in here and replaced it with a king-sized, black silk-covered mattress with a silver chrome frame.

Instead of a desk, he had a cozy, carpeted corner with books, arts and crafts supplies, and a small table for Lily to play and work on her assignments.

"Sue, you okay?"

"Why don't we have security cameras anymore?"

"Security cameras?" Crossing to the en suite, Alex went in, then came out holding a washcloth. "Why are you asking about that? You know why we got rid of them."

"Pretend I don't know."

"Pretend... you don't know?"

My intensity didn't let up. "Yes."

"Okay." Alex dropped down, cleaning up the spill. "The one we got was too sensitive. The floodlights went crazy over every squirrel and butterfly that went past. Then, if that wasn't enough, it started malfunctioning. The alarm would go off for no reason and scare Lily, and one night—at three in the fucking morning—it wouldn't turn off even though we entered the right code a dozen times.

"We got rid of it the next morning, and haven't gotten around to getting a new one."

Whoops. All of that did sound like something Sue would know. You don't forget an alarm waking you at three a.m. and screaming at you nonstop for the rest of the morning.

"Okay, thank you. I did know that," I fudged, "but I wanted to hear how it sounded from someone else. Because when I told Balogun all of this, she looked at me like I handed her the smoking gun."

"The smoking gun? Wait. The cops can't seriously think we had anything to do with Mr. C's murder— Which I can't believe I'm saying out loud." Alex groaned, falling back on his bed. "What the hell is going on around here, Sue? Why was there a murdered man on our doorstep this afternoon! How are we going to explain this to Lily?" Alex bolted up and grabbed my wrist.

I squeaked as I came plopping down next to him.

"Was everything okay when you picked Lily up from school?" Alex flipped on his side. Throwing his arm across my lap, he drew me close—drawing little circles on my hip.

The complete casualness of the touch brought back my shivers and clammies.

"Did you notice anyone weird? Anyone"—his grip tightened on me—"following you? Watching you guys?"

I shook my head. "No one. I didn't notice anyone hanging around the manor or lurking in the bushes either. I have to believe I would've noticed if someone was. I've been so on edge lately. All of my senses are on high alert."

"Same."

"But you're thinking what I'm thinking, aren't you?" I lay down next to him, meeting his eyes across the silken sheets. "This wasn't random. The person who killed Layton also killed my mother and Mrs. Prado."

"How can that be? Layton has nothing to do with your mother," he said. "They didn't even speak."

"He was upstairs when that beast went after my mother. Layton told me he was reading in the library the whole time, but we'll never know if that's true now. Maybe he saw something he wasn't supposed to, and the killer silenced him."

"Silenced him a day after some woman who attacked and tried to kill *you* was arrested for their crime? And hang on," he cried. "When did you decide Mrs. Finley was innocent?"

"I knew ten minutes into our conversation."

I told him why—explaining how she didn't know Mrs. Prado was dead until I told her, and she wouldn't have done a thing that would've taken her away from Colin.

"It makes sense," he gave in. "But it doesn't make sense that after getting away with two murders because someone else confessed to them, he'd kill someone else in the same way and draw the police's attention again. Why didn't he cut Layton's brakes or something? Make it look like an unrelated accident— And what the fuck am I saying?" Alex bolted up, tossing his head. "I'm talking about someone I knew. A real person with a real family—not a character in a game of Clue.

"Sue, I'm sorry, but this has to stop. I know she was your mother and that you cared about Mrs. Prado, but you've already been attacked once." Tender fingers stroked my neck. "The detectives have guns, training, and partners for a reason—because this is dangerous. Did you even consider for a second what you would've done if the person who stabbed Mr. C was standing right next to him when you opened the door!

"I can't— I don't even—" He hugged me, crushing me to his chest. "I wasn't even fucking here!" he burst out, surprising me. "This could've been so bad, and where was I? Not where I was supposed to be—with you and our daughter.

"Promise me." He pulled back, boring into me. "Promise me you're done playing sleuth, because I promise you we'll have a new security system installed around this entire place by this time tomorrow."

"That's good. We need one," I said softly. "But I can't promise I'll stop looking for the monster who killed my mother. I can't, Alex. Right now the cops are two for two with putting the wrong person in jail for the crime, and three for three with how many innocent people this shitbag has murdered while they're faffing around getting everything wrong. At this rate, a unicorn will find Atlantis before they find Omma's killer!"

The sad look he gave me made my heart shrivel that much smaller. "Baby, why is this so important to you? I know in the last few weeks of her life you two made peace, but you hated her." The words slapped me in the face. "You despised your mother with every fiber of your being, and going by the shouting match you two had shortly before she took a turn for the worst, the feeling was mutual.

"She was one hundred percent lucid and knowing when she called you filth. A worthless slut and her greatest shame. She said she never even wanted you," he rasped. "That your dad threatened to leave her for a woman who would give him children, so she gave in and it was *the biggest mistake of her life*.

"Sue." Alex cupped my cheek, sympathy etched into his face. "I heard her say that every day she was stuck with you was a waste of her time, her money, and her life. That she wished she caved in your skull and tossed you off the cliffs! Your own mother told you to your face that she wished she violently murdered you and disposed of your body.

"And then if that wasn't enough of a blow, she finished off by saying, 'I may not ever again know the peace of living in a world without you in it, but I will know the satisfaction of passing on and leaving you with nothing.'" He blew a hard breath. "And that was just what she said. The stuff you screamed back at her almost made me run in and pull you apart. I thought you were going to kill each other."

Alex held me close. "I know you're turning over a new leaf, and I love that, but you don't have to take it this far. It doesn't make you a bad person or a bad daughter if you choose to not risk your life chasing down a psychopath to get justice for a woman you hated and who hated you. Let the police do their job," he whispered. "Because you have an even more important one—to be the mother you deserved to the most perfect little girl in the world.

"Lily can't lose you too." His soft, full lips teased my trembling mouth. "I can't lose you."

So many horrifying and sweet truths demanding an answer, but I couldn't if I tried.

I had no idea that Sue and Omma had such a vicious fight. Omma's mental state had deteriorated by the time I stepped back into her life, but the few times she did mention Sue, she didn't bring up her name in anger or disgust.

Had Omma really forgotten saying those things to her child, or had their relationship gotten so toxic over the last decade, it was just another day for Omma—not worth remembering.

But even if Sue and Omma did hate each other in the end, what did that change for me? There were some things that a person just needed to do, and I needed to see the person who came into my home and made it an unsafe and frightening place again—punished.

My mother's killer couldn't get away with it. They simply couldn't.

"You won't lose me." I hugged him back just as tightly. "I finally have a fresh start—a new life. No one is going to take that away from me.

"Not this time."

Chapter Twenty

"All right, so we're looking at everything again." I opened Courtney's car door before she had the chance. "Back to the beginning."

"Good morning to you too." She let me tug her out and lead her outside past the gaggle of workmen. "Installing a new security system?"

"A super sensitive one that flips out over everything—even shifty squirrels. Lantana's no-violent-crime streak has officially hit the fan. We're not taking any more chances."

"Smart. Honestly, I'm doing the same thing." She paused by the coatrack to shrug hers off and toe off her shoes. "Tay and I have moved back in with Mom. Her security system is ten times better than the shop's, and right now I just need to know my daughter is safe."

"Is the shop still closed? Are you going to be okay for money?"

She gave me that *don't ask me silly questions even though they make me love you* look. "I'll be fine. I'm closed for the morning, but I'll reopen in the afternoon. Catch a little bit off of that lunchtime rush.

"Despite what Detective Dumbass and Dumbshit implied." She was calling Balogun and Kaplan that too. "I'm not broke or struggling. My bakery is the only shop in Lantana that serves upscale confections at Green Mart prices. All of the charity cliques hire me to do their desserts. I'm rolling in it."

"Oooh, yeah, baby." I wiggled, puckering my lips at her. "Shake that ass when you brag next time, put some more sexy on that sexy."

Courtney doubled over, laughing so hard she tripped over her feet and wheezed at my feet. "You're nuts! But I love it."

"And you're my partner." I helped her up, sobering up quickly. "I can't quit, but Alex was right about one thing last night. I've been reckless. It was idiocy in the extreme to confront Mrs. Finley alone. If Alex hadn't gotten out of the car and checked on me when he did, I'd be dead.

"We're in this together now, and we have to start by going over everything—checking to see what I missed." Pulling out my phone, I showed her the app, and all of its saved recordings. "Ready?"

"Ready."

That's how we found ourselves half an hour later, sitting over a rough sketch of the manor's floorplan in Sue's room.

"Goodness, this is like Clue," Courtney muttered. She was adorable in a pair of purple overalls with a purple bandana tying her hair up. You wouldn't have known she was locked in a holding cell only a couple days before. "Colonel Rhodes in the office. Master Layton in the library. Sir Spencer in the guest wing." She traced her finger across the floors. "If only we knew for sure where all the cops were, not just where they *claimed* they were."

"I know." I chewed my lip, wishing something would jump out at me. "Hard to be trusting after confirming one of them did let a wannabe murderer right up the stairs."

She tapped the page. "What about Nurse Agassi in the garden? Rhodes sounded pretty confident on the recording, claiming he saw your mom's nurse in the garden that night, but Agassi has pics of him in the bar with his friends an hour away, so who do we believe?"

"Hmm. Good question." I moved to my window. "Reynard made a good point that from the third floor, you'd be looking down at the top of a head. Rhodes could've seen someone with a similar haircut and thought it was Agassi."

"But you made a good point too," she shot back, tapping my phone. "With no lights in the garden, you'd need more than a piddly burning cigarette to make out anyone. We know the killer turned on the light when they went into your mother's room, why didn't they draw the drapes? Why risk someone noticing the light was on in your mother's room when it shouldn't be, and going to investigate?"

"All great questions." I peered out the window, thinking. "This is going to sound ghoulish, but I think we should recreate what happened that night. Try to see it from everyone's perspective."

She looked at me steadily. "I'm glad you said it first because I was thinking the same thing. I was also thinking... we need to start in your mother's room."

Courtney said it, and I agreed with it, but even though I left the room and followed her to Omma's, I didn't make it past the threshold.

I halted under the doorframe—flashes of that night assaulting me. The bloody walls. The overturned nightstand. My mother...

A gentle hand touched my shoulder. "I can do this if you don't want to."

I just nodded.

"All right." Courtney squared her shoulders, stepping inside.

Everything had been cleaned and all the items relevant to the investigation had been taken away, so there was nothing to see but an empty bedframe and bare night tables, but still, being in this space felt wrong.

"I'm the killer," Courtney began. "I come in with a weapon I concealed because even the dimmest-lit cop would've noticed someone skipping down the hall with a massive knife."

"That— That's true," I croaked, finding my voice. *Do this for Omma. Focus and do this for Omma.*

The urging got me to take one step inside, but just one step. "Also the... the cop guarding the main hall into the east wing would've noted a woman holding a bag large enough to conceal a knife. Women don't overlook stuff like that."

"Also true," Courtney agreed, sweeping the space. "Makes me think the killer had to be a man wearing a suit with pockets on pockets. Or even a knife hostler covered by a nice thick suit jacket."

"Yes, yes." Falling into the cold, hard facts of it helped pull me out of the trauma. "But we can't discount the fact that they could've stashed the knife and change of clothes somewhere beforehand, so that they could walk past the cops without raising suspicion, and then retrieve them when they were ready to act."

"But that still narrows things down," Courtney pounced. "Because they couldn't have retrieved it *before* they entered the east wing, so they had to grab it after, and then hide it in the same place so they could rejoin the party. How many hiding places between the guards and your mother's room could there be?"

That sent us running back into the hall, marking where all the guards were, where all the entrances into my mother's part of the east wing were, and all the rooms where someone could've hidden something to grab later.

"Unless this, this, or this guard was working with the killer, or are the killer, they would've flat-out said that someone walked past them into the hallway that led to your mother's room," Courtney said, pointing them out on our revised floorplan.

"Absolutely, and if that happened, the cops would not have spent all night compiling that list of everyone who went upstairs. They would've solely focused on the person who walked straight up to my mother's door. No," I said firmly. "I'm sure the only people the guards noted walking into this hallway that night were me and my entourage. And obviously I didn't do it with a cop and a nervous jeweler shadowing me."

"And there are no secret passageways or servant entrances to this part of the wing?"

I tensed. "No secret passageways," I forced out. "Not to this part of the manor. There is a servants' entrance, but it's not a secret. It goes from the wine cellar to the third floor." I tapped the door in front of me. "And it lets you out into the second-floor east wing right here."

Courtney swept left to right. "We're in a complete blind spot. No one would've seen someone enter the hallway here."

"And if they were careful," I said, moving down to where the hallway connected the main one leading out. "They could've run past to my mother's room while the cop standing there had their back turned."

"Can you enter this staircase through the wine cellar?"

I shook my head. "It's locked and bolted. Expensive glass bottles and little curious six-year-olds don't mix."

"What about the ground floor?"

"Also no. There's an entire entertainment center in front of the door. Someone definitely would've noticed, or heard, if that was moved," I said. "The only way into this staircase is from the second or third floor."

"So it does have to be someone who went upstairs," Courtney said mostly to herself. "At least the lazy dumbasses got that much right."

"It also means the killer could've stashed what they needed on the third or second floor with more than enough hiding places to choose from." I went to her side, leaning over her shoulder to trace the map. "They could've walked up to the third floor, gotten what they needed, slipped down there undetected, and then returned to the third floor and skipped past the cops without anyone knowing something went down."

"Anyone including Mrs. Finley?" she asked, brow cocked.

"No, not her." I showed her. "Finley was here by the guest rooms in the west wing. She'd have had to walk past three different cops to get to this back staircase in the east. I doubt that all three of those cops were her nephews."

She hummed, agreeing. "So, who was in the right place to get to these stairs without anyone seeing?"

"Unless someone's lying about where they were—and I can't confirm or deny that because Officer Davis refuses to give me the detailed charts of everyone's movements—that leaves Mr. Layton with a clear shot from the library to the stairs—"

"The same man who was just murdered," she burst out. "Murdered for a reason."

"No question. He did something or he saw something—we know that for sure now."

"Well, if he did it, going and stabbing himself in the spine for it is a weird fucking thing to do," Courtney said. "So that leaves him seeing something he shouldn't have. Who could he have seen at that time?"

"No one," I cried, throwing my hands up. "The only ones there were a bunch of cops and R—" I broke off, realization catching up and strangling my wayward tongue.

But it couldn't stop Courtney's.

"Rhodes," she whispered, pointing to his name on the floorplan. "Rhodes, whose office is right next to the entrance to this staircase. Rhodes, who could've hidden anything he wanted in his office."

A roaring sounded in my ears. "No."

No, no, no! Not the sweet, loving man who jumped between me and a bear, and laughed with Lily while they made terrible cookies. That man couldn't hurt anyone.

He couldn't hurt me.

"Babe? Babe? Sarah," she half shouted, snapping me out of it. "I'm not saying that he did it, but we're doing this for a reason. For the reason that you gave Mr. Layton—the poor man. If all the physical evidence is gone, the only thing to look for now is a liar.

"Rhodes said he went up to his office to get a new client contract, so if that's what he did, we can prove it," she insisted, shaking me. "Because he'll have a copy of that contract in his office. A signed and *dated* contract. We'll go up, find the contract, and rule him out. Then we'll focus on all the other liars."

"Yea— Yes," I seized, my shoulders loosening. "It's not like Rhodes worked that day, so a contract signed on the same day as the party proves what he told me. He didn't lie to me." I took off, rushing to the same back staircase. "He didn't do this."

Courtney chased me all the way upstairs to Rhodes's office. He didn't keep it locked, leaving us no barrier to get inside.

"This was my father's old office," I confessed. I took in the shelves filled with dusty tomes, the ancient Persian rugs, and the massive oak desk placed beside the rear window. "Never knew why he needed it since the only job he had was inheriting wealth, but I know I was never allowed in here growing up."

"Not even after he died?"

"Omma locked it up after he died. No one went in. Not even the housekeepers."

"That's kind of sad."

I fixed somewhere over her shoulder. "She had her reasons."

"Right." She clapped, snatching me out of the past. "You check his desk. I'll check these file cabinets." Courtney glanced at her phone. "And we have to be quick because I've got to open the bakery."

"Got it." I crossed to the desk, snatching the drawer handle and bending over to—

I froze.

"Sarah?" Courtney prompted when she noticed I hadn't moved. "What's wrong? Are the drawers locked?"

"It doesn't matter." I didn't recognize my own voice. "I don't need to open them."

"What? Why? Have you decided to take him at his word?"

"Why would I do that?" Rage burned me, shaking my voice. My vision blurred staring out the window. "He's a fucking liar."

***

That night, Lily and I were in the kitchen making dinner. She was the cutest little thing, standing on the stool with her tongue sticking out as she intensely concentrated on grating the cheese for the beef chili.

Rhodes walked in with his tie still on, looking exhausted from his twice-weekly commute to the New York office. "Evening, ladies. Smells like you're cooking up something delicious."

"We're making your favorite, Daddy." Lily lifted up a bowl full of nothing but cheese. "Chili!"

"Yummy." Rhodes dropped a kiss on her forehead, then turned to me.

I made like I had had to sneeze and caught his kiss on my cheek. "How was your day?" I asked, taking my chopped onion to the pot and tossing it in. "Anything interesting happen?"

"Nothing interesting. You?"

"Yes, actually." I beamed at him. "Courtney came over and we searched in your office to find the signed contract that sent you running upstairs during our anniversary party, but instead I discovered that the balcony to the room next door completely blocks the view to the garden, so you couldn't have seen Agassi in the garden that night. You couldn't have seen anyone."

The smile melted off his face. "Sue... it's not what you think."

"What I think is that your recollection of events that night were incorrect?" I chirped, highly aware of the listening Lily. "Am I wrong about that, or are you?"

"You're wrong if you're thinking what I believe you're thinking."

My smile widened. I must've looked like a lunatic. "What I'm thinking is what an awful time I had walking through every room on every floor of the southern corner of the east wing, where I discovered that the room where you can clearly see a man smoking in the garden below... is from the window in my mother's room."

"No, Sue, it's not—"

"So what were you doing in Omma's room at the same time as our unwanted guest?" I asked. "Were you catching up? Shooting the breeze?"

"Sue!" he barked, making Lily drop the grater.

"Or were you in there alone?"

"Daddy? Mommy?" Lily flicked between us. "What's wrong?"

Rhodes dropped his glare quick. "Nothing's wrong, baby. Mommy's just playing a game with Daddy. How about you have some screen time in the living room while—?"

"No," I sliced in. "You don't have to go anywhere, baby girl."

I opened the drawer by the stove, took out the iPad, and handed it to Lily. She happily turned on her show and went back to grating without missing a beat.

Rhodes did not look pleased. "Afraid to be alone with me, Sue? Seriously?"

"Why were you in Omma's room?"

He hissed through gritted teeth. "I wasn't in her room."

"Then why did you lie about seeing Reynard in the garden?" I snatched up the garlic and tossed it in. Yes, I was adept at angry cooking. All the nights I argued with Daniel over a boiling pot made me the expert.

"I didn't lie. He was there."

"Then the only way you could've seen him was if you were in Omma's room. You're spinning me a tale again!"

"No, I'm not! You can also see the garden from the room next—" Rhodes choked, eyes bugging.

"A-ha!"

He goggled at me. "A-ha? Did you just a-ha me? What kind of murder mystery show do you think we're in now, woman?"

"The kind where you've been caught in a lie." I dumped the tomato paste in the pot. "So tell me what really happened, or I'll keep imagining the worst."

He blew out a frustrated breath, scrubbing his face. "Can we at least speak privately—?"

"No."

Rhodes threw up his hands. "Fine, you win—here it is. That night, I did go up to the third floor, but I did it so that no one would see me take the servants' staircase down to the second."

He said it so readily, my breath stopped.

"Hera, help me, Rhodes," I croaked. "What did you do?"

"Not that," he cried. "Baby, please, believe me. *Not that.*"

"So why did you sneak around your own house just to contrive your way into a room you had no business being in? Please tell me the innocent reason for that behavior."

"It wasn't innocent." Rhodes's face was etched out of stone. "Your mother was blackmailing me. I went in there to find the proof she was keeping on me, and destroy it."

If anything could've dropped my jaw to the floor like a character in a Saturday morning cartoon, Rhodes just said it. "You—"

"Daddy, what's blackmail?"

We swung around, landing on Lily's smiling, curious expression. We'd both forgotten she was there.

"It's uh... It's when you get bad news in the mail."

"Oh no, Daddy, are you okay?"

He smiled soft. "I'm just fine, baby girl, but I need to talk to Mommy alone after all."

"No, don't—"

"Take your iPad into the living room." Rhodes spoke over me. "We'll call you when dinner's ready."

"Okay." She hopped off her stool and scampered off, leaving her auntie high and dry.

Rhodes was less than fazed at my glare. "You want to have this conversation? We'll have it, but not in front of Lily."

"Why wouldn't you want to spin more fairy tales in front of Lily? Kids love fairy tales."

"It's not a lie, Sue."

"Of course, it's a lie!" I hissed. "There's no way my mother was blackmailing you. She can't have been because you told me that the investigators turned up nothing! You've never done anything wrong, so how could my mother blackmail you? Huh? Huh!"

Rhodes fell back against the counter, shoulders slumping. The look of him said it all.

"I'm sorry," he whispered. "I was caught off guard when you brought it up. I'm just so fucking tired of this mistake haunting me!"

"The truth," I demanded. The ground beef, salt, and pepper were next in the pot. I stabbed more than stirred it as I stared him down. "Now."

"Okay, okay. This is the truth. When we came up with GloryBoi, we couldn't get the money we needed to get it off the ground, or pay out the initial winning bets," he began. "Micah's parents had no money to give us. Alex's parents wouldn't let him have early access to his trust fund, and my family wasn't going anywhere near a gambling app. Not after what my dad's addiction did to our family," he said. "So we heisted a ten-million-dollar diamond necklace, fenced it through some shady contacts I knew courtesy of my dad, and then we invented an anonymous angel investor."

I blinked. "I beg your pardon? Did you just say heist?"

He cringed. "I did, but I'm using it loosely. I'm Rhodes Newbury of the Chicago Newburys," he mocked, rolling his eyes. "My name and family connections have gotten me into the wealthiest homes in New York, Lantana, and Chicago. Back when we were at Columbia, I rolled with a particularly douchy group of rich fuck boys.

"We partied at each other's places every weekend, and there was one guy—Max Thompson—who couldn't resist bringing out the family jewels while he made a drunken fool of himself. The necklace was just hanging there around his neck while he snored on the pool table," Rhodes cried. "Micah said we should just take it, and Alex distracted everyone so we could. I was so desperate to make GloryBoi work and save my dad from himself, that I would've done anything—and that's what I did. Anything."

I nodded slowly, taking it in. "What happened when Thompson woke up and the necklace was gone?"

"He didn't even realize it was. He was so drunk off his ass, he didn't remember taking it out of his parents' room. It was a full three weeks later that anyone noticed it was missing, and in that time so many people had been in and out of that apartment, the police couldn't pin it on anyone." He scoffed. "And Thompson for damn sure didn't tell anyone that he regularly helped himself to the family jewels, so they just put in an insurance claim and moved on."

"And my mom dug all of this up?" Belief colored my voice. "When not even the police, the Thompsons, or anyone else figured out you three were behind it? Omma magically did."

He gave me a look. "There was nothing magical about it. Did you forget she sicced a forensic accountant on us? That guy went deep into our finances, and I mean so deep that he hacked us."

That blew my brows up.

"He dug through everything and uncovered the whole plot." He pointed. "Somewhere in your mother's office are old emails where we stupidly spilled the entire thing. It's true what they say—nothing can be deleted. The internet is forever."

"I... But..." I hated myself... but I was starting to believe him. "What could she even blackmail you for? What did you have that she wanted?"

Another cringe.

"What?" I snapped. "What did you lie about now?"

"It wasn't entirely a lie!" he burst out, not bothering to deny it. "When I opened the investment firm, I once again had no money because I donated the buyout payment. So, at the time, I did what your mother suggested and I went to your estate's lawyer with a business proposal."

"You can do that?"

He tipped his head. "Apparently, it's in your father's will that a portion of the funds can be invested in *income-generating opportunities*. Whatever keeps the money growing."

"Is that why the terms are so strict?" I asked—pieces falling into place. "Because you borrowed money from my father's estate?"

"That's exactly why," he replied. "I'll say this for your dad, he picked the perfect lawyer and executor of his estate. That man is fanatical about protecting your inheritance. The firm has to make the estate a certain profit every year, or he can and will demand the full amount of the investment be paid back."

"Rhodes!" I half screamed, clapping my hands. "What. Does. This. Have. To. Do. With. Omma!"

"It has to do with her because she initialed next to that penalty right along with me! *She's* the one who introduced me to the lawyer. *She* vouched for me. *And she* was on the hook with me if the firm went under," he said. "But she became my not-silent and unwanted partner for a reason. Because the lawyer agreed that in exchange for bringing a successful venture into the estate's portfolio, she'd receive a ten percent cut of the profits."

He looked at me through heavy lids. "You did know that your mother had zero money of her own, right? She lived on a pittance—her words—from the estate, and she hated it. That's why she was on me every minute of every single day to squeeze more money out of my business, but when she got her hands on those emails..." He whistled. "She demanded it all. Forget the lawyer. Forget the estate. Forget ten percent. She demanded my entire salary. Sue, I've been working for free for an entire year." Rhodes gave me a grim smile. "And I believe they have a word for that in this country. A history too."

Horror stole my breath. "R-Rhodes," I choked out. My gaze fell away, landing on the beans next to go in the pot, but making no move to touch them. "I don't... know what..."

"You don't have to say anything." Resignation laced his voice. "It's not like I told you. It's not like I told anyone," he confessed. "In the end, I fell back on the old Newbury motto: never let anyone see your pain."

The pain was ours. My chest ached like a dagger buried in my spine and forced its way through the other side. "I'm sorry," I said honestly. "Balogun said you can trust the opinion of someone's child over all. But it's not true. I didn't know my mother at all."

"She wasn't that hard to figure out, Sue. Your mother was accustomed to a certain standard of living." His eyes swept the grand home meant for fifty, but only housing five people. "And she wasn't going back to middle class. Not for anything."

"I understand that now," I confessed. "But what I don't understand is why you all of a sudden had to get your hands on those emails. She had them for over a year, so why now? Why when it didn't matter anymore? She was hardly blackmailing you from her deathbed."

His expression didn't flicker. "But she was."

"Excuse me?"

"She was still blackmailing me, Sue. After your mother got the news that she had months, not years, left, she brought me into that same fucking office and told me that she made *arrangements*," he spat. "She had digital files with all the proof of our crimes and GloryBoi's dirty money launch set to auto-send to the estate lawyer and the police the minute official word of her death came through."

I was wrong. Those were the words that dropped my jaw to the floor like a Tasmanian devil. "What!"

"You didn't mishear me." His voice was flat. "She was going to put all of us in jail. Omma claimed that it was one thing to keep quiet while she was here to *protect* you and Lily from us, but after she passed, you two would be alone with a bunch of thieving thugs, and she couldn't let that happen.

"So, yes, Sue, there was a reason why I suddenly had to get into her computer, delete the file, and destroy any hard copies. Because it wasn't until *now* that the situation became urgent."

"Because Omma didn't have much time left," whispered through numb lips. "The file was going to hit the LPD server any day now."

"Exactly. And before you ask," he plowed on, "I didn't fly into a rage and run into the room next door to kill Omma after failing to get into her computer. Because I didn't fail. I got in, deleted everything, and destroyed the emails.

"I was free," he hissed—hands out and beseeching like a starving man reaching for sustenance just within reach. "I was finally fucking free of a stupid mistake I made over ten years ago. I didn't celebrate that freedom by turning around and committing a worse one."

I was quiet for a long spell. So long, burned beef and smoke filled my nose—but I did nothing about it.

"How?"

He frowned. "What?"

"How did you get in?" No emotion lived in my voice, face, or eyes. "If it was so easy, why didn't you do it months ago? Why that night?"

His frown deepened. "It wasn't easy, Sue. Your mother only became bedridden in these last couple months. Before then she was alert and vigilant, waiting for me to make a move. She found someone who installed a program that would send the file immediately if her password was inputted incorrectly even once, or if the computer sensed an intrusion." He snorted. "Believe me, she took great pleasure in telling me that.

"No, the only way to get in was to find her password, and I didn't get my chance to search for it until—"

"I gave Reynard the night off."

Rhodes nodded, sweeping out a hand. "He dosed her up with heavy sleeping meds and left, and you were busy with the party. There was no one to stop me tearing apart her office to find the password. I found it taped to the bottom of the file cabinet—by the way." He tossed his head, rolling his eyes. "Your mother was clever, I have to give her that. To find it there you either had to flip the damn thing over, or take out all the files to drop it on its side, and then you'd have to put all the files back in the right place or risk getting caught.

"The first method is crazy loud, and the second method takes crazy long. Either way, you'd be caught before you finished."

I'd be honest, I was a bit impressed with my mother's ingenuity on that one.

"So... you're not lying to me," I said softly. "You were in her office and only her office?"

"Baby, I swear." Rhodes took a step. Then, another. "I can show you the password taped to the cabinet. I can prove it gets me into the computer."

"No, that's okay. I already know it," I mumbled. "The lawyer gave it to me so I could start gathering all the documents he needed. As much as she must've disliked him for carrying out Appa's harsh terms, she also liked him for the same reason you gave. He's fanatical about carrying out his clients' wishes. He's her executor too."

I put up a hand, stopping Rhodes in his tracks when he tried to get closer—tried to take me in his arms.

"Say the password, Rhodes—if you really know what only me, my mother, and her lawyer should know—"

"SarangSooMin3467," he rattled off without pause. "Or the translated version, LoveSooMin3467. I guess it's nice to know in the end that your mother could be sweet and sentimental."

Not so sweet, since Sarang was my name, and not a term of endearment attached to Soo Min, but there wasn't any need to explain that to Rhodes.

Sighing, I dropped my hand.

Rhodes bounded up and hugged me so fast, I squeaked as he crushed me to his chest. "Fuck's sake, woman." He held me tighter, sinking waves of love and comfort into my cold and brittle bones. "You know there's only so many times you can accuse a man of murder before he starts to get offended."

A soft laugh escaped me. "Ditto on how many times you can lie to a woman before she starts withholding blowjobs."

"Whoa, don't even joke about that."

We smiled at each other, the tension leaking from our bodies just a little bit.

"Well, then, in the spirit of honesty, I need to tell you that I... lied about one more thing."

My smile burned right off my face. "Are you serious? What now!"

He had the decency to look sheepish. "I didn't see Reynard in the garden that night—from the second floor or the third floor. I didn't see anyone," he said to my slackening jaw. "I made it up because I wanted you to suspect him, question him, even give his name to the police."

"What? Rhodes," I cried. "Why would you want that? Reynard is innocent—"

"He's not innocent." The look in his eyes silenced me. "Sue, when I went snooping through your mother's computer, I went through her emails. I don't think Reynard knows this, but the estate lawyer sends her a copy of every medical bill the estate pays on her behalf. It's all there in a million unread email invoices she never bothered to look at, but I looked."

"I— I don't understand. Was something wrong?"

"You know how it works," he said. "Staff submit the bills directly to the estate. We don't even need to see them. Well, in the last few months, our good nurse Reynard has been loading the invoices with fraudulent charges and no doubt pocketing the difference."

"What!" I lurched back, gaping at him. "Are you sure? How do you know this?"

"I'm sure. I saw all these treatments and services that I know for a *fact* Omma never received. Weekly acupuncture sessions, weekly massages, tai chi at the Coldstone Wellness Center in upstate New York, and the best one, Eversaic medicinal pills at five thousand dollars a fucking bottle," he tossed out. "The thing is, I looked into Eversaic when a client asked me if it was a good idea to invest in their growing company, and I told them no, because Eversaic sold nothing more than overpriced multivitamins. And even if they didn't, I've never seen a bottle of the stuff on your mother's pill caddy. Have you?"

I stiffly shook my head, throat tight.

"Just like I've never seen her allow a stranger to give her a massage, let alone stick needles in her body."

"The lawyer trusted her nurse," I squeezed through dry lips. "If he said she needed it or she did it, he just believed him and paid the money. That piece of shit used my dying mother to make himself rich."

"Sue..." Something in his eyes chilled me. "I'm afraid there's more."

"More? What else could there be?"

More sympathy stole across his face for the first time since our conversation began. For me?

No, I thought, backing up farther. *For my mother.*

"I saw a lot of charges on those invoices," he began, "but none of them were *real* drugs needed to fight nausea, pain, fatigue, bone loss, or weight loss."

My brain went offline, refusing to supply an explanation. "What does that mean?"

"It means that when he started working for your mother, she was on all of those things, but in the last couple months, she was still on the cancer pills, but he wasn't giving her anything to combat the effects. I think..." The pity in his eyes ripped my heart out. "I think he was purposely denying her the meds she needed to be well. He was making her sicker, weaker, and basically medically torturing her to keep Omma dependent on him, and therefore keep the money coming."

"Rhodes..." I clapped a hand over my mouth, a horror I couldn't name poisoning me. "How could you keep this from me!?"

"I had no intention to," he cried. "I went to tell you immediately so we could beat his ass together, but then—then—then you screamed! Everyone came running and we discovered Omma was killed.

"After that, I didn't know how to tell you or the police what I found without admitting I was in the room right next door with a huge fucking motive when the murder happened. Those lazy bastards would've driven off with me in the backseat next to your friend," he said. "That's why I made up that shit about Reynard being in the garden below Omma's window. I wanted to give you a reason to doubt him. To dig into that creep and find out what he was hiding.

"I know he didn't kill her—because he was an hour away and you don't kill the golden goose—but he was the reason your mother was so weak and out of it she didn't have a prayer of defending herself when that monster stole into her room. And he deserves to pay for it."

"You're fucking right he does!" I almost ripped the dial free turning off the stove. Storming out of the kitchen, Rhodes's shouts for me to stop were nothing but buzzing in my ears.

That cheating, fraudulent bitch realized he walked into a scam-rich environment, and he took full advantage. Who questions it when a doctor or nurse says a patient needs a certain treatment? Who wants to be the heartless shitbag who denies a dying woman said treatment? The lawyer approved every charge Reynard sent his way, trying to do right by my mother, and that bastard took advantage of the fact that no one knew his treatments were bogus or nonexistent. And if that wasn't enough...

Bile surged up my throat, threatening to spew on the staircase.

Reynard was torturing her. Denying the basic, humane care his oath demanded, just so she never got the idea that she didn't need his services. Just so that we never decided that we didn't need his help, and could care for her ourselves.

"It's disgusting!" I screamed, tearing down the hall to the east wing. "How could anyone be so evil? You're no better than the monster who killed her!"

"Sue, I agree with you completely, but don't confront this guy." Rhodes chased after me. He grabbed my hand but didn't try to slow me down. I might've attacked him if he did. "Let's call the police. We have the invoices proving fraud. They'll handle him."

I shook free, practically sprinting to get ahead of him. "Yeah, they'll handle him—after I'm done!"

"Sue!"

I charged up to Reynard's door and pounded on the wood, shrieking through the barrier like a madwoman. "Open up! Reynard, get the fuck out here!"

Bang! Bang! Bang!

"Open the door!" I banged on the door. "I know what you did to my mother, you thieving bastard! Get out and face me like the sniveling worm you are, bitch! Take this beating like a man!"

"That's not much of an incentive to open the door," came a dry voice.

My glare would've peeled his head like a grape if I was given the superpowers I asked Santa for as a child. "Break it down," I ordered Rhodes. "Break it down, and *drag him out of there!* We will be kicking his ass together after all!"

"I will not be doing that, and *we* will not be doing that." Rhodes fished his phone out of his pocket. "I'm calling the police. We'll give them the proof; they'll take it from there."

I wasn't given much choice on the matter. Reynard was a grown man who expected privacy, so he had his own lock installed in the door that could only be opened with his key. Said door was a thick, heavy oak, so the chances of me and my chicken legs kicking it in was nil.

I paced the whole time I waited for the cops to arrive—the anger building in my chest. Anger I didn't know where to place. As much as I wanted to crack Reynard's skull for what he did to Omma, wasn't I partially to blame for asking no questions? For not even bothering to check the invoices, or Omma's pill caddy to see what was in those bottles?

I blindly trusted that complete stranger too, and my mother paid the price.

"Uh, hey, guys?" Micah rounded the corner, leading Officer Davis and his partner behind him. "Did you order a couple of cops? Because the Lilybug and I were hoping for Chinese?"

"Order some Chinese, please, Micah, this is going to take a while—*because the evil, twisted, bitch baby won't come out!*" I shouted, kicking the door. "The police are here, you sick fuck, and we're all going to swear we saw nothing when they beat you with their nightsticks!"

"We don't carry nightsticks anymore, ma'am," said Officer Mulvaney, Davis's partner, "and we must now ask that you step back from the door and explain what's going on."

"It's simple." Rhodes grasped my shoulders, gently drawing me to his side. "While going through my mother-in-law's documents, we found some medical invoices submitted by Mr. Agassi that don't add up. The short of it is that he was medically torturing Omma by denying her the meds she did need, and stealing from the estate by charging services and treatments that she didn't. And before you ask," Rhodes said to their shocked faces, "we have proof."

"Theft, fraud, elder abuse," I cried. "You can't let that shitbag get away with this!"

"He's not getting away with anything." Mulvaney unstrapped her gun. Taking my place, she tried the knob, then started banging just as hard on the door as me. "Mr. Agassi? Mr. Agassi, we are officers with the Lantana Police Department and we need you to open this door immediately."

"Do you have a key?" Davis asked, herding us farther back.

"No," Micah chimed in. "Reynard put the lock in himself. He had the only key."

"Don't you have a battering ram?" I demanded.

"It doesn't ride shotgun," Davis shot back. "Are you certain he's in there?"

"I'm sure. His car is in the driveway."

"Wait— We have an axe in the wine cellar," Rhodes spoke up, taking off down the hall. "Tell him to open the door or we'll break it down."

Mulvaney did just that. "Open this door, or we'll break it down, Mr. Agassi."

That's how Rhodes, Micah, Alex, Lily, and I ended up watching from the end of the hall as Davis took an axe to his door, reducing the beautiful carved oak to splinters while his partner trained her gun—ready and willing to take the abusive bastard down.

"Why's he doing that, Mommy?"

"Because Reynard was very naughty, so now Santa's undercover elves are taking him away to the North Pole, where he'll spend the rest of his days mining coal—"

With Lily riding on his shoulders, Alex mumbled under his breath, "Thank you for giving her the G-rated version—"

"—like the raggedy-ass bitch he is," I finished, earning a giggle from Lily and a gusty sigh from Alex.

"Mr. Agassi!" Davis sunk his final whack, finally splitting a hole beside the lock that was big enough for his hand to fit through. "We are coming in. Do not move from your current spot. Remain calm and put your hands on—" The door swung open. "Fuck!"

Davis rushed in, dropping the axe on the carpet. "Sabrina, call it in! Get an ambulance here now!"

"What?" I cried, breaking free. "What's going on!"

"Mrs. Kim, stay back. Stay back!"

I ignored Mulvaney. Sprinting down the hall, I skidded to a stop beside her, and fell on my ass—hands clapping over my mouth.

I now knew why Reynard refused to answer us. It wasn't because he was a cowardly bitch.

Wide, unseeing eyes peered into my soul, sending a silent plea for forgiveness as Davis felt his neck, waiting for the lack of pulse to confirm what his foaming blue lips already did.

He's dead.

Chapter Twenty-One

"This isn't so bad." Courtney stuck her head in the en suite—oohing and aahing to lift my spirits. "You can think of it like a staycation."

"Argh," I groaned, flinging myself down on the couch. "The only one thinking of this like a vacation is Lily. Four people have died in our home or outside of it within the last three weeks. None of us can relax anymore."

I looked around the plush hotel room. Two sectionals claimed most of the space in the sunken living room. Beside it was the mini-kitchen—already loaded with prepared food from room service. In the bedrooms, foam-topped mattresses waited to welcome us with downy arms, and don't get me started on the Jacuzzi tub in the bathroom.

The Lantana Royal Suites delivered on the luxury, but not on the number of bedrooms. It wasn't often they needed a suite for four adults and their daughter, so Lily had her own room, I had the main bedroom, and the guys were sleeping on the pullout couches while alternating every night who slept in the bedroom with me.

It was fine, and it was safer, but it wasn't home. We hadn't been in our actual home for over a week. We moved out and into the hotel the morning after Reynard died.

"Are you okay?" Courtney dropped next to me and rested my head on her shoulder. "This whole thing has got to be wrecking your head."

"That's an understatement," I muttered, cuddling into her side like a baby. It was just me in the hotel room again. Rhodes and Micah were at work, and Alex was with Lily at Taekwondo. We signed her up the week before. When you lived in a town that was going to shit, it was never too early to start learning how to defend yourself.

"I have no idea what to feel right now," I said. "I was ready to bust into Reynard's room and punch his teeth down his throat, but I didn't want to trigger the man into killing himself!"

"You can't know he did that because of you," she argued.

"Lucky for me, I can. The coroner determined he swallowed the pills no more than an hour before we found him. During that hour, I was pounding on his door, screaming that I knew what he did and the police were going to haul his ass to prison." I squeezed my eyes shut. "He obviously panicked and..."

Courtney hugged me tighter. "He made his own choices, babe. First, to steal from and abuse your mother, and then to swallow a handful of pills instead of facing the consequences. Do not spend a second of your time blaming yourself. Reynard Agassi was the lowest, most vile scum. He doesn't get to become a saint in death."

She was right. I knew she was right. But guilt didn't always listen to truth.

"What are the police saying? Can they recover what he stole?"

I shook my head. "They're being way more forthcoming about the investigation into Reynard than they are about Mrs. Prado's, Layton's, or Omma's, but unfortunately, they still don't have much to say.

"Reynard's bank accounts were empty. He didn't have more than three hundred dollars to his name, but Rhodes calculated that he stole over two hundred thousand."

"Fucking hell!" Courtney gaped at me. "He got away with that much and no one knew? How?"

"He charged a whole mess of experimental, natural, or Eastern treatments that Omma never received. All the money that was supposed to pay for them just went right in his pocket." I scoffed. "There wasn't any sign either. He was careful not to suddenly roll up to the manor in his new Maserati, but whatever happened with the money, he spent it fast and hot."

"Dick."

I couldn't agree more.

Courtney dropped her head back on the couch, sighing. "Not to keep you even more depressed by switching to another dismal topic, but have you considered that Reynard could've killed Omma?" she asked. "I know Rhodes was lying about seeing him in the garden, but when you threw that lie at Reynard, he was so fast with that alibi. Even then I thought it was a little too convenient that he had a photo with the clock in the background ready to go the second you asked."

"I did consider it," I confessed. "I mean, I was looking for an evil bastard that wanted to hurt my mother and that turned out to be Reynard the whole time. Of course I considered that he might've killed her too, but why?

"He couldn't use her illness to steal from the estate if she was gone. If anything, he had more motive to keep her alive. It just doesn't make sense that he'd kill her."

"Good point. Only a fool kills the golden goose," she said, echoing Rhodes. "Have you thought of anyone else it could've been? Last I heard, Mrs. Finley refused a plea deal. The case is going to trial just like you said, and she's going to use this charade to give her and Colin's trauma a platform while the real killer skips into the sunset."

"There's no one, Court." My lips burned uttering those words. "Rhodes said he was in Omma's office, and I believe him. Reynard didn't have a motive. Mr. Layton was silenced before he could tell us what he knew—if he knew anything. The only question left is where your boytoy, Mr. Stevens, went when he left the party"—I gave her a knowing look—"but I guess you know something about that."

She smirked unashamedly. "He went upstairs to get the condom we used when we fucked in the downstairs closet."

"And there you go."

She laughed, but quickly sobered. "There has to be something we missed. I don't know, maybe Mrs. Finley did do it. Sometimes the simplest explanation is the correct one."

"Then what's the simplest explanation for why Mrs. Prado was killed? What's the explanation for who killed Mr. Layton when Mrs. Finley was safely locked in a holding cell?"

Courtney had no response for that.

"I'm sorry, Courtney, but I just don't believe what the detectives are saying now. That Mrs. Finley killed Mrs. Prado and Omma, and an unknown assailant who hated Layton Lager went after the heir." I slid her a look. "Before telling me to butt out of police investigations, Davis told me that there have been some serious disputes between Lager factory workers and management. The workers have been complaining about unsafe working conditions, terrible pay, and crappy benefits.

"One of the floor managers even socked Layton Senior, Charles's dad, in the face when an argument between them got out of hand," I said. "Davis didn't confirm or deny, but it's pretty clear they're looking at the factory workers as the main suspects in Mr. C's murder. That's a lot easier than admitting the middle-aged attempted murderer in their holding cell is lying."

"Okay." Courtney shifted on the couch, taking my hands. "I want you to look in my eyes and hear me. It looks bad right now. It feels like we've hit a dead end, but we haven't. No matter what, we won't stop until we discover the truth and put the right psychopath behind bars. Got it?"

"Got it," I mumbled.

"Uh-uh, you have to do better than that. Got it?!"

"Got it!" I belted out. "We're taking that bitch down!"

"Fuck yeah, we are!" She clapped. "But we're not doing that this minute, so distraction time. Let's do something that'll put a smile on your face. Oooh," she cried. "This fancy hotel has a nice bar. Wanna get drunk and dance on the tables till they throw us out?"

"You got a taste for the bad-girl life, didn't you? You can't wait to go back to jail."

She fell over herself cracking up.

"Not that, but can you help me with something?" I got up, went into the bedroom, and came back holding two laptops. "The videographers sent us all of the footage from the party. We're supposed to pick our favorite moments, and their boss will cut it all together into movie magic." I handed her Alex's laptop. "There are hours' worth of stuff from ten different cameras, so I need help going through it."

She hesitated. "Babe... are you sure?"

I swallowed hard, sinking on the couch. "I know it seems ghoulish. Trust me, part of me almost deleted all the videos, but now..." I looked away. "That was the last night—the only night—we were all happy in that house. Up until nine thirty-fucking-seven, the men of my dreams were in love with me, my best friend was back in my life, everyone was in awe of me, the daughter I always dreamed of slept soundly, and the mother I always wanted finally had a good relationship with me.

"That's what I want to remember," I whispered. "That brief stolen time where we were a happy family."

"I get it." She rested her cheek on my shoulder, saying more without words than she did with. "I do."

That's how an hour later, the two of us were tipsy on champagne while watching me dance like a lunatic from every camera angle.

"Hera in heaven, why didn't anyone tell me how stupid I looked?"

"We tried," Courtney mourned. "Oh, how we tried."

I snorted, spraying my sip on my laugh, and setting Courtney off giggling.

"Pull up the video from camera eight," Courtney ordered. She had long ago ditched her coat and shoes, and was now stretched out on the sectional in her bright pink minidress. "It says that guy got the outside shots of the workers in the kitchen and all that. I want to see the dude who sneezed on his hands and didn't wash, and the lady that flicked her booger in the pudding."

"What the hell, Court, what have you been doing in that bakery kitchen!"

Naturally, that set her off laughing so hard she fell off the couch and took me with her. We howled on the floor like a couple of loons—more than a little under the influence of the alcohol.

But I didn't care.

This was the first time I laughed—really laughed—since the very same night we were watching in the video. But instead of all the trauma and the pain from that night, just for a minute, we got to indulge in how happy I was for the first time in ten years. You could see it in my eyes from every angle that I had gotten back something I lost—hope.

As commanded, I queued up the video from the eighth cameraman. It actually would be nice to get some shots of the cooks preparing the feast. Even better if there was video of the cake being born.

I could ask them to speed through these scenes, I thought as we watched the camera leave the ballroom and moved down the hall to the kitchen. *Watch the cake go from plain to decorated in fast-motion, and then—*

"—can't fucking stand all this playing nice and smiling through."

Courtney, the cameraman, and I jerked to a stop as a loud voice came through the speakers.

"That wrinkled old bitch set us up and stole our money," growled a familiar voice. "You and Dad had to sell the house. Everything you saved for retirement is gone. It's not right that *Omma* gets to drift away on a bed of goose feathers while you're clipping coupons and cutting Dad's gout medicine in half to make it stretch farther!"

"Of course it's not right," Marsha Spencer hissed. "But what can we do about it?"

The naughty cameraman stuck to the wall, slowly moving closer, not away, from the alcove their voices were coming from.

"I'll tell you what I want to do about it," Micah snarled. "I want to grab a knife, go upstairs, and stab that witch in the heart—"

The video abruptly cut out. In a blink, the picture was back and the camera guy was filming in the kitchens, getting a close-up of the making of the strawberry tartlets like nothing ever happened.

Courtney and I gaped at each other, eyes wide.

"Babe," she rasped, the color draining from her face. "I think I found your psychopath."

"Ladies."

We screamed, whirling around as Micah walked in carrying his coat over his arm.

"Whoa," he crowed, smiling that sweet, devilish smile. "I know the wind messed up my hair, but I don't look that bad. No need to scream."

"What are you doing here?" I blurted. "You're supposed to be at work."

"That's where I was headed when my assistant called and said my client canceled the meeting." He tossed his coat over the bar. "So I came back to be with my hot-ass wife."

We stared at him.

"What?" Micah looked down, inspecting his clothes. "Why are you looking at me like that?"

Courtney said nothing. She just scrolled back the video, and hit *play*.

Micah's hissed threats hit the air... and his grin melted away.

His blank expression settled into stone. "Baby, I know what it sounds like but—"

"But what, Micah?" I shot up and nearly tipped over. I did have too much to drink. "What can you possibly be about to say next that will make up for the fact that you lied to my fucking face, and you still kept lying after I bared my soul to you!"

"Baby, I—"

"Don't baby me," I blared. "You told me that you found out weeks ago that my mother had nothing to do with you and your parents getting conned out of your money, but if that was true, why were you cursing her out and wishing you could kill her the exact way she was killed long after she was exonerated?"

Micah flicked between me and Courtney. I couldn't begin to guess what he was thinking.

Sighing, his lips parted—

"And don't you dare open your mouth and lie to me again," I hissed. "If you do, I'm gone. I'm packing my shit and I'm leaving."

"Okay, okay," he said, holding up his hands. "No lies. No omissions. No half-truths. I did track down a man in Atlantic City who was scammed by the same con artist. He told me the conman worked by finding an in with a family member or friend, but what I left out is that the family member is part of the scam. They do it... for a cut of the money."

"A cut... of the money..." My alcohol-laden brain stalled.

Courtney wasn't so speechless. "Hold on, you're saying Omma introduced that conman to your parents knowing what he'd do? She was in on the whole thing so that she could steal from you too?"

"That's exactly what I'm saying."

Courtney gaped at him. "And she called me a trashy slut!"

"But—but how could she do that?" I croaked. "Why would she do that?"

Micah tossed his head, crossing to the window. "My family isn't like the others around here. We lived paycheck to paycheck. I only got into Titan Prep on scholarship. Same for Columbia.

"When everything with the buyout got nasty, my *coping habits* got worse," he said. "I was drunk every night and hungover every morning. I told you that after Alex, Rhodes, and I gave in and took the money, I gave it all to my parents, but they didn't know what to do with that kind of money either. They just stuck it in a savings account and ignored it."

"They should've invested it," Courtney piped up. "Diversified portfolios. Property. 529s for the grandkids. You don't want that kind of money just sitting in a savings account."

He threw out his hands, his lips twisted in a mirthless grin. "That's exactly what everyone—literally all of our new rich friends—said. Especially, my new mother-in-law. She never missed a chance to chide them for being clueless, new-money boneheads that didn't know how to handle their money properly. But she really upped the pressure after Lily was born.

"Being the out-of-line, overstepping prude Omma was." Micah spoke through gritted teeth. "She had Lily DNA tested without our knowledge. She found out I'm Lily's bio father, and she brought that test to my parents—laying it on even thicker that if our *unnatural arrangement* ever broke up, I'd be the one legally on the hook for providing for Lily's future.

"With that in their heads, my folks gave in," he breezed—his nonchalant voice not matching the look in his eyes. "They took the contact info of the *great financial advisor* she knew, and that was that." He snapped his fingers. "All the money was gone."

A pregnant pause birthed a litter of awkward silences as I tried to reconcile the mother I knew with the manipulative monster he was describing.

"Is that why you suspected her from the start?" Courtney asked. "Because she was so pushy—even to the point of a DNA test."

"I didn't suspect her at all," Micah said, surprising us. "Omma and my parents never had these conversations in front of me. I didn't have a clue. Remember, we were still living in New York then. It wasn't until a year after the conman got away with all the money that my parents finally told me the full story of how they were steered into their path.

"I knew immediately Omma wasn't innocent. Just like you said, Thorne, she was too pushy. She played too hard on my parents' insecurities, and then brought her own granddaughter into it." He snorted. "I don't know what her cut was, but any percentage of seven billion dollars is a lot of money. She just couldn't let it go."

"What happened when you confronted Omma?" asked Courtney.

They were doing all the talking, because I couldn't get a word out.

"She denied it, of course. She even burst into tears—oh so wounded that I could accuse her of such a thing." His fists balled. Micah was still angry—even then. "But she did feel terrible for *trusting the wrong person*. She said she couldn't forgive herself for being taken in by him too, and even more so that her relationship with her family was now in jeopardy. Her solution to make it all up to us was to sign over the manor."

"Sign it over?" Courtney repeated. "Just like that, she gave you her home?"

Nodding, he looked to me. "Sorry, Sue, but that was another thing I lied about. We didn't buy the manor from Omma to help her pay her medical bills. She transferred ownership to us and we had to take it. We just couldn't afford living in New York anymore."

"Wow." Courtney dropped back on her heels. "I guess that was nice of her to—"

"It wasn't," Micah sliced in, eyes narrowing. "She did not give us that fucking manor to be nice. As always, we were too naïve and too late to figure out her real goal. After we moved in, she *refused* to move out. Just like that, she had her hooks in all of us—trying to run our lives, and most of all, trying to run Lily's. It wasn't enough that she fucked up Sue— No offense, baby.

"She was trying to ruin Lily's childhood too." He clicked his tongue, turning his glare onto the horizon. "Some days I wondered if the con was ever about the money at all. I think she was just a lonely, sour old woman who didn't know how to have real relationships with people, so instead she schemed to make them dependent on her."

Courtney slowly turned to me, worry lighting in her eyes.

It took me a minute, but I found my voice. "That's a sad story, Micah, for all of us, but nowhere in there did I hear proof that you didn't kill my mother."

"What? Of course you did!" He advanced on me. "Sue, why would I kill Omma? She was already dying! I wanted her out of my life, my daughter's life, and my marriage, and the cancer was taking care of that for me! What would killing her have accomplished, because it sure as hell wouldn't have gotten my money back."

"Maybe it would've." I faced him head-on, chin hard and set. "Maybe you got tired of waiting and you wanted to trigger a little thing called an inheritance. All the money Omma had stashed would go to me, and you'd get it by getting custody of Lily and claiming every cent as child support."

"That's ridiculous," he deadpanned. "Omma very loudly announced that she was cutting you out of her will. You wouldn't have inherited my money. I wouldn't have gotten any child support."

Shit. I forgot I'm the twin who wasn't cut out of the will. I'm supposed to be the one who was!

"But—but that doesn't mean you didn't do it," I scrambled. "You can kill a person just because you hate them, Micah. She stole from you. She took everything your parents worked for, and then she turned her poison on Lily. That's more than enough reason to want someone out of your life for good."

"Sure it is," he agreed, tipping his head. "But in my case, all I had to do was wait."

I clamped down hard on my lip, frustration roaring in my chest. We just kept coming back to that. Why kill a dying woman?

My mind suddenly latched on to his previous words. "Yes, all you had to do was wait, but you didn't want to. I heard you in the video, saying it wasn't right that Omma would get to drift off peacefully instead of dying like a witch should.

"You didn't want to wait, Micah. You wanted her to be punished in *this* life, and there was only one way to do that."

"Baby"—I squawked when he laced his fingers through mine—"I know that sounded bad, and it's even worse because I lied to you on top of it. But I never laid a finger on your mother. I could never have hurt her."

"Why?" I shook him loose. "Why is it so beyond the realm of possibility that you went upstairs and did exactly what you said you wanted to do?"

"Because I love you," he exploded. "I love you and I could never do anything to hurt you. Especially not in those last few weeks when everything changed between you and Omma... Especially not when everything changed between you and me."

A band latched around my chest, squeezing the air from my lungs. And if I couldn't breathe... I couldn't fight him taking me in his arms.

"For the first time in ten fucking years, we were happy. *You* were happy," he whispered. "But the look on your face when you walked out of that room that night...

"I could never put that look on your face. Not even for seven billion dollars."

I put my hands between us, shoving against his chest.

"I love you."

No, stop. These are just more pretty words. Words I don't deserve.

"I love you."

My fists pummeled those hard, inked pecs—thrashing this way and that as he held me tighter.

"I love you."

"Stop it! There's nothing happy about this family. There's nothing real!" Pressure built behind my eyes, fueling the strength in my arms. My blows fell hard, ripping grunts from his lips. "It's all a lie. I'm a lie!"

"So what if you are?" Micah's gaze burned into me—into my soul. "You're my lie, and this is our fucked-up family, and I wouldn't change a thing because I love you. *I love you.*" The words sank deep into my heart. "And I'll say it as many times as you need to hear it.

"You and me—we're forever."

I almost hit him in the face wildly shaking my head. Behind us, the door silently clicked shut on Courtney's exit. "No! If you knew the truth about me—"

"I'd choose you anyway."

"You can't say that."

Capturing my gaze, he grinned that sweet, perfect grin. "I just did."

I broke down. Collapsing against him, I did something I hadn't been able to do since this all began—

Cry.

***

"So, lay it on me." Micah popped the bubbles covering my boobs, unashamedly revealing my nakedness.

I would've rolled my eyes if they weren't sore and puffy from crying. As wretched as it was to bawl my eyes out on his tie like a little girl, I felt lighter than I had in weeks. Finally, the pit was shrinking.

"What else don't I know about you?"

I relaxed against his chest—warm and safe in our bubble bath in a way I hadn't felt for years. Our legs entwined in the soapy water, the two of us blissed and unhurried as I lazily stroked the erection poking my back. "One for one?" I suggested. "I give you a secret. You give me one."

"Deal."

"I'm afraid of mascots."

"What?" he cried, bursting out laughing. "Mascots? You mean like the big suits, or the dancing performer in them?"

"The dancing performer in the oversized, animal suits. They just freak me out," I mused. "Big reason why I avoid sporting events."

Micah chuckled without shame. "Well, then if we're going with irrational fears, I'm afraid of dentists. I take crazy good care of my teeth so I never have to see one... and I haven't in the last fourteen years."

"Years? Years!" Giggles floated out of me like bubbles. "You haven't been to the dentist in over a decade, grown man? How have you gotten away with that?"

"All that matters is that I have." He flashed me the cheesiest, big-tooth grin. "No one's complaining about this smile."

"No one, including me." I laid a big smooch on him. "My turn. When I was little, I wanted to wrestle crocodiles like Steve Irwin."

"Really? Why?"

"He just seemed so fearless," I admitted, picking up the pace a bit and making Micah tense against me. "And so free. The world and all the dangers in it just didn't scare him. I wanted to be like that."

Gentle fingers stroked my hair and brought me in for a sweet kiss on the temple. This was one of the things I loved about Micah. For as many infuriating things he'd say on a daily basis, he still knew when it was time to say nothing at all.

"Rhodes stole for the first time when we took that necklace," Micah dropped, surprising me. "But by that time, I'd been stealing from his rich friends for months."

I met his eyes, reading the shame in them even then. "It was hard feeling like you had to keep up with them, wasn't it."

"Yeah." Micah flashed a mirthless smile somewhere over my shoulder. "Alex and Rhodes are my boys—no question. They never pulled that competitive shit with me, and they never acted like money mattered. But money attracts money," he said. "That's just how it is. When you're wealthy, you hang out with people who can do all the same stuff you can, and pay for the same toys and events. And who can watch you do all of that without writhing in jealousy.

"That's why Rhodes and Alex always ended up in a group of trust-fund babies." He tipped his head. "Being the good guys they were, they always invited me to join them when they were hanging out with their friends, but unfortunately, their friends were dicks.

"Whenever Alex and Rhodes had their backs turned, they were making some slick-ass comment or digging at me. The first time one of those guys told me I should work off the beer Alex bought me by sucking his dick like a good little leech—"

My jaw fell open.

"—I made up some lie about needing to use the bathroom, and instead went upstairs and stole a fifty-thousand-dollar watch from his room." He blew out a breath. "And so it went every time those assholes pissed me off. All culminating in me pressuring one of my closest friends into grand larceny.

"If it helps, I chose Max Thompson because he date-raped a girl on campus, then used his family's money to buy her silence."

"What! Oh my gosh."

Micah clenched his jaw—angry at the mere memory. "Rhodes and Alex didn't know what he did, but I knew because the vile piece of shit sidled up to me at a party one night, drunk off his ass, and whispered that us poors were so pathetic, all you had to do is throw some money at us and we'll do anything—even let a man get away with rape."

I grabbed my mouth, horror bleeding through my pores. "Fucking hell, that poor girl. Vile monster is right! Why does Rhodes even feel guilty about stealing from that shitstain?"

"Because all I told them is why that guy made an easy target. I didn't say anything about what he did," he said. "I wasn't going to pretend like I was some kind of hero when I was first and foremost acting for my own ends." He looked away. "I was able to track her down later and contact her. I told her that if she ever decided to go through with pressing charges, I'd be a witness. I'd stand up in court and tell them what he confessed to me. But she never responded."

"It can be hard to face these things," I heard myself say. "Hard to talk about. Even harder... to not be believed."

"I know." He flicked my nose, teasing my smile back. "I don't blame her. I blame that rapist piece of shit. In senior year, he tried drugging and attacking another girl, but her roommate came in and beat the shit out of him with her hockey stick. He still slurs his words." Micah smirked. "I don't know what it says about me that I smile whenever I tell the end of that story. I also don't know what it says that I got so mad at your mother for stealing from me, when I stole from people for months.

"I guess karma does come for everyone in the end."

I hummed, reclaiming my place against his chest while my hand reclaimed his cock. "I don't know that I believe in karma. Or even justice," I admitted. "I believe we make our own. Those rich fuck boys valued material things over decency to other human beings, and for that they lost their precious things. That shitbag violated women and their bodies in the worst way, so he got a taste of what it's like when someone ignores your screams and hurts you.

"To me, you can only balance the scales in life if you step on them, and there's nothing wrong with laughing at a raggedy bitch who got stepped on."

Micah blinked at me.

"What?" *Oh shit, did I go too far?* "What's wrong?"

"Wrong? What's wrong?" Micah grasped my chin and planted a kiss on me so heated, my nipples sprung free of their bubbly cage. "I'm so pissed at you, I can't stand it."

"What?" I cried in alarm.

Anger and lust battled for dominance in his eyes. "Why in the hell did you hide the most delicious parts of yourself from me for ten years!"

The world spun and I went flying, splashing down and dumping half our bath on the floor.

"No more," Micah barked, coming down on top of me. "I'm fucking the rest of your yummy secrets out of you right now. I won't stop until you're hoarse."

"Mica— Micah!" I squealed, eyes rolling up in my head when all nine inches of him kicked down the door and barged through my entrance. "You don't have to fuck it out of me, I'm giving it up for free!"

"A man has to be sure."

I was laughing my head off until Micah slammed his cock home, making me gasp that laugh right back down.

"Favorite color?"

"Micah!"

Micah set a punishing pace, drilling against the porcelain like he was trying to make me come out the other side.

"Resisting already?" he tsked, and then if possible, pumped even harder. "Give it up, Kim, or you won't walk right for a week."

My moans were screams. One foot scrabbled for purchase, the other hung over the tub—kicking and jerking with each soul-wracking, pleasure-filled surge that ransacked my body with every strike of that secret spot.

"P-purple! Yes, yes, fuck yes! It's purple!"

He grunted. The hard line of his muscled shoulders and arms rippled. The tigers danced with my tits as he launched on and off the tub like a springboard. "Next. Who's better in bed? Me, Rhodes, or Alex?"

"What the—!" I might've whacked his arm if my eyes weren't too crossed for me to see. "I'm not answering that!"

"I see." He managed to sound mournful even as he plowed my pussy like a land hoe. "Then you've chosen war."

"Micah," I laugh-screamed. "Don't—"

"Now, I'll have to break you."

Micah latched on to my nipple, trying to suck the happy slut clean off while bouncing me off his lap.

If he was trying to get me to talk, he was going entirely the wrong way about it. I couldn't summon anything to my lips other than grunts, moans, and screams.

My body came alive under his power. Both secure and captive in his arms, every cell exploded with white-hot heat and contracted my walls around his thick, bulging cock.

The man was so big he was stretching me out like pliers, but despite his incredibly inappropriate question, I couldn't rank him against Rhodes if I wanted to. Sex with Rhodes was incredible in all the ways, but also different ways. And even though I never had the pleasure of bedding down Alex like a bale of hay, our bodies were two alternating currents that would electrocute anyone who touched us. I felt alive when I was near him—even if that spark of life was fueled by raging annoyance.

The fact was that all of these men had a piece of my soul, and that truth had only gotten deeper and stronger since we were reunited ten years later.

"I love you," I cried, riding on an orgasmic wave of rushing, crashing ecstasy.

"Course you do, but that was not the answer I was looking for."

"Micah!"

He struck that spot and I burst, exploding all over his cock and screaming myself hoarse as ordered. My pussy clamped down on him, milking and pumping him for every grunted drop.

We went boneless, collapsing in the two inches of water left of our bubble bath.

"Wow," I breathed. Grabbing his face, I kissed the crap out of him. "You've been holding out on me, baby."

"No, *you're* holding out." My eyes grew wide in face of his devilish smirk. "But I'm going to get the truth out of you, woman, if it takes all day and night." Micah bit my nipple, chasing pleasure and pain through my body until it escaped as a breathy moan. "There's nowhere I'd rather be."

***

"He, in fact, did not fuck me all day and night," I confirmed. "If only because Lily came bursting into the hotel room, calling for me, so I had to scramble my butt out of the tub and get dressed. But, Court..." I shuddered. "You've never had an orgasm until you've had an orgasm from Micah and Rhodes. I mean... wow."

"I'll take your word for it," she replied, amusement lacing her voice. "But sweet and sexy Mr. Nicolas Stevens is supplying my orgasms these days, and I'm a one-man girl."

"Since when?"

"Hey!" she barked, making me bust up on my end of the phone. "But seriously, babe, it's good to hear you laugh again. You sound like you're getting your happy back. I love that for you."

"Thanks." I glanced over my shoulder.

Alex and Lily were at the living room table working on her homework. Micah was setting the table and Rhodes was in the kitchenette dishing the takeout. Yes, this was my happy.

"But I'm not quite there yet. This pit in my stomach will never go away. Not until I know the truth of what happened to Mrs. Prado, Layton, and Omma. Not until the killer is caught."

"You've ruled everyone out?"

I shrugged. "As much as an amateur detective trained on crime shows and mystery books can. There's just no one left to talk to," I said. "I know we tossed around the idea that one of the cops could've done it, but we just keep coming back to the same problem: why now?

"Any grudges someone had against my mother was going to be settled by the cancer. It makes no sense that someone would go out of their way to murder an old, sick woman that couldn't hurt anyone anymore. There had to be some reason," I hissed, falling back in the familiar pattern that quickly. "An urgency. A desperation that drove them to kill Mrs. Prado and strike in a house full of cops."

"Well, there could be someone who knows." There was an odd note in her voice. "You haven't actually spoken to everyone yet. You haven't... gotten the truth about that night from everyone yet."

I frowned. "Who do you mean? Are you talking about those catty women from New York? Because I..." I dropped my voice. "I've got Sue's phone and I can confirm they are the kind of friends that don't give a shit about you unless you're right in front of them. Sue hasn't even texted them for months. I doubt all that ignoring each other whipped up a homicidal rage."

"Those New York women aren't who I was thinking of," she said. "I was talking about Alex. You haven't spoken to Alex, Sarah. You haven't asked him what he was doing upstairs that night."

"Uhh, because I know." I let out a little laugh. "Court, it's okay. He already told me that he went upstairs to call his aunt and check on Lily."

"Uh-huh."

My face froze, unease crawling up my spine. "Court, he didn't do it. He didn't go upstairs until after nine thirty-seven. The police only made him come to the ballroom the morning after because they wanted to know if he saw or heard anything strange. Not because he was a suspect."

"Okay, maybe all of that's true. But I do feel pressed to point out that anyone can mess with a broken clock and put the hands back to whatever time they choose. Like to before they came upstairs," she said, opening the floor up beneath me. "But if I'm wrong and Alex— The same Alex who was just as threatened by Omma's dying plot to send proof of their jewelry theft to the police. And the same Alex who must've lost his billions in terrible circumstances too, or Rhodes wouldn't have said he was supporting a family of *five* all on his own—"

"Hold on—"

"If that Alex is telling you the truth, then it'll be easy to prove," she stated. "There will be an outgoing call to his aunt on the night he said and at the time he said, and if there isn't, then he didn't go upstairs to talk to Auntie. He went upstairs for another reason, and then he lied to your face about it. And thanks to a couple dumbass cops and a broken clock, he's been getting away with that lie.

"Smart, charming, disarming people like Alexander Montgomery tend to be very good at looking innocent, and isn't it lucky that he started being all of those things the day after your mother died—when up till the day before, he was still acting like an ass."

Stiffly, I turned to Alex, my gaze latching on to the handsome, smiling man laughing with my niece.

"And what if it goes even deeper than that?" Courtney continued—unaware she was pulling my heart out through my butt. "I thought it was odd when I first heard your recordings, but the more I thought about it, the stranger it was. Every time you questioned one of the guys, they immediately lied, shifted blame to someone else, and then confessed to a lesser sin when caught in that lie.

"Rhodes turned you on to Agassi and his fraud. Micah *happened* to see Mrs. Finley sneaking around upstairs. And then it was, *yeah, sure, I lied, but I was only in Omma's office deleting the evidence that would've put me in prison.* And *for sure, she stole seven fucking billion dollars from me, but I got over it.*

"They just keep pointing the blame every which way except at each other or themselves, even though the people who hated Omma most in this world were always sleeping right down the hall from her. Honestly, they likely would've been the main and only suspects from the start if it wasn't for a conveniently thrown anniversary party that filled their house with cops, suspects, witnesses, and a bloody knife that found its way into the bag of a woman who had a very public shouting match with Omma the last time she saw her," she cried.

"And another thing—"

I hung up.

Ending the call, I quickly turned off my phone—reducing it to nothing but a black brick.

"Oh, yeah, good idea," I said, raising my voice. "I can pick you up—Hello? Hello?"

I turned on Alex, beaming away. "Alex, my phone died. Mind if I call Courtney back on yours?"

"Sure." He picked it up off the table, typed in the code, and tossed it to me without hesitation. "Oh, did you remember to order my tom yum goong?"

"Of course." I was already in his recent calls, swiping through as fast as possible without being frantic. "Told them to slide me some of that sweet, sweet mango sticky rice for my man too. They didn't want to do it at first, but I bribed them."

Alex chuckled. "Did you happen to bribe them with the stated price for the mango rice?"

"Works every time."

His chuckle rolled into a belly laugh. "Well, then, I owe you a thank-you."

I scrolled faster—still stuck in the calls from the week before.

"You okay?"

"Yeah." I forced a laugh. "Just trying to remember the last number. You know, all those experts might be right about screens and technology. The impact on our memories and attention span is..."

The date of the party shown proudly on the screen, where it did indeed log a call from Alex to his aunt... in the morning. There was no other incoming or outgoing call between them for the rest of the day. There was no call between them that night.

"Shocking," I finished, meeting his eyes over the screen.

You lied to me. You didn't go upstairs to make a call, Alexander Montgomery, so why did you feel the need to lie about where you were in your own house?

Unless you were somewhere you shouldn't be.

Quickly, I hit the phone app and tapped in Courtney's number. The forced smile remained on my lips as I backed away, breaking free of his gaze as the call picked up.

"Hello?"

"Court, it's me."

"Sarah? Thank goodness," she cried. "Why'd you hang up on me like that? Are you okay?"

"No, that's not a problem. We're about to have dinner, but the guys will keep a plate warm for me."

"What? What are you talking about?"

"Yeah, I'll swing by your mom's, pick up Taylor, fill her full of burgers and soda, then bring her home," I said. "You finish up your order."

"You need a reason to go out and you don't want them to know the real reason why." Courtney was nobody's fool. "Are you in danger? Just yes or no."

"Nope," I breezed, drifting into the bedroom.

"Where are you really going? I'll meet you there. Back you up."

"Nah, that's okay." I quickly went to the dresser to gather my purse and keys, straining to keep the voice floating through the open door relaxed. "You don't owe me. Anything to cement my destiny as best auntie ever."

A presence loomed behind me.

"Sarah—"

"See you soon, bye."

Click.

"Everything okay?"

I turned around, the smile already fixed on my lips by the time it met Alex's eyes. "Everything's good. Courtney's assistant called out sick, and she's finishing up a big order by herself. It's taking longer than she planned, so she needs me to pick up Taylor." I gave him a crooked smile. "First rule of not burning down your business and home—don't leave when the stove's on and the oven's running."

"Good rule," he agreed, chuckling.

"I shouldn't be long." I sidestepped him and made for the door. "Save a plate of the spicy shrimp for me, yeah?"

"Rhodes will do that. I'll go with you."

"No need." I didn't slow my steps. "You're busy helping Lily with her homework."

"Micah can do that too." A hand slipped around my waist, snuggling me against his chest and sinking me in a cloud of cedar and cinnamon. "It'd be nice for us to have some time alone together."

I forced out a giggle. "Except, we won't be alone. There'll be a five-year-old in the car." I turned in his hold, peering at him through my lashes. "But if you really want some alone time with me, naughty boy, then let's make it count.

"Stay and order some candles and dessert from room service." I winked. "When I get back, we'll see about ending that dry spell—*hard*."

A pleasantly pleased grin stole across that handsome, charming, disarming face. "Really? Are you sure?"

"Oh, I'm very sure." Rising on tiptoe, I kissed him. My lips burned everywhere they touched his. "But no ice cream," I continued, nipping his nose. "Despite what the movies say, eating ice cream off each other is not as sexy as it sounds. It's just a sticky, runny, cold mess."

"No ice cream." Alex winked right back. "You got it."

With that I hurried out, tossing a quick goodbye to Rhodes, Micah, and Lily on my way to the door.

I need to go back to the manor. I need to retrace it all in my own steps, and see it through my eyes. There has to be another explanation. Another perfectly valid reason why Alex wouldn't share the real reason why he went upstairs.

Alexander has been the most closed off to me, but that was only because he thought he was dealing with his lying, cheating, gaslighting wife. The same wife who already knows him. He has no idea that our relationship is beginning again with a ten-year gap in the middle.

I'm sure if I just look through everything again with no interruptions and no false explanations, I can fill in the gaps on who these men I love have truly become—

—because killers cannot be the answer.

I threw open the door. "Ah!"

"Ah!" Balogun cried out, grabbing her chest. "Goodness, Mrs. Kim, you scared the daylights out of me."

"I scared you?" I held my racing heart in the same way. "What are you doing here?" I flicked over her shoulder to her partner, Kaplan, and a woman I didn't recognize. She wore a cream pantsuit and a kind smile. "What are you all doing here?"

"May we come in?" Balogun asked. "There's something important we need to discuss with you and your husbands."

"I— Uh—" I glanced over my shoulder. "I was just on my way out. Can we do this tomorrow?"

She didn't budge. "I'm afraid it really is important."

"Sue?" Rhodes stuck his head out of the kitchenette. "What's going on?"

"The detectives are here," I replied, backing into the room. "They say they have to talk to us."

"We do." Kaplan's large presence entered our suite, trailing me. He spotted Lily. "Would it be possible for us to speak to the four of you in private?"

Micah frowned, but agreed. "Lilybug, take your iPad into the bedroom. We'll be right out here if you need us."

Lily happily took her pad and went, completely unconcerned by the no-nonsense, unsmiling faces that were unnerving me.

"What's the problem?" I asked, then straightened. "Wait, is it good news? Have you finally caught the real killer and let Mrs. Finley go? She should be surrounded by family while she grieves her son, not surrounded by bars and cinderblocks."

Detective Kaplan gestured to the couch. "Please."

Our dinner cooled on the counter as Rhodes, Micah, Alex, and I claimed the sectional, and the detectives and their friend sat in the armchairs across from us. The way the seats were divided, it felt like we were in an interrogation room.

Balogun released a deep breath. "The first thing I must do is apologize to you, Mrs. Kim."

"Who? Me?" I cried, whipping my head around like she was talking to someone else. "Why?"

"Because you told us we had it wrong. You said all the deaths on your property had to be connected, and we needed to look harder. While we were doing our jobs and following the evidence," she stressed, "it doesn't excuse us for not listening to you... especially as you turned out to be tragically correct."

"What does that mean?" Rhodes leaned over, taking my hand. "Right about what?"

"Our investigation into Mr. Layton's murder took a new and terrible direction this week, and it has shed light on the recent events in a way that has been both chilling and illuminating," Balogun said. "I won't beat around the bush. We believe that Mr. Layton was blackmailing your mother's former nurse, Mr. Agassi, into giving him drugs he didn't want a record of receiving.

"I say *we believe*, but the evidence is ample. Prescriptions with Madame Kim's name on them were found in a hidden compartment in Mr. Layton's car."

"So, he was an addict?" Micah questioned.

She shook her head. "These drugs don't get you high. For a woman, like Madame Kim, they are a harmless acid reducer, but for men they have a powerful side effect. Which is why they are rarely prescribed to men," she said. "These drugs cause low libido, or in simpler terms, chemical castration."

"Chemical... castration?" I repeated slowly. "I don't understand. Why would he want that?"

"He wanted them because he was a pedophile," Kaplan stated bluntly. "Who was clearly afraid he couldn't control himself, so he wanted the drugs to do it for him."

The four of us gaped at him, the wind collectively whooshing out of our lungs.

"What?!"

"Pedophile?" Micah shouted, jumping up. "Oh my God, Lily!"

And then we were all jumping off the couch and sprinting across the living room.

"Wait— Wait!" Balogun and Kaplan cried, shooting out in front of us. "We understand, believe us we do, but that's why Mrs. Zeller is here." Balogun pointed to the woman getting up from the couch. "She's a child psychologist with our department. She's here to interview Lily."

"That piece of shit never touched her," Alex roared. "I was in the room for every lesson. I never left them alone. And if he ever fucking thought of it, I'll dig him up and kill him again!"

"We're sure you protected your daughter to beyond the best of your ability," Mrs. Zeller soothed, "but we wouldn't be doing our due diligence if we didn't have a conversation with Lily to be sure. So, if one of you wouldn't mind sitting with Lily while I chat with her, the rest of you can hear what the detectives have to say."

She said it in a nice, soothing psychologist voice, but her tone still brokered no argument.

It took some tense discussion with her, and then among ourselves to decide that Alex would go in with Mrs. Zeller to talk with Lily.

Only after the door shut behind them did we heed Balogun's fifth request to claim our seats.

"And you're sure," I pressed. "You're certain he was taking those pills because of... *that*... and not a bad case of heartburn?"

"You can get heartburn pills from any pharmacy," Balogun said. "You don't need to steal or commit fraud for them. But when you have the kind of photos hidden on your laptop that Mr. Layton did—"

A low, furious growl ripped from Rhodes's throat.

"—it becomes clear Layton was more interested in the side effects, not the main purpose of those pills," she finished.

"So he was a fucking pedophile and he got stabbed in the back for it," Rhodes barked. "Good riddance."

Kaplan inclined his head. "We understand your feelings, but as we said, more has come to light as we've dug further into the matter. As Mr. Layton, Mr. Agassi, and Madame Kim are no longer with us, we may never know the full details, but this is what we believe happened."

"Mr. Agassi was being blackmailed into providing Mr. Layton with those pills," Balogun said, picking up the trail. "Seeing as there were no monetary transactions between them, or large withdrawals from Mr. Layton's bank account—blackmail seems most likely.

"At some point, this arrangement was discovered by your mother, Mrs. Kim," she said, blowing me back. "Likely after the death of Mrs. Prado."

"Mrs. Prado?"

She nodded. "To understand how this medical fraud went on for so long, we contacted your family's lawyer. We don't believe he had any knowledge of Mr. Agassi's criminal activity, but he did say something that made everything clear," she told us. "He said that none of this would've happened if Mrs. Prado was still running the household. When we pressed him, he explained that invoices, expenses, and even medical bills went through her first. She oversaw every single penny, and never submitted a charge to him that she didn't verify five ways to Sunday."

Rhodes, Micah, and I exchanged incredulous looks. "So that's why—!"

"Yes," Kaplan stated, voice hard. "That's why Mrs. Prado couldn't be rehired. That's why she had to go."

"Oh my goodness," I breathed, horror stamping my spine. "This is all my fault. If I hadn't rehired her— If I hadn't—"

"No." Balogun shot forward and did something I wouldn't have expected from her. She held my hand. "You cannot blame yourself, Mrs. Kim. You were trying to help and protect your family and your household. You had no idea there were those within your own home who were trying to do the opposite."

"But— But what does that mean?" Rhodes burst out. "Did Layton kill Mrs. Prado, or did Agassi?"

"We believe it was Mr. Layton," Balogun confirmed. "She was killed on Sunday morning. He didn't have class, or anything scheduled as far as we could dig up. He could've been anywhere, including skulking around on your property."

"And the murder of Mrs. Prado was the first domino to fall," Kaplan continued. "Agassi and Layton must've fallen out over her death. No doubt Agassi had been justifying his actions up to that point. He was keeping children safe by supplying Layton with those pills. He was a good man—a hero even. But no hero can call himself that after causing the death of an innocent woman.

"It's possible the two of them got into an argument that was overheard—"

"By my mother," I whispered through numb lips.

Kaplan just nodded. "Why kill a dying woman?" he asked softly. "That's what we continually came back to, but the answer turned out to be simple. You'd do it if she discovered something you needed her to take to the grave immediately. A secret that simply couldn't wait for *any day now*."

I was hollow and numb. It felt like my soul was scraped out with a rusty spoon. "Layton was afraid that in her moments of lucidity, my mother would tell me there was a murderer and pedophile in our house," I rasped. "So he killed her too."

Micah put his arm around my shoulders, squeezing me tight. "But how?" he asked. "How did he get to her? He told my wife he was in the library on the third floor. Your cops were up there too. If he skipped downstairs to the east wing second floor, surely he should've been your top suspect from the start if you... knew..."

Balogun's headshaking made him trail off. "The tenacious Officer Davis couldn't let go of the idea of secret rooms, halls, and entrances in your manor. They are, as he told you, era-appropriate. Especially for manors along the coast," she said. "So he dug up the old blueprints in city hall. There weren't any secret cellars for moonshine, but he did find a network of old servant staircases. One such staircase goes straight to the third floor to the hallway leading to your mother's room."

Rhodes frowned. "But those aren't a secret. We know about that staircase. We could've told you that ourselves."

"Sure," Kaplan agreed, "but what we didn't know until we lined up the officers' positions with the blueprints, is that the entrances to those staircases are both in a blind spot. Blind spots perfectly placed to stop all nine officers from seeing someone slip out of the library, go down a floor, kill Madame Kim, and then return to the library without being seen."

"It also explains why he skulked around the second floor first," Balogun put in. "Most of the officers on the second floor reported spotting Layton wandering around *exploring* the mansion."

"Why the fuck would he need to explore?" Micah snapped. "He'd been there a thousand times before."

Balogun tapped her nose. "But they didn't know that. They just saw a curious looky-loo. They didn't realize he was scoping out their positions, and confirming no one would see him go up to the third floor... and then sneak back down."

I squeezed my eyes shut, head falling into my hands. "I should've seen that. That shitbucket told me to my face that he hid out in the library all night because he hated the party. He didn't want to be there. It didn't occur to me that he could've just gone home if he was having such a horrible time," I said. "Why would he spend all night in our library? Unless he had another reason for being there."

"That's the question we also asked ourselves," Kaplan confirmed. "Nothing about his movements or his actions that night made any sense... unless he had an ulterior motive."

"So he killed Mrs. Prado, Omma, and framed Courtney all to protect his secret," Rhodes finished. "What a fucking monster."

"And it was that monster your family would've been left alone with after Agassi left," Balogun said. "Agassi's job was over. He no longer had a reason to live in your manor, and he no longer had the means to supply Layton with pills. That man would've continued to have access to your home, and your child, with you all none the wiser. So, to right his wrongs in his eyes—"

"He killed Layton." I sighed, rubbing my aching temples. "He knew what time he'd come for Lily's piano lesson. He knew he could intercept him with a knife in the back before I even opened the door."

"Yes."

"And then wracked with guilt over everything he'd done, and all the lives—innocent and guilty—that had been taken," I said, "Reynard killed himself."

Balogun met my eyes. "Yes."

Micah, Rhodes, and I met each other's eyes.

"I guess..." Micah sighed. "Maybe it says something for Reynard that his last act was to protect our family—protect Lily."

"It would've said more if he reported to Lantana Day that there was a pedophile teaching at their school," Kaplan said. "It would've said more if he hadn't stolen from an old, sick woman and gotten himself into the position of being blackmailed. It would've said more if he'd come straight to the police after Mrs. Prado's murder. If he had done those things, nothing that followed would've happened."

"If you had listened to me, a couple of things wouldn't have happened too," I flung back. "I *asked* you for a chart showing where all the officers were positioned. I *told* you that Courtney didn't hurt anyone and was framed. And I *said* that Mrs. Prado's murderer had to be the same person who returned and killed my mother. I told you all of these things but you dismissed me as a hysterical idiot and ignored me!"

Stony faces looked back at me. Stony... and contrite.

"You're right," Balogun said, her grip on my hand firming. "While it's true we couldn't share details of an investigation with you, or simply take your word on who's innocent or guilty... it's also true that we should've spent more time listening to you, and less time dismissing you. Two senseless deaths would've been prevented if we had."

Rhodes pointedly removed Balogun's hand, and laced his fingers through mine instead. "What about Mrs. Finley? You said a lot of *we believe* and *it's possible*," Rhodes said. "If you don't have proof it was Layton, how will you combat her false confession?"

Balogun straightened. "We didn't need to combat it. We simply explained to her that if she didn't tell us the truth, she ran the risk of allowing a pedophile to die as an innocent victim—with people the world over crying over his memory and memorial. We asked her if she truly wanted a man like that to be made a saint in death.

"She recanted immediately." Balogun flicked to me. "She admitted that she crashed your party hoping to get to either one of you—you or your mother—she didn't care. But you were surrounded by guards, Mrs. Kim, and Madame Kim's room proved too difficult to find. She never got near any one of you." She gave me a stern look. "That is until you walked right through her front door."

"Not my smartest move," I said simply.

"Quite."

"There is one more thing," Kaplan spoke up. "Mrs. Finley has asked to speak to you. She says there's a matter you both need to settle, and she asks that you do so as soon as possible."

I stiffened. *The matter of me not being Soo Min Kim. I was wondering why she hadn't yet told the world I was an imposter. I guess now I know.*

"Obviously, if you don't wish to see her—"

"No, I'll see her," I cut in. "Actually, I think that's a good idea. If we talk, I know we can settle things, and any remaining charges she has for assaulting me can finally be put to rest."

Balogun shared raised brows with her partner. "Put to rest? Mrs. Kim, whatever else she may have lied about, she still came to your home with the intent to harm you and your mother. We don't put to rest attempted murder."

"She got nowhere near my mother or me that night," I corrected. "And she only attacked me in her home that morning because I provoked her. I told her something she wasn't ready to hear so soon after losing her only child."

Kaplan opened his mouth. "Mrs. Kim—"

"All of this will be resolved with one conversation," I said firmly. "Mrs. Finley is giving me a chance to do that, and I will." I gave them both a crazy look. "Is this really what you want to do? Press charges against a depressed, middle-aged woman whose son was basically murdered by medical neglect? I'm pretty sure she's been punished enough."

Kaplan threw up his hands, frustrated with me. "Fine. You're the victim. If you intend to stand in the way of these charges, it'll only make the case that much harder to prosecute, but are you certain?"

"I'm cert—"

Lily's door opened. Rhodes, Micah, and I were up and across the room before Mrs. Zeller stepped a foot out the door.

"Goodbye, Lily, it was very nice to meet you."

Our sweet girl waved heartily, smiling her wide, missing-tooth grin. "Nice to meet you."

I dropped down in front of Lily, making her giggle when I pulled her in for a tight hug. Peering over her shoulder at Alex, he met our eyes... and shook his head.

"Oh, thank goodness," I cried, peppering her face with kisses. I didn't notice I was crying until my own tears coated my mouth.

"What's wrong, Mommy?" Lily hugged me tight—trying to comfort me like the precious girl she was.

"Nothing's wrong, baby," I hiccupped. "I just love you so much."

"I love you too." Twisting around, she pecked my cheek, then patted my forehead. "There, there. Everything's going to be okay."

I swear my heart burst into confetti.

Micah squeezed in and threw his arms around her. Then, Rhodes was at my back—pressing his warmth and solidity against me as he rested his forehead against Lily's, and right behind him was Alex, throwing his arms around us all.

A very confused Lily became the jelly center of our donut, but we couldn't let her go.

I couldn't let her go.

Courtney was right about one thing. These men and this little girl were my family, and for once, family was going to be the thing I clung on to, not the boogeyman I ran away from.

Chapter Twenty-Two

"That's why I'm not going to run away," I whispered as I stepped inside the manor. "No more lies."

The arrival of the detectives, the psychologist, and the news they brought with them pushed aside everything Courtney told me and the fears that came with them.

I made up an excuse to the guys about Courtney's mom driving Taylor home, so she didn't need me anymore. We then spent the rest of the night showering a bemused but happy Lily in love and attention—letting her choose the games, show me funny videos on her phone, and then draw each of us portraits that weren't half bad for a six-year-old.

It wasn't until she and the guys were sleeping soundly in their beds and pullout couches did I slip out of the hotel room and into the night. That's how I found myself in my childhood home at three in the morning.

Slowly, I moved from room to room, flicking the lights on as I went. Memories tumbled into my head one after the other.

"We can't get sucked back into her spinning, swirling vortex of psycho," Alex said so long ago. *"Not when we're so close to being rid of her for good."*

I thought they were talking about me, but when I confronted Rhodes, he said no. He claimed they were talking about an investor... who turned out to be my mother backed by the estate.

I stepped into the kitchen, brushing my hands across the countertop as another memory assaulted me.

"So why would you want to throw a lavish and obscenely expensive party to celebrate a marriage that's dead?"

Alex looked in my eyes, and smirked. "Dead? It's not dead yet, baby."

"Hell no," Micah breezed. "The old girl's still got some kick in her."

"That's right," Rhodes threw in, sharing a grin with his fellow brother-husbands that stood my neck hairs on end. "Can't tap out before they call T.O.D. That would be wrong."

"But when it is dead," Alex whispered, his smile widening as he turned away. "That'll really be something to celebrate. I promise you, my dear wife, that's going to be the party you care about."

The guys were so weird about it when I wanted to cancel the party, but again, Rhodes had an explanation ready to go. They needed our anniversary to lure big clients to the firm—get us on a healthy financial track again.

But what if not?

What if everything they told me was bullshit? What if Detectives Kaplan and Balogun had only *maybes* and *we believes* when talking about Layton because he didn't have a thing to do with Mrs. Prado or my mother? What if, like Courtney suggested, there was a reason Alex flip-flopped so suddenly after the party?

He had been so cold and distant up to that night, but then the next morning, he was sweet and charming—going on about how he refused to go to New York and leave me alone. Was he just trying to comfort his wife after she lost her mother... or was it more?

"Every time you questioned one of the guys, they immediately lied, shifted blame to someone else, and then confessed to a lesser sin when caught in that lie.

"They just keep pointing the blame every which way except at each other or themselves, even though the people who hated Omma most in this world were always sleeping right down the hall from her. Honestly, they likely would've been the main and only suspects from the start if it wasn't for a conveniently thrown anniversary party that filled their house with cops, suspects, and witnesses."

"They would've been the main and only suspects if not for that party." My feet carried me out of the kitchen and onto the stairs. "They—all three of them—had everything to lose."

I looked it up after Rhodes confessed to me. The statute of limitations was up for stealing the necklace, but unfortunately for the guys, they didn't stop there. They then fenced it, laundered the money they received, and funneled back into a business built on dirty money. The clock for those crimes starts when the crime is discovered, and those were going to be discovered after Omma's death.

My mother truly did have the means to put my sister's husbands in jail, and she intended to do just that. They *all* had motive to stop her. Especially when she started rapidly declining and the end drew near.

"But what would you do to stop her?" I asked the walls as I topped the stairs. "Was it enough to get rid of the evidence? Or did you need to silence her for good—sending your secrets to the grave that much sooner?"

Naturally, the walls had no answers for me, but their rooms had to. There had to be some clue or hint as to what their true endgame is, and if they achieved it that horrible night.

I started in Micah's room. I'd been in there enough times to know he wasn't keeping anything incriminating out in the open, so instead I searched his drawers, closet, vents—everything.

I wasn't even sure what I was looking for, but if these men murdered my mother one night, and then crawled up my pussy the next, then one thing was for sure—they didn't love me.

They didn't love me. They didn't want me. They had no interest in a future with the four of us together. There was simply no way they could convince themselves we could ride off into the sunset with my mother's blood on their hands, so maybe I was never meant to be riding with them.

Plane tickets. I crossed the hall to Rhodes's room. *Stashed packed bags. Stacks of hundreds hidden in a shoebox. There'll be proof that all of this was a lie.*

I blew through Rhodes's room, ransacking the place in a fit of fervor.

I pulled out the drawers, dumped them, and checked their bottoms. I turned out the pockets of every coat and pants. I checked under and behind all the furniture. I kicked the baseboards to see if any of them were loose, and hiding something behind them.

Rhodes's bedroom turned up nothing, so I tore across to Alex's.

The distance between this quadruple was felt from the moment their concern morphed into hostility after I walked in with a bleeding head.

Their bedrooms were in an entirely different wing from Sue's. They cut her out of the family finances and parental decisions. Every kind thing I said or gesture I made was met with narrowed eyes. But when they changed, I believed I had something to do with it.

That my love, respect, and care for them had melted the frost around their hearts, and we were truly beginning to build a loving, safe family.

"But what if I was wrong?" I yanked out Alex's bedside table drawer and dumped its contents on the carpet. "What if you all were keeping me sweet so that I'd ignore every glaring red flag!" I kicked over the table, looking for something taped under it like Rhodes claimed the password to his incarceration was stuck to the bottom of my mother's file cabinet. "Does a man really trust that deleting a file is enough, or does he go a step further and silence the witness so that not even in a morphine-hazed dream can she ever admit the truth?"

I dove into Alex's closet and tore everything from its hangers. "Does a man really swallow it all and let it go when his mother-in-law helps a con-man steal from him and his parents? All to make him dependent on her so she can keep controlling his life?"

The closet in tatters, I stumbled over the clothes piles and grabbed Alex's desk chair—slamming it against the wall housing the vent. "Was I really so desperate to get back everything I'd lost—love, motherhood, security—I ignored all the signs, so I could live in the fantasy Sue stole from me?"

How familiar this was, standing on a chair to reach this vent—the only place my secrets and true thoughts were safe... until they weren't.

But of course it was familiar, because Alexander was sleeping in my old bedroom.

I unscrewed the vent cover and flung it over my shoulder. Sticking my hand in, I slapped around, searching for what? I didn't know. I just had to be sure that—

Crinkle.

My fingertips brushed against something. Straining on my tiptoes, I stuck my hand in farther and grabbed it, pulling it out.

"Ah!"

The bag opened and unloaded its contents on my face. Something struck my forehead and bounced off while cloth smothered the light. I battered it away and snapped down, gaze falling on the white suit at my feet.

I recognized it immediately. It was the suit Alex wore the night of the party. I knew from the silver buttons setting the suit apart. But it wasn't the same as I'd seen it before, because this suit, was covered in blood.

I didn't know how long I stood there, staring at the blood-covered suit, and the tiny flash drive lying next to it. I just knew I was up on that chair long enough for my legs to ache.

Long enough for the full, horrible truth of that night to dawn on me. All the lies I'd been told. All the ways I'd been steered and maneuvered. All the smiles to my face while the knife struck my back.

I stood there... and everything became clear.

Stiff, cramping legs bent and dropped onto the floor. Carefully, I tucked the clothes back into its plastic bag, and picked up the thumb drive. I didn't know what was on it, but I could guess it was worth killing for.

There was only one thing to do with it all now.

I hurried down the stairs, the car keys already clutched in my hand and ready to take me away from here. *It's early, but Courtney will forgive me for waking her up. I need her with me when I go to the police stat—*

"Hey, babe."

I screamed. Whirling around, the light fell on my blown eyes and terrified face as he emerged from the front sitting room.

His smirk didn't fade even as his gaze drifted down to the items in my hand. "Now, what are you doing with that?" Alex drawled, grin widening. "I've been looking all over for it."

I breathed hard, breaths coming in rapid pants. Knees shaking, hands trembling, chest constricting, I stumbled over my feet—backing away as Alex slowly moved between me and the door.

"Alex, what. The. Fuck?" My voice was no more than a strangled rasp. "What are you doing here? You scared the life out of me."

"Well, so did you," he mused, shrugging. "When I woke up and found you gone, I got worried." He cocked his head—that eerie smile even more unsettling the wrong way up. "It was when you took my phone to call that friend of yours, wasn't it? You looked through my call logs and saw I never called my aunt that night." He snapped his fingers. "Rookie mistake."

I backed away until I hit the stair railing. What could I do? Did it even make sense to run? How far could I possibly get?

"You lied to me." My hand shook holding up the plastic bag. "You lied about everything. You were in my mother's room that night—*you!* And then you turned the clock back and swaggered into a change of clothes so that no one was the wiser. And this whole time, you've sat back and watched me—watched all of us—twist ourselves into knots trying to figure out the truth. You've watched people die!

"How could you, Alex? How could you!?"

He blinked lazily in the face of my rage. "All right, sure, I may have told a few fibs—"

Fibs?!

"—but, honestly, I'm finding all of this outrage a bit hypocritical. I mean, who are you to talk about liars when you're not Soo Min."

A deep, chilling quiet pierced my soul.

"This whole time you've been pretending to be my wife while fooling my daughter, and sleeping with Micah and Rhodes." He cocked a brow. "Naughty, naughty imposter."

"I— I don't know what y-you're t-t-talking about." Everything went white and cold. I didn't know what a stroke felt like, but it had to be this. "You're cr—"

"Oh, please, save it." Alex straight rolled his eyes. "You got the look down, but for personality and mannerisms it's an F-minus. The woman I married is cruel, selfish, greedy, and narcissistic. But you…?" he cried, leaning back and holding his hands out to me. "You're perfect.

"You're sweet, smart, funny, loving, and gorgeous."

I couldn't help it. Even then, his compliments made my heart flutter.

"You are my fucking dream girl, whoever-the-hell-you-are, and a change like that simply doesn't happen overnight." He gave me a wry look like I was a misbehaving parrot. "So, come on, out with it. You're Sue's sister, right? Her twin sister? Either that or you're some psycho fan who got plastic surgery to look like my wife."

"Sister," I snapped. "I'm her twin sister, Sarang."

That irritating smirk melted away as understanding dawned. "Sarang? So that's why Omma kept calling you that." He cursed under his breath like he was pissed he missed something obvious. "The whole time I thought she was being sweet, but I should've known better. That woman did not have a sentimental bone in her body."

"Don't you dare!" I shouted. "Don't you dare speak ill of my mother now after you—after you—!"

He cupped his hand to his ear, making a show of leaning in. "After I what?"

"After you killed her!"

"And there it is," he crowed. "You've accused literally everyone else on the planet, it was only a matter of time before you worked your way to me. The only problem is that I didn't do it.

"I didn't kill your mother."

"Then how do you explain this?" I ripped the tux out and shook it at him. "Let's hear your slick-ass explanation for why the clothes you were wearing that night are covered in blood? Are you going to claim it's someone else's blood?"

"No," he drew out. "It's Omma's blood."

"I—" I choked. He came out with it so easily, my heart stopped.

"But I didn't get blood on it from killing her," he breezed, "and you can see that for yourself. The person who attacked Omma would've been covered head to toe, whereas I only got some smeared here and there on my tux."

I couldn't breathe. "What the hell is wrong with you? How can you stand there casual and *lying* like you did nothing wrong?"

"Because I did nothing wrong." He took a step and I shouted, making him throw his hands up in surrender. "All right, all right, chill." Alex actually sounded a bit annoyed with me. "It's not as big a deal as you're building up in your head. I did go into your mother's room that night, but she was already dead," he dropped on my head like a ton of bricks. "The minute I saw her, I knew my time was up. I needed to find *that* thumb drive before a forensic team found it for me.

"I'd been looking for it for months—"

Visions flashed through my mind of that first day when I walked into Omma's room and found Alex being all shifty and suspicious.

"—and I wasn't going to pass up my chance," he continued. "Reynard was gone for the night. Everyone was downstairs preoccupied with the party, and there was an entire three-hour window before you were expected to look in on her. I had to find it, and stumbling on her dead body wasn't going to stop me."

The callousness in his voice reflected the emptiness in his eyes.

"All that looking around got some blood on me," he said, nodding at the plastic bag. "But I finally found it in one of the bed posts. I unscrewed the top and there it was." Alex shook his head, a tiny smirk tugging at his lips. "Excellent hiding place, I've got to give Omma credit for that. I wouldn't even have thought to look there if the internet hadn't given me the idea. Truly well done."

I gaped at him. *He's nuts. A true and proper psychopath stands in front of me.*

"Anyway," he said. "I had to climb on the bedside table to reach it and I accidentally knocked over the clock and broke it. It occurred to me that I could use that to my advantage, so I moved the hands back." He shrugged. "Simple, see? I didn't kill your mother."

"Simple, huh? Fuck you!" I bellowed, blowing his brows up. "Because you're lying. You're *still* lying! I don't believe for a second that you were in her room and Rhodes was kicking it next door, and neither of you knew! What's even on this flash drive? Did you think it was another copy of the emails? Is that why you three planned the second dumbest heist in history!"

Alex cracked up. "Hey, no need to be mean," he hooted. "Our first one wasn't that dumb. We did get away with it after all."

"You doorknobs spilled all the details in trackable, recoverable emails! You went to the same fucking school, why wasn't it possible for you to do all your planning in person without a record?"

He blinked at me. "I... uh... Damn, that's a good point. Shit, maybe we are doorknobs."

"You are! And instead of owning up to it and accepting the consequences for being thoughtless idiots, you guys killed my mom to cover it up."

"Again, we didn't kill your mom. If we wanted her death, why wouldn't we have smothered her with a pillow or slipped something in her morning tea? Here's a newsflash, baby girl, people don't ask that many questions when an old lady dies of seemingly natural causes. They just assume it was natural," he said. "Truth is we could've gotten her out of the way whenever we wanted, but that's not what we wanted."

"We, we, we," I hissed. "So you admit you were in this together."

"I admit that it was Rhodes's job to find the password and delete the email, and my job to find the backup evidence on the flash drive," he said. "Micah was supposed to stay downstairs and make sure you didn't feel the urge to check on your mom sooner, but then he saw one of the officers sneaking Mrs. Finley into the downstairs pantry." He beamed at me. "Obviously, she wasn't there to steal jars of our imported marmalade. Micah figured her presence might come in handy, so he popped upstairs at one point just so people would believe it when he said he saw Mrs. Finley upstairs.

"But no part of the plan involved killing Omma, because, as I said, she was already dead when I went in there."

My mind spun. Was any of that true? Was he lying to me again? Was he trying to get me to let my guard down, so he could do whatever he followed me here in the middle of the night to do?

"Why?" I rasped. "If you're telling me the truth, explain why? Why was it so important for you to get this drive, that you stepped over my mother's body to do it? You truly did something so cold and inhumane just to save yourself from some charges over the creation of a business you sold over ten years ago! This"—I shook the drive—"matters to you so much!?"

Hard eyes met mine. "It matters more than anything. It's all that matters," he growled. "You don't know this. I mean, you literally don't know this since you haven't actually been here for the last seven years, but I have nothing—fucking nothing—except for Lily."

I reeled back. *Lily?*

"And your mother wanted to take her from me too."

"What are you talking about?" I demanded. "How could my mother possibly take Lily from you?"

Alex scoffed. Crossing his legs at the ankle, he leaned back against the doorframe—raking me up and down like he pitied me.

Or envied me.

"You have no idea," he repeated. "Your sister has always seen us as trophies—billionaire trophies—except the billionaire part didn't work out so well for her. We all wanted to break up with her after that video of her throwing coffee on the waitress went viral, but Rhodes didn't even get the sentence out before she blurted that she was pregnant."

I sunk down to the floor. I could already tell I wouldn't like this story.

"We couldn't leave our baby alone with that woman," Alex stated, blunt as a truck, "so we agreed to the wedding and commitment ceremonies. All done very quickly, because Sue claimed she didn't want a big belly in the wedding photos.

"But while we were on our honeymoon, we caught her drinking." His fists balled even then. "We confronted her, and she confessed that she wasn't pregnant. She never was. She only said that because she was *afraid to lose us* and *what we had was too special to end*. But because we were still fucking pissed, she turned it around on us and said we were the jerks who only wanted to marry her for the baby. We were assholes. We lied about loving her. We only wanted to use her for her uterus. On and fucking on she went—blaming it all on us.

"She even went so far as to say it didn't matter that she lied. If we wanted to break up with her, we should've just done it. It wasn't like there was a real shotgun forcing us down the aisle. We made our own choices." He scoffed. "Can you believe we actually walked away thinking we were the jerks?"

"Yes." I didn't know I spoke until his face changed, flickering with surprise. "Sue... Sue was..." I swallowed hard. "Sue was always very good at making a person feel worthless for her mistakes."

"Was?"

I realized too late what I said... but I wasn't going to lie—not anymore. "Was," I said, voice flat. "She's dead."

Alex nodded slow. "How?"

"In the car accident." I couldn't believe we were doing this—talking normally like I wasn't holding the proof and the evidence of my mother's murderer in my hands. "She tracked me down to bring me home to see Omma before it was too late. I hit a deer, crashed the car, and she died. I came here thinking I could just hide out with my mother, send her off peacefully, and then start over in a new life.

"I didn't know she was married to the three of you," I stressed. "I didn't know Lily existed."

"Hmm. Well, I guess that's something. At least you didn't come here intending to deceive us. But it doesn't change the fact that you did it anyway."

Hera, help me, his expression didn't give a hint of his thoughts away.

"Yeah, I don't think I'm going to accept criticism from you, murderer."

Alex laughed out loud. "Damn, you're feisty. It's very sexy."

I blushed like a dumbass.

"And I wish I could say I'm not a murderer but..." His gaze flicked to the thumb drive. "There's still so much more to this story." He clapped, making me jump. "So, let's get back to it. We left off at the point in the story where we found out just how far your sister would go to get what she wants. Naturally, legally, she was only married to one of us, but Rhodes is our boy. Micah and I couldn't abandon him to her swirling vortex of evil manipulations. Especially because the next time she told us she was pregnant, it was real.

"Looking back, I think she thought we were holding out on her," he said. "Sue was living her dream life in New York—spending our money like water—but all the big, major, insane purchases she wanted, like a nine-figure condo in Manhattan and a private jet, we said no to.

"I truly believe she thought a baby would give her more leverage," Alex confessed. "If not in the marriage, then certainly in the divorce."

I bit hard on my lip, holding back my thoughts on the matter, because they wouldn't have been words of disagreement.

"With Lily on the way, she got even more pushy, and insistent, and threatening about us needing to give *the baby* the life she deserved, and if we kept refusing to give her *full access* to the family finances, she'd leave and get full custody of Lily," he said. "After that, we were forced to tell her that we'd been living on the dwindling profits left over from when we owned GloryBoi, because Rhodes gave all of his buyout money away, Micah put his share in an account controlled by his parents, and I never got paid a cent—"

"What?"

"—and Sue hated us from that day on."

"Whoa, hold on," I cried, shooting up. "What do you mean you never got paid a cent? You didn't receive your share of the buyout?"

Alex shook his head, tipping his chin to the ceiling. "Rhodes told us that he shared this part with you, so you already know those bastards came after us when we refused to sell GloryBoi. They dug around in our pasts. With Micah and Rhodes, there was nothing to find. The same couldn't be said for me."

"What do you mean? What did they find?"

Alex chuckled, shaking his head. "They found out—and you're really going to get a kick out of this one—that I'm not Alexander Montgomery."

A high-pitched, buzzing noise sounded in my ear, drowning the alarm bells going wild in my head. "Excuse me?" I sidestepped toward the exit leaving the great hall. "What did you say?"

Alex? tracked my movement like a hunter. "I said I'm not Alexander Montgomery." He tipped his head. "Or at least, I wasn't born Alexander Montgomery. My real name is Fritz Calloway."

"Fritz... Calloway?" Surprise stopped my inching in its tracks. "That's a stupid fucking name."

Fritz barked a startled laugh. "No arguments here. My birth mother was a drug addict who walked right out the damn hospital two days after giving birth to me... without me. I ended up in the system, of course. Foster care until I was eight, then a group home from eight to twelve."

I held his gaze. "And then..."

A mirthless smile curled into his cheeks. "And then when I was ten years old, one of the older kids in the home started... doing stuff to me."

My muscles locked up.

"I was small and weak." Alex's low, deep voice filled the room. "He was bigger and stronger. He didn't think there was anything I could do to stop him. He didn't think anyone would believe me if I told. He found out he was wrong on both counts when I stabbed him with a penknife I stole from a kid at school.

"When the caregivers came running in and found him bleeding on the floor with his pants down, they believed me when I told them why."

I gave in, releasing the long, slow breath bursting to get out of my lungs. The buzzing quieted, leaving way for a blanketing silence.

"He died in the hospital a week later," Alexander continued. "The director of the home didn't want anyone to know that everyone in charge missed that he was abusing me to the point I had to kill him, so they covered it up. They said he was jumped on the way home from school by an unknown assailant that was never caught, and not even a little blemish went into my file.

"That's why the Montgomerys had no idea when they adopted me." Alex tried again to take a step closer to me.

I let him.

"They changed my name," he went on. "Like I was a fucking puppy, not a person, but I didn't complain. I let them drive me off to my new life of mansions, butlers, and playrooms with a whole-ass slide and jungle gym in it. The only thing they wanted in exchange is that I be the perfect little robot boy they'd never been able to have.

"I got great grades, I joined all the clubs, I got into the prestigious Titan Prep, and then into Columbia." *Step.* "They were so proud... until the conglomerate sent their worst after us, and their PIs dug up the history of Fritz Calloway. They ended up interviewing one of my old caregivers who told the PI the whole story of how I'd gotten away with murder, and with that weapon in their arsenal, the conglomerate forced me to sign on the bottom line and give them my share of the business for free."

The question left my lips unbidden. "Did they tell your parents too?"

"No, *I* told my parents." *Step.* "After the buyout was announced to the media, dearest Mommy and Daddy came knocking with their hands out." He looked away—anger finally bleeding through his serene mask. "I guess it's true what they say: a wealthy person never has enough money.

"Even though my folks never had to work a day in their lives, a millionaire is not a billionaire, and they wanted to be billionaires. They *hounded* me for a cut of the money," he forced through gritted teeth. "They got nasty, Sarang. Fast."

I jerked to hear my name leave his lips.

"They started going on about how I was an ungrateful brat who they plucked out of the gutter. That the *least* I could do was repay their *investment* in me."

Bile burned my throat. "That's disgusting."

"Yes, it is." *Step.* "You want a master class in how *not* to treat your son or daughter, Connie and Richard Montgomery could teach it to you."

"You had to tell them you didn't have any money to get them off your back."

"And then I had to tell them why." Alex stepped again—only three feet away and drifting closer. "They wouldn't accept that only Micah and Rhodes got paid, and not me, so I had to tell them I was blackmailed with a murder I committed when I was eleven years old.

"They haven't spoken to me since."

"I'm sorry," I said, and I meant it.

He shrugged. "It's no matter. Honestly, the three of us were never that close. Growing up, I only ever saw them as absent roommates who paid the housekeepers and chefs. Them walking out of my life was no great loss. No," Alex said. "The only family I've ever really had is this one."

My eyes drifted down to the flash drive. "And Omma threatened that when she hired her own investigators to look into you, and they spoke to your same former caregiver."

"Yep," he hissed. "Real fucking chatty, she is."

"This," I whispered, "is what you couldn't let get out."

"That has been the fuse lighting the slow destruction of my life." His eyes flashed as he moved ever closer. "I never got a cent of that fucking money, so I became the useless fifth wheel dragged behind the car. I got all jaded and paranoid after the conglomerate dug up my deepest secret and my parents ditched me. I was scared to go after anything because it felt like at any moment, someone would pop up and blackmail me into giving it all away.

"When Lily was born, I threw myself into raising her, and for a long time, living life just as her dad was good enough," he said. "I didn't care that I lived in a house I hated, in a town I hated, with a wife I hated. I had a daughter who needed me, and that was all that mattered. But then things got so bad with Sue, it was looking like divorce, and Omma decided to make sure her daughter got every cent and more out of all *three* of us—only one legal husband be damned."

"Omma blackmailed you too." It wasn't a question.

"She didn't even go to Sue with the information in the end. What she found on Rhodes, Micah, and me was just too good to give up, and she wasn't going to let Sue drain us dry before she got the chance."

"But you didn't have any money? What could she want from you?"

"Lily."

My lips parted, but nothing came out.

"Omma never approved of how we were raising Lily." *Step.* "We were too soft, too permissive, too lax, too this, too that. I think she thought when she tricked us into moving in, she'd finally get her hooks into Lily through

Sue, but Sue was way too uninterested in being a mother to bother enforcing Omma's rules, and Rhodes, Micah, and I just ignored her.

"But when she got the truth about what happened to Jason Earnst, that was the jackpot. She told me that if the three of us didn't sign custody of Lily over to her, and if I didn't get the fuck out and disappear, she'd put us all in jail," he said. "Divorce seemed inevitable back then, so it was quite a threat. When we left, we'd leave alone."

"But— But it can't have been that simple," I burst out. "You could've fought the charges. Even the murder charge! It was self-defense and you were *eleven*."

"It was a cover-up, Sarang. The cover-up of a child's murder in a state-run facility. Compounded by the fact that said child killer then grew up to be a money-laundering thief," he dropped. "The only thing the jury would've seen is a dangerous felon that escaped justice for too long. They would've put me away, and I'd have lost the only thing in my life worth having—three-fifths of this family."

"So what happened?" I couldn't help myself. If all of this was more lies, they were the most engrossing lies I'd ever been told. "You obviously didn't leave. The four of you didn't get divorced."

"What happened is Sue got hit with those lawsuits, and suddenly her useless husbands weren't so useless after all. Rhodes leveraged the firm to pay everyone off and keep her out of jail. Micah has a bunch of big clients who loan out the keys to their summer and winter homes in the off-season, giving Sue endless escapes to lie low and figure out how to blame everyone else for her problems, and I continued to love and raise Lily, so she didn't have to.

"Suddenly, trading us for richer husbands didn't seem so likely, so she settled for the ones she had. After all, who wanted to be attached to the bird-poop lady?"

"Who indeed."

Step. "Omma kept pushing for Sue to dump us, but Sue refused while the lawsuits were ongoing, and she definitely fucking refused when Omma let slip that Sue could walk away with Rhodes's firm, and Omma could walk away with Lily." He whistled. "Wow. Did that blow up in her face."

"It did?"

"Oh, yeah. Sue did not want a firm she had no idea how to run. Your sister was born to be famous, loved, and adored, and investment managers did not have worldwide fans. And besides, who would fund her rise to fame if she signed away her only bargaining chip?"

It took me a sec, but then I got it. "You can't get child support if you don't have custody of the child."

"Ding, ding, ding," he sang. "When Sue found out your mother was maneuvering behind her back to force through the divorces, send her free nanny away"—he gestured to himself—"and rob her of future child support payments, she lost her flipping mind. She blew up on Omma, telling her that if she didn't back off and stay out of our marriage, she'd sell the manor right out from under her, and the five of us would take off. She'd never see any of us again.

"That threat hit the bull's-eye. Because Omma had just—"

"—found out she had cancer," I finished, hearing the pieces fall into place. "She was scared. Afraid of dying. Afraid of being alone. But most of all, afraid of dying alone. She took her finger away from the nuclear button because she wanted you all to stay here in the manor with her, but a ceasefire isn't a surrender. She planned to have the last laugh by making sure this..." I held up the drive. "...was released after she died."

"Yes." Alex took that final step, surrounding me in his spicy-sweet cinnamon cloud. His thumb and forefinger closed on the drive. "But I didn't kill your mother, Sarang. There wasn't any need or point. She kept my secret for an entire year. She was obviously content with knowing our lives would be ruined after she died. All we needed to do was find the email and backup drive, and destroy it without her knowing. Then she'd just peacefully pass on, and that'd be the end of the whole sorry fucking episode.

"I got the drive that night and hid it, and the clothes, under a loose step in the servants' staircase. When I went back to get it the next morning, it was gone. I thought the cops took it, but then they arrested your friend. You were protesting her innocence so hard, it occurred to me that maybe you found the clothes and drive, but you didn't know what to make of it. You were hanging on to it until you figured out what to do with me."

I made a strangled noise. "That's why you suddenly started acting all nice and sweet to me."

"Well, I certainly wasn't going to piss you off when you had the key to my freedom in your hands," he said. "But it's different now. You know the truth now." I felt him tug on the drive. "I'm innocent, Sarang, so what I'm going to do now is burn the drive and the clothes, and we're all going to move on with our lives."

Alex tugged a little harder as he reached down, closing on the plastic bag with his other—

"My father started raping me when I was eight years old."

Alex froze—stopping dead with his head hovering over my cleavage and body bent at the waist.

"There is a secret passage on the second floor that leads to a secret room," I went on—my tone flat. "No doubt it was made for the reasons Davis suspects. As a hiding place for alcohol during Prohibition. But what it became... was my hell."

Slowly, Alex straightened... and let go of the drive and bag.

"Appa was clever," I forced out. "When he'd come into our room in the middle of the night, he dressed head to toe as a clown. The stupid outfit, the big shoes, the red nose, and the face paint. No detail spared because he knew if I ever told anyone about the evil clown who'd sneak into my room at night and carry me through the walls to a room where he'd hurt me, no one would believe me.

"And no one did."

No smirk. No laugh. No trickster's grin. Alex's bravado faded away, leaving behind nothing but true and naked horror. "Sarang... I..."

It was okay that he was speechless. Not even someone with a history like his could be expected to know what to say in the face of such evil.

"Even with all that fucking face paint on, I knew it was my father doing those things to me, but when I tried telling Omma, she didn't believe me," I croaked. "She thought I was just a little kid having nightmares, and it didn't help that every time I turned to Sue and begged her to tell Omma that the clown was real, she'd lie."

"She'd lie!?"

My lips twisted. "Oh, yes. You see, Appa was only doing it to me, not her. I got to deal with the monster every night, and Sue got the saint every day. Our father would shower her in treats, presents, candy, pets—anything she wanted. And all Sue had to do was keep telling the world I was a liar. That no one was coming into our room at night, and I was making it all up for attention."

I made a noise under my breath. "I know what you're thinking. She was a young, impressionable child being groomed by a predator. By her own father. She didn't know any better. All the fault lay with Appa, not her." I inclined my head. "And sure, I guess I can say that's true.

"But that wasn't what Omma thought when she woke in the middle of the night and found my father's side of the bed empty, and me missing from mine. She panicked," I confessed. "She searched the whole manor for me but I was gone. Then, she woke up Sue and ordered her to tell her what happened. Where did I go?

"Scared, Sue finally admitted that everything I said was true. Our disgusting, vile, pedophilic father was dressing as a clown, taking me from my bed at night, and dragging me to a room hidden in the walls.

"And just like that, Omma got a rolling pin from the kitchen, burst into the room, found him on top of me, and cracked my father over the head—killing him."

"Killing?" he rasped.

"Killing. She didn't slow down. She didn't ask for explanations. She didn't hesitate. She killed her husband, dragged his body outside, and threw it off the cliff."

Alex's head snapped around, staring at the walls that hid the cliffs as if he could see through them to that very scene all those years ago.

"As much as I've come to despise my mother over the many years," I continued, pulling the words through a strangled throat. "As much as I've cried, cursed her, and wished she'd change everything about herself, I've never been fully able to hate her, because all I could remember is that when faced with the truth—she chose me.

"She protected me, and made sure that he'd never hurt me again," I said. "But while our relationship was able to stay together with a frayed thread, her relationship with Sue never recovered. She couldn't forgive Sue for lying to her face all so she could receive a few toys and lollipops. Omma looked at her differently from that day on, and Sue *hated* it. Of course she fucking did," I spat. "There's nothing a malicious narcissist hates more than someone who sees right through their bullshit.

"But because of the narcissist part I mentioned, it wasn't Sue's fault, and it wasn't even Appa's fault," I cried. "It was mine."

"Yours?" Outrage stole across his face. "How the fuck was it your fault?"

"Don't ask me, Alex. I shared a womb with that bitch, and still no one on this planet understands her less than me. She was awful to me! She would constantly throw the sexual abuse in my face and say nasty, disgusting things like that I liked it or I wanted it."

Alex's jaw straight dropped.

"I'd tell Omma, and Omma would punish her, but that just fueled Sue's fire and made her more resentful of me. The parent who favored her was gone, and now she was stuck with the parent who favored me—and that was just unacceptable.

"By middle school, she was running around calling me Appa-fucker."

"What the hell?!"

I just gave him a *see? I hated her long before you did* look. "She always waited until the teachers turned their backs to say it, and when I flipped out on her, she'd feign innocence—knowing I was never going to explain what she said, or what it meant. But that didn't stop my friends and classmates from hearing that nickname.

"At first, they thought Sue was talking about Appa, that flying bison from the anime. They figured I just really liked that show, but then we got to eighth grade, everyone got cellphones, and they found out Appa has another meaning in Korean—Dad.

"The first time a kid asked me if it was true I fucked my father, I marched straight up to Sue and punched her in the face." I smiled grimly thinking of how hard she went down—screaming and wailing. "We got into a fight—which Sue lost—and Omma stopped questioning if we needed to be sent to different schools.

"*I* went to Titan Prep," I said, shocking him, "and Sue went to the local high school. *I* am the one who approached you that day in the auditorium, made that crack about Micah's fly being down, and scored a date with you three."

"Holy shit." His goggle-eyed surprise would've been funny, if there was anything about this story that was funny. "Are you serious?"

"As a heart attack. It was *me* you guys felt a spark with," I said, "but that day, Sue sabotaged the stage with our face on the video cameras, and framed me. The principal didn't believe it was her. And after Sue's tutor swore up, down, and sideways that Sue was with him the whole time, my mother didn't believe it was her either.

"I was thrown out of the house the next morning, and Sue went on that date with you guys." I held out my hands, lifting my shoulders. "The rest is history."

"Wow..." Alex stumbled back. "I just... wow."

"It's okay. I wouldn't know what to say either. None of this seems real. Like, how could there be a real life that someone is living with evil twins, pedophilic clowns, homicidal mothers, and the twisted schemes and plots that destroyed all our lives. It's like something out of a movie, except it isn't," I said. "It's real and I know it's real because no one is ever going to gaslight and make me doubt my reality again.

"Ever since I got my first recorder, and then my first cellphone, I've recorded everything." Dropping the bag, I took out my phone and showed him the screen.

Alex paled when he saw my recording app open and doing its work.

"Everything that people say to me and all that they do, I keep it all, Alex, and that's how I know... you love me."

He snapped up, his chest heaving as his body tensed and coiled like a snake.

"You, Rhodes, and Micah. The way you laugh with me, joke with me, tease me, touch me, and hold me—it's real," I said softly as I closed the distance to him. "And I know this because even before you started making nice with me to protect yourself, you had already started thawing. You probably thought I missed your covered laughs and smiles when I made a joke, or how your eyes always followed my ass out of a room.

"You want me, Alexander Montgomery. You wanted me that day in the auditorium, and you want me just as much if not more now." The veins shown stark in his neck and forehead. He tracked my approach with bared teeth—a predator backed into a corner, readying to strike. "What we have now isn't three-fifths of a family, it's a whole one. A real one. And it's one worth fighting for, so this is what's actually going to happen now."

Taking his hand, I dropped the drive on his palm. His surprise compounded when I followed that by dropping the bag at his feet.

"You didn't kill my mother." As it left my lips, I knew it was true. "Because the man who was falling in love with me just wouldn't do that to me. He'd never hurt me like that."

Alex looked from me to the drive—agog. "Just like that? You believe me?"

"I do." I cupped his face, smoothing out the lines between his brows. "It's over, baby. It's finally over. The cops have their killer, and I've had enough of being Soo Fucking Min," I groaned. "First thing we're going to do is move out of that hotel, and start packing this place up. You guys can get started on putting the manor for sale, and I'll contact the lawyer as myself, collect my inheritance, and finally give Omma the funeral and goodbye she deserves.

"Once she's laid to rest peacefully, we'll— I don't know, charter a boat and leave this miserable place behind."

Alex blinked at me. "We?"

"Yes, we?" I cocked a brow at him. "You don't really plan to be parted from your dream girl, do you?"

A slow grin lit up his beautiful, sinful eyes. "Girl, I wouldn't be parted from you if you killed me. And forget my fucking dreams because the reality is so much better."

"Then stop talking," I whispered, leaning in, "and kiss me already."

Alex snapped me to his chest before I finished my sentence. Flinging away the evidence that could put him away for life, Alex cupped the back of my neck and crashed his lips on mine.

The world fell away.

All the blood, pain, and tragedies of the present and past—none of it touched us as our bodies fit together—two puzzle pieces left in the box, finally becoming whole.

Alex didn't mess around or ask for permission. He broke the seal and tangled with my tongue, teaching it the true meanings of ceasefire and surrender—and I surrendered.

I went limp in his hold, giving in to pure, explosive bliss. Fireworks lit in my mind. Electricity surged through my veins. Waves crashed through my body, making me writhe and shiver in his strong, steadying arms.

I moaned into the kiss, giving myself over to him completely.

We were all liars and thieves. We wore masks to hide our true selves, and battled the harsh realities of the world with coldness and duplicity. We ran from the right ways to live, and the proper ways to be, but when we were done running, Micah, Rhodes, Alex, and I ended up in the same place—

Together.

Alex heaved me squealing over his shoulder and marched out the door. "Enough. I've held myself back for too fucking long. We're going into that car and fucking in the backseat."

"Alex!" I cried, laughing my head off next to his shapely tush.

"After that," he said, "we're going home. To our family."

"Yes." I smiled as he began undressing me before we hit the door. "To our family."

Chapter Twenty-Three

The week after Alex and I made our peace, and made love in a truck, I lay down in Sue's bed, mulling over all the things that had happened, and would.

It had been a long and terrible road for all of us, but finally, our new start was beginning. Alex and I went back to the hotel and announced to Rhodes and Micah that we were leaving Lantana.

Enough of living in a miserable, haunted house. We were selling the thing, taking the multimillion-dollar check, and making the manor someone else's problem. With the money from the house sale in our pockets, we'd have enough to return to New York.

Rhodes could devote himself full-time to the New York office—the most profitable branch. Micah would quadruple his potential client pool. Alex would apply to med school—finally embracing his life as Alexander Montgomery without the fear of Fritz Calloway taking everything good away. And I'd stay home with Lily while doing my captioning work during school hours.

Together, we'd build something real, faithful, and happy for all five of us—leaving the ghosts of Lantana behind.

Micah and Rhodes agreed so fast, they had their bag packed before we finished our speech.

I smiled up at the ceiling, content in a way I'd never been in this house before. When I sat beside that totaled car, wishing Sarang Kim had died instead, I had given up on myself in every way. I truly believed there was nothing else for me. Nothing left to fight for.

I thought I was dragging myself away from that accident to hide in my nightmares until hate and revenge helped me eke out a new path.

How wrong I was.

So much more was waiting for me here. Everything was waiting for me here.

Love, understanding, and hope. The trust and innocence of a sweet, perfect child looking at me to guide her. A second chance, all too brief, to laugh and make good memories with my mother. Sharing laughs on the couch with the sister I had all along.

Everything I thought I lost in this house, I got back again, and now I could walk away with no regrets.

There was finally something to look forward to.

Splash.

A noise sounded outside my door. Checking the clock, I saw it was pushing two in the morning.

I gave it a few minutes before getting up, putting on my slippers, and padding out the door. The gasoline fumes punched me in the nose—scrunching my face and making me cover half of it with the sleeve of my robe.

Still, I didn't slow—following the splashes through the darkened hallway and silently down the stairs.

I truly was a specter following them unseen through the gloom as they made their way to the kitchen. Stepping inside right behind them, I threw on the light—beaming at the round-eyed, pale face that whirled around on me, snapping the gas container behind her back like I couldn't see and smell the evidence.

"Hello, sis," I chirped. "About time you showed up. I almost fell asleep waiting for you."

Soo Min gaped at me, frozen amid the puddles of gasoline she'd been splashing about our kitchen.

"So how you been?" I leaned against the wall, folding my arms. "The afterlife been treating you okay?"

Sue's eyes rolled in her head, flicking from side to side calculating her chances of getting to a safe distance, lighting the match, throwing it, and beating it out of here before I chased her down and stomped her into the floor.

"This— This isn't what you think—"

"You know, I've been hearing that a lot lately, and most of the time, it wasn't what I thought," I admitted, "but what I'm thinking now is that you're trying to burn down the manor with the last of your family inside"—I stared pointedly at the container—"and I'm pretty sure I'm right."

"You're not!" she shrieked.

Soo Min looked pretty fucking stupid. Not that there was ever a time that I didn't think she looked like a drooling moron—my biological copy be damned. But still, standing there in her big rubber boots; tight, black romper; hair piled on top of her head in a messy bun; a white mask covering her face and mouth; and a yellow fanny pack hanging around her middle, I could once again only think—

Drooling moron.

"You have no idea what's going on here, you gutter-trash bitch. You couldn't possibly understand—!"

"That you murdered our mother and got your accomplice, Reynard, to frame Courtney for it?"

Her jaw went slack behind the mask.

"And that was after you murdered Mrs. Prado and that poor girl from the post office, Tracy Williams?" I beamed even wider when she dropped the container, stumbling back. "See? I understand just fine."

Sue's jaw worked. "H— How—"

"How did I figure it out?" I tsked. "See, this is the problem with narcissists. You get so hopped up on your own supply, deluding yourself into thinking you really are smarter than everyone, that you seriously underestimate your opponents."

I rolled my eyes. "Sue, I was onto you since three days after you killed Omma—when the call from the lawyer sent me into her office armed with her password. I found quite a bit tucked in the many files on her computer. Quite a fucking bit. But still," I said, "I probably still might have been fooled if you hadn't told me your motive straight to my face, and put the proof in my hands."

"What? What the fuck are you talking about! I never did anything like that!"

"But of course you did." My airy tone didn't waver. "Don't you remember? It was on the very day that we were reunited for the first time in ten years. You handed me the reason Omma had to die—her will. The will... that disinherited you."

Her eyes narrowed. "So what? Fuck that will, I didn't care about that. What's ten thousand dollars, a shit car, and some rotting furniture mean to me? SueNaturals is a global brand. I make ten thousand dollars in a week."

No, bitch, you literally don't! Hera in heaven, you can't stop lying for ten seconds. "Whether or not that's true—and we both know it's not—"

"Yes, it is!"

"No, it's not!"

"Is," she shrieked. "Is, is, is!"

"Agh, you're such a fucking child," I exploded—losing my cool, chill *gotcha* vibe fast. "I know ShitNaturals is in the toilet—pun intended. Bird-shit face cream, anyone? What the hell were you even thinking?"

"It's not my fault!" Incensed eyes burned me over the mask. "Asian cultures have been making face creams from bird droppings for centuries. How was I supposed to know people would get a fucking rash?"

"Because they were using the droppings from a *specific* species after it had been sterilized! They didn't just scrape Polly Wanna Cracker's shit off the newspaper and dump it in a jar!"

"Well, I know that *now*!"

"Ugh!" I screamed, throwing up my hands. "Enough of this. It doesn't even matter except it's probably one of the many reasons Omma decided to disown you. You'd become a massive embarrassment that made Omma the joke of the charity clique. The real reason she started hiding away in the last year is because of you." I scoffed. "Not that you gave a shit about that or her feelings.

"You only started to care when you discovered what it truly meant to be disowned by Omma. What she personally had to leave didn't matter. It was all about Appa, and the estate." Holding up a finger, I gestured for her to wait while I fished my phone out of my robe and pulled up the photo I took three days after losing my mother. "*I, Jong Woo Kim, leave the entirety of my estate to my daughters, Sarang Kim and Soo Min Kim, to be transferred to them upon the death of my wife, Ha-eun Kim—*"

I raised my eyes, my grim sneer returning. "*Upon the condition that my wife hasn't disinherited one or both of them. If she disinherits one, the entirety of my estate is to be bequeathed to the other. If she disinherits both, my entire estate is to be liquidated and donated to—*"

"Blah, blah, blah," I finished, turning off my phone. "We both get the gist. When Omma cut you out of her will, she didn't just rob you of ten thousand dollars and some rotting furniture. She snatched over eight hundred and seventy-two million dollars out of your greedy little grasp, and you couldn't have that."

"No."

I raised a brow. "No?"

"That's right. No." Sue straightened, ripping off her mask. "You think you're so clever. Think you're going to get me to incriminate myself? Ha! Nice try, but you're not recording some big, blubbering confession from me on the other phone you're hiding underneath that incredibly unflattering robe." She gave me a nasty smile. "I didn't touch Omma, and I never even knew Appa's will had that clause in it. None of this had to do with me. You're making this up like you make up scary clowns and secret plots against you. It is just another ploy in your endless bid for attention."

I weathered her speech patiently. "Fine. If you don't want to explain how we got here, then I'll do it for you. When Omma decided to change her will and cut you out, she didn't go to her friends and ask them to witness the new will. She couldn't. She was still isolating out of pride, and she didn't want our family drama to be the main topic trending on the Ajumma Gossip Network.

"So, she did what many people do, she called the post office and set an appointment with the notary, and during that appointment, one of the postal employees offered to sign her will as Omma's second witness"—my gaze sharpened—"Tracy Williams."

If I expected Sue to gasp or give some kind of reaction to my reveal, I was sorely disappointed.

"The other witness," I went on, "was Mrs. Prado. Of course she was. Omma trusted her. She ran our house with an expert hand for years. She was also a good, honest woman. She would make sure Omma's wishes were carried out. That's why it was always your plan to kill her, but when Reynard heard that we were hiring her back, the first thing he did was call and warn you.

"You didn't want Mrs. Prado back in this house. You didn't want her figuring out I wasn't you and asking too many questions about where the real Soo Min was. You didn't want her explaining just how massive my coming inheritance was. That's why you," I hissed, "called Mrs. Prado back the night before and changed the time of our meeting.

"She had no idea she was talking to you instead of me. So when you told her to come a little earlier, she did it," I said. "You ran up on her as she was getting out of the car and stabbed her in the back before she could think to fight back. Then, you dragged her into the fountain and covered her with leaves.

"That done, you drove her car away, waited for Christie and her fleet of vans to show up, and then parked the car back on our property to make it look like she arrived later and therefore died later than she did. You wanted all the people running around the manor to confuse and flood the suspect pool," I said. "You wanted me, Rhodes, Micah, and Alex to have solid alibis for her death, because Mrs. Prado's death wasn't the main event, and you needed all your pieces in place for the main event."

"Hmm, no," Sue sang. "I have no idea what you're talking about. As always, you're rambling on about nothing and making a complete fool of yourself, Sarah. Gods, it's so embarrassing sharing a face with you. Imagine what it's like waking up every morning and seeing a complete loser staring back at you."

"You'd be seeing that even if I didn't exist, bitch." I flipped her off. "At least until your reflection runs away from your stank-ass breath."

"Fuck you! I could gargle with diarrhea and my breath would still be minty-fresh compared to yours."

I gasped, clapping my hand over the "O" of my mouth. "Goodness, Sue, don't tell me you're hawking Diarrhea Mouthwash next for ShitNaturals. What is with you and excrement? It's getting weird now."

Sue snatched an oily frying pan off the stove and flung it at my head.

I ducked, dropping to the floor and whipping out my second phone as she charged me. "Back off!" I belted. "Everything I've said is being recorded as a voice note headed straight for Officer Davis. Come near me and I hit send."

Her expression was terrible. Straight snarling like a wild animal, Sue took one jerky step back, then another.

"Better." Standing up, I cleared my throat. "Now, where was I? Oh, yeah, I'd gotten to the part where the real winged specter of death swooped down and murdered the sweet woman who was like a second mother to us, but I really should back up to how you faked your death."

Sue bared her teeth at me. "Sure, go ahead, but you should know, Officer," she called, raising her voice, "that everything this psycho says is a lie. If I really died, why did she steal my identity and pretend to be her dead twin? What kind of Appa-fucking nutcase does that?"

I clenched my jaw, refusing to rise to her bait. "The car accident was faked," I gritted out. "It all seemed real to me, but in actuality, it was just another performance.

"The deer wasn't real," I dropped. "Or I should say, it was real, but it wasn't alive. It was a stuffed deer mounted on a rigged pulley hooked up to fishing line. When I came flying around that corner, Reynard pulled and sent that oversized horned doll flying into the street. I crashed, conked my head on the dash, and was out.

"That gave you and your boytoy plenty of time to put some torn-up deer limbs and blood on the road, and replace my sister with your body double, Tracy Williams."

"Tracy Williams?" she snorted. "The girl who was just at the post office signing strangers' wills? Now she's in the car with you pretending to be me? Honestly, you've got to stop watching all those murder shows, they're messing with your brain."

I went on like she hadn't spoken. "I've seen photos of Tracy Williams all over the news. She was approximately our same height and body type. It was crazy how well that worked out for you. You didn't have to go and kill *another* innocent person to pass off as yourself. You just had to dye Tracy's hair, put her in your clothes, and smash her face enough that all I could identify was her eyes. *Our eyes*," I stressed. "I saw a body next to me with purple eyes and believed it was you, because of course I did. Humans take shortcuts in their understanding. The simplest explanation is their favorite.

"What came next you couldn't be sure of, but that's why you spent the whole car ride going on and on about how perfect your life was, while digging at how shitty mine was," I said. "You were needling and manipulating me into concluding that my life would be better if I took over yours... so I did.

"I cleaned up your crime scene and threw Tracy Williams's body off a cliff, and that's how she washed up on Bonsai Beach shortly after." My voice shook. "Because of me."

She hummed again. "Wow. You're confessing to a lot of serious felonies, little sis, but I'm still not hearing any proof that I was involved. Who in the hell told you I was working with Reynard? I barely ever spoke to him."

"You more than spoke to him. You're the reason why he dumped a shiny career in the trash," I said. "He didn't start charging all those fake charges to the estate because he woke up one day and suddenly decided to become a monster. He did it because he was waking up every day in bed with a monster." I smiled. "You.

"You started sleeping with him and got into his head. Who knows what you said to convince him to start stealing from the estate for you. It was probably some boohoo sob story about the husbands who canceled your credit cards and blocked you from the joint accounts. Or maybe it was the tale of the mean mommy and lawyer who had an iron grip on your inheritance. Either way, it worked.

"And when you realized all you needed to get half a billion dollars was for Omma to die, you convinced Reynard to start shortchanging her care, denying her the meds she needed to be well—all around trying to drain the life out of her even faster, so she'd just finally fucking die," I cried. "But too bad for you, our mother was a tough old broad. Six months she was on hospice—six months!

"She just kept hanging on with no funeral in sight, and you couldn't fucking stand it. But," I stressed, "you were going to struggle on to the end until Omma did the one thing that sealed her fate. She cut you out of the will, giving everything to me, and she told you so in a loud, screaming match that the whole manor heard." I whistled. "I don't know what set her off, but it had to be bad for her to say she wished she bashed your head in with the rolling pin and threw you off a cliff."

I snapped my fingers. "Maybe she found out you were using her nurse to steal from her while you counted the days until she died." I shook my head, tsking. "I know parents are supposed to forgive their kids anything, but even Hera, the goddess of motherhood, would throw her kid off a mountain for that.

"Either way, you were *not* going to sit by and watch everything go to me, so you put your plan into motion," I continued while Sue rolled her eyes. She was really going to stand there and play it like I was spinning fairy tales. "I always thought it was a little weird how everyone kept mentioning the fight, and how vicious it was. It happened just before I arrived, but the Omma I walked in on was weak, dreamy, and asleep twenty hours out of the day. How was it possible that only a couple weeks before, she had enough energy to crush your spirit to dust, but now all of a sudden she was too weak to lift her eyelids?" I held out my hands. "But then I read those invoices... and saw the bulk order of sleeping pills, morphine, and a mess of other hallucinogenic drugs that keep a person out of it, and pliable.

"Reynard was doping her," I announced. "Carefully keeping her sailing on a river of happy drugs so she wouldn't know which way was up, and it was all because Omma made the mistake of showing you the newest copy of her will *before* she turned it over to the estate lawyer. He had no idea you'd been disinherited—confirmed by the fact that he believes he's been talking to Soo Min over the last couple weeks, and he's told me all the details of Soo Min's coming inheritance, when in actuality, Sue doesn't get shit.

"With the doping going off without a hitch, the next thing to do was pluck your nature-made replica out of Willingsworth and put me in place in time for the party. Because it was *all* about the party."

Sue groaned. "Is there an off-ramp from Delusion Highway to the real world? And if there is, can I get off there now?"

"Oh my gods, can you shut the fuck up for five minutes," I screeched. "I swear, if you ever stopped running your mouth, you'd die!"

"This from the boring bitch who's been blathering on about nothing for the last ten minutes!"

"It's not boring. I'll give you that much, Sue, your plot to kill your own mother wasn't lazy or boring in the least. You thought of everything," I threw back. "You commissioned the dress and rented the jewels knowing it'd come with a million bodyguards. You needed *Soo Min* to have a rock-solid alibi with witnesses and a dozen video cameras on her at the same time *Soo Min* murdered her mother. Everyone else would be a suspect... except you.

"You stole the guys' credit cards and paid for that over-the-top, eye-wateringly expensive party because even though you told them you were done with them and wanted out, you needed them to stick around long enough to attend the party and then collect the refundable deposits," I said. "They were in financial straits. They couldn't walk away from sixteen million dollars, and if they were staying until after the anniversary party, they had to attend the party—not doing so would've looked too strange to all of their families, friends, and clients.

"You left nothing to chance," I hissed. "Everything from it being a white party to Reynard securing a photographed alibi was planned out. That night, after Reynard left and we were all partying, you slipped out of his locked bedroom out of sight of every guard, killed Omma, and then shot under the bed when you heard the footsteps.

"Alex came into the room searching for the drive, and you witnessed it all. That's why the clothes and the drive disappeared from under the step. You watched him duck into the servants' entrance, and then you took it with you, because you couldn't risk the police finding his hiding place.

"You didn't want any of us—Rhodes, Micah, Alex, Reynard, or me—to be suspects in the murder. Reynard because he was your accomplice, and the rest of us because you had special plans for us." I shook my head at her, lips twisting. "You didn't want to share that inheritance, Sue. Not with me, not with your soon-to-be ex-husbands, and"—I choked, stomach heaving—"not with your daughter.

"That's why you were waiting for Reynard to officially move out, so you two could come back and burn this place down with all of us inside," I said. "The cops would come, peel my crispy corpse out of the ashes, compare my dental records, and reveal I was Sarang, and you—who planned to be a million miles away when Reynard started this fire—would receive the devastating news, and then step forward to play your new role of grieving daughter, sister, mother, and widow."

I clicked my tongue. "But don't feel too bad for Reynard having to do your dirty work, because you promised the lovesick fool that he'd ride off into the sunset with you with everyone none the wiser. You had your pick of murder-suicide motives to stop the police from investigating the arson too closely," I said. "Either one of the guys did it because you cheated, asked for a divorce, and demanded custody of Lily, *or* your psycho twin would be the one who came back for ten-year-old revenge, and killed everyone you loved.

"Either way, we'd be dead, and you wouldn't have to share a cent of the money."

Sue listened in stony silence. "Wow," she rasped. "That was a scary story. Too bad that's all that was—a story. I never did and never would hurt my mother," Sue said loudly, speaking for the recorder. "I woke up and came downstairs for a drink of water, and found you splashing gasoline about the place like the psycho twin you are." She beamed at me. "You need help, Sarah. Please, put down the container and let me—"

"You know what? Fuck this!" Whipping around, I flung my phone out of the kitchen and smashed it to pieces against the dining room wall. "No more lying, Sue! NO MORE LYING!"

She blew back, eyes widening at my shout like she was a little afraid of me.

"You're not spinning your bullshit web of lies on the night you walked in here ready and willing to murder your six-year-old daughter! Your own child! You tell the truth and admit what you did or I swear"—I snatched up the frying pan she unwisely threw at me—"I swear, the next time I throw you off a cliff, you will be a battered corpse!"

"Sarah!"

"Admit it!" I charged her.

Screaming, Sue raced around the island—putting it between her and me. "Stop it!"

"Your own daughter!" Spittle flew from my mouth. "The sweetest, cutest, kindest little angel, and you were going to kill her because your new, fancy, rich life doesn't include bandaging scabby knees or paying for nannies?! What kind of demon are you! Argh!" I roared, sending her running when I charged again. "You fucking soulless monster!"

"I'm not a monster! This is for her!" Sue ripped open the fanny pack and unearthed a vial and syringe. "See? See?!" she shrieked like those items were supposed to mean something to me. "So Nari wouldn't feel any pain. She won't even wake up! This is *for her!*"

I gaped at her, going limp and nearly dropping the pan. "Are you fucking kidding me right now? That's how you justified killing your own child in that sick, screaming horror show of a mind? At least she won't feel it?!"

"It's not my fault," she roared, eyes bugging. "I never wanted kids. I never wanted those stupid, limp-dick wonders! They're the ones who tricked *me*! They made me believe they could support me and my dreams, when the whole time, they pissed away or gave away all the money they got from that idiotic gambling app!

"I wasted ten years of my *life* with them! I gave them everything! I even gave them a frickin' kid so they'd stop whining about me doing what I had to do to stop them ditching me when I needed them the most. They never supported me!" Sue cried, hand slashing the air. "They never understood me! They never sacrificed a thing for me while I sacrificed everything.

"All those shit-for-brains bitch boys have done is take, take, take, so forgive me for getting fed up!" She snapped, throwing her arms up. "The last thing I was going to do was let them use Lily to drain me of my money through child support. They had to go," Sue said matter-of-factly, gesturing at the gas container. "But Lily can't join me when I move on from this place, so instead of letting my only child end up in some horrible foster home..." She held out the vial and syringe again. "I'm sending her on peacefully and painlessly, because I love her."

I could only stare at her, jaw slack. I've said it before and I'd say it again, Soo Min might have been my twin, but there was no one on the planet who understood her less than me. "You really are fucked in the head."

Her face twisted in a furious snarl. "That's rich coming from you. Did you enjoy living my life these past few months, Sarah? Tell me, what do you call a person who pretends to be her dead sister all so she can sleep in her bed and fuck her husbands? Hmm?" She cupped her ear, leaning in for my answer. "Have they even thought of a word for that level of fucked up?"

"Yes," I breezed. "All of them are synonyms of liar or duplicitous. Not great descriptors, sure, but it's nowhere as bad as the words they call a sick bitch who gets five people killed, and then plots the death of five more."

"Hey," she barked, eyes flashing, "it wasn't five! It was only Omma, Prado, and that post office bitch—and only because they left me no choice. Appa's money is mine. It belongs to me! I was his favorite. I was the one he loved. I wasn't letting some sad, jealous old cunt and her accomplices interfere with my father's true wish—for me to be his heir. But I had nothing to do with that teacher guy getting killed, or with what Reynard did to himself."

"Fuck's sake," I snapped, rolling my eyes. "Of course you didn't kill Reynard or Layton. I did that."

Sue froze with her mouth half open. "What did you say?"

"I killed them," I droned, looking at her like the dumbass she was. "Duh. But don't convince yourself their deaths weren't your fault too, because it absolutely was. I saw almost right away what Layton was. First, with him indulging Lily so much she got sick at the school carnival, and then again when he tried to convince me to let him drive Lily home alone.

"My hackles were already up, but then he sealed his fate when he made that strange comment about if the manor would be searched again. After talking to Davis, I went straight upstairs to Lily's room, tore it apart, and found the camera that bastard hid in her bathroom vent during the party when he was wandering around our home—*exploring*." Rage tightened my grip on the pan handle. "Thankfully, a little thing like that was only set up to record, not broadcast, so he had to come back, retrieve it, and plug it in to see the video, but I took care of him long before that happened."

I cocked my head, flashing her a mirthless smirk. "I want to thank you for persuading Reynard to bulk order all of those sleeping pills and drugs. There was plenty left over for the cupcake I laced and gave to Layton outside of school that afternoon, right before he was set to drive over to our house.

"Those fast-acting babies dropped him right on our doorstep. All I had to do was take the knife I stashed in the shoe cupboard and plunge it in his back," I sang. "Thanks to you making sure the guys didn't buy another security system, I got away with that, and with taking his car keys and stashing a few of Omma's pills in his car."

I shrugged. "So many of the pills Omma actually needed to take were just sitting there, piling up while the two of you medically tortured her. So I just searched all the side effects until I found one that had the worst effect on male libido, and stashed them in his car. I didn't need to do more than that," I said. "A man like Layton was bound to have all the evidence the cops needed to bridge the gap, hidden on his hard drive.

"And then, there was Reynard."

"Rey— Reynard?" she croaked, looking at me like I was the one who horrified her.

"He helped you torture and kill my mother. Of course he had to fucking go. The minute I realized you faked your death, I knew you had to have an accomplice that helped you pull off the bullshit hit-a-deer con. I knew who that accomplice was when I saw the invoices, and realized just how easy it would've been for Reynard to sneak you into his room the day of the party, so you could kick back and wait.

"That's why I volunteered to help him bring his boxes down to his car when he was moving out," I said. "The stupid fool handed me his keys, I made a copy of his room key, and after lacing his dinner with a little something extra, I went down to the kitchen to cook with Lily, and confront Rhodes." I let out a gusty sigh. "I wasn't expecting Rhodes to reveal that he knew about the invoices and what Reynard had done, but after he did, it would've been too strange if I'd taken it in stride.

"I had to flip out and go running up there—shouting and pounding on his door." I laid my hand over my heart. It was racing like it had that night. "Thankfully, I'd already let myself in and out of Reynard's room that day. I planted the pill bottle of the stuff *Reynard* crushed up in his food, so it all looked self-administered."

"How—?" Her jaw worked. "How could you?! You killed Reynard! I loved him!"

"Oh, please." I rolled my eyes so hard, I hurt myself. "You're not capable of love, Sue, so spare me the theatrics, especially because, as I said, you're the one who got him killed. If you hadn't recruited him to help you kill my mother, he'd be skipping off to his next job right about now. Instead, he died on the dirty floor like the rat he is.

"Same for Layton," I growled. "I knew what he was right away, Sue. And you would've known too if you paid a lick of fucking attention, but you didn't, and that slimy piece of shit entered Lily's orbit. You wouldn't do what you needed to do to protect her. In fact," I cried, stabbing a finger at that fucking vial. "You've become an active threat to her, so now... she's mine."

She jerked back. "Yours?"

"That's right." Certainty settled into my bones. "Expelling a person from your vagina doesn't make you a mother. Any of half the world's fucking assholes can do that. No," I whispered. "Motherhood is borne in pain, and blood, and sacrifice. It's borne in the all-consuming truth that you'd burn the world down to protect your child's smile.

"Omma was nothing to me for ten years," I gritted. "She was just the gaslighting bitch who called me a liar, but then... she killed Appa. She saved me from him, and from that day on, I had a mother.

"Lily has a mother now, and that was never you. She can go on, living a happy life after you're gone, because she won't have missed a fucking thing. She'll have me and I will always be there for her. I will always... choose her."

I released a long, slow breath—rising to my full height. "And now, to repay the debt I owe to the woman who chose me..." I took a step around the island. "You have to go."

"What?" Sue backed away. "What are you saying?"

"I'm going to kill you, Sue," I slowly drew out. "Obviously. That stupid little voice-note stunt was for show. No one outside of this room is going to know what truly happened here. The police have wrapped up their investigations into the murders at Kim Manor, and I'm not about to make them question that story. It's just you and me now, Sue, and this was always going to end one way."

"You— You wouldn't! You *couldn't* kill me!"

"Uhh, I very much could." I stepped in time with her, both of us moving around the island as I hefted the pan. "You killed my mother and then broke in here to kill my daughter. You're way too fucking homicidal and psycho to have on the loose."

"She's my daughter!" Sue dared to argue while holding that syringe in her hand.

"And who are you?" I flashed her owl eyes. "You're nobody, and I'm Soo Min Kim—just like you wanted."

I burst into a sprint and she flashed. Dropping the vial, she snatched her phone from her fanny pack—holding it up like a weapon. "Not so fast," she hissed. "See, I can send things to the police too, Sarah. I found the dirty little file Omma was keeping on my husbands and made a copy." She shook the phone at me. "If you don't back the fuck off, I'm hitting send on the draft email waiting and ready to go to the LPD."

"The four of you are never riding off into a fucking fairy tale. Either they die here, or they die in prison." She smiled nastily as she pulled up that very email—proving she was not bluffing. "You pick the kinder ending."

"Hmm," I mocked. "Okay, sure. I pick killing you, snatching that phone from your cold dead grip, deleting the draft so no one ever sees it, and then living happily ever after with my fam—"

Sue dove to the right. Snatching up the container, she heaved it at me.

I dropped the pan, screaming as I threw my hands up over my eyes, mouth, and nose. The container smashed into the side of my head and dropped me down hard—crumpling in a puddle of gasoline.

I didn't have a chance to recover before one hundred and twenty pounds pounced on me. "You crazy, evil, husband-stealing bitch!" Sue seized my throat, and squeezed. "You took everything from me! My father died because of you! My mother hated me because of you! All I'm trying to do is get what I'm owed, *and you're ruining that too!*" she screamed in my face—her purple eyes bleeding red... or that was me.

I gasped and kicked, hands flailing and slapping at her face. My feet slipped in the puddles, gaining no purchase as red crowded the corners of my vision. Everything was fading away, but not so fast that I didn't see her remove one hand, lean over, and press *send*.

"I deserve that money! I earned that money!" Her grip tightened ever still, both hands returning and throttling the last of my wretched gasps from my throat. "No one's going to take it from me! Not that saggy old bitch! Not those dickless shits! And not you," she hissed—true hatred twisting her face. "Never *you*."

Help! My kicking feet slowed. My blows stopped falling. *HELP!*

"Die," Sue shrieked. "Die! D—!"

Sue jerked, her head snapping to the right. Grip loosening, she dropped like a sack of shit—tumbling off me and collapsing on the floor.

Rhodes stood over me, clutching the frying pan in his grip. He dropped it next to his wife's head and fell on me, gathering me in his arms. "Are you okay, baby?" That was the signal that sent Micah and Alex running out of the shadows.

They fell around me, hugging and kissing me all over as I just fought to breathe.

"We were waiting for you to say the code word," Micah said, stroking my hair as Rhodes carried me away from the kitchen, the fumes, and Sue.

"But when I heard Sue shouting *die, die*," Rhodes gruffed, "I had to make sure you were okay."

"I'm... o-okay," I croaked out. "But—"

I dissolved into a hacking, coughing fit. They were right. I spent too much time inhaling the fumes. I should've killed the bitch first and explained the rest to her corpse. "But you were r-right, Alex," I wheezed. "Sue made a c-copy of the drive... and sent it to the police."

The guys exchanged looks... and grinned.

Smirking away, Micah kissed me soundly on the lips and said, "Plan B it is, then."

Final Chapter

The sun crested over the horizon, lighting the waves into an undulating blanket of shimmering sapphires. A stiff wind blew off the sea—cold and bracing like a bucket of chilled water over the head. I'd never been more awake, or more clear.

Beside me, Rhodes pounded the spokes—securing the tripod to the earth. It wouldn't do for our final goodbye to blow into the sea.

Fingers slipped through mine, lacing up tight. I smiled wanly into Micah's eyes.

"Are you ready?" he asked softly.

"I'm ready." I peered over my shoulder at the manor freely burning to ash.

Flames greedily consumed the steepled roof and ornate gables. It climbed the towering turrets, blew out the stained glass windows, and ravaged the halls and rooms—secret or otherwise. The high ceilings crumpled. The delicately carved trim warped.

Before my eyes, my childhood home burned to the ground.

"There's no turning back now," I whispered. "By now, everyone can see the smoke in the air. I can already hear the sirens."

It was true.

Sirens called faintly on the air—fire trucks certainly, but under their noise would most likely be police cars.

"Meaning we're out of time," Alex said, falling in on my other side. "Let's do this."

Nodding to us, Rhodes opened the video app, and pressed record.

The three of them wore the handsome, perfect white suits they wore the night of our anniversary—the last night we were all together, and happy.

For me, I wore a simple cotton gown and no shoes. I didn't need them where I was going.

"Hello," Micah began. "If you're here and you're watching this, then by now, you know what we've done. You know we stole the Thompson necklace—"

"—you know we funded GloryBoi with dirty money—" Rhodes continued, taking his place beside Micah. Together, we stood at the edge of the cliff.

"—and you know I'm Fritz Calloway," Alex went on. "I killed my abuser when I was eleven years old, and the directors of the group home I lived in lied and covered for me, to save my chance at a future. A chance that's over now."

"For all of us," I finished. "The police will be on their way to take my husbands from me, but no more. I've lost my parents, my sense of safety, and my hope in humanity. I won't lose the men I love too. So, we're leaving," I rasped, my gaze falling down the long drop below. "Together."

"We've already sent Lily on," Micah gasped, choking on a sob. "Our sweet girl is truly among the angels now."

"And now it's time for us to go wherever we belong," Alex announced as we all grasped hands.

"Goodbye."

Launching off, we jumped.

I tried to hold it in, but broke in less than a second. I screamed.

Wind, water, and terror rushed into all of my wide, gaping orifices. My dress flew and slapped me in the face, covering my eyes and making the coming impact a horrifying anticipation.

We smacked the icy water and it immediately took its revenge. Water surged into my eyes, nose, and mouth wrapping its unseen claws around me and dragging me down to its depths.

And then stronger, surer hands held me tight, and guided me to the surface.

Alex, Micah, and Rhodes wrapped around me—holding me safe and secure as the waves tried their hardest to bash us against the cliff face.

"Hurry!" She waved frantically from the boat, flinging life buoys at us like frisbees. "Grab on!"

We did one after the other, letting her strength and our feet power against the waves and help us onto the boat.

Mrs. Finley handed out the last towel as Micah climbed on. "How did it go?"

"Perfectly," I chattered out. Damn, that water was cold! "But the fire trucks are already on the way. We need to be a speck on the distance before they arrive."

Hard eyes pinned me. Mrs. Finley pointed to the cabin. "After you."

She said it to me, but I didn't have to move. Micah, Rhodes, and Alex went down into the cabin, and emerged carrying a thrashing, shouting Sue.

Padded cuffs secured her wrists. A gag saved us from the spewing filth. Otherwise, she was dressed exactly like me, from the bare feet to the red hair tie.

The three of them carried her to the edge of the boat and ungagged her.

"—do this," Sue screamed. "I'm your wife! I love you! You can't kill me. You wouldn't!"

Empty eyes and blank faces reflected back at her.

"Trust me, sweetheart," Rhodes drawled. "This part of the plan got a lot easier to stomach when we heard you confess your plan to burn our daughter alive."

"We don't love you," Alex said, "and you never loved us."

"Fuck you," Micah dropped—the end of his goodbye.

Eyes white with fear latched on to me. "Sarah? Sarah! Please!"

Rhodes and Micah secured her hands as Alex uncuffed her. She fought that much harder, shrieking as she tried to claw their faces off.

"You can't do this!" she pleaded with me. "I'm your sister! Your twin!"

I rolled my eyes. "Bitch, you were literally going to kill me even though I'm your twin. Why do you think these pleas for mercy are going to work? You weren't going to spare any mercy for us."

She turned so fast, I missed it when I blinked. "You don't deserve any mercy, you trashy, husband-fucking slut! You stole my life!" Her eyes bulged out of her head—red with madness. "You deserved everything you had coming to you! You all did!"

"Enough of this," I snapped, throwing off my towel. "I'm not going down your it's-everyone's-fault-but-mine rabbit hole again. I'll just let Satan explain it all to you in hell."

"You won't get away with this! You won't—"

"Mrs. Finley," I breezed, ignoring Sue completely. "Would you like to do the honors?"

"With pleasure." Hefting the rock, she struck Sue in the temple, snapping her head to the side and ending her screaming for the final time.

Together, she and I dumped her over the side.

I felt nothing as her body hit the water. Even less as she floated away. Truth was, my sister died when I was eight years old—leaving nothing but the gleeful monster who enjoyed every second of my torment.

She couldn't hurt me anymore. She couldn't hurt my loves anymore. And most of all, she couldn't hurt Lily anymore. A lot of things were done wrong in my relationship with my only sister, but this...

...this was the sole thing done right.

I knew that before we got to this moment, but the certainty settled in over the past week.

After Alex and I had our heart-to-heart, we went back to the hotel, and I told the guys everything—including that I was actually Sarang.

Micah and Rhodes exchanged looks and then replied, "Duh."

They both explained to my astonished expression that they both figured it out at different times, but they definitely figured it out. I was just too different from the wife they knew. There was no way I was the same person.

When I asked why they didn't call me out, they said by that point they'd fallen in love with me, and they didn't want to do or say anything that might scare me off.

All of that was shocking enough news, but then I explained who I believed the killer really was and why they did it. I told them that Soo Min obviously wanted the inheritance Omma tried to give solely to me, and to make her plan work, she had to kill me like she killed everyone else who'd seen the true will.

"But if I was the only one left who has to die, she would've done it already," I explained. "It doesn't make sense that she's waited this long unless it's not just me. She wants to get rid of everyone who can lay claim to *her* money... and that includes her husbands and child."

They denied that it could be true at first. For a whole day and night, we went back and forth until I proposed a simple test. If Sue was waiting for us all to finally be alone in the house so she could pull something, I'd catch her in the middle of it and prove it. And if that happened, we needed to have an escape plan waiting, because she still had information that could destroy our lives.

The guys agreed and that set off a flurry of activity. I went to the prison to speak to Mrs. Finley. I told her that I believed my sister was still alive, and if she wanted revenge against the sister who truly wronged her and her son, I could make that happen.

Mrs. Finley said yes so fast, I didn't even get a chance to explain the plan. With her on board, I pressured the detectives into letting her go. I pressed on the point that she never would've gotten in my home in the first place if one of their own hadn't let her in, and her assault against me hadn't left any damage. I was fine, and I'd tell the jury that, along with what a massive waste of time and taxpayer money this trial was. They'd inevitably vote not guilty, and there would've been no point to any of it.

In the end, the detectives agreed and released her with no charges. Her next step from there was to charter the boat so it couldn't be connected to us.

Our next step was to send Lily, Courtney, and Taylor on an impromptu vacation to New York. We wouldn't have Lily anywhere near her unpredictable, homicidal birth mother.

Micah even bought a child-size mannequin that we covered with a blanket and carried into the house under the cover of night, just in case Soo Min was watching from somewhere. We needed her to believe we'd all come home.

With all of that done, we waited... and she came.

"There's one thing I don't get," Alex mused. "Why did she stash my bloody clothes and the drive in my vent? What was the point?"

"I know exactly what the point was," I told him. "Before he died, Agassi tipped Sue off to how suspicious I was of everyone—including you guys. She purposely stashed those things in my old hiding place because she wanted me to find it... and she wanted me to think one or all of you killed Omma. Even though she planned to kill us all and it didn't even matter, she wanted us to spend our final days fractured and fighting. Because she *hated* watching us fall in love."

"Wow," Micah breathed. "That's a whole new level of vindictive."

"Yes, it is, but now, it's over," I said. Behind me, I heard Mrs. Finley start the engine. "The inhabitants of Kim Manor are all officially dead. When— If Sue's body washes up on shore, cops will just assume the rest of you weren't so lucky and washed out to sea."

My men— My loves— My husbands held me as we sailed away.

"You know, I'm not going to miss being Fritz Calloway or Alexander Montgomery," Alexander mused. "Both of those poor bastards had the worst luck." He stroked my cheek. "They had to spend most of their life without you."

I once again blushed like the silly mare I was. "Don't worry, baby. Sarang has an almost-billion-dollar inheritance coming her way. She'll buy you whatever name you want."

Micah put up his hand. "Let the record reflect that I did not fall in love with you for your money, but all the same, I'm very much looking forward to you becoming my sugar momma." He captured my lips in a searing kiss that rocked me on my feet. "As long as it comes with lots of sugar."

"Oh, I can confirm for the record, it will."

"We should change out of these wet clothes and check on Lily," Rhodes reminded. "Although, I'm sure she's having a great time with Auntie Courtney and Cousin Taylor on their impromptu trip to New York."

I laughed. "One hundred percent, there will be a million cheesy, touristy photos waiting on my phone. We were all wrong, guys. It's Courtney who's going to beat us out as Lily's favorite."

Rhodes smiled into my eyes—making my heart flutter even then. "Good news is, we've got the rest of our lives to challenge her title." His kiss was just as sweet, and just as hot. "Let's go get our daughter."

Alex compounded my heart palpitations with a kiss of his own, nipping my bottom lip as he drew back. "And start our new lives."

"Together."

***

Five Years Later

"Hello, everyone, and thank you for joining us on this special tour."

Our group of ten stepped off the shuttle. Whistles rippled over the group as we got the first look at the great, green expanse rolling out before us.

The tour guide stood ramrod straight in an expensive blue pantsuit with matching sapphire earrings. Her hair was pulled back in a sharp bun, and her makeup was lightly, but charmingly applied. She carried a clipboard, but did us the favor of keeping it at her side as she shook our hands and greeted us.

"Now, we are going to show you around and give you the opportunity to see with your own eyes all of the incredible things that we've achieved here in the mere year that we've been open..." She gestured at the fleet of golf carts, and the drivers waiting to man them. "But before we do, I'd like to give you the context of exactly what you're going to see.

"We are standing on over one hundred acres of land," she began, "and on this land we have the largest food bank in the state, the second largest clothes bank in the state, and five free clinics with doctors and surgeons on-site who can, and do, perform all emergency procedures and operations. We have single homes—full and proper homes complete with full kitchens, bathrooms, and bedrooms for all the unhoused members of our community who walk through our gates.

"No more bunk beds, gyms stuffed with dozens of people inside, or trudging through a cafeteria line," she said. "We return privacy, dignity, personal space, and choice to those who've lost everything. And yes, that applies to adults who come here alone, and those who arrive with a family—all are allowed to reclaim their own space again.

"And within that space, they have access to cooking classes, GED classes, applications to our microloan program, parenting classes, elder care services, mental health specialists, driving classes, and legal aid and lawyers on retainer. We offer substance abuse programs, gambling addiction programs, employment assistance, job assistance, and jobs for those who graciously choose to work for this great community.

"We have not one, or three, or five, but six libraries," she said, "three community centers, two movie theaters, and two sports facilities. For the minors and underage runaways that come to our doors, we have group homes, yes, but what makes us different is that we don't assign five-to-ten children to one caregiver—no," she affirmed, voice firm. "We assign one, I repeat, one caregiver to one child."

"One?" someone remarked.

"One." She smiled at us. "One person to love, care, and devote to this child who has found their way here through circumstances that were most certainly tragic. And while that child or teenager lives with us, they'll receive a full education in a traditional school environment, or even a non-traditional one—for those with special needs who require a different pace or accommodations.

"While living at the shared home, every child has their own private room, but when they're outside of that room, they're free to enjoy the theater, the soccer field, the basketball courts, swimming at the community center, or just kicking back with their friends. They have a home here," she stressed. "Not a facility or a program. But a home."

She paused, taking in a deep breath. "And last, I must mention the program closest to my heart, our disability support and service program. Here we are fully equipped to care for and support children and adults with all disabilities. I can attest that one of the fears the parent of a child with a severe disability has is: what will happen to my child if something happens to me? Who will love them, who will care for them? Who can they trust?

"And while I pray that no force in this world will ever s-separate a parent from their child," she croaked, "I also need the world to know that it's *here*. This is the place where they'll be loved, respected, and cared for by people they can trust."

"Wow." The group burst into applause, adding more color to the guide's cheeks than was already given by the balmy Florida morning. "Amazing. Simply fantastic."

"Truly impressive," the woman to my right agreed. "You certainly have a lot to offer, but you're also very out of the way. We are miles from the nearest town. How is the average person in need supposed to get here?"

"That is a great question, and thank you so much for asking it," the guide replied, "because we had the same question when we chose this location, and the answer was simple. We have partnered with every major rideshare company in the country. The only thing a person in need has to do is give our name, and they will be driven—for free—to the many pickup locations we operate in all fifty states.

"Pickups within the continental US will be driven here by shuttle. Pickups in Hawaii and Alaska are given flight vouchers directly to our nearest airport here in Florida, where we again, are waiting to receive them."

That got a round of impressed looks and raised brows.

"But isn't there the potential for abuse in this free-for-all," called the grumbly voice of the cynic who spent the whole shuttle ride bitching and moaning behind me. He clearly wasn't pleased that his wife wanted him to donate their yearly charity tax write-off to this place. "What if all these people you're giving free food, houses, and money to are just a bunch of freeloading wastes who would be making something of themselves and contributing to society if you didn't make the need to do so obsolete?"

The guide didn't lose her smile. "Also, a very great question. This is a fear that many of our potential donors have. You're good people," she said. "You want to make sure that every cent you donate goes to people in need, and not to those who seek to take even more from those without.

"That is why during the tour, I will go in depth into our vetting and application process, criminal record check, security, and our close and personal relationship with local law enforcement," she said. "I do not mind telling you that we had an incident three months ago with a man who did pretend to be unhoused, so that he could gain access to our grounds.

"We went through all the standard motions, which included taking a photograph and sending it to every man and woman who came here escaping partner violence. One of those brave women immediately identified the intruder as the violent husband she traveled three states to escape. That man was arrested and escorted off the property without ever stepping foot past the welcome center."

Another round of applause lit the air—me clapping loudest of all.

"I assure you, Mr. Bryant," she continued when our claps subsided. "We are just as determined, if not more so, to ensure that everyone who comes here, does so for the right reasons."

"Yes, well... uh..." Bryant clearly didn't know what else he could say that wouldn't make him sound like an ass judging people who were down on their luck and struggling. "Very good to hear. Thank you."

The guide tipped her head. "Any more questions before we begin the tour?"

"Just one." A blonde woman at the head of the group raised her hand. "What made you think of this? I mean, this is truly the most comprehensive charity and social service I've ever come across. You've taken everything a person could need and brought it under one umbrella. Why?"

The guide smiled. "That is what we have done here, and as much as I wish I could take credit for this vision, the idea was born in the mind of a smart, talented, brave, honest young woman who once found herself in need of many of these services, but didn't know where or how to get them.

"She dreamed of one place—one home—that would become the place you go, when you have nowhere else to go," she said. "She entrusted me with her faith, and half a billion dollars—"

That set off a few chuckles.

"—to make her dream come true," finished Mrs. Finley as she found me in the crowd, and winked. "And so, I did so in the name of her friend, and my son." Stepping aside, Mrs. Finley gestured to the grand sign stamped bold and proud on the gates. "Together we created Colin Finley's Home for Everyone."

***

I broke off from the tour group and caught the shuttle back to my car. Hopping in, I made the short drive home.

Sure, I didn't need to visit on my off days. Mrs. Finley was the best administrator ever. She had everything in hand, along with a capable team, but still, every now and then I liked to see what we created together, and plant myself in the middle of a group of potential donors and do my best to sway them.

Soon, I was rolling up on our oceanfront mansion, the smile already on my lips.

The home I bought was night and day from the dusty, drafty haunted manor we left behind. This beauty was an all-white, two-story luxury retreat with private cabanas by the pool, a tennis court, a firepit on our private stretch of beach, home theater, exercise room, game room, and a separate guesthouse with three bedrooms and four bathrooms for when Courtney, her husband formally known as Mr. Stevens, and their two kids, Taylor and Joey, came to stay for the summers.

With everything we could possibly need inside, we didn't have much reason to leave our haven—which was good since my husbands were all legally dead.

After leaving Lantana behind for good, we lay low in Europe while the news repeated broadcasts of the burning of Kim Manor and the quadruple suicide of Kim Manor's inhabitants. As it happened, Sue's body did wash ashore and they were able to bury her properly—but, as expected, finding her sealed the deal on Rhodes, Micah, and Alex. They were officially declared dead, and the Lee family was born.

Sarang became Soo Min who officially became Sarah Lee. Rhodes became Elijah Lee. Micah traded his name in for Roman Lee, and Fritz Calloway went from that to Alexander Montgomery and finally to Brooks Lee. Then, there were the kids...

I pushed inside. "I'm home."

"Mommy, Mommy!" Two torpedoes came at me from opposite sides, blocking my chance of escape.

I laughed as Ha-joon and Ji-ho tackled a leg each—trying to fell me like a tree. "Hello, my babies, have you been misbehaving while I was away?"

"Yes!" the twins cried, more than pleased with themselves.

I looked down at my boys, my heart bursting at the seams and overflowing with love. I still remembered the day the guys and I went back for our second IVF appointment and were told that we couldn't proceed because I was already pregnant.

That news dropped me on my ass, but it was the news that I was having twins that crumpled Micah, and then we doubled the faints when Alex and Rhodes discovered our babies had two different fathers, and they were the two.

Naturally, between an Asian mother, Black father, and white father, we gave birth to fraternal twins that couldn't look less alike. All they shared were adorable cherub faces and big, calla lily eyes like their momma, but there was no telling the boys that they weren't identical. The three-year-olds were the most adorable goofballs who liked to change clothes, pretend to be the other, and then shriek with laughter when they "tricked" us. But even sweeter than the innocence of babes was how much they loved each other.

I knew from day one that Ha-joon and Ji-ho would be nothing like me and Sue. They would always be there for each other and have the other's back. Family would always be something safe to them.

"There you are, sweetheart." Micah's mother, Marsha, padded into the front room and kissed me warmly on the cheek. "How was the tour? Did we get any new donors?"

"We got all of them," I said, making Marsha clap with excitement. "Which is worth celebrating with some... ice cream!"

"Yay!" The boys took off running for the kitchen, championing their coming victory of the icy treat.

"Where's Lily?" I asked.

"Where else?" Marsha tossed an amused look over her shoulder. "Wreaking havoc on the beach with Taylor. I tell you, Sarah, it's the biggest injustice of her life that Taylor has to leave at the end of every summer. The two are closer than sisters."

I groaned. "Believe me, I've tried to get Courtney to move down here, but she's opening up another location in New York, and she insists she needs to be close by to supervise everything. Florida to New York is too long a commute."

She planted her hands on her hips. "Well, you tell her that they love cookies and cupcakes just as much in Florida as they do in New York, so she can just as well open a location down here and do all her supervising right next to her best friend and godchildren."

"Yes, ma'am, I will tell her."

Laughing, she took off for the kitchen. "Lunch will be ready in an hour. Micah took his father and Rhodes out on the boat, but they promised to be back by then. We're all eating together now that the Stevens family is finally back home."

Home.

Oh, how I loved that word. My home where I was surrounded by all the people I loved. My home where I was finally safe to be myself with people who encouraged and supported me. It was my guys who gave me the push I needed to go back to school and get my law degree. Even when I thought

I'd have to drop out to carry and care for the twins, they held on to me the whole way through, and became feeding, pampering, burping, rocking machines—completely taking on the care of our babies while I studied and passed the bar on my first try.

Now, I was one of the lawyers on retainer for Colin's Home.

As for Micah, he was never going to fake his death and let his parents believe that they not only lost everything, they lost their only child too. He let them in on the plan first thing, and then flew them over to live with us after the heat died down and the investigation was closed. Now, Marsha and Arthur got to spend all day in a mansion with their grandbabies. They both agreed this retirement was way better than the one my mother stole from them.

But Micah, Alex, and Rhodes were not retired. Even though they could've kicked back and cruised through life on my inherited millions, the good and kind men I married felt compelled to join the Colin's Home family.

Rhodes now taught financial literacy and investment classes. When he wasn't doing that, he was leading a support group for family members touched by gambling addiction.

Micah also followed his talents. He was officially the home's football coach. There were a lot of kids to teach, so he held practices five afternoons a week, and taught business classes five mornings a week.

That just left my Alex, who'd finally gone for his dream and applied to med school. He wasn't finished with that or his residency yet, but he already knew he planned to work for one of the Colin's Home clinics.

I padded upstairs to my home, soaking in our beautiful, light, airy home for the millionth time. Gone were the dark walls, pressing hallways, and dreary rooms. Everything was cream, light gray, and baby blue. This home of a thousand windows always had them open and letting in the sunshine—making us all one with the sea and sand.

Topping the stairs, I made for my bedroom at the end of the hall. I had a particularly tricky case brought to us by a man who came to Colin's Home with his two children. Because he didn't have a steady job or live in a safe area, his ex-wife was given custody of the kids. Unfortunately, said ex-wife was married to an unsafe man, and he simply refused to leave his children alone in a house with him.

Trapped and scared for his children, he picked the kids up from school and drove through four states to find safe haven here with us. Dad was looking at some serious charges—kidnapping at the top of the list—but I chose this career path because I wanted to give a voice to all of those scared kids out there who aren't believed. And no matter what it took, I would make the system listen to these little kids, and their desire to stay with the parent who loved them so much, he'd give up his freedom to see them safe.

Walking inside, I found a surprise on my bed.

"Oh, hello," I teased, grinning. "What brings you by?"

Alex grinned right back. "I've brought you a package."

"What package?" I asked, peering around.

Alex shamelessly grabbed his unmentionables. "This package."

"Wow." Giggling, I crossed to my desk. "Did it take you all week to come up with that line?"

"Hey, go easy on me. I'm new to this seduction thing," he cried. "I've spent the last five years shacking up with this hot-ass piece of tail."

"Oh, have you?" I winked at him over my shoulder. "Tell me more about her."

"Quadruple threat. Funny, smart, kind, and sexy. She wakes a mighty beast in my pants whenever I look at her."

I could not contain myself. Alex had me blushing as hard as I was giggling.

"Problem is," Alex continued, "I haven't been inside of her in the past seventy-two hours, and that needs to be rectified immediately."

"Oooh, agreed," I purred.

Alex was pushing against his forties, and he was still one of the sexiest men around. He grew out his soft, dusky locks, so now they fell over his eyes—drawing my hands to them a dozen times a day to bring back those perfect, hazel orbs.

Thanks to daily runs on the beach, Alex was in even better shape than he was in high school. Every inch of him was hard, tanned, and muscled, and going three days without rubbing myself all over those muscles was torture.

"But I've really got to prep for this case," I said, reaching for him. He came over and dropped a kiss on my lips. "I'm sorry, baby. Let's break our no-sex streak tonight. We'll con Courtney into hosting a sleepover for the kids, and get the bed to ourselves for once."

"Hmm. I'm not sure I can wait." He tapped his chin, screwing up his face as he looked to the ceiling. "I have no choice. I'm just going to have to seduce you. Let's see if you can really hold out until tonight."

My brows were halfway past my hairline. "All right. Challenge accepted."

Alex moved to the bed, peeling his clothes off as he went. A damp patch formed in my panties before his belt hit the ground. Let's be honest, I didn't stand a chance.

His shorts were kicked off, followed quickly by his boxers. I openly raked him up and down.

Alex was perfect from head to toe. There wasn't a single bit of him that wasn't hard, ropey muscle—even his ass. He turned and I dropped down in my desk chair, drinking him in.

I'd ridden Alex's cock in all kinds of fun ways, but I still drooled every time he unleashed it. Alex was long and thick—just the right size to make a girl scream while stretching her past her limit.

Holding my gaze, he leaned back over the side of my bed, reclining on his elbows. I swallowed hard as he grasped his cock.

I watched rapt, biting my lip at the rising pressure in my middle.

"Sure you don't want to give in now?" Alex asked, lazily stroking the base. "I'm pretty sure you won't make it past the massage oil."

"Let's find out."

Tipping over, Alex got the oil from the drawer, and poured it directly on his cock.

He started stroking—slow and lazily as though he had nothing but time. "This could be slipping and sliding inside you right now, Lee. Right." *Stroke.* "To." *Stroke.* "The." *Stroke.* "Hilt."

I gripped the seat, holding tight. This was new. Usually, Alex and I were too busy tearing each other's clothes off to waste time with teasing. I kind of wanted to drag this out for as long as I could last.

The problem was... how long would that be?

"Show me, baby," I rasped. "Do it harder. Faster."

"Yes, ma'am."

Increasing his pace, Alex pumped and primed his cock like a fire hose. "Yes, baby," he groaned. "Fuck, you feel so good, Sarah. Ride that dick, you perfect, tasty little treat."

I sucked in a hard breath, straining to pop my lungs as my legs crossed and clenched hard. I didn't know watching him was as good as the real thing. Pinpricks of sweat dotted my skin. The heat building within me was rising to a fever pitch. He wasn't touching me, and I wasn't touching myself, and I was still on track for an incredible orgasm.

Alex stroked faster still. Rising off the bed, he bucked in his hand—drilling the phantom me to pieces. "Damn, you're so gorgeous. A fucking goddess descended from the heavens. I want to put you on your knees and cum on those delicious tits. Make you beg for it while I paint your pouty lips, then drill that dick-hungry pussy from behind."

My nails dug half-moons into my palms. This mix of praise, compliments, and dirty little promises was working like magic.

I fought to stop myself. I really did need to get some work done!

"Suck that dick, baby. Take it fucking all."

My hand shoved between my legs, slipping under my dress and sliding three fingers into my slick, moist heat. "More."

Alex climbed on top of the bed, rising tall on his knees. He thrust hard into his palm—pumping like I was ass up and face down in front of him. "Shit. Perfect round ass like yours is just begging to be spanked. And that's what I'm going to make you do, *beg*."

I bit my lips hard trying to stem the breathy moans leaking through my teeth. I rocked on the chair—driving my fingers deeper, sending electric shocks through my body with every brush against that bundle of nerves.

It wasn't enough.

"You belong to me, Sarah Lee. I want all of you from that strong, defiant mind to your yummy pussy. You don't leave this bed until you've wet these sheets so many times, you—"

Jumping off the chair, I toppled it with a crash that snapped his neck up. His eyes bulged in time for me to tackle him.

"Whoa?" We bounced off the mattress in a tangle of limbs. "Impressive. You held out twice as long as I thought you would."

"Don't stop," I demanded, straddling him. "Fuck me."

Grabbing my waist, he smirked like the self-satisfied ass he was. "What about work?"

I dropped my dress on his face. My bra followed. "Now."

"As you wish."

The world spun. Before I knew it, I was blinking up at the ceiling.

Pinning my hands over my head, Alex tore my thong off one-handed. Why was this man so hot? Everything he did was sexy.

Alex kissed me hard and rough. Our tongues clashed in a fury of sparks, grunts, and moans. My whole body was alive with need and excitement. I was a live wire. If anyone touched me, the shock would blow us all to nirvana.

We broke apart gasping. My head was spinning—dizzying. I either giggled or growled for more, I couldn't be sure.

My eyes blew open to moist heat claiming my nipple. Alex sucked me in his mouth—flicking and torturing the happy nipple with his tongue while the other surrendered under his rough, calloused fingers.

I melted into the sheets, moaning and crying out as loud as I wanted. Why not? We had my bedroom soundproofed. The guys would not stand for me to hold back.

Alex kissed his way down my stomach, popping goose bumps in his trail. Anticipation heightened as he lifted my knees and draped them on his shoulders.

A firm swat landed on my backside.

"Ah," I cried—part surprise, part pleasure.

"On your knees."

I flipped over so fast, I hit myself in the face.

Alex grasped my hips and rocked me back on his hardness. I moaned as our bodies ground together, practically purring under his roaming hands.

"Gods, you're beautiful. Every fucking inch of you is perfection."

Thwack!

I bucked under the surprise spank, my core heating up to melt.

"Wow, you're revved up today," I gasped. "I really fucking like it."

He probed my folds, pushing one, then two fingers inside. My eyes rolled up in my head as his knuckles tapped a fast beat against that bundle of nerves. I cried out when he was suddenly gone, until his tongue replaced his fingers.

Alex ate me out like a buffet. I reached for the bedpost as he tongue-fucked me, head bobbing against my ass, I had to anchor myself or I swear I would've floated away. Every cell, every pore, every follicle was brimming with the perfect pleasure of great fucking sex.

"Gods, this pussy is so delicious. Want some?"

I didn't have a chance to register what that meant before he pounced on me. Squealing happily, I laughed in our sloppy, dirty kiss. This was everything I ever wanted. Guys who could make me laugh as hard as they could make me cum.

Alex dropped back and took me with him. Holding me firm, he dropped me on his lap. I shivered with need when he pressed his tip to my entrance.

"Three days since I've watched these beauties bounce," he growled. "We're fixing that right the fuck now."

Smiling, I braced myself on his knees. "Yes, sir."

Alex bucked, pushing in and turning my laugh into a cry of ecstasy. The feel of him stuffing me to bursting would never get old.

He set a mind-scrambling, punishing pace. Pulling almost all the way out and thrusting back in. We devolved into a chorus of screams, grunts, and moans.

Grabbing his arms, I met him thrust for buck, driving him deeper still. Alex was striking that spot every time. I was boiling over to a fever pitch, my orgasm coming fast.

Alex struck that spot a final time, and I came hard—body rocking and writhing on top of him. I lost control and tipped over, nearly falling off the bed as wave after wave of pleasure crashed over and drowned me. Alex came on my heels, spilling his release inside of me.

We likely both wanted that to last longer, but we never had a chance. Three days without, we were both at the edge of our limit.

We collapsed in each other's arms, grinning at each other like fools.

"Now that was a fun work break," I breathed, throwing my arm across his chest. "What brought that on?"

He smirked wolfishly. "Can't a man have screaming hot sex with his wife in the middle of the afternoon just for the hell of it?"

"He most certainly can." I smooched him. "But I get the sense you're in a particularly good mood today. Did something happen? Are you planning a surprise for me?"

Alex froze. "Well, see, that's not fair," he cried. "Because now I'm a bad husband if I say I'm not planning a surprise for you. What kind of jerk am I for not planning a surprise for the fine-ass wife who gives me screaming hot sex in the middle of the day?"

I poked his side, giggling. "You better say you are, then."

"I am," Alex stressed. "Definitely. But that's not the *only reason* I'm in a good mood."

"What is it, then?"

Alexander smiled at me. "It's this," he whispered. "It's you. It's our three perfect, amazing kids. It's getting to live and co-parent with my two closest friends in the world. It's chasing my dream for the first time in my life. It's being surrounded by the people I love most in this world.

"For a long time, I had three-fifths of a family," he whispered. "Now I have the whole thing... and it's because of you."

Tears flooded my lids, spilling down as his sweet, whispered words washed over me.

"How could I not be happy, baby?" Gentle fingers brushed away my tears. "Five years ago we died, and this is heaven."

"No." Lacing our fingers together, our wedding rings glittered and shone side by side. "This is better."

***

ABOUT THE AUTHOR

Ruby Vincent is a writer and lover of contemporary, fantasy, and paranormal romance. She loves saucy heroines, bold alpha males, and weaving a tale where both get their happy ever after. Use the QR Code to check out her website and more of her books.

www.ingramcontent.com/pod-product-compliance
Lightning Source LLC
LaVergne TN
LVHW040036080526
838202LV00045B/3365